Falling for You Again

FOUR SEASONS

Falling for You Again

CATHERINE PALMER & GARY CHAPMAN

TYNDALE HOUSE PUBLISHERS, INC.
Carol Stream, Illinois

Visit Tyndale's exciting Web site at www.tyndale.com

Check out the latest about Catherine Palmer at www.catherinepalmer.com and about Gary Chapman at www.garychapman.org

TYNDALE and Tyndale's quill logo are registered trademarks of Tyndale House Publishers, Inc.

Library of Congress Cataloging-in-Publication Data

Palmer, Catherine, date.
  Falling for you again / Catherine Palmer and Gary Chapman.
  p. cm.
  ISBN-13: 978-1-4143-1167-8 (sc)
  ISBN-10: 1-4143-1167-2 (sc)
  1. Married people—Fiction. 2. Older couples—Fiction. 3. Marriage—Fiction.
4. Missouri—Fiction. I. Chapman, Gary D., date II. Title.
PS3566.A495F35 2007
813'.54—dc22   2007024430

Printed in the United States of America

13 12 11 10 09 08 07
 7 6 5 4 3 2 1

FOR AUNT PEGGY AND UNCLE AL CUMMINS.

Thank you for loving me and my family so many years.
I'll never forget the "three-ring circus" at Ngara Road, the laughter down the
hall on prayer meeting nights in the house on Ol Donyo Sabuk Road, Uncle
Al's booming voice preaching at Parklands, and Aunt Peggy's sweet Texas
accent teaching me what being a young lady truly meant. From one member
of the "girl Cummins" to my dear "boy Cummins" family, I love you.

C.P.

Ruth and I are happily incompatible.

BILLY GRAHAM, *when asked*
the secret of being married fifty-four years to the same person

A good marriage is the union of two good forgivers.

RUTH BELL GRAHAM

NOTE TO READERS

There's nothing like a good story! I'm excited to be working with Catherine Palmer on a fiction series based on the concepts in my book *The Four Seasons of Marriage*. You hold in your hands the third book in this series.

My experience, both in my own marriage and in counseling couples for more than thirty years, suggests that marriages are always moving from one season to another. Sometimes we find ourselves in winter—discouraged, detached, and dissatisfied; other times we experience springtime, with its openness, hope, and anticipation. On still other occasions we bask in the warmth of summer—comfortable, relaxed, enjoying life. And then comes fall with its uncertainty, negligence, and apprehension. The cycle repeats itself many times throughout the life of a marriage, just as the seasons repeat themselves in nature. These concepts are described in *The Four Seasons of Marriage*, along with seven proven strategies to help couples move away from the unsettledness of fall or the alienation and coldness of winter toward the hopefulness of spring or the warmth and closeness of summer.

Combining what I've learned in my counseling practice with Catherine's excellent writing skills has led to this series of four novels. In the lives of the characters you'll meet in these pages, you will see the choices I have observed people making over and over again through the years, the value of caring friends and neighbors, and the hope of marriages moving to a new and more pleasant season.

In *Falling for You Again* and the other stories in the Four Seasons fiction series, you will meet newlyweds, blended families, couples who are deep in the throes of empty-nest adjustment, and senior couples. Our hope is that you will see yourself or someone you know in these characters. If you are hurting, this book can give you hope—and some ideas for making things better. Be sure to check out the discussion questions at the end of the book for further ideas.

And whatever season you're in, I know you'll enjoy the people and the stories in Deepwater Cove.

Gary D. Chapman, PhD

ACKNOWLEDGMENTS

So many people affect the writing and publication of a novel. For their beautiful example of a long marriage, I honor my parents, Harold and Betty Cummins. I also thank the many missionary families I grew up with in Kenya whose enduring marriages I have tried to emulate. For sharing both laughter and tears, my longtime friends are treasures I cherish. Janice, Mary, Roxie, Kristie, BB, Lucia, I love you. My prayer support team holds me up before God, and I can't thank you enough, Mary, Andrew, Nina, and Marilyn.

I also thank my Tyndale family for all you have meant to me during these past ten years. Ron Beers and Karen Watson, bless you for making this series not only a reality but a pleasure. Kathy Olson, I can't imagine having the courage to write a single word without you. Your careful editing and precious friendship are truly gifts from the Lord. Andrea, Babette, Mavis, Travis, and Keri, the amazing sales team, the wonderful design department—thank you all from the bottom of my heart.

Though I often leave them for last, first on my list of supporters, encouragers, and loved ones are my family. Tim, Geoffrey, and Andrei, I love you so much.

Catherine Palmer

Fall always brings changes to Deepwater Cove," Charlie Moore said as he sat at Patsy Pringle's styling station in her Just As I Am beauty salon. "And I don't mean the good kind."

"Now you stop talking like that, honey," Patsy chided, brushing the back of Charlie's neck. "Especially on a Friday afternoon in my favorite month of the year. There's nothing like a September weekend to lift a girl's spirits—and I won't have you trying to squash 'em flat."

Patsy finished brushing the wisps of hair off Charlie's neck. Then she turned him around and let him have a look in the mirror.

He checked to see that his sideburns were even; then he nodded.

"Good work, Patsy. You always fix me up right."

She smiled and patted his shoulders. "I have a feeling this autumn is going to be one of our prettiest in years, Charlie. The leaves are starting to change colors already, and a cool breeze is blowing in off the lake. I don't know why you'd think we're in for a rough season."

Charlie shook his head. "History, Patsy. Look at our history. A year ago, the last of the Hansen kids went off to college, and, well . . . you know things got pretty difficult for Steve and Brenda."

"What else happened in the autumn, Charlie?" she asked. "I've owned this salon for umpteen years, and I can't remember a single bad thing."

"That's you, Patsy. The eternal optimist." He leaned back in the chair, adjusted his glasses, and began. "Last fall, we had the Hansen problem. The year before that, flu took two of our widows—one in September and the other in early November, as I recall. And don't forget the year the pizza restaurant went belly-up, the main bank in Camdenton shut down its local branch, and the new tavern set up shop—all of them right as summer ended."

"Well, I have to admit I'm no fan of Larry's Lake Lounge. Why is it that bars never go out of business? That rankles me," Patsy declared, whisking the cape from Charlie's shoulders and helping him from the chair. If he didn't know better, he'd think the young woman was trying to hurry him along.

Charlie started for the cash register. "I'm with you on that one, Patsy. Too many young guys waste the better part of their time and their money there. Never understood it myself."

"And don't forget the fall colors," Patsy said. "I know folks enjoy going on tours to look at the leaves changing along the East Coast and up toward Canada, but land's sakes, why don't they open their eyes right here? The Ozarks has some of the prettiest fall colors God ever painted on a tree."

"Sumac," Charlie said as he tugged his wallet from his pocket. "Now there's a red you won't often see in nature."

"See what I mean? Fall is a wonderful time of year."

Charlie chuckled. "I reckon you're right, Patsy. Plus, most of the out-of-towners are gone, and we don't have to put up with all their fireworks, speedboats, and barhopping."

"I love the excitement and fun the summer crowd brings, but I don't mind too much when they leave. There's a kind of peace that settles around us—even though we've still got plenty to do. Fall festivals, bake sales, church hayrides. And the high school homecoming parade, trick-or-treaters, Thanksgiving—"

"All right, all right," Charlie sputtered, holding up a hand. "If I stay here any longer you're going to talk the blues right out of me, Patsy Pringle. I was just working up a good head of melancholy and pessimism, but you're fixin' to ruin the whole thing." He shrugged. "You've plumb worn me down with all your zip-a-dee-doo-dah. I won't have any choice now but to be in a good mood, which means I'll go home and infect Esther, who'll get all chipper and talk my ear off."

"Esther's due here in about twenty minutes for her weekly set-and-style," Patsy said. "In fact, I was surprised you didn't come together."

"I'm not going to sit through that ordeal again. I did it once and believe you me, once was enough. Nope, I think I'll head home and start putting the vegetable garden to bed."

Patsy sighed as she studied him. "Charlie, I just want you to know that every time I see you and Esther together, I feel like there's hope for the world. You're both so kind and helpful—and sweet as apple pie to each other. How long have you two been married?"

He scratched the back of his neck. "Well now, that takes some figuring. My seventieth birthday is just around the bend, and I was born in . . ." He paused, lifting his eyes to the ceiling as if the numbers were written up there in the wallpaper border. "And we got married in . . . hmmm . . ." He calculated some more. "Good gravy, we'll be coming up on fifty years before we know it. Who would have thought?"

"Well, you're a wonderful example for the rest of us," Patsy said. "If I had ever gotten married, I would pray to have as happy a home as you and Esther."

"You make it sound like things have always been perfect." He reached across the counter and touched Patsy's nose as if she were a child. "You know better than that, kiddo."

She laughed. "I guess so, but I can't imagine what could come between you."

"Well now, we've had our ups and downs, Esther and me. More good times than bad, but we've worked hard to make it that way. You ever heard that opposites attract? That's us. She's a talker, and I'd rather read a book or watch TV. I'm up at the crack of dawn, and she'd sleep till eight or nine if she didn't drag herself up to make my breakfast. We're kind of like sunshine and rain, you know. You've gotta have both to keep things growing."

❧

"I'm late, I'm late!" Esther Moore hooked her purse strap over her arm as she hurried into the kitchen. "Cody, where did you put that stack of mail I set on the table by the door?"

"Mail?" Cody Goss turned from the sink, where he was scrubbing the gray and white speckled pot Esther used to fry crappie and catfish. "Is mail the same as letters? Because I read in my *Giant Book of Myths and Legends* that King Arthur and his knights wore *mail*. And also, the other day at the post office, I had to sign a paper to be a soldier if ever the president wants me to fight, and I checked the box that said *male*. So that's three kinds of mail. There might be another *mail* that I don't even know about, because I also found out that *tail*, which rhymes with *mail*, can mean—"

"I'm talking about letters," Esther cried. "Not half an hour ago, I put a stack of envelopes on the little table in the living room, and now they're gone."

Gracious sakes. Esther dearly loved Cody Goss, but sometimes the young man could drive her right up the wall. Cody had appeared in Deepwater Cove this spring as a homeless, bedraggled stranger. Since then, he had been helping clean some of the neighborhood houses and shops—earning minimum wage and carefully building his savings account. After vacuuming, dusting, and tidying the Moores' home, he often spent the night in their spare bedroom, and both Esther and Charlie enjoyed his company.

"The side table by the couch," Esther clarified. "This afternoon, Charlie paid our bills before he went to get his hair cut. Then I wrote a birthday card for one of my grandkids and a get-well card for Opal Jones. I put stamps on every envelope and set them right there by the door. Where did you move those letters, Cody?"

He blinked at her, his blue eyes shining in the afternoon sunlight that slanted through the kitchen window. "You don't have to put a stamp on Opal's envelope," he told her. "Since Opal lives right across the street and three houses down, I could take that card over there and give it to her."

"Yes, but Charlie and I support our federal postal service, because—" Esther cut herself off with a little growl of frustration. "Cody Goss, where did you put my mail? If I don't get those letters into the mailbox on time, Charlie will pitch a fit. That means I'll have to knock on the back door of the post office and remind them that Charlie used to be a mail carrier, which might make me miss my appointment with . . . with . . ."

She shook her head. "Well, where am I going, Cody? You've got me so flustered I can't even remember."

"You're driving over to Tranquility to get your weekly set-and-style at Patsy's salon," Cody said, his fingers dripping soapy water on the vinyl floor as he trudged past her. "And there's your mail, right on the table by the couch. See?"

Esther would have dropped her teeth but they were still attached. There sat the stack of letters, exactly where she'd laid them earlier. But she would have sworn that when she looked for them a moment before, they were gone.

Now they were back. Just like that.

"Did you put them there?" she asked Cody.

"*You* put them there," he replied. "The only letters I ever touch are the ones that come from my aunt in Kansas, when she writes to say she loves me and please eat my vegetables. She also mails me ten dollars every month, and I put that into my savings account, which

I hate to tell you is something you can't see at the bank even if you ask very nicely. Did you know that, Mrs. Moore? I asked to see my savings account one time, and the bank lady said sorry, but no. She told me an account is not a box with money in it. It's just pretend. An account is nothing but numbers inside a computer. You have to have faith that those numbers are the same as dollar bills, which is exactly like having faith that God is real even if you can't see Him."

Esther stared at Cody as she gripped the stack of letters in one hand and her purse in the other. What on earth was he rambling about? His aunt? Savings accounts? God?

"Cody, one of these days you're going to drive me to drink," Esther said as she opened the front door.

"I can't drive; remember, Mrs. Moore? I'm not yet smart enough to get my driving slicers."

"Driver's license!" she called over her shoulder. Then she began to mutter. "*Driver's license* not *driving slicers*. Oh, that poor boy is a dim bulb. I don't care what Charlie says about him being smart as a whip. He's never going to make it in this world without help, and I shouldn't even be leaving him alone in the house."

Wearing heels a little too high for the occasion, Esther tottered over to the carport. She set her purse and the mail on the roof of the sturdy Lincoln Town Car she'd been driving for decades. Fiddling with her car keys, she tried to find the one that unlocked the door. The car was too old to open electronically. That was okay with Esther, who had a hard time getting used to automatic door openers, television remote controls, cell phones, computers, and other modern-day necessities. A person could go crazy trying to understand the new technology.

Finally Esther got the car unlocked and slid behind the steering wheel. She was definitely going to be late, thanks to Cody moving the mail all over the house. It was one thing to have the boy help with the dusting and vacuuming. But if he kept putting things where they didn't belong, Esther would have to talk to Charlie about letting him go. After all, she had been cleaning house for forty-eight years, and she could certainly keep it up a while longer.

Through the open front end of the carport, Esther could see the purple martin birdhouse Charlie had built and set up on a tall metal pole several years ago. It was listing a little to the left, and she would have to get him to straighten it. The trees that dotted their large backyard were starting to turn. It wouldn't be long before Charlie would be out mulching and putting everything into his compost bin.

As she turned the key in the ignition, Esther reflected with pride on her husband's fine garden. Every year they had the tastiest, freshest, plumpest vegetables in the neighborhood. Nothing pleased Esther more than to drop off a pint of ruby red strawberries as a get-well gift or leave a surprise basket of peppers and onions on someone's front porch. She pulled the car's transmission lever into reverse and pressed on the gas.

Just as the Lincoln began backing out of the carport, Esther saw her purse slide off the roof and land on the driveway. Oh, what now? She quickly put the car in neutral and pressed the brake.

Charlie had his mind on tomatoes as he drove around the curve that led to his clapboard house with its neatly manicured lawn. Feeling a little itchy for change, he had tried some different varieties this year. In the past, Esther had wanted only beefsteak and cherry tomatoes. Beefsteak for their sandwiches and cherries for their salads. But Charlie had put in three new plants as an experiment—pear-shaped red romas, a yellow variety, and even one that had a hint of purple to it. To his surprise, Esther thought the new tomatoes tasted delicious, and she had enjoyed showing them off at Deepwater Cove's Labor Day barbecue.

Having decided to be bold with peppers in the coming spring, Charlie was pondering the difference between sweet bells, anchos, and jalapeños when he heard a loud bang from the direction of his carport.

Charlie stepped on his brake, gaping in disbelief as Esther's long bronze Lincoln flew through the air, sailing off the four-foot-high concrete wall that divided the driveway from the backyard and then slamming down a good ten feet onto the lawn. On its way, the car had taken out two of the wooden support posts holding up the carport's roof. Now the hood popped open and the horn began to blare. And the car kept going, careening across the grass as steam billowed from the engine and the hood bounced up and down like a jack-in-the-box lid. Somehow the Lincoln swerved around the purple martin house before grazing the trunk of an oak tree and mowing down a walnut sapling. Then it hurtled toward the thin strip of beach and the lake edge beyond, with only the shed blocking its way.

His heart frozen in his chest, Charlie put his own car in park and threw open the door. Was someone stealing the Lincoln? Had it rolled down the driveway on its own? Or could that dark shape in the driver's seat be his wife?

"Esther?" Charlie took off at a dead run. The Lincoln was now barreling toward the shed. Charlie had built it a few years earlier to store his riding lawn mower and tools. Just as the car reached the shed door, it veered to the right.

"Mrs. Moore! Mrs. Moore, stop!" Cody Goss suddenly burst from the house, leaped off the end of the carport, and raced past Charlie. "Mrs. Moore, the post office is the other direction!"

With the Lincoln's horn still blaring, Charlie could hear little else as he watched the car miss the side of the shed by inches. It pulled around in a tight curve, swayed toward the lake again, and then rolled to a sudden stop beside a lilac bush. Smoke billowed out from under the hood, and steaming water gushed onto the ground. The unremitting horn sounded louder than ever.

Cody reached the car five steps ahead of Charlie, but as the young man grabbed the handle, the door swung open.

Esther surged up from the driver's seat, shoved her way past Cody, and headed up the slope in her high heels. "Where's the mail?" she shouted. "I've got to get to the post office before it closes."

"Mrs. Moore, you had an accident!" Cody called after her as she marched toward Charlie, arms flapping in agitation.

"Esther, what on earth?" Charlie caught her by the shoulders and forced her to stop. "Are you all right, honey? What happened?"

"I can't find the mail," she snapped. "Cody keeps moving it, and I'm late for the post office. Those bills aren't going out today unless I—"

She looked up at her husband and seemed to see him for the first time. "Charlie?"

"Esther." He wrapped his arms around her and drew her close. "Oh, sweetheart, you scared me half to death."

"I don't know . . . I'm not sure what happened, Charlie."

"You drove the Lincoln out the wrong end of the carport. You've been in an accident, honey. Let's sit you down."

"Where's my purse?"

"Here, sit on my jacket."

"On the grass?"

"Yes, right here. I'll help you." He pulled off his lightweight jacket and spread it out for her. Then he eased her down onto the lawn. "Now catch your breath, Esther."

"What did Cody do to my car?" She glared in the direction of the shed. Cody was leaning into the driver's side of the Lincoln. A sudden silence sounded loud as he somehow managed to turn off the horn.

"Look at that boy," Esther grumbled. "He's gone and wrecked my car. I knew we never should have taken him on. You think you can trust someone, and then . . . where's the mail, Charlie? I've got to hurry to the post office. And my hair. Good heavens, I'm late for my set-and-style."

As she checked her watch, Charlie noticed a discoloration on her wrist. "You're hurt! Esther, honey, let me see your other arm. Oh, for pete's sake, sweetheart, you're all bruised up."

"Esther? Charlie, what happened?"

He looked up to see their neighbor, Kim Finley, hurrying across the lawn with her twins in tow.

"Charlie, is Esther all right?"

"We heard the crash!" Lydia sang out.

"Your carport roof is caving in, Mr. Moore," Luke added as they neared the couple seated on the grass. "You lost the two middle support posts."

Behind them, Charlie noticed Brenda Hansen and Kim's mother-in-law, Miranda Finley, moving toward the scene. Suddenly it seemed like half the neighborhood was descending on the Moores.

"I wish Derek was here," Kim cried as she knelt in the grass at Esther's feet. "He's got all that first-aid training. Charlie, it looks like she might have hit her head. Her face is beginning to swell."

"Whose face?" Esther asked. She was looking from one person to another. "What's wrong? What happened?"

"You drove the wrong way out of the carport," Cody told her. "You meant to go backward, but you went forward. We need to call 911 right now, because that's what you do when someone has an accident. Even if they don't look hurt too much, they could be hurt inside, and that's why the doctor needs to check them. I saw it on TV when I was at my aunt's house. They said to call the ambulance no matter what."

"I've already called." Brenda Hansen, crouched beside Esther, took her hand. "Do you remember getting into your car?"

"Well, that's what I've been trying to tell everyone. I need to get to the post office. And Patsy's expecting me for my set-and-style."

Charlie had noticed a lump growing in his throat, and he tried to speak around it. "After you got into the car, honey, why did you put it in drive instead of reverse?"

Esther gazed at him, her blue eyes misty. "Did I do that?"

"Do you recall driving off the end of the carport?"

"I saw the birdhouse; that's all." She blinked a couple of times, and then she turned to where the car was still sending up clouds of steam. "I looked up, and the birdhouse was coming right at me, so I turned the car a little bit. And then there was a tree."

"Two trees," Cody said. "You did some fancy steering, Mrs. Moore. You missed the birdhouse, the trees, and even the shed."

"Well, what do you know. . . ."

"We know you scared us halfway to deaf!" Cody exclaimed. "I still can hardly hear. But I got the horn to quit, and here are your keys. I switched off the engine all by myself."

Charlie reached up and took the keys. The Lincoln wouldn't be going anywhere soon, if ever again, he realized. The front end looked somewhat like an accordion, and the smell from the smashed radiator still hung in the cool late-afternoon air.

"I hear the ambulance," Esther said. "Oh, goodness, I don't think that's necessary. But I guess we ought to go and thank them anyway for coming out this far."

As Esther moved, Charlie saw her pretty face crumple in pain. "You sit right here with me, Esther," he said, tucking her under his arm. "Just the two of us. We'll sit here together, and everything will be fine."

CHAPTER TWO

Charlie couldn't keep his eyes off Esther, who lay sleeping in the hospital bed. Though her injuries from the car accident appeared minor—mostly bruising and abrasions—the doctor had decided to keep her there for a couple of days. *"Tests,"* he'd told Charlie. *"I'd like to run a few more tests."*

What did that mean? Wasn't Esther going to be back to normal once those dark spots on her arms and face healed up? And why wasn't she talking more? Esther had always been a chatterbox, but now she mostly slept or just looked out the window at the hospital parking lot.

Pastor Andrew had driven to the hospital the moment he heard about the accident, and he'd been back every day since. Usually the minister focused his attention on Esther—talking to her, reading the Bible, praying with her. Today, instead of walking straight to Esther's bedside, he sat on the chair next to Charlie's recliner and studied the silent television set for a few minutes.

"I notice you've got the TV on, but you haven't glanced at it once," Pastor Andrew said finally. "You keep looking at Esther as if you'd never seen her before. What's on your mind, Charlie?"

"I've never seen her like this," Charlie admitted. "I even considered telling Charles Jr. and Ellie they'd better come see their mother. But the doctor says it's not that serious, and the kids are both so busy that I decided against it. But she's got me worried."

Pastor Andrew nodded. Charlie liked the tall, lanky fellow who wore glasses a little too big for his face and suit coats a little too short for his arms. He had led Lake Area Ministry Bible Chapel—LAMB Chapel, as folks called it—for more than ten years. He took his role as pastor of the flock seriously, and he was forever visiting folks in their homes or dropping by the hospital or nursing home.

When Pastor Andrew preached a sermon, about all he did was choose a passage from the Bible and teach the congregation what the verses meant and how they ought to affect a person's life. Which Charlie figured was exactly what most folks needed. Pastor Andrew had been to a Bible college, but he didn't go for fancy messages with highfalutin lingo like some ministers.

Charlie had been raised in a church where the pastor was more interested in sounding grandiose than in teaching truth to his flock. Not Pastor Andrew. In fact, he regularly got garbled, off track, or tongue-twisted during his sermons—a fact that endeared him to everybody. One Sunday, he told the congregation that they should not be lax in doing good. "The truth is obvious," he announced in a stern voice. "We've got a laxative problem around here."

Esther and Charlie had laughed over that one later, and they still occasionally reminded each other not to have a laxative attitude. It was one of the many little jokes between them—lines from movies, silly puns, memorable events—things only the two of them understood. One word or a meaningful glance could trigger the very same thought in both of them. As Charlie gazed at his wife, he wondered if they would ever share such intimate moments again.

"Has she been talking to you much?" Pastor Andrew asked Charlie now. "I wonder if she remembers the accident. I can't get her to tell me about it."

"Right after it happened, she had all kinds of energy. She was talking, but she was confused. She thought Cody Goss had wrecked her car and made her miss her weekly set-and-style at the beauty parlor. She kept talking about the post office and insisting that she was fine. I thought the accident had just shaken her up a little, and she'd be back to her same old self in no time. But now . . . I don't know . . . it's like she's gone off somewhere, and I can't get her to come home."

"Home? This world is not Esther's real home, Charlie. You know that, don't you? Her Father's getting things ready for her—for all of us who belong to Christ—to come home forever."

"I hate to disappoint you, Pastor, but heaven is the last thing on our minds. Esther's even got Thanksgiving dinner all planned out. There's a turkey in the freezer. On the day of the accident, she was on her way to her hair appointment, and then we had planned to eat dinner at Aunt Mamie's Good Food—the Friday night all-you-can-eat shrimp special. I can't figure out why Esther just lies there sleeping or staring out the window."

"Maybe it's the medication. Do they have her sedated?"

"They did at first. I'm not sure now. The doctors and nurses mean well, but they talk so fast you can hardly make heads or tails of what they're telling you. They rattle off their medical jabber—names of medicines and tests and body parts. The doctor told me he thought Esther might have a broken clavicle, and it about scared me half to death. I typed the word into my computer, expecting the worst, and it turns out a clavicle is nothing more than a collarbone. And Esther's wasn't broken after all, just bruised."

Pastor Andrew gave a low chuckle. "Sometimes they forget we're all just regular people."

Charlie nodded. That was what he liked best about his minister. Pastor Andrew was a regular fellow with a wife and two kids, a man who planted a vegetable garden every spring, took his family boating on the lake in the summer, and organized a pancake breakfast for the deer hunters every fall. Only difference was, God had given him a special gift, and that was to shepherd a flock—which he did to the best of his ability.

"Did the doctor tell you what kind of tests they're running?" Pastor Andrew asked.

"He told me a lot of different things, and I tried to write it all down on the back of an envelope I had in my pocket. But that didn't do me much good. Couldn't spell much of it, so I couldn't read it, so I couldn't look it up. I guess I'll have to wait until they tell me what they've found out."

For a moment, the two men studied the motionless woman in the bed nearby. A chill ran down Charlie's spine, as it did every time he looked at Esther. How could this have happened? Why did she step on the gas pedal instead of the brake? Old people made those kinds of mistakes, and Esther wasn't old. They were both still in their sixties—not for long, but even so. It didn't make sense.

"Why all the sunflowers in the bouquets around her bed?" Pastor Andrew asked.

"Esther likes them. They're her favorite kind of flower." Charlie hung his head. "You know, I didn't even realize that until the bouquets started coming in. Finally, this morning when Kim and Derek Finley brought over an arrangement with nothing but sunflowers, I asked about it. Kim acted real surprised that I didn't know how much Esther loved sunflowers. But I didn't. I never gave it a thought till I went home last night. We've got sunflower wallpaper in the kitchen, sunflower towels in the bathroom, and a wreath of artificial sunflowers on the front door. I've been married to that woman almost fifty years, and suddenly I'm finding out all kinds of things about her that I never knew."

"What else?"

"Take a look at this." He picked up one of Ashley Hanes's jewelry boxes from the rolling cart near Esther's bed. "I'm sure Esther told you that she's been helping a young lady in our neighborhood build a small business. Well, I got roped into it too. We sort beads and string them onto fishing line. Anyhow, in the past few weeks, Esther and I have discussed every color in the rainbow and a few more besides. We've talked about patterns and shapes and earrings and necklaces and what all, till I'm just about beaded out. Then yesterday, Ashley Hanes showed up with this."

He lifted a delicate, three-strand necklace out of the box. "Ashley tells me she made these beads especially for Esther. And you know why? Because purple is Esther's favorite color. Purple! I never knew that. Never thought about it, never asked her, nothing. Last night, I got to thinking back, and I remembered that Esther wore a purple gown to our high school prom. *Orchid*, she called the color. Big flouncy thing all covered in netting and lace. We've still got that dress up in the attic somewhere. So before I went to bed, I took a look at Esther's side of the closet. Lo and behold, nearly everything the woman owns has some shade of purple on it."

"I suppose there are always a few surprises left in a marriage," Pastor Andrew observed.

"I reckon so." Charlie fell silent, wondering what else he might have missed in the past fifty years. "It wasn't too long ago I found out Esther was self-conscious about her cooking. Her mother had made her feel inferior in the kitchen. Turns out every time I took her to a restaurant for dinner, Esther thought it was because I didn't like what she was planning to make that night. But she's a wonderful cook."

"She sure is. I've enjoyed her Sunday pot roast many times." Pastor Andrew clapped a hand on Charlie's shoulder. "Well, I'd better get home before my wife starts thinking I've forgotten it's family game night. She's a whiz at Scrabble, and I can beat her at checkers any day of the week. The kids always want to play Uno, but there's only so much of that you can take."

As the minister made to stand, Charlie suddenly caught his arm. "Pastor Andrew, what would *you* do?" he asked, the words tumbling from his lips before he'd thought them through. "What would you do if you lost your wife?"

The pastor settled back into his chair. "I'd be heartbroken. I love her, and I can't imagine being without her."

"That's it. That's the thing. I don't know what life is like without Esther. I can hardly remember back that far. We're so comfortable, you know—kind of like a summer afternoon when you're sitting on the porch swing looking at the lake, and suddenly you realize that everything is right. You wouldn't change a thing. That's Esther and me. We trust each other. We like each other. We even laugh at the same old jokes over and over. The bottom line is that we're happy, Pastor. Esther and I are happy together."

"That's a blessing, Charlie. Not too many people can get to your place in life and say that."

"I know it's a blessing, but it has a downside. Chances are, one of us will die before the other. I don't even know how to think about such a thing—and I never intended to. In my mind, I'm the one who's supposed to go first. The statistics are stacked against me. I'm a man, I smoked cigarettes when I was younger, and my father had a stroke at sixty-three. Esther's always been so vibrant and busy. Sometimes she acts as young and silly as she did when we first met. But when I see her like this . . . well, I don't know what I'd do if she passed away before me."

Pastor Andrew let out a breath. "I could give you pat answers, Charlie. Hold fast to the Lord. Take comfort in knowing your spouse will be joyful in heaven. Read your Bible. But the truth is, each person has to work through loss in his own way. There's no quick and easy prescription. You will take it one minute at a time, one hour at a time, one day at a time . . . and after a while, you will realize you can go on. You can survive after all. And eventually, you can even figure out how to be happy again."

Charlie nodded. "You've never steered me wrong before, Pastor, so I'll trust you about this. Well, I guess you'd better get home to your checkers."

The minister stood. He walked to Esther's bedside, laid a hand on her shoulder, and murmured a brief prayer.

As Pastor Andrew left the room, Charlie thought about calling the kids, but there really wasn't any news to report. So he settled back into the recliner and closed his eyes. With Esther so near, breathing softly, he knew it wouldn't be long before he was sound asleep.

"This meeting of the Tea Lovers' Club will now come to order." Ashley Hanes cleared her throat and raised her voice. "Hey, everyone! Be quiet so I can start the meeting."

Cody glanced at Patsy, who was eyeing the young redhead standing at a table near the window. "Ashley's not doing it right," Cody whispered, leaning against Patsy's shoulder. "Mrs. Moore always clinks her teacup with a spoon until people stop talking."

"Shh," Patsy said, elbowing him. "Esther asked Ashley to take over today, and she's doing her best."

"I miss Mrs. Moore," Cody told her. "She keeps minutes in her purse instead of in her watch. I think that's smart, because I've lost two watches already. One I accidentally dropped down the garbage disposal when I was grinding up leftovers at the Hansens' house. The other one I ran over with the lawn mower at the Moores' house."

Patsy tried to keep her focus on Ashley. She was hoping for some current news about Esther, and she wasn't really in the mood for Cody. "Scoot over, Cody. You're dropping cookie crumbs into my teacup."

"I think you're mad at me."

"I'm not mad. But you can't drape all over folks like that. And for your information, Cody, there are two kinds of minutes. The minutes that a watch counts, and the minutes that are a record of a meeting."

"You're upset because Pete Roberts is letting his beard grow again, aren't you, Patsy? You go to church with him, and you eat at Aunt

Mamie's, and you fish off the dock with him. But you wouldn't go to the football game last Friday night, so he's growing out his beard. You didn't do what he wanted, and now he won't do what you want. Mrs. Moore told me that's how it is with love. It's like a seesaw, back and forth, up and down."

"Cody, for mercy's sake, keep your voice down." Patsy smiled at Opal Jones. She was grateful for once that the ninety-four-year-old widow wasn't wearing her hearing aids. "Pete and I are not in love, Cody, and no, I didn't want to go to the game with him."

"Because it would be a date—and there are three kinds of dates. There's a fruit that grows on a palm tree, and there's a number for a day of the month, and there's the girlfriend kind of date. That's what Pete wanted, but you—"

The tinkling sound of Ashley tapping her teacup with a spoon finally brought silence to Cody and the others gathered in the tea nook inside Just As I Am. Patsy turned away from the young man and hoped that he would stop talking about Pete Roberts.

"Hi, everyone," Ashley said into the silence of the room. As if the sound of her own voice startled her, she suddenly blushed bright pink beneath her freckles. "Well, I'm not used to talking in front of people, but anyhow . . . I went over to visit Mrs. Moore this morning—she came home from the hospital yesterday—and she asked me to read the minutes of the last meeting."

"Is Esther on her feet yet?" one of the elderly women asked Ashley. "She's not bedridden, is she? I heard they kept her in the hospital for two extra days because they had to run tests, and that sounds like cancer to me."

"Or kidney failure," someone else suggested. "She's been having a few problems in that area lately."

"It's nothing," Ashley asserted, cutting off the hum of rumors zipping around the room. "The doctor didn't find anything seriously wrong with Esther, just the usual stuff. She has high blood pressure, like always. Her cholesterol is up. And her bones are weak."

"Osteoporosis," one of the neighborhood's widows clarified. "Bone loss. You girls need to drink plenty of milk and get your exercise while you're young, or you'll wind up all stooped over when you get old. You'll be a hunchback."

"A thumbtack?" Opal Jones asked, turning to Patsy. "I've got a box of thumbtacks at home, and paper clips, too. I used to have a stapler, though I never was sure how to load the blame thing."

"Ashley's talking about Mrs. Moore," Cody explained loudly, leaning across Patsy's teacup to address Opal. "Mrs. Moore is sick in her bones and her blood, but that's the usual stuff."

Opal squinted at Cody for a moment. "Well, I'll be."

"Mr. and Mrs. Moore are going down to Springfield in a couple weeks," Ashley continued, breezing on almost breathlessly. "They both plan to have their neck arteries checked out along with a few other things. Mrs. Moore told me she feels pretty good except for the bruises."

"I heard her face is as purple as a ripe plum," someone spoke up. "They say her eyes are almost swelled shut."

"Like she got run over by a Mack truck," another woman added.

"What I'd like to know is why on earth Esther drove off the end of her carport. Did she tell you what happened that day, Ashley?"

Before the young woman could answer, someone else chimed in. "She knocked down the two central posts in their carport, you know. The roof would have collapsed if some of the neighborhood men hadn't hurried over to brace it up."

"Brad helped," Ashley said, mentioning her young husband. "So did Steve Hansen and Derek Finley. Mrs. Moore said to tell them thanks, and when her arms aren't so sore, she'll be mailing notes to everyone."

"Mrs. Moore buys stamps to support the United States Postal Service," Cody informed the others. "That's because Mr. Moore used to be a mailman. It doesn't matter if you live right across the street. Mrs. Moore will put a stamp on her letter and stick it in the mailbox, and you won't get it for two days instead of letting me run over to your house and give it to you."

"Thanks, Cody," Ashley said, awarding him one of her infrequent smiles. "That brings me to what I want to say. As everyone knows, Mrs. Moore's car ran over the backyard flower bed and one corner of Charlie's vegetable garden. I think we should all go over to the Moores' house and do some repair work. This weekend, the men are going to take down the temporary supports under the carport roof, and Brad is going to show them how to rebuild it. So I thought that would be a good time for us to help out too."

"Ashley, you forgot 'old business,'" Cody inserted. "That comes before 'new business' in the minutes."

One corner of Ashley's mouth turned down. "Who cares about that, Cody? Everyone remembers what happened at last week's meeting. We're not stupid."

"I might be. Before I came to Deepwater Cove, some men beat me up and told me I was stupid and dumb and a moron."

"Well, you're not," Ashley declared. "People are different from each other, and it doesn't matter. Like I have red hair, and kids used to tease me. But then I wound up marrying Brad Hanes, so there."

"So there," Cody echoed.

"If you want to come rebuild the Moores' garden beds," Ashley continued, "we'll start on Saturday morning. And I think we all should try to help, because Mrs. Moore is a good friend to all of us."

"She brought me fresh strawberries," Brenda Hansen said. "Last spring, I was struggling over the fact that all my children were away at college. One day Esther came over to the house with a basket of strawberries from Charlie's garden. It made a big difference in how I felt."

"Esther helped plant flowers in front of my house," Patsy added. "I didn't have time to work on the garden bed, but she took care of everything."

"Let's not forget it was Esther who organized the Fourth of July picnic and the Labor Day barbecue." Kim Finley rarely spoke during the meetings. But on the matter of Esther Moore, she had a definite opinion. "Before the accident, she told me she was hoping we could do something as a community around the Thanksgiving holiday. I think that's a great idea, and I'd like to offer to chair the committee on behalf of Esther. I want to plan something really special."

"New business," Cody muttered.

"I'll help you, Kim."

Patsy turned to find that the voice belonged to Bitty Sondheim. She had slipped into the meeting unnoticed, and Patsy was glad to see her. Bitty owned the Pop-In, a small fast-food restaurant on the other side of the salon. Coming from California, she hadn't quite figured out how to blend in with her Missouri neighbors.

In a room full of women wearing sweaters with autumn leaves, scarecrows, and other fall motifs, Bitty had on a red tie-dyed dress with a purple fringed shawl tied around her waist. A long blonde braid ran down her back in contrast to the carefully coiffed, curled, set, gelled, and sprayed hair on the other women. More amazing yet, while everyone in the room wore sensible shoes and socks—some bearing patterns of pumpkins or orange leaves—Bitty had stuck her bare feet into a pair of sandals with such heavy soles and thick straps they looked fit to climb the Alps. Plus, she hadn't bothered to paint her toenails.

"Thanksgiving is my favorite holiday," Bitty said. "I have so much to be grateful for, especially this year. And besides, I need to make up for my bad attitude at the barbecue."

"Don't worry about that," Ashley told her. "Your frustration led you to create those Hearty Homemade Wraps that Brad and the other guys in his crew eat for lunch nearly every day. I was sick of making bologna sandwiches and hearing him gripe about them. You pretty much saved my bacon."

Patsy took a last sip of tea as Ashley glanced through the minutes Esther had written out before the accident. Clearly the younger woman had decided most of the information wasn't worth mentioning as she flipped through the pages. At last she raised her head. "Okay, that's it for this meeting."

With a faint smile, she sat down.

Patsy was about to head for the hot water urn when Brenda Hansen stood. "I don't believe Ashley mentioned her bead business. Ladies, Christmas is just around the corner, and the necklaces are going fast. If you want to get your orders in, you'll need to hurry. Miranda Finley has put together a lovely brochure, and the Moores have been sorting and stringing beads. Now that Esther is out of commission for a while, if anyone wants to help Charlie, that would be great."

"I'll help him," Miranda said. "I have time on my hands now that my grandchildren are back in school."

Like Bitty, the newly arrived St. Louis transplant Miranda had her own sense of style. But while Bitty was wild and wacky, Miranda appeared to have stepped out of a fashion magazine. Today she wore a pair of taupe linen slacks and a matching sweater set accented with gold jewelry. Her deeply tanned skin set off her spiky blonde hair. Patsy couldn't help but wonder how she and her daughter-in-law, Kim, were getting along these days.

Ashley spoke from her chair. "I'm going into bracelets and headbands too. That means you can order for your kids or grandkids, if you want. And thank you, Brenda, for letting me use your basement craft room to make my beads."

Brenda beamed. Ever since her elder daughter, Jennifer, had returned to the area to prepare for training as a missionary, Brenda had seemed more cheerful. But Patsy suspected that Brenda's radiance had a lot to do with her joy in the rebirth of her marriage. These days, she and Steve worked almost side by side, refurbishing and decorating houses and putting them on the real estate market.

"I'll tell Mrs. Moore we're going to fix her flower bed on Saturday," Ashley was saying as the women began to lay their napkins on the tea tables and pick up their purses. "I'll let her know we like the idea of a Thanksgiving get-together too. But I'm not writing out a meeting report; that's for sure."

Cody elbowed Patsy. "Minutes," he murmured. "I may not be very good at telling time, but I could do a better job than Ashley with old and new business. Once when I was supposed to be vacuuming the Moores' house, I saw one of Mrs. Moore's books on the shelf, and I read the whole thing. I know all about *Robert's Rules of Order*, and I'm probably better at parliamentary procedure than anyone in this room. So there."

Patsy gaped as Cody rose from his chair and headed for the pastry case. *So there.*

CHAPTER THREE

Esther studied the array of wilting flower arrangements on the bookshelves and end tables around her bed. What on earth was wrong with Charlie that he couldn't remember to water them? The man had to be told what to do every minute of the day or he'd let the whole house fall to wrack and ruin.

"Charlie?" she called out. "Are you watching TV again?"

"That talk show's on." His voice drifted in from the living room.

"The one where people get into fights and throw chairs at each other?"

Esther could picture her husband stretched out on his brown leather recliner, rumpled socks on his big old feet, wearing baggy exercise pants and jacket, a bowl of popcorn perched on his stomach. She ought to haul herself out of bed and go bop him on the head. Charlie Moore would make the worst nurse in the world.

As for cooking—well, the meals he had fixed since she came home from the hospital were so bad even the dog turned up his nose. Poor Boofer. He didn't understand why Esther and Charlie were no longer taking him on long walks or driving him around the neighborhood in their golf cart.

As Esther edged her legs toward the side of the bed, Charlie's head appeared in the doorway. "Whatcha need, sweet pea?"

"You *are* watching that awful show, aren't you?"

"Me and plenty of other people. It wouldn't be on TV if it didn't bring an audience. The show isn't so bad, Esther. In fact, it's interesting."

With a sigh, she leaned back on her pillow. "You miss your old mail route, don't you? Chatting with people, finding out the latest news, checking on the condition of folks' houses and yards, petting their dogs. That's why you like the show, isn't it?"

He shrugged. "Maybe so. I've always taken an interest in people and what they're up to."

"Because I'm such a bore." She focused on a bouquet of sunflowers, pretty heads bowed in resignation at their coming death. "If I hadn't talked you into taking early retirement, you wouldn't be stuck at home with an old woman who can't even get out of bed."

"Now that's just plain silly, Esther, and you know it. I was happy to retire, and I enjoy our life here at the lake. You're not an old woman who can't get out of bed. In fact, it's high time for you to sit up, put on your clothes, and walk around again. You haven't been out of that bed since breakfast. The doctor told me you should be able to leave the house and walk to the mailbox by now. Let's go outside; what do you say?"

"I don't want to walk," Esther said. "My bones ache, and I look like I got into a fight with Joe Louis or Muhammad what's his name."

"The bruises are fading faster than you think. How about if we walk to the bathroom together, and you put on some makeup? You'll feel better once you realize you're almost back to normal."

Her eyes suddenly misting, Esther tried to stop her lower lip from quivering. "I'll never be back to normal, Charlie. I'm fading away, losing my mind. I probably have Alzheimer's."

Charlie sat down on the bed beside his wife and kissed her tears. "Why are you talking this way, honey? What's gotten into you?"

"Old age! I put the car in drive instead of in neutral, Charlie. I stepped on the gas instead of the brake. And I have no idea why. I'm old and frail and falling apart—can't you see that?"

"No, I can't. Everyone makes driving mistakes now and then. Derek Finley hit a deer one night last week. Said he tried to avoid it, ran his truck off the road, almost overcorrected, and would have landed upside down in the ditch if he hadn't been paying attention. Just the other day, Brad Hanes rammed into a parking meter and scraped the front fender of his brand-new pickup. You couldn't call those men old or frail."

"Deer are unpredictable. That's not the same as what I did. And Brad was drunk. That's why he ran into the parking meter. Ashley told me all about it. She was devastated, poor thing. All that money down the drain to fix the truck, and a DWI on Brad's record too."

"That'll be his second one this year," Charlie remarked. "I wonder if he's got a drinking problem."

"Ashley wants so badly to have a perfect marriage, but she's struggling. I think she married Brad because she was amazed and flattered that he took notice of her in the first place. The girl has no idea how pretty she is with all that long red hair and those big brown eyes. She married him before she gave it a second thought, and now she's stuck with a drunk who spends money left and right. He's never home, you know."

"Brad is a kid, Esther. He's got to learn what being married is all about. We were kids once too, remember? We had some hard times."

"I know. . . . I remember what I did to you. . . ." Her voice quavering, Esther pulled the sheet up over her face and pressed it against her damp eyes. "I forced you to give up your dream when you were young, and I did it all over again when I made you retire. I ruined your life. Oh, I might as well have died in that crash. I'm going to pass away anyhow, and then you'll be free of me."

Unable to stop crying, Esther saw the past flashing through her mind like an old flickering movie reel. So many things she'd done wrong. So many ways she had failed her husband. Her children. Her friends. Even God.

"Now what's this all about?" Charlie murmured, tugging the sheet out of her hands. He ran a finger down his wife's cheek, as he'd done so many thousands of times before. "Esther, I love you. You've made me a happy man, and I can't bear the thought of losing you."

As he spoke, Charlie slipped his arms around his wife and lifted her to his chest. Holding her firmly, he rubbed her back for a moment. Then he began to shift her toward the edge of the bed.

"You're going to get out of this bed right now, Mrs. Moore," he declared as he pushed aside the sheet and drew her to her feet. "You're going to put on some real clothes. And we're taking Boofer for a walk. Don't even try to argue, because I'm sticking to my guns on this one."

Sniffling, Esther leaned on her husband's arm as she shuffled toward the bathroom. She truly did feel old now. Much older than before the accident. Driving the careening car across the yard, she'd had a strange sense that she was propelling herself toward death. Toward an unexpected ending, neither planned nor prepared for.

She hadn't died, but she had seen the end of life. She had looked it in the face. And the experience had aged her.

"How about these?" Charlie asked, holding up one of the many identical pairs of elastic-waist slacks—each in a slightly different color—that Esther had purchased at her favorite store over the years. He plucked a hanger from the closet. "This shirt ought to be easy to slide over your arms without causing any pain. I'll help you with the buttons."

"Charlie, you've got a pair of brown slacks in one hand and my Fourth of July blouse with American flags all over it in the other. What are you thinking, you big galoot? Don't you know how to match outfits after all this time? For pete's sake, you're just like the kids. How many years did I work on teaching them manners? They still forget to put their napkins in their laps, and they chew with their mouths open as bad as they ever did."

Pushing away from her husband, Esther sorted through her clothes until she found a nice blouse with chocolate and tan stripes. "Brown goes with brown," she instructed Charlie as they headed for the bathroom. "And here's the sweater I usually wear with this outfit. See these red, brown, and gold leaves embroidered down the front and on the pockets? That's because it's an *autumn* sweater. In autumn, you wear brown, gold, russet, cranberry, and plum."

"What about your favorite color?" He paused a moment and then said, "Purple."

"Didn't I just list plum as an autumn shade? What color is a plum, Charlie? Honestly, sometimes it's an uphill battle with you."

As she spoke, Esther managed to slip out of her gown. Charlie propped her up on one side, and she balanced herself on the edge of the sink with her free hand while she worked to get her feet into the trouser legs. Such an effort! She secretly wondered if she had broken something and the doctor had failed to notice. Her body felt like one of those forgotten Easter eggs discovered a few days after the hunt—still in one piece, but cracked all over.

"My, my, my," Charlie said as Esther pulled on her blouse. He waggled his eyebrows at her. "You are one good-looking gal. You've got my heart beating so hard, I think I'm beginning to feel a little frisky."

Rolling her eyes, Esther brushed his hands away and buttoned her blouse by herself. Wouldn't you know it? Here she was, half dead, sore all over, recovering from the most harrowing experience of her life, and all her husband could think about was how frisky he was feeling. How many times had the man seen her body in various stages of dress and undress? She would never have believed that at sixty-eight years of age and after forty-eight years of marriage, Charlie Moore still had just one thing on his mind.

At a glance in the mirror, Esther groaned. But she truly didn't look as bad as she had feared. While Charlie hovered, she patted powder on her nose and slicked on a pretty shade of lipstick. Her hair was awful, and she knew she would have to miss this Friday's set-and-style at Just As I Am, but what else could she do? She couldn't go out in public in such a state. Tugging a gold silk scarf from her drawer, she tied it around her white hair. Then she stepped into a pair of soft brown leather shoes and looked up at Charlie.

"There. I'm ready for a walk."

He grinned and offered his arm. "Shall we promenade, madam?"

Esther looped her arm through Charlie's and let him escort her through the house. Beside himself with joy at the emergence of both his owners in sweaters and jackets, Boofer hopped down from the sofa and began racing around their feet, barking like crazy. The pudgy black mop was clearly certain that a walk was in the offing.

When Charlie pushed open the front door, Boofer darted outside and dashed toward the mailbox. A brisk wind hit Esther and nearly knocked her backward. She realized at once that she should have worn a coat. The sweater wouldn't keep her warm enough in the biting breeze.

"One of us is going to come down with pneumonia in this chill," she predicted as they made their way across the front porch and down the steps.

Charlie glanced at her. "People don't get pneumonia from cold weather, remember? You read it in one of those women's magazines. Germs or some such is what causes colds and pneumonia. You're the one who told me that."

"I did? Well, I don't remember. My mother always said a cold wind never did anyone any good."

She lifted a hand and waved as Derek Finley drove by in his Water Patrol truck. "He's such a nice man," she said. "He treats Kim like a queen. As far as I know, he never brings up her past—that awful husband she had to escape with the twins in the middle of the night. But Kim really made something of herself. A dental assistant. That takes skill, you know. A person doesn't just walk into a dentist's office and start cleaning teeth. Kim went to technical school."

When Charlie didn't respond, Esther continued down the path in silence. The houses that surrounded theirs were shut tight against the cold. Dreary square boxes under brown tree limbs. But inside there would be fires and hot chocolate and happy chatter. Suddenly it seemed to Esther that everyone in Deepwater Cove was young and busy with life. Even the neighborhood's widows sashayed out to their bridge games, club meetings, shopping trips, and luncheons.

Esther sighed. "I'm going to die, Charlie," she murmured.

His arm stiffened under hers, and he paused on the sidewalk. "Now what kind of nonsense are you talking, woman? You just got a few bruises, and they're almost gone."

"But don't you see? That accident proves it. Anything can happen."

"Sure it can. Folks die all the time—young, old, and in-between. Happens to every single one of us at some point." They began walking again. "The accident didn't mean you're about to kick the bucket, Esther. For crying out loud, you sure are grumpy these days. I wish you would get back to being pert and peppy. This is getting tiresome."

Esther heard her husband complaining, but she couldn't focus beyond her own thoughts. "I just never gave it much consideration. Dying. I always believed I had a lot more interesting, important things to do. But now that I think about my life, it wasn't much. I didn't go to college or get a job like Kim and so many others. I was no beauty queen, and I never won a single blue ribbon at the county fair. I didn't have the voice to sing in the church choir, and I gave up teaching Sunday school because my heart wasn't in it. All I really did was look after the kids and keep you fed and clothed. Now I spend my time getting my hair fixed or meeting with the TLC or sorting beads. I've never done a single significant thing. And I kept you from your dream too."

Charlie gave a low whistle, his traditional sign of frustration. Lips pressed together, he opened the mailbox at the end of their driveway. Esther could see that Christmas catalogs were starting to trickle in already. There were a few bills too. Nothing important.

As Charlie shut the mailbox, he turned and faced his wife. "Esther, are you afraid to die?"

She glanced away as tears once again sprang to her eyes. "Who wouldn't be? Death is an awful thing. And then you go to heaven and have to play a harp for the rest of eternity. I swear, Charlie, sometimes I lie there in bed and wish I'd never been born."

"I cannot believe what I'm hearing out of your mouth. It's like that crash scrambled your brains and left me with a different wife. Perk up, pumpkin. Please."

She shrugged. "Have the kids called today?"

"Not yet. Give them time."

"You would think I could have done a better job raising them, since that's all I had to do. But look at them. Charles Jr. works in an onion factory. Onions, of all things. And then there's Ellie—she made such a mess of her life it's a wonder she's even alive."

"Charles *manages* the onion company, Esther. He's got a fine wife and two sweet kids. Sure, Ellie made some mistakes, but God brought her back in line, just like we prayed. She makes a good salary running the church youth program. You can't complain about that. She always wanted to live in Florida, and now she does and bought herself a condo there too."

For some reason, Esther had forgotten what her daughter was doing these days. Ellie had been in and out of so many jobs through the years. How long ago had she accepted that church position? After what the child put her parents through, it was a wonder to Esther that any church would want Ellie on its staff.

Arms still linked, Esther and Charlie headed back toward the house. "Well," she said, "there's no question I steered your life onto the wrong course. I was selfish and insisted on having my way."

"Now listen here, woman!" Charlie halted and clamped his hand on his wife's shoulder. "I want you to stop talking this kind of nonsense, right now. We've had a wonderful life, raised two great kids, and are happily retired. I look back on the years with a sense of accomplishment and gratitude. God has blessed us, Esther. Why can't you remember that? We've got a nice house, enough money, good friends, and plenty to eat. Our marriage has been wonderful, and I'm happy we took the path we chose. I don't regret a thing. Do you? Can you honestly disagree with anything I just said?"

Esther gazed at Boofer, who was happily sniffing around the flower bed. The lawn was already brown in patches. The impatiens and begonias had begun to get leggy. It wouldn't be long before the first frost would turn them into piles of green mush. Esther ought to get out and tie up the chrysanthemums. They were beginning to flower and get too heavy to hold their heads up.

Was that how she would end her life? Drooping her head until finally she turned into a pile of mush? Esther could vaguely remember when budding mums had filled her heart with bubbles of joy. The first cold autumn breeze made her laugh out loud in relief at the end of another long, hot summer. She had savored the changing leaves, the smell of chimney smoke, the promise of snow.

Now all she could think about was steering her car past the birdhouse and the tree trunks as its hood flopped up and down. She remembered the look on Cody's face when she pushed her way out of the steaming car, its horn blowing so loud she couldn't hear herself think. She recalled the hospital, people in wheelchairs, the odor of antiseptic.

"Oh, Charlie," she said, leaning into him. "When my car flew off the back of the carport, I feel like I landed in another world. Suddenly life seems so serious to me. No, that's not right. Death seems serious. Life seems trivial. I can't make myself *care* about anything. Why have I spent time and money getting my hair done every Friday? Why did I think a Labor Day barbecue was important? Why have the colors of my outfits mattered so much to me, Charlie?"

"Because those things are all part of who you are. You like sun-flowers. Purple is your favorite color. You're talented at organizing parties and picnics. You get huffy if I dare presume to mismatch your shirt and your slacks because you take pride in your appearance. And I'm glad you do."

For the first time since the accident, Esther felt a smile tickle her lips. "I guess I do still care about that, after all."

"And we're both getting pretty tired of me burning the beans and leaving lumps in the mashed potatoes. You still care about eating a good meal, don't you?"

"I suppose so."

"It's all just life, honey." He slipped his arm around her shoulders and helped her climb the steps onto the porch. "Barbecues, dogs, good food, and sunflowers are part of life, and that means they mat-ter. God wants us to serve Him, but we're to take pleasure in our world too. Even the hard parts—Ellie in trouble, Charles's wife hav-ing miscarriages, your accident—those things are part of life too. Now, let's get back to enjoying it together; what do you say?"

Esther watched Boofer race ahead of them and stand at the front door, his tail wagging his entire body. She grinned. "You sure are wordy for an old man," she told Charlie, giving him a coy glance. "Sometimes I think all you do is talk and eat."

At that, he reached down and gave her backside a gentle swat. "I'm good for a lot more than that, sweetheart. And you know it."

Carrying a piping hot tuna-noodle casserole up the Moores' front walk, Patsy Pringle spotted three figures crossing the street toward her. Although the brisk wind chilled her bare legs and tossed the ruffled hem of her skirt, Patsy paused to wait for them. In a moment, she recognized Jennifer and Jessica Hansen, accompanied by Cody Goss.

"Hey, Patsy!" Cody called out. "We're bringing supper to the Moores. Lasagna!"

"Lasagna?" Patsy rolled her eyes. "Oh, for pity's sake, I thought it was my day to bring a meal. Isn't this Friday?"

"Today is Saturday, Patsy!" Cody bent over, slapped his thigh, and laughed. "We'll have to get you over to Brenda's basement and teach you how to read a calendar."

Both young women giggled as they reached out to hug Patsy.

"I came home for the weekend," Jessica explained. The younger of the two Hansen girls, she was a sophomore in college and newly engaged. "Mom and Jen and I are working on wedding invitations. Cody's helping too. I can't believe how many people are on our list."

Jennifer nodded. "I think Mom has invited the whole church, and Dad keeps adding real estate clients."

"My job is to tie an apricot ribbon through a hole in each invitation," Cody said. "Apricot is Jessica's wedding color. Everyone is wearing apricot, even me."

"Gracious!" Patsy sized up the handsome young man and wondered how Cody would look in an apricot tuxedo. "Well, you can tell me more about it inside. Let's get out of the weather before our casseroles get cold."

They hurried across the porch to find Charlie Moore waiting for them at the front door. "Come on in, everyone! Bless you all for volunteering to bring us dinner. We might have starved from my bad cooking."

Patsy laughed as she hurried past him through the door. "Brr. This cold snap has about frozen off my fingers and toes."

"Look at this, now!" Charlie said, assessing the lineup in his living room. "What do we have here? Two beautiful Hansen girls. One dashing Cody Goss. And the glorious Patsy Pringle."

"Patsy's an apple," Cody piped up.

"*Ample*," Patsy clarified, feeling a flush heat her cheeks. "It's something between Pete Roberts and me. Well, not *between us* like a secret or anything. There was a time when . . . oh, never mind. Come on, girls. Let's put our dinners in the refrigerator. What do you want for supper tonight, Charlie? Lasagna or tuna-noodle casserole?"

"Two dinners on one night. Now that's what I'd call ample." Rubbing his hands together, Charlie followed them into the kitchen. "I know—let me get Esther out of the bedroom. She'll want to have her say in this decision."

Before long, Charlie had his wife by the arm and was escorting her into the living room, where everyone had settled. Patsy stifled a gasp of surprise at the sight of her friend. Usually coiffed, dressed in a classy outfit, and wearing a faint trace of perfume, Esther hardly looked like herself. Still in her bathrobe, she shuffled over and collapsed into a chair. Her white hair—about which she was positively vain—had gone flat on one side, with nary a curl in sight.

"Esther!" Patsy cried. "Are you sick?"

"No, it's just the accident. It threw me off."

"Off the carport," Cody said. "I was standing right over there in the kitchen, looking out the window, when I saw your Lincoln go flying through the air, Mrs. Moore. For a second, I thought I was watching a TV show back at my aunt's house in Kansas. But then I saw the smoke and heard the horn—and I realized it was really happening. That's when I hightailed it outside."

"The whole incident is a blur to me now." Esther fiddled with her hair. "I'm worn to a frazzle. I can't seem to find the energy to do anything."

"I've got you scheduled for your set-and-style next Friday," Patsy told her.

"Oh, I won't be able to go out by then. I'm a wreck."

"How about if we move your appointment up to Tuesday? You'll feel so much better once we do your hair."

"I don't know." Esther waved her hand. "It's not that important to me now."

"But you've always loved getting your set-and-style," Patsy protested. "And what on earth are you doing in your bathrobe at this hour of the day, honey? We need you back in action."

"That's right, Mrs. Moore," Cody said. "I'm sorry to tell you this, but Ashley Hanes does *not* know how to do minutes at the TLC. She doesn't care a bit about parliamentary procedure. I bet she hasn't even read *Robert's Rules of Order*. She did new business first, you know. Then she said she wasn't going to read old business because we were smart enough to remember it—which might be true, but all the same, it's not right. You better come next week, or the TLC will go straight to pot."

When Esther didn't speak, everyone turned to Charlie. Looking bemused, he shrugged. "In the last few days, we've talked till we're blue in the face. If anyone knows how to talk things through, it's Esther and me. She's tried to tell me how she feels, but I still don't understand why she's so worn-out. The doctor said nothing was broken, and her bruises are nearly gone. She's as healthy as a horse except for an occasional headache, but Esther seems to think she's on her deathbed."

"Who can think about death when there's so much to live for?" Jessica asked.

The younger of the two girls, she had been Camdenton High School's homecoming queen her senior year. Patsy had styled her hair for the big event. Though she didn't like to brag, Patsy felt it was one of her best updos ever.

"Mrs. Moore," Jessica continued, her voice rising in animation. "I was hoping I could count on you to serve drinks at my reception. The punch will be raspberry flavored with apricot sherbet balls floating in it. And we're having a chocolate fountain, too! Have you ever seen one? Melted chocolate pours out of the fountain just like water, and you dip strawberries or bananas or whatever you want into it! We're putting a huge apricot bow with apricot carnations at the end of every pew too. The church is going to be gorgeous!"

For a moment, no one responded. Jessica's face sobered, and she glanced uncomfortably at her older sister.

Then Esther spoke up.

"Sherbet balls?" she queried. "In the *punch*? Those are going to melt in the first five minutes, Jessica. You'll be left with a bowl full of apricot goo."

"Really? I never thought of that."

"You need to find something you can freeze good and solid. That way it'll keep its shape the whole way through the reception. And have you given any consideration as to what to do with the punch cups? If you invite as many guests as you mentioned, you'll have empty punch cups sitting all over the place. I think we're going to need someone to keep the fellowship hall tidied up. How about if we put the Finley twins to work? They'd look so cute roaming around with silver trays."

"What a great idea! We could dress them both in apricot!"

"I doubt you'll get Luke into anything apricot, but you can try. He's as cute as a bug's ear."

"I'll talk to Kim about it at church tomorrow. I've been reading all the bridal magazines, Mrs. Moore, but there are so many things to plan. I'm scared I'll forget something really important. Do you want to know the main problem I'm having right now?"

Esther leaned forward. "What is it, sugar?"

"The guest book. Do you think an ostrich quill pen is too over-the-top? It seems like it would be so pretty, but I'm just not sure."

As Esther gave her opinions on the topic of ostrich quill pens, Patsy looked across the living room at Charlie. For the first time since they'd entered the house, he was smiling.

CHAPTER FOUR

Come on, Boofer. I mean it now."

Charlie pulled his golf cart into the carport and turned off the motor. As usual, his loyal traveling companion refused to budge. The plump little black mutt viewed the golf cart as a magic carpet that would take him to foreign lands where he could view vistas heretofore unknown. Who would want to leave such wonders?

Though Charlie drove the same path around the Deepwater Cove neighborhood two or three times a day, the experience thrilled Boofer as if he'd never seen the place in his life. Each smell, each dashing squirrel, each gust of breeze delighted and amazed the dog, who literally grinned the entire way along the road. By the time Charlie had stopped the cart to chat with neighbors, surveyed the lake, picked up the mail, and accomplished whatever other tasks he'd assigned himself, he was ready to head into the house for a while.

Not Boofer.

He sat firmly adhered to the golf cart's vinyl seat, refusing to move, until finally Charlie pretended he was abandoning the stubborn dog. "Well, have it your way, Boof," Charlie said, as he did every day. "I guess I'll go see what's on the stove for dinner."

The moment he opened the screen door that led into the house, Charlie heard Boofer leap from the cart and scamper toward him, tiny black claws skittering on the cement carport floor. Before the man could set one foot inside, the dog had hurtled past him and was racing around the house, looking for Esther.

This evening, Charlie's wife was once again a queen in her realm. Esther had returned to her kitchen.

But things were not as they once had been. True, Esther still rose every morning to make Charlie's breakfast, and she prepared their sandwiches for lunch. But that was about it. Women from the church still regularly brought casseroles or pot roasts to the house. And nearly every afternoon at around three o'clock, Ashley Hanes showed up to help Esther start putting dinner together.

Sometimes the young woman dropped by earlier in the day to string necklaces while Esther sorted and organized beads. Though Charlie liked Ashley well enough, it often startled or even distressed him to find her inside the house. It was his private haven, the cocoon he withdrew into for rest and refreshment. On the other hand, Ashley's presence was about the only thing that perked up Esther's spirits. The pair of them chattered so much that it became a verifiable hen party.

Two weeks had passed since the accident, and Charlie had expected his wife to be back to her same old self. But just about every day Esther announced that she felt frail. Or weak. Or tired. Her hips, her back, her neck, her eyes, even her skin—something was always out of whack. Once in a while she told her husband she was feeling "goofy," to which Charlie had silently replied, *So what else is new?*

"Where've you been, sugar?" Esther called over her shoulder as Charlie hung his jacket in the closet by the door. "Ashley and I are in a bind. The other day, Cody broke the can opener, and we need you to open these beans or we'll never get them into the pot in time."

"*You* broke the can opener, honey," Charlie gently reminded his wife.

"I did not. Why would you say that?"

"You put the blame thing in the dishwasher, Esther. An electric can opener. I still can't figure out what you were thinking. Ruined the motor. Honestly! Nobody puts an electric can opener in the dishwasher."

"Oh well," she said, brushing him off with a wave of her hand. "Come over here and help us—my knuckles have been aching all day. It's the weather, I suppose. You know what the cold does to my joints."

"Yup," Charlie said. Another ailment to add to her collection.

"Ashley tells me she's never even seen the nonelectric kind of can opener," Esther went on. "Can you believe it? That's modern technology for you—good old tools lie in a drawer unused and forgotten. It's a throwaway world, Ashley, and don't ever let anyone tell you different."

With a sigh, Charlie stepped up to the counter. "Evening, Ashley," he said, hooking the hand-turned opener onto the lid of the can of beans. "How's the necklace business these days?"

"I'm swamped." She glanced at him, her big brown eyes framed by masses of long red hair. "Mrs. Finley—Miranda, not Kim—gets the credit for a lot of my sales. She and the twins made up brochures and sent them to friends in the social clubs she used to belong to in St. Louis. Those women are ordering necklaces so fast I can hardly keep up. Seems like I'm always down in the Hansens' basement craft room making beads or printing out orders from my computer or running to the post office with a bunch of boxes to mail. I really do appreciate all the work you and Mrs. Moore have done sorting beads for me. It's been a huge help."

"No problem." Charlie gave the can opener a final twist, and the lid popped open. Truth to tell, if he never saw another bead in his life, it wouldn't bother him a bit. He handed Ashley the can. "Watch the edge of that, now. It's sharp."

"Wow, you're right, Mrs. Moore," Ashley said, dumping the contents into a saucepan. "These beans aren't nearly as green and pretty as the ones from your garden."

"Nothing beats fresh vegetables, right, Charlie?" Esther flashed her husband a pretty smile. "If *someone* had troubled himself to plant enough beans this summer, we wouldn't need to be opening cans. We'd have bags of beans from our own garden sitting in the freezer."

Choosing not to remind Esther that it was she who had urged him to limit the number of rows in his garden this year, Charlie set off toward the laundry room. Esther had said she was tired of cleaning and freezing vegetables, he recalled. *"Why not just open a can from the grocery store?"* she asked him. *"It's much simpler, and the beans are almost as good."*

As usual, he had done his wife's bidding. Now he was paying the price. He had conceded her original point. The garden *was* too big, and it took a lot of time and work.

Charlie loved his garden, though. Since Esther wasn't interested in buying a motor home, taking a cruise, or even venturing out of state to see the grandkids, he knew he'd be stuck at home again next summer. He might as well take his garden back to its previous size, no matter what Esther said.

Hearing Ashley's voice in the kitchen reminded Charlie of something that nagged at him every time he made a round in his golf cart. Back in the summer, Brad Hanes had begun building an addition onto the couple's small house. The young man had informed Charlie that it was to be a garage for his new truck. But Ashley had told Esther the room would be a nursery for the baby she was hoping to have one of these days.

Either way, not long after Brad erected the frame and put on a semblance of a roof, construction ceased. Now the Hanes property—never much to look at in the first place—had become an eyesore. Charlie had done some investigating. He learned that not only had Brad failed to obtain a building permit, but he hadn't gotten construction permission from the subdivision's governing board. To top it off, debris lay scattered everywhere—piles of flagstone, heaps of dirt, stacks of shingles, and several moldering cardboard boxes filled with vinyl siding.

Halting on his way to the laundry room, Charlie looked back toward the kitchen. "Say, how's that addition coming along, Ashley?" he said over his shoulder. "I don't believe I've seen Brad working on it for a while."

A moment of silence was followed by Esther's voice. "Charles Moore, if you don't stop griping about Ashley's new room, I'm going to give you a good chewing out. Leave her and Brad alone. They'll finish it when they have time—which is a scarce commodity when you're young."

"Yeah, yeah, yeah," Charlie muttered under his breath. Surely in four months the Hanes kids could have found a few hours to straighten up the clutter. If there was one thing Charlie couldn't stand, it was a mess.

He ambled into the laundry room, opened the dryer, and began folding clothes—a new activity he'd undertaken in recent days. Charlie hadn't signed on for this job when he married Esther. But life had changed since her accident—in more ways than one. He laid one of his undershirts on the dryer and smoothed it out with his palms. As he began to fold, he could hear the women still jabbering away in the kitchen.

"I don't think Brad's ready," Ashley was saying. "At least, he tells me he wants to wait awhile—till we're more settled, you know."

"How much more settled can a couple be?" Esther asked. "You've both got good jobs, and you own a lovely home. Most of all, you have empty arms and a heart hungry for the sweet babble of a baby."

Sweet babble? Charlie thought, recalling the two babies he'd helped raise to adulthood. *Howl* was more like it. *Wail. Scream. Screech* until the roof raised a good foot or two.

He chuckled at the memory of himself and Esther—practically

kids themselves—frantically racing around trying to figure out how to stop the babies from squalling. Charlie sighed and began to match and roll the white cotton socks Esther had taken to wearing in bed a few years back. Time sure went by fast. Their two children were adults now, one of them with offspring of his own.

Over the years, he and Esther had matured into adults, and then—slowly and insidiously—they had begun to fall apart. Joints began to ache. Backs went out. Hair thinned, and so did bones. Even though Pastor Andrew had offered up a rosy picture of the afterlife, Charlie didn't like to think about it. He enjoyed his wife and the marriage they'd built. It was impossible to imagine an end to their summer-time of gentle breezes, sweet fragrances, and love beyond measure.

"Our jobs are the problem." Ashley's voice was plaintive as Charlie carried a wicker basket of clothing toward the bedroom. "If I could work days like Brad, then we'd be together in the evenings. But with me waitressing at the country club almost every night, he's left at home alone. Days and weekends, I'm working on my beads all the time. Brad says he doesn't like to sit around and watch TV by himself. I can't blame him, but I wish he wouldn't go over to Larry's."

Charlie grunted. Larry's Lake Lounge was a popular local tavern. Brad Hanes's pickup was usually parked outside it every afternoon by four. Charlie couldn't be sure how long the young man stayed there playing pool and drinking beer with his buddies, but two DWIs on his record didn't bode well.

That kind of thing had never been a problem between him and Esther, Charlie reflected as he arranged his clean clothes in the chest of drawers near his side of their double bed. After a day on his feet delivering mail, he had wanted nothing more than to head for his home, his family, and one of Esther's delicious meals. Usually he and Charles Jr. had played catch in the backyard until Esther called them inside. After dinner, he often pulled both kids onto his lap and read them stories until bedtime. Those had been golden years.

Opening the top drawer in Esther's dresser, Charlie discovered that the space was neatly divided into little boxes filled with Esther's jewelry. Bemused, he realized he had no idea where his wife kept her lingerie. Another thing he'd failed to notice. The second drawer down held scarves and the girdles Esther had stopped wearing years ago. Charlie pulled out a girdle and held it up to the light. Studying the web of elastic and the dangling stocking clips, he shook his head. Amazing contraption.

He pushed the drawer shut. Didn't Esther use her dresser for clothing? Pulling open the bottom drawer, he noted stacks of old Christmas cards tied with faded ribbons. Into each collection Esther had slipped a piece of paper noting the year the cards had arrived. Here were birthday cards and letters from the kids too. A small white leather Bible lay on a pair of white silk gloves. Where had that come from?

Charlie lifted the Bible, opened it, and read the inscription. *To my beloved Esther on our wedding day. Charles Edgar Moore.*

Well, how about that? He didn't even remember giving the Bible to Esther, and here she had kept it all these years. Maybe she had worn the gloves that special day too. Charlie drew them out and fingered them gently. Such fine, pale fabric. He thought back on the afternoon of their wedding—and the surprise, embarrassed confusion, and eventual joy of the ensuing night. Now *that* had been quite an event for both of them.

Smiling as he replaced the Bible and gloves, Charlie noticed a large manila envelope with Esther's name and the address of their first apartment scrawled in a hand he didn't recognize. Feeling a little sheepish for snooping, he slid the envelope out from under the stacks of Christmas cards. Was this something else he had given Esther and forgotten? He certainly had no memory of the envelope, but then he hadn't recognized the Bible either.

Reaching inside the manila packet, he drew out a sheet of paper on which someone had penciled a sketch. Not a sketch exactly—better than that. It was a full-blown portrait. A woman with dark hair; intense eyes; and a warm, beautiful smile gazed back at him.

It was Esther.

A shiver of recognition racing down his spine, Charlie stared at the portrait. But this wasn't Esther Jennings, the cute brunette he'd met in high school and married shortly after graduation. This was a curly-haired, doe-eyed, seductive dream girl.

Sure, it was Esther. But—wow. Somehow the artist had captured a side of her that Charlie had never seen. If he'd been anywhere near *this* Esther, he surely would have remembered it.

Swallowing, he dropped his focus to the signature at the bottom of the sketch. *George Snyder*, it read. And beneath the name, a short phrase had been penciled: *I will always love you, Esther.*

"Did you know Ashley has never made gravy from scratch in her entire life?"

Esther's voice echoing along the hall startled Charlie. Quickly he slid the portrait back into the envelope, slipped it under the old white Bible, and pushed the drawer shut.

"Can you imagine that, honey?" Esther's head appeared around the doorframe just as Charlie dropped down onto the bed beside the laundry basket. His wife was giggling as she spoke. "I had to come tell you so I could watch your reaction. Not once. Not a single time. Do you believe it?"

"Nope. I don't believe it." Charlie feigned an expression of wonderment and shook his head. Though he had no idea what Esther was talking about, he felt pretty sure he would agree with her no matter what. Hoping she would hurry back to the kitchen, he leaned over the wicker basket and began reorganizing the folded clothing. Who was George Snyder? Why had he sketched Esther? And when?

"Neither brown nor white!" Esther was saying. "I told Ashley I'd teach her, because I am the gravy queen. Wouldn't you agree with that?"

"Yup. Sure would."

"You don't sound as though you mean that, Charlie." Esther's face sobered as she moved into the bedroom. "I know your mother always made a tasty gravy. And my mother was . . . well, you and I talked about how she felt about my cooking. But I thought you liked my gravy."

Charlie repositioned the sock balls for a third time. "Esther, I like your gravy. You know I do."

"You don't sound sincere."

"*I like your gravy!*" he bellowed, surprising himself with the intensity of his own voice. He stood from the bed and jerked open the closet door. "Where in blazes do you keep your socks, woman?"

"Right there in front of your nose." She marched to the closet and pointed out a set of shelves she'd had him build inside it a few years back. "If you don't like my cooking, why don't you just admit it? That way I won't embarrass myself trying to teach Ashley how to make a gravy no one will even want to eat."

Charlie plunked his wife's socks and lingerie on the shelf. Wishing Esther would leave him alone for once, he turned his back on her and examined the items remaining in the laundry basket. If that portrait in the drawer wasn't the strangest thing, he didn't know what was.

George Snyder. The name had a familiar ring, but he couldn't quite place it. Esther had never mentioned having had a boyfriend before Charlie started dating her when they were high school juniors.

So why had this George Snyder fellow written that he would always love her? Love was love. Not admiration. Not simple affection. Not respect or appreciation.

Love.

"Well, if that's how you feel," Esther huffed, "I certainly won't make the effort to pass along my culinary skills. But you might have let me know what you thought of my gravy before we'd been married nearly fifty years, Charlie Moore. I can't count all the times I've served it to you, and you never said a word. Mashed potatoes and gravy. Chicken-fried steak and gravy. Roast beef and gravy. Turkey and—"

"What are you jabbering about, Esther?" He swung around to

face her. "Can't you see I'm trying to figure out where to put this blame-fool laundry? It's bad enough I'm stuck in the house day and night, but now you've got me washing clothes, sweeping floors, and vacuuming carpets. I've about had it up to here, and I mean that."

"For your information, Cody Goss can do just as good a job with the laundry and the floors as you. Better, in fact. I don't know why you asked him to stop coming after my accident."

"What? You told me to keep him out of the house. You thought he might have had something to do with your Lincoln rolling forward instead of backward. You said he made you nervous."

"Cody—make *me* nervous? Don't be silly, Charlie. I love that boy. He wouldn't hurt a fly."

"Esther, he had been telling you he wanted to learn how to drive a car. You thought he might have fiddled with your Lincoln."

"And maybe he did. How will we ever know what happened that day?" She caught her breath and pressed a hand against her chest. "You blame me, don't you? You think the accident was my fault—just like the other bad things that have happened in your life. I made you turn down that job promotion with the postal service. I raised our daughter so poorly she turned into a drug addict. I begged you to retire early even though you wanted to keep working. And now you're stranded at home because I drove off the end of the carport and totaled my Lincoln."

Charlie set his hands on his hips. "Look here, Esther. I've had enough of this moaning and groaning. Ever since your accident, you've concocted one thing after another to whine about. If it's not your achy joints, it's your failures as a wife and mother. You'd better snap out of it, or I'm going to load up Boofer and head for California to see Charles Jr., Natalie, and the grandkids."

"You would leave me here alone?"

"You're never alone. Not hardly a minute. Women march in and out of here at all hours of the day and night. You've got enough casseroles in the freezer to feed two armies. You've got Cody to clean the house. You've got Ashley, your beads, your tea club, your hairdo appointments—what do you need with an old man like me anyhow? I might as well go visit my grandchildren and have a little fun."

"Well, why don't you just do that!" she snapped. Turning on her heel, Esther set off down the hall toward the kitchen.

Charlie sank onto the bed again and scratched his chin. Boy oh boy. That woman could really get his goat sometimes. No doubt she'd recite the details of their little spat to Ashley, who would award Charlie the evil eye the minute he wandered into the vicinity.

He really was getting cabin fever, and the thought of winter coming on didn't help a bit. A trip to California would be an adventure. Charles Jr. and his pretty wife would welcome a visit from him. The grandkids were teenagers now, and it would be fun to attend a high school football game or theater production with them. But Charlie knew he couldn't really leave Esther in Deepwater Cove alone. Not without a car. Not without someone to watch over her and make sure she remembered to take her medicines and to drive her to church or the grocery store.

Nope, he was glued to Esther about as surely as a postage stamp to an envelope. Like the mail he had carried so many years, Charlie and his wife belonged together. Letter, envelope, address, and stamp—communication went nowhere unless all the parts were in place. Neither did a marriage.

Tonight, after Ashley Hanes went off to work, he would sit Esther down and do what he did best. Talk . . . and listen. Better than any man he'd ever met, Charlie knew how to get his wife to open up and spill her heart.

He stood and picked up the laundry basket. As he laid out the rest of the clean clothes on the bed, Charlie realized there was only one topic he didn't have a clue how to broach. That was George Snyder, his portrait of Esther, and his vow to love another man's wife forever.

Early Tuesday morning, Patsy pushed open the door to the Pop-In and found the little café already crowded with customers. It had taken Bitty Sondheim most of the summer to figure out that the Missouri palate was far different from what she'd been used to in California. Now, with cold weather settling into the lake area, folks poured in for her gourmet coffees, fluffy omelets, and sizzling luncheon wraps.

From the moment Bitty opened at dawn until she shut down at two in the afternoon, her place was hopping. Far from competing with the tea area in Patsy's salon, the Pop-In had actually brought new clientele both for tea and for beauty treatments. Even more important to Patsy, she had found a good friend and ally in Bitty. Like herself, Bitty was a single woman of a certain age and bodily proportion who enjoyed a pleasant chat or a shopping trip to the nearby outlet mall.

"Hi, Patsy!" Bitty waved over the heads of her customers. "Come in out of the cold. I'll be with you in a minute."

Much to her chagrin, Patsy had taken to eating lunch at the Pop-In frequently. Though Bitty's vegetarian pita wraps were tasty enough, most folks—including Patsy—preferred her crispy, deep-fried concoctions of meat, potatoes, bread, and a few vegetables tucked away in the middle somewhere. Bitty had dubbed her revolutionary creations Hearty Homemade Wraps, but they were known around the lake as "heart-attack-in-a-sack" wraps. With a load of carbohydrates and cooking oil, they packed a lot of calories. Just this morning, in fact, Patsy had noticed that her slacks were a little hard to button at the waist.

"Mornin', Patsy." Pete Roberts was edging through the crowd to her side. He tipped the brim of his ball cap in greeting. "I guess you've heard the news. You planning to talk to Steve and Brenda about it?"

Though she tried her best to keep her calm poise in Pete's presence, Patsy felt her heart stumble as she looked into the man's bright blue eyes. True, he was growing his beard again, and his hair looked a little shaggy on the ends. But she would never forget the moment he had showed up at the Labor Day barbecue. She simply could not get that tall, dark, handsome fellow off her mind. Every time she saw Pete now, he looked different to her. So rugged, so charming, so downright dashing that she was halfway scared to death of him.

"Yes, I heard the news," Patsy managed. "I figure it's none of my business, though."

"I'd have thought you'd be steaming about it."

"Why should I get upset? I've known for months that he had a crush on her. He's tried to tell her two or three times already. In fact, I think he blurted it out point-blank at the barbecue last month. A handwritten message in a birthday card shouldn't have come as a surprise to anyone."

For a moment, Pete looked confused. Then one corner of his mouth curved up. "You never cease to amaze me, pretty Patsy Pringle."

She prayed she wasn't blushing. "And why is that? I'm the same as the day you met me."

"You're *never* the same."

"Are you fixing to tease me about changing my appearance again?" She fingered the golden curls of her favorite hairstyle. "I happen to enjoy being a blonde. I colored over the auburn three days ago, and I don't expect I'll change this shade for quite a while. You might as well get used to it."

He laughed. "What are you talking about, girl?"

At the sight of his warm smile and the sound of his deep chuckle, Patsy knew for sure she was turning pink. "What do you think I'm talking about, Pete Roberts? My hair."

"But I asked if you'd heard the news about the tanning salon moving in."

Patsy felt the blood drain from her cheeks. "A tanning salon? Where?"

"Here. In Tranquility. Someone's been talking to Steve Hansen about subletting half of the tattoo parlor. They want to set up tanning beds, work on fingernails, and do body piercing."

"Fingernails?" Patsy breathed out.

"I figured you would have heard about it by now."

"No. Nobody said a word. I thought the news you were talking about was the birthday card that Cody sent to Jennifer Hansen. The ladies next door are just buzzing about his profession of love. But I already knew how he felt about her."

"Cody Goss is in love with Jennifer Hansen? The missionary?"

"She's not a missionary yet. She's studying to be one at Hidden Tribes Learning Center near Camdenton. Are you sure they said nails? I don't give a rip about the tanning bed or the body piercing, but I do a big nail business all year long."

"Fingernails is what I heard. What did Jennifer say to him after she read the card?"

"Same thing she always does if he starts getting too affectionate. 'Everyone loves you, Cody. You're so sweet.' Is it the kind of manicure with the black polish and crazy designs, or is it my kind? You know, French nails and warm paraffin treatments and all that."

"Honey, I wouldn't know a French nail from a French fry. Do you think he got his feelings hurt, because I noticed he's been kind of moping around every time he stops by to get a hot dog."

"Pete Roberts!" Bitty Sondheim sang out. "Your order's ready. One plain omelet with a hazelnut coffee."

"Hazelnut coffee?" Patsy stared at the tackle shop owner and part-time engine repairman.

Pete shrugged. "A man can drink flavored coffee if he wants to, can't he?"

Patsy had never known Pete to drink anything but the black, tar-like sludge he brewed in the coffeemaker in his tackle shop. "Well, I guess so," she said.

"I've been known to down a hot mocha latte when the mood hits me just right." He leaned over and whispered in her ear, "You sure missed a good football game last Friday."

The bristles on his chin against her cheek sent a shower of goose bumps straight down to Patsy's toes. She tried to back away, but in the crowded room, it was impossible.

"I listened to the game on the radio," she told Pete. "Last-minute touchdown for the Lakers."

"Say, Patsy, how would you like to go to a movie with me on Saturday night?" He paused a moment; then he moved a little closer to whisper again. "I'll shave."

Seeing as she was about to shiver the top button right off her too-tight pants, Patsy couldn't do a thing but nod. Pete winked at her and went to fetch his breakfast. Staring after the man, she watched as he paid Bitty for the meal, greeted a few fellow customers, and then headed for the door.

"Pick you up at five," he called to her over his shoulder as he left the Pop-In.

Several people smiled and elbowed each other.

Trying to appear disinterested, Patsy stepped up and placed her order. "My usual," she told Bitty.

A three-egg omelet stuffed with potatoes and dripping with melted cheese was exactly what Patsy needed to calm her shattered nerves. But the sudden image of herself on Saturday evening—trying to fit into her favorite purple turtleneck and matching pencil skirt—brought her breakfast plans to a skidding halt. What would Pete think if the fabric was stretched too tight or, heaven forbid, a seam suddenly ripped open?

"On second thought, Bitty, just give me one of your plain omelets. Maybe a sprinkle or two of cheese."

Bitty took the change in stride. "Coming right up."

"A cheery good morning to you, Miss Pringle," Charlie Moore sang out as he stepped toward her. "You're looking lovely, as usual."

At the sight of the white-haired gentleman and his little wife standing arm in arm, Patsy smiled. "Hey there, you two lovebirds. Esther, your hair's so pretty today. You're not pulling a Benedict Arnold on me and trying out a new salon, are you?"

"Don't be silly, Patsy," Esther said, touching her well-sprayed coiffure with her fingertips. "I did this myself, and it's just awful. Last week I wasn't up to attending the Tea Lovers' Club or having my hair done. I didn't even make it to church on Sunday."

"She's been feeling puny," Charlie inserted.

"Anyhow, I've got no choice but to get out on my feet today."

"How so?" Patsy absently tucked a sprig of Esther's hair into place. "Where are you off to at this hour of the morning?"

"Springfield," Esther told her. "We've got doctor appointments."

"Gonna have our arteries checked," Charlie clarified. "Make sure we don't have anything gumming up the works. Might have to auger 'em out to keep us both ticking for a few more years."

"My accident, you know. One little mishap, and the doctors insist on examining you from head to toe."

"And inside out."

"I feel perfectly fine," Esther chirped. "Charlie's got all those years of carrying mail behind him. We're fit as a pair of fiddles. Seems like a waste of time to drive all the way down to Springfield, but we're planning to do a little Christmas shopping at the big mall there. You know how I love to give presents."

"And get 'em too." Charlie grinned at his wife.

"Esther, you do the prettiest wrapping in Deepwater Cove," Patsy told her friend. "Last year, you tied a white crocheted star onto the gift you gave me, remember? I saved it to hang on my Christmas tree."

"It was a snowflake, not a star, and be thankful you've still got it. There won't be any more of those, I assure you. I nearly wore my fingers to the bone with all that needlework."

"Order's up, Patsy!" Bitty announced. "One cheese omelet. I threw in a few potatoes for you too."

With distressing visions of skirt seams splitting, a competing manicure business moving in next door, and Pete Roberts looking at her with moony blue eyes, Patsy almost forgot to pay for her breakfast. As she passed Charlie and Esther on her way to the door, she saw the elderly man bend down and gently kiss his wife's cheek. Clenching her sack, Patsy stepped out into the crisp autumn morning and hurried toward her salon.

Just As I Am. She read the sign silently. *The good Lord loves me just as I am,* she told herself. *Remember that, Patsy Pringle.*

What is plaque, anyhow?" Esther asked. Seated beside her husband in the car, she gazed out the window at the majestic Ozark hills as they drove toward Camdenton. Cloaked in shades of red, gold, and brown, the trees were reaching the peak of their colorful display. Esther had always loved autumn at the lake. Brisk breezes ruffled the water and whispered through the leaves. Docks emptied as people tucked their boats away for the winter. Canada geese flew overhead, squirrels hunted for nuts, and deer bounded into the woods from the roadside.

"Some kind of sticky goop, I guess. The doctor said it was a mix of cholesterol, calcium, and . . . what was it? Oh, fibrous tissue."

Behind the wheel, Charlie looked as he always had. Handsome and earnest but with the hint of a smile at the corners of his mouth. Esther studied the rays of the setting sun as they lit up a farmer's stubbled field and round bales of hay.

"I don't like the idea of anyone putting a balloon into my arteries or poking around in there to clean them out," she fretted. "I'm not sure I'll agree to that. Why do you suppose I have plaque and you don't? We've been eating the same meals all these years."

"Probably walking my mail route kept the blood pumping."

"As if I didn't walk just as much as you—running after those two kids, doing my chores, cooking three meals a day. And in case you've forgotten, I used to mow the lawn too."

"How could I forget a sight like that? You in your pedal pushers with those shapely legs. When I knew you'd be outside mowing, I used to try to get home from work early."

"Did you really?"

"Sure." He glanced over at her. "I liked the red pants with the polka dots. You were as cute as a bug's ear."

"I cannot believe you remember those crazy pants, Charlie."

"They're burned into my memory."

She giggled. "Do you still think I'm cute? Sometimes I feel like I'm nothing but an old wrinkled sack. My curves have gone flat. My hips keep spreading. My neck looks like a turkey wattle."

"Don't forget your plaque."

"Oh, Charlie, stop teasing me!" She gave him a playful swat. "I used to think I was kind of pretty. Some people even called me beautiful."

She sat back to wait for him to make one of his usual sweetly flattering remarks. Instead of responding, Charlie frowned and adjusted the sun visor. Esther waited a little longer for him to speak up, but he said nothing.

"Is any of my beauty left?" she asked finally. "Do you still find me attractive, Charlie? In a sweetheart kind of way?"

Charlie fell silent for so long that Esther decided he must be figuring out how to tell her the truth—her looks were gone, her mind was fading, and even her arteries were clogging up. Well, so what if he did think that? Charlie Moore was no Prince Charming himself. He pooched out around the middle, and he couldn't see the end of his own nose without those trifocals. What once had been a head of hair to rival Elvis Presley's pompadour was now a scattering of straight white wisps.

Just when she'd given up on him answering her question, he spoke. "You know, Esther, a name came to mind the other day, and for the life of me, I can't place it." He looked at her. "George Snyder. Does that ring a bell?"

Esther's hand tightened on her purse strap. "I haven't heard that name in years. What on earth made you think of George Snyder?"

"So you do remember him?"

"Somewhere back in the past. But you never answered my question, Charlie."

"What did you ask?"

"If you thought I was still attractive."

"Of course you are."

He sounded awfully grumpy for someone paying a compliment. Esther couldn't imagine what had unearthed Charlie's memory of George Snyder. She had filed away that era of her life a long time ago.

"What's wrong with you, Mr. Grouch?" she asked. "Are you getting sleepy? The last thing we need is another car accident."

"I'm not sleepy. I'm just wondering when we knew this George Snyder fellow."

"You always insist you're not sleepy, but you are. We both missed our after-lunch nap today, and I can tell you're getting drowsy. You'd better let me drive, Charlie."

"I'm fine."

"No, you're not. Pull over to that rest area up ahead. Let's swap places."

"Oh, for pete's sake."

"Don't argue with me, Charlie. I saw your eyelids drooping way back there in Buffalo. We've got a half hour to go till Camdenton and then another twenty minutes to Deepwater Cove. I insist on taking the wheel."

"It's getting dark, Esther."

"Which is exactly why I should be driving."

"If you hadn't frittered away so much time choosing Christmas cards, we'd be home by now. Did you have to read the inscription on every single box, Esther?"

"Pull over right this minute, Charles Moore, and I mean it. You are tired and hungry and irritable, and I'm not riding another mile with you in the driver's seat."

To Esther's immense satisfaction, her husband steered the car off the roadway and parked under a tree at a rest area. Esther pushed open her door. "Yes, I had to read every inscription. We can't send out cards that just say *Happy Holidays* or *Warm Wishes for the Season.* A Christmas card ought to celebrate the birth of Jesus, don't you think?"

Charlie was muttering under his breath as they swapped places. If there was one thing about her husband that drove Esther nuts, it was his habit of mumbling. She had no doubt he was griping about something she'd said or done, but he was too big a chicken to say what.

Through the years, her husband had been a good listener—a sit-down-and-talk-things-out kind of man. If an important issue came up, they both knew how to have a good discussion and clear it all up. But Charlie preferred to let the smaller things slide—except for that exasperating muttering.

As Esther pulled the car out onto Highway 54, she recalled the topic of their most recent conversation. Christmas cards—yes. That had been a bother. But of greater concern was Charlie's mention of George Snyder. Esther had no desire to dredge up memories of that long-ago time, and she certainly hoped Charlie would lay it to rest too.

"I may take a few names off our Christmas list," she told her husband. "Last year we sent out nearly a hundred cards. That's too many, don't you think?"

"Doesn't make much difference to me," he said. "They're all your friends."

"*Our* friends."

"Esther, I've had a few buddies through the years. Guys I enjoyed visiting with at work. A neighbor or two I didn't mind having over to barbecue some burgers. But as for friends, that's always been your department."

"I never thought of it that way, but I suppose you're right." Esther switched on the headlamps. If traffic was light, she always used the brighter beams in case a deer wandered onto the road.

"You don't have friends because you never learned how to give a gift," she told him. "If someone gives you a present, you can be sure they care about you. When I was in the hospital, Ashley Hanes made that beautiful necklace for me, and I knew right away that she valued my friendship. Why do you suppose I've spent so much time with her lately? I'm teaching her how to cook. It's my way of repaying the gift she gave me."

Charlie leaned his head against the backrest. "Men don't give each other gifts. Can you see me presenting Steve Hansen with a new tie or a box of chocolates?"

Esther laughed. "Maybe not, but you could take him to lunch. Or offer to help him rehab one of the houses he's trying to sell."

"No thanks. I don't intend to get into the remodeling business ever again."

Esther reflected on the first house she and Charlie had purchased. After two years in an apartment—with one baby crawling around and another on the way—she'd been about to go stark raving mad. They couldn't afford much, but they had put money down on an old fixer-upper in a nice neighborhood. Charlie worked his mail route during the day and spent his evenings and weekends repairing the house. Those had been some trying years, now that she thought about it.

"If you don't want to have close friendships, that's fine," she told him. "But I intend to keep mine—except for those I'm thinking of crossing off the Christmas card list."

"How come you keep every card you ever got, Esther?" he asked. "The other day when I was putting laundry away, I saw them all bundled up in your bottom drawer."

"I don't save all my cards. Just the special ones. I tie them with ribbons and mark down the year I got them. It may sound silly to you, but each card is like a little gift. A love token. That makes it precious. Sometimes I take the cards out and look at them, remembering and feeling grateful for all the love I've known through the years."

Charlie grunted. Esther pursed her lips as she drove. Muttering again. That was one of the things she had learned about a long marriage—the husband would always have some unchangeable traits that nearly sent his poor wife around the bend. For her, it was Charlie's muttering. And always forgetting where he'd put things. Not to mention leaving the kitchen cabinet doors open. Clomping around in his house slippers. Blowing his nose like a foghorn. Chewing a toothpick for two hours after every meal. Well, she could go on and on.

If she chose to focus on the negatives about her husband, Esther realized, she probably could come up with enough irritants, aggravations, disagreements, and downright hostilities to just about warrant a divorce. But then she would lose *him*. Charlie had so many wonderful, endearing qualities. She certainly couldn't have found a kinder, better, steadier, or more faithful man to spend her life with.

"George Snyder," he suddenly spoke up in the darkness. "Ever figure out where we knew him?"

Esther's heart stumbled. "Would you just shut your eyes and go to sleep, Charlie? You're pulling long-forgotten names out of an old hat, while I'm sitting here trying to figure out who to cross off our Christmas card list. Do you suppose Clara Gibson even remembers us? She babysat the kids for us a few times. You remember—that old lady with the white streak in her hair? Should I eliminate her?"

When Charlie didn't reply, Esther drove on in silence. Thank goodness. They were both worn-out from missing their naps and running around the city of Springfield all day, so maybe he would doze the rest of the way home.

What had made him think of George Snyder anyway? Esther hardly remembered the man. Well, that wasn't quite true. Who could forget those amazing blond curls and sapphire blue eyes?

She and Charlie had been in their first apartment for about a month when their neighbor knocked on the door to ask if Esther could spare an egg. George had been mixing up a cake, of all things. A man baking a cake? Esther had actually giggled in his face. He explained that he'd accidentally dropped his last egg on the floor; then he stood in the doorway while she fetched one from her refrigerator. They had chatted a moment or two before he headed back down the corridor to his own apartment.

Esther wouldn't have thought another thing about him, but that afternoon George Snyder had knocked on her door again. This time he carried a plate with two slices of lemon chiffon cake—a gift of appreciation for the borrowed egg. Her heart softening, Esther had invited the golden-haired young man into the living room, brewed a pot of tea, and nibbled on that heavenly cake while they sat and talked.

George was an artist, he had told her. At least, that was his goal. His father's recent death had provided him with a small inheritance, and he was using the money to pay for the apartment and a course of art lessons. George dreamed of moving to New York, where he could paint magazine covers like Norman Rockwell's famous illustrations or sketch celebrities as Al Hirschfeld did. Esther had happily donated all her back issues of the *Saturday Evening Post, Ladies' Home Journal, McCall's,* and *Look* to George's artistic endeavors. He responded as though she had given him a treasure more valuable than gold. When she asked to see some of his artwork, George promised to show her the portfolio he was compiling. They talked so long that Esther barely had dinner on the stove when Charlie walked in the door that evening.

Glancing over at her husband now, Esther saw that he had laid his head against the padded seat back and was already snoozing. Glad that she had insisted on driving, she relaxed and allowed herself to drift back in time to those awkward early years of marriage. How lonely she had been in her new role as the wife of a mailman. Without children or a job, she had felt terribly isolated in the tiny apartment . . . until George Snyder showed up asking for an egg. Things had certainly changed after that.

Esther leaned her own head against the seat back and focused on the road ahead. The yellow lines flashed beneath the car's headlights as she steered toward Camdenton. In the silence of the growing darkness, she reflected on the man who had brought such luminosity, such turmoil, and such joy into her world.

How odd to remember him now, after all these years. To recall the hours of chatting, playing dominoes, watching television together on the old tufted sofa. George had given Esther so many gifts. Copies of his favorite books . . . wildflowers from the park near their apartment building . . . a chip of broken Italian tile he had found near the train tracks . . . and sketches . . . so many lovely sketches . . .

Charlie woke to the sparkle of streetlights flickering through the windshield. It took a moment to realize he was in the car, and he glanced over at Esther. Head lolling and eyes closed, she was sound asleep.

A wash of disbelief poured through Charlie's veins when it dawned on him that his wife was sitting on the driver's side of the vehicle. Her hands held the steering wheel, and she snored softly as the highway became the main street of Camdenton.

"Esther!" Charlie jerked forward and grabbed the steering wheel. "What in blazes are you doing, woman? Wake up!"

Jolting to consciousness, Esther let out a shriek and began to fight

Charlie for control of the wheel. "Let go," she cried, slapping at his hands. "You're going to run us off the road!"

"You were asleep!"

"Give me that steering wheel, you big ox! Can't you see we're nearly at the stoplight in Camdenton?"

"Are you awake now?" he demanded, still struggling to steer. "Pull over, Esther! Pull into that gas station. Right there—that one!"

"What on earth? Charlie, you are going to be the death of me!" She turned into the parking area of the gas station and stepped on the brake. "This is the craziest thing you've ever done, Charles Moore!" she snapped at him. "I was just coming into town when you woke up and started grabbing for the steering wheel. You nearly ran us off the road—do you realize that? We could have been hurt! We might have hit somebody!"

"You were asleep, Esther," Charlie growled back at her. "I woke up, looked over, and you were snoring away as if you were home in bed."

"I was not!"

"I saw you with my own two eyes. Now, put on the parking brake, and we're going to swap places again."

"I will do nothing of the sort. You must still be out of it yourself to be spouting such nonsense. Are you trying to tell me that we were *both* sleeping?"

"Yes, we were—rolling down the highway, the two of us sound asleep."

"That's ridiculous. Here we are in Camdenton, exactly where we were headed. Do you think I drove all the way from the rest stop in my sleep?"

"I have no idea when you drifted off, Esther, but I know for a fact that when I opened my eyes a minute ago, you were out like a light."

Esther dropped her hands into her lap. "Well, that's impossible."

"I would have thought so too. But it's true."

"You heard me snoring?"

"Just like always."

"How did I stay on the road?"

"Beats me." He let out a breath.

If this wasn't the craziest thing that had ever happened to Charlie, he didn't know what was. Two people driving down the highway—who knew how far—and both of them sound asleep.

Esther adjusted the hem of her sweater. "It *is* awfully warm in this car. I don't know why you always want the heat turned up so high. No wonder we got drowsy."

Charlie stared at his wife. "Have you been hearing me at all? You were driving this car in your sleep."

She glanced across at him. "I remember slowing down at Macks Creek. That little spot in the road has always been a speed trap."

"And after Macks Creek?"

Esther shrugged. "Well, anyway . . ."

"What's that supposed to mean?"

"It means that maybe I did snooze for a little bit. But we stayed on the highway, and here we are safe and sound in Camdenton. So let's trade seats again and get on home."

Gritting his teeth, Charlie pushed open his door. A gust of nippy night air filled his lungs as he walked around the car, passing his wife in silence. He was awake now, for sure. They both settled into their seats and buckled up. Charlie let off the brake and drove back out onto the road.

At the intersection of the two highways that formed the center of Camdenton, he stopped at the red light. Turning finally from Highway 54 onto North Highway 5, Charlie thought of himself and Esther inside the car, rolling down the road, sound asleep. They so easily could have dropped a wheel onto the shoulder, run into a drainage ditch and flipped over, hit a deer, or smashed head-on into another car. The horrible possibilities were endless. God must have sent a host of extra-vigilant guardian angels to surround and watch over the slumbering pair.

The very idea of what had occurred tonight was downright crazy.

If he wasn't still half scared out of his wits and half mad at Esther, Charlie might even find the event comical. Who ever would have thought such a thing possible?

In the silence of the car, Charlie heard Esther coughing softly. Or maybe she was crying. Hard to tell. The sound continued until Charlie decided he ought to comfort her. As he reached out toward his wife, he realized that the snuffling noise he'd been hearing was suppressed laughter.

"Esther?"

At that, she tossed back her head and burst out in a gale of giggles. "Oh, I'm sorry for upsetting you, Charlie, but don't you think it's the funniest thing in the world? Driving along and both of us snoring away?"

"*You* were snoring," he muttered.

"I'll bet you were too." She made a valiant effort to stifle her snickers, but in a moment she began hooting with hilarity all over again.

"What if we passed someone, and they looked in the car and saw us?" she gasped out between chortles. "What must they have thought? A couple of old fogies taking naps! Oh my stars, I have no idea how I did it!"

Charlie wanted to stay angry and worried. Twice now, Esther had put her own life in grave danger. With this latest stunt, she might have killed them both. What if she was fading faster than he'd thought? Her arteries weren't in the best shape. Her blood pressure was troublesome, and her bones were brittle. Could she be growing a little bit senile, too?

There was evidence pointing to that conclusion. Putting the electric can opener into the dishwasher. Wrecking her Lincoln in the backyard. Now he had to add this foolishness of his wife driving down the highway asleep. And that didn't even take into account the disturbing sketch she had kept hidden in the bottom drawer of her dresser. What was going on with Esther? And what else lay ahead for Charlie?

"I'm going to have to write to one of those late-night talk shows and offer myself as a guest," she said, tee-heeing as she spoke. "'Meet Esther Moore—the Most Amazing Driver in the Universe! Watch as she sails her car through the air and then negotiates an obstacle course of birdhouses, sheds, and trees. See her drive while sound asleep, effortlessly missing potholes and eluding armadillos!' Don't you think it would be funny, Charlie? Honestly, it's such a silly thing!"

Charlie tried to muster a grin. "I guess you could find some humor in it—seeing as it turned out okay in the end."

"It was hilarious!" she said. "I can't wait to tell Patsy Pringle when I go into the salon Friday for my set-and-style. She'll get a big kick out of it, and then the story will be all over the place. I'll be known as Esther the Wonder Driver. Maybe the newspaper will write me up; what do you think?"

Charlie harrumphed. Reaching out, he took his wife's hand. "Esther, you'd better be glad it wasn't a Highway Patrolman writing you up."

Or the county coroner, he thought.

As Charlie drove on toward home, Esther began warbling one of her favorite songs. She had told Charlie about learning the words in elementary school and singing them with her family every Thanksgiving.

"'Over the river and through the wood, oh, how the wind does blow!'" she trilled. "'It stings the toes and bites the nose, as over the ground we go. Over the river and through the wood, to have a first-rate play; oh, hear the bell ring, "ting-a-ling-ling!" Hurrah for Thanksgiving Day!'"

The car pulled into the carport of the house in Deepwater Cove, and Charlie gratefully switched off the ignition. Esther elbowed him for the umpteenth time, and he finally joined in. "'Over the river and through the wood,'" they sang together, "'now Grandmother's cap I spy! Hurrah for the fun! Is the pudding done? Hurrah for the pumpkin pie!'"

CHAPTER SIX

Early on in the history of the Tea Lovers' Club, every member had agreed they would not elect a president. Neither would they have a meeting agenda, minutes, dues, or any of that folderol. But the following Wednesday when Esther Moore stood and began tapping a spoon on her teacup, Patsy was delighted to see the older woman assume her usual self-appointed role as club leader.

Having gotten the group's attention, Esther opened her purse to take out the notebook of meeting minutes. At that, everyone in the room began to clap, and she looked up in surprise. Then her face broke into a radiant smile, and she clasped her hands together at her throat.

"My goodness, aren't you all sweet to welcome me back to the TLC?" she said as the applause faded. "I can't tell you how much I've missed visiting with everyone. There is nothing like a sick spell to make you appreciate your friends. In this case, TLC stands for Tender Loving Care. Charlie and I are grateful to each one of you who brought food to the house. If you can believe my husband, we've got enough in our freezer to feed the whole neighborhood twice over."

"Do you have hot dogs?" Cody Goss spoke up. He was seated at Patsy's table along with Brenda Hansen and her two daughters. Cody hooked his hands into his pockets. "I hope it isn't bad social skills to say that I like hot dogs, and if you have some extra ones, Mrs. Moore, I would volunteer to eat them."

"Hot dogs are just about the only thing we don't have, Cody." Esther gazed tenderly at the young man for a moment. "Oh, honey, I have missed you so much. You haven't been to the house except the one time with the Hansen girls."

"I'm too scared. I don't want Mr. Moore to get mad at me again. You told him that I tinkered with your car the day you drove off your carport, even though I didn't."

As always, Cody spoke his true thoughts without considering how they might be taken. Patsy loved that about Cody. It was hard to find a person who never lied. It was even harder to find someone who didn't bother to put on a mask or twist words around to protect feelings. But that was Cody Goss. Other than Jesus Himself, there probably had never been a more honest man in the history of the world.

Esther was brushing him off with a wave of her hand. "Don't be silly, Cody. Charlie and I both know you didn't touch my car—and we're not upset with you. Somehow I just drove in the wrong direction. After what happened the other day, I've decided to call myself Esther the Wonder Driver." Grinning, she glanced around at the group. "If you can believe this, I drove part of the way home from Springfield in my sleep! Charlie was snoozing right beside me in the passenger seat—both of us snoring to beat the band."

When she laughed, a titter of giggles from around the tea area joined in. Patsy found the story amusing, but it worried her that Esther and Charlie had done such a thing. It was a wonder they didn't have an awful accident.

"I don't think that's funny," Cody spoke up. "I'm studying for my driver's license test, and you're not supposed to sleep while you drive a car. You have to be alert at all times."

"Of course you do," Esther said. "Unless you're Esther the Wonder Driver! Anyway, all that's behind us now, and it's time to focus on our meeting. Since I haven't been here for a while and no one took minutes . . ."

Here she paused and glanced at Ashley Hanes, who flipped a hank of long red hair over her shoulder, obviously unconcerned about falling short in her duties as club president pro tem.

"Does anyone have old business to report?" Esther asked, holding a pen poised over her notebook.

"Old business," Cody said, standing. "Last Saturday, the men got together to repair Mr. and Mrs. Moore's carport. The two Mrs. Finleys organized the ladies to fix up Mr. Moore's broken garden fence and repair the flower bed. All these things were knocked down by Mrs. Moore when she drove off the back of her carport. Also, Mrs. Finley—the older one—helped Ashley Hanes by separating beads because Mrs. Moore was laid up in bed and Mr. Moore couldn't do it all by himself while taking care of his wife. Ashley is getting lots of Christmas orders from rich ladies in St. Louis. They want necklaces, earrings, and bracelets made out of Ashley's beads. Mr. and Mrs. Moore went to Springfield to get their veins checked; young ladies need to drink milk or they'll become hunchbacks; and Mrs. Jones has thumbtacks if anybody needs to borrow one. That's all."

Cody sat down to a second burst of applause from the roomful of women. Registering pride, he looked across the table at Jennifer Hansen. Immediately, she leaned over to whisper something to her sister.

Patsy had heard a disturbing rumor that Jessica was thinking of dropping out of college after her wedding. Maybe even before the big event. This would be a blow to the young woman's parents. Steve Hansen had worked his tail off to sell enough real estate so all three kids could go to college debt-free. Neither he nor Brenda were graduates, and they had big dreams for their offspring.

"Cody, you have amazed us all," Esther was saying now. "What an excellent recitation. I may have to put you in charge of old business from now on. And though I haven't been out and about much, Charlie tells me the carport and the backyard are in tip-top shape thanks to our dear neighbors. Such gifts you've given us! I don't know when I've ever felt more loved."

Patsy drank the last sip of her tea and hoped the official part of the meeting wouldn't last much longer. She wanted to enjoy another cup of Earl Grey and a chat with her friends before returning to a long lineup of clients in the salon area.

"New business," Esther announced. She looked around and then swallowed. "Well, I don't believe I can think of a thing. Does anyone know of a plan in the works?"

"Patsy Pringle is going to the movies with Pete Roberts on Saturday night," Cody announced. "He already shaved."

Struggling to keep her cool, Patsy glared at Cody. Point-blank honesty could have its disadvantages, after all. To keep from chewing out the young man, she excused herself from the table and headed for the hot water urn. Though she focused on listening to the uplifting Color of Mercy CD playing in the background, Patsy could hear the women conversing. She hoped they weren't talking about her and Pete.

She had agreed to see a movie with the man, but now she was doubting the wisdom of that decision. As she waited for her tea to steep, Patsy hummed along with the words to one of her favorite songs by the local trio. *The Potter has us on His potter's wheel*, the chorus went, *molding, stretching, shaping us to His will.*

The idea of being prodded and pressed and spun around like a lump of clay had never sat well with Patsy, even though she knew the message in the song was taken straight out of the Bible. All her life, Patsy had needed to be strong and independent, forging her way toward a station in life that would make her proud. But pride was exactly the opposite of what God wanted from her. He demanded submission and surrender. How did Pete Roberts fit into God's plan?

Was she supposed to let him near . . . or run away before she got fried in her own grease?

"How about a Thanksgiving parade in Deepwater Cove?" Esther was suggesting as Patsy made her way back to the table. For some reason, the woman seemed to think parades were essential to every holiday.

When no one responded, Opal Jones proposed a day trip around the lake to look at fall foliage. A committee formed to check into it, and then Miranda Finley once again pleaded for help with Ashley's business. This time a round of hands went up to volunteer for bead duty. Next, someone mentioned Halloween, and that brought up a discussion about whether or not trick-or-treating was a sin.

Still dwelling on what to do about Pete Roberts, Patsy paid scant attention when Miranda stood to give a short history lesson on the origins of the holiday. Pagans, druids, Celts, Romans, and one saint or another all seemed to have contributed to the controversial event.

Patsy herself had never celebrated Halloween. When she was young, her family had been too poor to buy or make costumes or to use up gas driving from one neighborhood to another so Patsy could collect candy. Nowadays, she decorated the salon for autumn with hay bales and pumpkins outside the front door and a few garlands of colorful leaves inside. She left the witches, ghosts, and spiderwebs for folks who liked that kind of thing.

The moment Miranda finished her speech, Jennifer Hansen rose to offer her own opinion. "The question I have about Halloween," she said, "is whether it's beneficial in any way."

"It's beneficial to the kiddos, honey," one of the widows piped up. "They come home with all that candy to eat. Besides, I enjoy making popcorn balls every year, and the little ones are so cute when they traipse around the neighborhood as fairies or pirates. To my way of thinking, there's nothing evil or wicked about it."

"Whether or not Halloween has satanic influences," Jennifer replied, "we have to ask ourselves if it glorifies God. If an activity isn't beneficial to us and it doesn't exalt the name of the Lord, then I don't think it belongs in our lives."

"You brush your teeth, don't you, Jennifer?" Miranda asked, her voice tinged with a faint hint of derision. "How does that activity 'exalt the name of the Lord'?"

The retort provoked another hubbub of discussion among the TLC members. As Patsy nibbled on a homemade chocolate-chip cookie, she decided that the outspoken young Jennifer was going to make an excellent missionary—if she could keep from getting herself into a knock-down-drag-out with Miranda Finley first.

"All right, ladies ... and gentleman," Esther called before things got out of hand. "If that's all, we'll close this week's meeting of the Tea Lovers' Club."

At that, Jennifer sat down and so did Miranda—thankfully at separate tables. Patsy let out a breath. She liked both women. Jennifer was especially dear to her, but lambasting folks in the name of the Lord just wasn't Patsy's way. She knew God could use all kinds of people on His side, though. Bold or shy, dumb or smart, fat or skinny, it didn't matter at all as long as a person was willing to do what He asked. Patsy had no trouble imagining Jennifer as a messenger for the Lord—hacking through jungles to pour out the Word of God on some unsuspecting tribe.

"I don't know what Halloween is, but I do know that Satan is bad." Cody addressed the women at the table. "I remember what the Bible says. 'Submit yourselves therefore to God. Resist the devil, and he will flee from you. Draw nigh to God, and he will draw nigh to you. Cleanse your hands, ye sinners; and purify your hearts, ye double minded.' James 4:7-8. *Nigh* means near, so that verse tells us to stay near God if we want Him to be close to us and keep the devil away."

The moment of stunned silence that always followed one of Cody's scriptural recitations was broken by Jennifer. "That's exactly right," she said. "Whether we believe it or not, we're in the midst of a battle between good and evil. We all need to wear our spiritual armor and be ready to fight for God."

"I fight for God," Cody told her.

Jennifer looked at him. "I know you do. You're one of His best soldiers."

"I can say lots of Scriptures."

"Your father was wise to help you memorize all those verses."

Cody's face sobered. "My daddy used to read the Bible out loud a lot. He called it the Good Book. He said I was a great rememberizer. And I am. Also, I can read and write whatever I want to now that Brenda taught me how. I can paint good too. And I work hard all the time doing chores for people. But I can't do numbers. My daddy tried to explain them to me, and finally he said, 'Cody, you are a hopeless case.' He was sure right about that."

"We're still working on math," Brenda Hansen told the others. "I'm not giving up and neither should Cody."

"Oh, I've figured him out!" Jessica gasped. The younger of the two daughters leaned forward across the table, glancing from woman to woman. "I just figured Cody out! We're learning about people like him in the Abnormal Psychology class I'm taking this semester."

"Abnormal?" Jennifer frowned at her sister. "Cody's not abnormal."

"I know! But he is different—and that's because he's autistic!" Jessica beamed as if she had just laid a home-baked, flaky-crusted, meringue-topped chocolate pie on the table.

Autistic? Patsy looked at Cody, who was grinning and nodding his head.

"Jessica's right," he said. "If you turn around, everyone, you'll see my paintings right over there on Patsy's wall. Seven ladies with pretty hairdos. Seven *beautiful* ladies."

He focused those sapphire blue eyes on Jennifer Hansen, whose lovely face—framed with different colors and styles of hair—was clearly the subject of every single portrait in the wall mural Cody had painted that summer. With a slight smirk, he shrugged.

"I never knew I was artistic until Patsy bought me a sketchbook and some pencils. But once I got to drawing and painting, nobody could stop talking about my talent. Mrs. Moore said I am an artistic genius, and she knows because she has a friend who makes illustrations for magazines in New York City. I guess God fixes people exactly the way He wants them to be. There's not a thing I like to do better than paint, paint, paint. If you looked in my room in the back of the salon, you would see what I mean. It's full to the brim of pictures. Whenever I have spare time, all I do is be artistic. I'm glad you figured it out, Jessica, and if you want, I would be happy to paint a picture of you in your wedding dress."

Once again, Cody had managed to silence the entire table. Patsy considered excusing herself and getting back to work, but she had a feeling she ought to stay. Something was hovering over the table—something unpredictable and worrisome.

"*Autistic*," Jessica said. Reaching out, she laid her hand on Cody's. "*Autistic* is different from *artistic*."

"Uh-oh." Cody glanced at Brenda. "Did I do bad social skills?"

She shook her head, then turned to her daughter. "Jessica, I think you should save your theory for another place and time."

"But there's nothing shameful about being autistic, Mom. That's the whole problem with disabilities. In class, we learned that back in the olden days, people with physical or mental disabilities were hidden away, even locked in cages."

"Cages?" Cody stiffened. "I'm not going to live in a cage. I am not an animal."

"That's exactly what I'm trying to say. These days we make all kinds of accommodations for people with *physical* disabilities. We have handicapped parking spaces, wheelchair-size toilet stalls, ramps, elevators, you name it. But those with mental, social, or developmental disabilities are still misunderstood and mistreated. It's as though we think they have something to be ashamed of—but they don't!"

"I am not an animal," Cody repeated. "I am not a dog. I am not a bear. I am not a fish. I am not—"

"Stop." Jennifer slipped her arm around Cody's shoulders for a brief hug. "No one is going to put you into a cage. I promise."

Cody gazed at her, his blue eyes deepening. "I love you, Jennifer Hansen."

"I know," she whispered. "You're a wonderful guy . . . and I love you, too."

Patsy nearly choked on the last crumb of her chocolate-chip cookie. Oh, boy. This was not a good thing. Autism. Cages. Love. What next?

"Everyone in Deepwater Cove loves you," Jennifer went on. "Everyone. That's because you're kind and good-hearted and smart."

"Not to mention handsome as all get-out," Patsy put in. She couldn't refrain from drawing attention to Cody's good looks—at least some of which were due to her own efforts.

"He's wonderful . . . and he's autistic, Jen," Jessica said. "I'm sure of it. I just turned in a term paper about that disability. There's a spectrum of different kinds of autism from mild to severe. I think Cody fits a type called Asperger's syndrome."

"What's an Asperger?" Cody asked. "It sounds like one of the vegetables my aunt kept feeding me. Asp . . . asp . . . asparagus."

"Cody, most people with Asperger's syndrome have special interests, even giftedness in certain areas. They can be very intelligent and skilled, especially in their main areas of curiosity—like you are about painting or memorizing Scripture or learning to read and write."

Jessica looked around at the women. "Who would have thought that someone who didn't know a single letter of the alphabet would be reading in a few short months?"

"I can read anything," Cody boasted. "I learned my letters and words from Brenda, and now I've read all the books about painting in the Camdenton library. That's because I have asparagus syndrome."

"*Asperger's* syndrome. See how Cody keeps mentioning his painting? People with Asperger's usually will lead the conversation right back to their topic of interest no matter what else you may have been discussing. They struggle a bit with social skills—like understanding body language or knowing how to keep from getting into other people's space."

"Oh, boy." Cody put his hand on his forehead. "That's true. My social skills are nearly as bad as my numbers."

"No, they're not," Jennifer argued. "You have better social skills than a lot of people I know. Especially those who discuss others' difficulties in public."

The two golden-haired sisters glared at each other for a moment. But Jessica wasn't about to be silenced by her older sibling. "She's right, Cody. You have a lot of social skills. But still, it's not always easy to figure out the right thing to do. Also, I know you like to follow a schedule, and that's another characteristic of Asperger's syndrome. Plus, people who have it can sometimes be clumsy in sports like swimming or activities that involve motor skills."

"I don't like swimming," Cody told the group. "I am not a fish."

By this time, Patsy was growing alarmed. Jessica's description did fit Cody pretty well. But what was this syndrome, really? And more important, what did it mean for Cody?

"People with Asperger's are sensitive to sounds," Jessica continued. "I remember Mom telling us about Cody's reaction the day Pete Roberts fired up a chain saw next door."

"I screamed and ran into the woods," Cody said.

"I know. And I bet you like certain foods more than others."

"Hot dogs." Cody nodded. "I like hot dogs a lot."

"And you always want your chocolate cake cut into . . . ?"

"*Squares,*" everyone at the table said in unison.

"I like squares better than triangles," Cody said firmly.

"There's nothing wrong with being autistic," Jessica told the group. "It just makes life a little more challenging. People with Asperger's syndrome say they have to guess at what 'normal' is. Cody always looks at Mom to find out if he's saying something out of line, because he truly doesn't know. He has trouble reading facial expressions. It's hard for him to interpret the world."

As Jessica finished speaking, she looked at Cody. "There's nothing wrong with who you are—and don't let people tell you there is."

"Okay," he said, shrugging.

"But what does this syndrome do?" Patsy asked. "Can doctors cure it? The truth is, I wouldn't want to change a thing about Cody, but can we help him?"

"I don't need any more help, Patsy." He smiled at her. "I'm happy because I have work to do and places to live and people who say I'm a genius. A genius is a very good thing to be. I wish everyone could be autistic, but sorry. It's just for the ones God chooses to give it to. Even if a long time ago some mean men beat me up and called me dumb and stupid, I know that I can say more Scriptures than any of them and paint better pictures and also clean houses."

By now, Jennifer—clearly upset over her sister's amateur diagnosis of Cody—was using a napkin to blot the tears that had begun to roll down her cheeks.

The young man glanced at her and then patted her gently on the back. "Don't worry, Jennifer," he said in a low voice. "You don't need to cry. The older Mrs. Finley doesn't know Scriptures like we do, so that's why she talked to you in a mean way about Halloween. The Bible says, 'Why am I evil spoken of for that for which I give thanks? Whether therefore ye eat, or drink, or whatsoever ye do, do all to the glory of God.' First Corinthians 10:30-31. That means you were right—everything we do is supposed to glorify God. Even brushing our teeth. Look."

His lips parted into a wide grin, displaying his set of fine white chompers. At that, Jennifer began to giggle through her tears ... which made Jessica laugh, and then Brenda.

Finally Patsy, too, began to chuckle. If Cody could be happy with autism and view it as God's gift, maybe she ought to give Pete Roberts more of a chance. What if this twice-divorced former alcoholic—who appeared to be a disability worth shunning—was actually someone special the Lord had prepared just for her?

CHAPTER SEVEN

Charlie and Boofer were cruising down the lakeside road in the Moores' golf cart at about four in the afternoon when they noticed something suspicious. Always alert for anything unusual in a neighborhood, Charlie kept a keen eye trained on Deepwater Cove. Mail carriers had been known to save people's lives. Finding an elderly person who had fallen inside a house and couldn't get up, discovering someone who had slid on a patch of ice and was lying nearly frozen in a ditch, noticing a nonworking air conditioner in the home of a bedridden invalid—any of these could mean the difference between life and death. Charlie considered himself one of the best in this unwritten aspect of the job.

If Esther hadn't talked him out of taking the job as a postal inspector and moving to Washington DC for training so many years ago, he might have risen to a high level in the agency. He certainly would have been paid better and built up a bigger pension. Not to mention the satisfaction he would have had in investigating postal violations. It would have been almost like working for the FBI or the CIA.

But Charlie didn't like to think about the old days and that long-buried conflict with his wife. They never spoke about what had happened—at least, they hadn't until Esther started bringing it up again. No, Charlie was retired now, and he had a new field of service. Deepwater Cove.

Just at the bend in the road, he and Boofer both heard a faint scraping sound. Ears perked, they looked at each other, and Charlie spoke the words he felt sure his dog was thinking.

"Something's amiss."

Slowing the golf cart to a crawl, Charlie peered along the water's edge and up into the woods beneath a large limestone bluff. Most of the leaves had turned, and a few trees were already bare, making it easier to see into the dense growth.

"What've we got there, Boof?" he asked in a low voice.

The little mutt sniffed the air. Charlie did the same. Smoke from burning leaves mingled with a mouthwatering aroma from someone's barbecue grill. Pork steaks, by the smell of it. Charlie wouldn't mind a nice pork steak, but he and Esther were still working their way through all the casseroles in their freezer.

A flash of dark blue appeared between two trees and then vanished. "There!" Charlie said. "Someone's down by the Hanes kids' house, Boofer. That's not right. We just saw Ashley headed over to the Hansens' basement to make beads, and Brad is always at Larry's Lake Lounge this time of day."

Boofer stood up on the seat and began panting in anticipation. Charlie stroked the black dog's head as he eased the cart along the road toward the house. What if someone was stealing the supplies for Brad and Ashley's spare room? The piles of lumber and siding had been lying around so long that a passerby might think they'd been abandoned. Still, it wasn't right to trespass. And it certainly wasn't legal to take another person's property.

"See anything?" Charlie asked the dog. "You know he's there, don't you, fella? We'd better get our protection ready."

Flipping open a compartment on his dashboard, Charlie took

out the small Mace can he always carried in case of emergencies. A mail carrier knew to take these kinds of precautions. As the cart approached the small, forlorn house at the edge of the road, Charlie stepped on the brake. Suddenly the crash of falling lumber echoed across the lake, followed by a string of swearwords foul enough to make Charlie wince.

Boofer let out a low growl that quickly rose to a torrent of staccato barks. Leaping off the golf cart before his master could stop him, the dog rushed toward the shell of the Haneses' unfinished room.

Charlie slipped the Mace can into his jacket pocket and hurried after him. "Boofer! Come back here, you little rascal!"

Charlie gritted his teeth at the sound of a man shouting at the dog. The scalawag had better not touch Boofer; that's for sure. Cusswords flew through the air as the small black mutt yipped and yapped. Ducking his head, Charlie climbed into the framed-up room in time to see Brad Hanes take a step backward away from the dog and tumble over a stack of roofing shingles.

"Boofer, stop!" Charlie shouted before the animal could attack the hem of Brad's blue jeans. "Sit!"

Obedient, even a little sheepish, Boofer plopped down on the bare ground and turned baleful brown eyes on his master.

Charlie commanded his dog to stay; then he climbed over the shingles and stretched a hand toward the young man. "Sorry about that, Brad. Boofer heard you moving around back here, and he took off like a lightning bolt."

Declining Charlie's assistance, Brad stood and brushed off the seat of his jeans. "Crazy dog," he muttered. Hanging his head, he rubbed his eyes with a hand as though he had a headache. "What do you want, Mr. Moore? I'm kind of busy here."

Charlie dipped his hands into his pockets for warmth and studied the young man. Tall, good-looking, built like the star athlete he'd been in high school, Brad wore a hooded gray sweatshirt and a pair of old jeans. He was too young to have lost any hair or developed even a wrinkle, but his shoulders sloped as if he were carrying the weight of a hundred years.

"I don't need a thing," Charlie said. "Boofer and I were just taking our usual afternoon cruise around the neighborhood."

Eyes still downcast, Brad nodded. "Okay. Well, I'd better get back to work."

Charlie sensed that something was wrong. Handsome young bucks like Brad Hanes didn't act this way. Brad had always been something of a show-off, a cocky fellow who seemed to have the world by the tail. This hangdog look surprised Charlie.

"So, you're building a garage?" he asked, turning away from Brad to examine a weathered stud. "You planning to make it wide enough for Ashley's car and your truck?"

There was a moment of silence so long that Charlie almost looked around to see if Brad was still there. The younger man finally spoke up.

"I sold the truck."

The last thing Charlie had heard was that Brad had dented his prized possession while driving under the influence. "I don't blame you for selling it," he said, noting a six-pack of beer on the floor near a sawhorse. "I expect you can use one of your company's vehicles if you need to haul anything. No use making big payments—though the truck sure was a pretty piece of machinery. You had the engine purring like a cat."

Examining the exposed framework, Charlie could see that it wouldn't be long before most of the studs Brad had erected would begin to sag and lean. Nails would rust. Lumber would warp, shrink, expand. By next summer, termites would have found the structure. Within a year, Missouri's poison ivy and wild honeysuckle vines, weeds, carpenter bees, mud dauber wasps, and various other vegetation and pests would creep onto the construction site. In two years, the potential room would be nothing but a pile of rotting lumber.

"You've done a good job framing this up," Charlie said. "I've built a fair number of things in my life—garden sheds, decks, front porches—and I'd say you're off to a great start."

"Look, Mr. Moore, I didn't get the building permit," Brad said. "If that's what you're here about, I didn't get it, okay? I didn't talk to the Deepwater Cove bylaws committee either. I don't have time for that kind of—"

At this point the young man spoke a word that stiffened Charlie's spine and just about knocked his glasses off his nose. Mail carriers were as down-to-earth as anyone else, but he didn't recall any of his colleagues talking to each other with such coarse language. Maybe construction workers were a different breed, but if so, it was a shame.

"Excuse my French," Brad said, "but I'm tired of you asking Ashley about the room. And now you come snooping around our place with your dog. It's my project, and I'll finish it when I get around to it."

Charlie knotted and unknotted his fists inside his pockets. He realized he had two choices about how to react to Brad Hanes: He could rear back and punch the kid's lights out. Or he could stand still for a while and try to figure out what was behind all this hostility.

Seeing as how punching Brad Hanes was not exactly Christlike and would likely result in Charlie's own hasty downfall, he decided to ponder the situation.

"I never studied French," Charlie muttered, more to himself than to Brad. "Guess I'm not exactly familiar with that kind of language."

He watched Boofer scurry around, sniffing at the tools and lumber. In a moment, he heard a sigh come from Brad's direction.

"I'm sorry, Mr. Moore. I apologize."

Charlie turned in surprise. As he focused on the young man, he suddenly noticed that Brad's eyes were red-rimmed. Was the boy that upset?

Charlie tipped his head in acknowledgement of the apology. "Thank you. That means a lot coming from a fine young man like you. I'm glad to see you're back at work on the room. I noticed Ashley on her way to the Hansens' house a few minutes ago. She'll be making more beads, I guess. That wife of yours works day and night on her necklace business."

Brad kicked at a nail lying on the plywood boards he had set across the floor joists. He ran a finger across one eye and then the other. This time, Charlie knew something was up. Either Brad and Ashley had been in a newlywed battle or something else was troubling the boy. Charlie had learned to "fish" for answers when someone was reluctant to talk. Deciding this might be a good course, he bent down and picked up a length of asphalt shingling that had spilled from a torn packet.

"I've always liked a green roof on a house with clapboard siding," he remarked, examining the material more closely than necessary. "When I was growing up, we had a green roof. Every time I see one, I get a feeling of home. I guess you'll be reroofing the whole house eventually. That'll look nice."

Charlie paused a moment, searched Brad's face, and then cast his fishing line into the deep waters. "What's troubling you, boy? You look lower than a mole's belly button this afternoon."

Brad gave a momentary scowl and then leaned over to grab a hammer off a sawhorse. "Nothing's troubling me. I'm fine. I just need to get to work."

"I guess so. I shouldn't bother you any longer, though I've got to say I'm surprised Ashley's not here to keep you company. She tells Esther she really misses her husband."

"Ashley's schedule and mine don't match up. I work days; she works nights. We hardly see each other." He fiddled with the hammer. "I don't care. Makes no difference to me what she does with her time."

"Now that's something I would never say about Esther. I always liked knowing where my wife was and what she was up to—especially so we could work out free time to be together. That was hard sometimes, with me working and her raising the kids, but it mattered a lot to us."

"I guess that's how marriage was in the olden days."

Charlie felt the sting that Brad obviously intended. Sure, he might have said such a thing when he was a young man and full of himself. He remembered a time when he thought he would live forever . . . when he considered himself the finest husband, protector, friend, and lover a woman could ever want . . . when his own agenda was paramount in his mind . . . when his dreams appeared within easy reach.

Experience and a long string of years had taught him reality. Taught him that what mattered most was his love for God, family, friends, country. He wasn't the greatest or best at anything. But he was good enough, and that's all that really mattered.

"Olden days, golden days," Charlie muttered. "Yep, Esther and I were plumb crazy about each other. But that changes through the years. It sure does."

He waited patiently, like a fisherman slowly reeling in a lure. It wasn't long before Brad bit.

"What do you mean it changes?" he asked in a sullen voice. "You and Mrs. Moore are still married. Don't you love her anymore?"

"Sure I do. But I'm not crazy in love. I'm into it way too deep for that sort of foolishness. You see that Boston ivy over there? The red vine climbing up the pine tree? If you look close, you'll notice that the ivy has worked some of its little feet right into the bark of the tree. And parts of the bark have grown around the ivy's stem. That's how Esther and I have come to be. We're firmly attached. Two different people, but stuck together good and tight. A chilly wind can't tear us apart. A winter frost won't even begin to kill our love for each other. You and Ashley are that way, aren't you?"

Brad dropped the hammer into his toolbox. "Are you kidding? I don't even know why we got married. She's mad at me most of the time."

"Mad at you? That can't be right. She helps Esther with her cooking nearly every day, and she sings your praises until I have to leave the room for fear that my wife will start judging me next to you."

"No way, Mr. Moore." Brad turned and faced the direction Ashley had gone. The small muscle in his square jaw flickered with tension. "She's a . . . well, I won't say the word."

"And I thank you for that."

"It's just that she's on my case day and night. Why don't I pick up after myself? Why don't I do the laundry once in a while? Why don't I put my dishes away?"

"I've heard those questions many a time."

"That's why I eat lunch at Bitty Sondheim's Pop-In nearly every day. If I came home for a quick bite, Ashley would gripe at me the minute she got in from work. She expects the house to look like something out of one of her stupid decorating magazines. Pillows stacked up on the bed, dishes put away, shoes in the closet. It's ridiculous."

"Well now, I don't know about the pillows, but Esther does like her kitchen to stay clean."

"Ashley bought bed pillows we're not supposed to touch, let alone sleep on. I mean, we *live* in that house, you know? Nobody's going to take pictures of it or show it off on some dumb 'parade of homes.' I can't even put my feet on the coffee table without her pitching a hissy fit."

"Mmm. Sounds like a woman. It took me years to figure out what made Esther melt in my arms. It wasn't my paycheck. It wasn't my fine physique. It wasn't even this handsome face."

Charlie rubbed his chin as if admiring himself in a mirror and saw that he'd finally drawn the hint of a smile from Brad. The young man sat down on an upturned bucket and shook his head. Boofer wandered over and nudged Brad's hand with his nose.

"I don't have a clue what makes my wife tick," he said, stroking the dog's furry head. "Ashley used to be crazy about me, Mr. Moore. Every day, she was all over me—kissing on me and cooking for me and hanging around my neck like she was one of those dumb beaded chokers she makes. Now I'm a drunk, I can't manage money, I'm lazy, I'm boring . . . she even tossed the Big D on the table."

"The Big D?" Charlie raced through a mental dictionary, but all he could think of were words that fit his own life. *Dementia. Despair. Dread. Death.*

"Divorce," Brad said, standing again and muttering foul words under his breath. "What is the deal around this place? It's like I live with a bunch of bozos. No offense, Mr. Moore, but you people are so old you don't have any idea what's going on in the real world. Deepwater Cove . . . why did Ashley want to buy a house here? It's like living in a cemetery. There's nothing to do. Nobody to talk to. You're not even allowed to shoot fireworks or ride a motorcycle or dive off the dock or do anything fun."

He kicked his toolbox this time, and Charlie began wondering what would be next. Jamming his hands into the pockets of his sweatshirt, Brad glared at the lake. Charlie recognized himself as a young man. Frustrated, angry, clueless. His first few years with Esther had been a joy—as well as a mishmash of confusing messages and awkward turns. Did she love him? Or hate him? Was he Sir Lancelot? Or a buffoon?

"I'm old, all right," Charlie conceded, though he figured he was a lot more spry than Brad gave him credit for. "But I'm not too old to remember wondering if I'd done the right thing when I married Esther. Wow, that woman was a handful. She never stopped talking. Sometimes, right out of the blue, she'd start boohooing like it was the end of the world. Usually I had no idea what had set her off, though it always turned out to be me."

"Sounds like Ashley. That's the worst thing about her. She's always got to talk, talk, talk. She wants to tell me about her whole day and all the people she met and what everyone did and said. If I don't hang on every word and then make the exact right response, she gets furious."

Charlie chuckled. "Esther had strong opinions too. I expected them all to be focused on how wonderful I was and how glad she was to be my wife. I sure missed that by a mile. In fact, now that I think about it, Esther is still moody and opinionated."

"Ashley says I never listen to her. Well, she's right. Who cares what Brenda Hansen thinks about couches? And as for Cody, that kid's a kook. Ashley says he's so cute and handsome and sweet and funny and blah, blah, blah. Sometimes she acts like she's in love with *him*."

The hurt in Brad's voice told Charlie exactly what he needed to know. The young man deeply loved his wife and wanted to please her. The thought of losing her to another man, even a "kook" like Cody, was enough to rankle him. That meant there was hope for this troubled young marriage. It might seem like only a spark of affection was left between the two, but Charlie had a lot of faith in God's ability to stoke the fire.

"Tell you what," he said before he'd given himself the opportunity to think it through. "How about if I help you with this room addition? I've got the time to round up a building permit and take your plans to the bylaws committee. I'm a pretty good hand with a power saw and a nail gun, and I know the ins and outs of a toolbox. Maybe if we whip this thing out before next summer rolls around, Ashley will realize you're still Prince Charming."

Brad eyed the older man. Clearly he didn't think much of what he saw. "She's not going to be happy even if I do finish the garage," he said.

"What if you finish a nursery?"

With a grunt of acknowledgment, Brad shrugged. "Yeah, but I've got other things to do after work."

"I imagine Larry's Lake Lounge will stay afloat without any more contributions from your paycheck. What do you say, Brad? Think a youngster and an old geezer can put up with each other long enough to turn this pile of lumber into a bona fide room?"

"I don't know, Mr. Moore." Brad stalked the construction area like a caged panther. "Maybe I should just get out. If she hates me that much, why stick around? I don't need it, you know? I earn a good living, and there are plenty of other women willing to treat me right. I don't see the point in busting my can to build this room for Ashley if she's already planning to divorce me. I ought to cut my losses and leave while I can."

"You don't want to do that, do you? Have you even made it to your first anniversary, kid? You have to pass that milestone at least."

"Like I said, no offense, but you're too old to know what things are like these days. People get divorced all the time. It happens, Mr. Moore. Most of the kids in my graduating class had parents, stepparents, half brothers and sisters, stepbrothers and -sisters. That's the way things are."

"It may be the way things are, but it's not the way God wants them to be. He'd prefer that a man and wife stick together and try their best to work through problems. Sometimes they can't, but I suspect sometimes they give up too quickly. I've got nearly fifty years of marriage under my belt. And that's with Esther—which has to count for a lot."

Brad chuckled. "Ashley thinks Mrs. Moore hung the moon. I've gotta tell you, though—and I don't mean anything bad by it—but living with your wife would drive me right around the bend. What's the deal with her hair, Mr. Moore?"

"Oh, it's her style. Every curl in place." Charlie reflected on the way Esther darted to one side if his hand ever went near her head. The few times he'd managed to touch that glowing white crown, he had discovered it was as crisp and solid as the chocolate shell on a dipped ice cream cone.

"Well, I guess so then," Brad said. "It's all right with me, anyhow. I'm sure Ashley won't mind either."

"What's all right? Esther's hair?"

"No—you and me. Putting up the new room together. If you'll get the permits, I'll make sure we have what we need for the next step. I think I can get a good deal on some insulation, and the contractor I work for will probably let me borrow big tools we'll need—as long as we use them on the weekends. I'll talk to him about the project tomorrow. It'll be easier with two of us, even if you're not that strong. I get off from work around three. How does that sound to you?"

Charlie frowned for a moment, realizing all at once that he'd committed himself to a long-term project just as winter was coming on. Not only that, but Brad Hanes was one rough kid. Smart mouth, foul language, big ego, and probably on his way toward alcoholism and divorce. The idea of trying to work with a man who had been drinking didn't please Charlie in the least.

Besides that, Esther would be home alone. These days, that might be a problem. Just the day before, he had seen her take a mug out of a dishwasher loaded with dirty dishes. Before he could stop her, she filled the mug with coffee and walked off humming a tune. She had no idea what she'd done. Hadn't even looked to see whether the mug was clean. Though it wasn't a big deal, the number of these little glitches had been growing. Charlie was troubled, to say the least.

"Aw, never mind," Brad spoke up. He took a can of beer from the six-pack and popped the top. "Ashley married me, and she'll have to accept me for who I am or get out. I don't care about this room. It was a dumb idea in the first place."

"Now, hold on." Charlie studied the young man, who was taking a long swig. "Tell you what. I'll help you, but only under certain conditions. No beer on the job. And you've got to pull your fair share of the labor. I'm off during the mornings, but I don't intend to work out here by myself. You do your part, I'll do mine, and we'll get her done."

Brad tilted his can again and eyed Charlie. "This is my property. I can drink whatever I like."

"Not if you want my help."

"No cussing. No beer. I guess that means no weed either, huh?" He grinned.

"You've got plenty of weeds around here, but not the kind that might land us in jail. No weed, Brad."

"All right." Crushing the can, he studied it for a moment and then hurled it into the woods behind the house. "I'll see you tomorrow, then."

With a nod, Charlie whistled for Boofer and headed back to the golf cart. He had made several poor decisions in his life, and he figured this one might be right up there with the worst. As his little dog settled on the vinyl seat beside him, Charlie put the vehicle in motion. They would be home again soon, and no doubt Esther would be aflutter with delight that he was going to help the husband of her dear, sweet Ashley.

But something Brad had said during their conversation bothered Charlie a lot more than the thought of working with a no-account young tough.

"There are plenty of other women willing to treat me right," he had boasted.

A wandering eye had to be one of the most common signs of a struggling marriage. Were things ever that bad with Esther? Had she been so frustrated with her hardworking, inattentive, and more than a little demanding husband that she'd been susceptible to the attentions of another man?

George Snyder. The name filtered through the fog of memories inside Charlie's brain, as it had so often since the day he'd found the sketch in the bottom drawer of Esther's dresser. But this time it hit a bump and skidded to a standstill.

Charlie stopped the golf cart and looked out at the lake. He knew that man. George Snyder had lived down the hall from the Moores in their first apartment. He was blond, blue-eyed, friendly, and in Charlie's eyes, basically a bum living off the trust fund his father had left him. He didn't hold down a job, and his head was full of fantasies. An artist . . . that's what he planned to become. An illustrator for big city magazines and newspapers. Charlie had barely given the fellow the time of day.

But Esther had been home alone from the moment her husband

left the apartment until he returned each evening. Alone. Lonely. Hungry for conversation. In need of company.

Despite her unhappiness, she had begged Charlie not to take the postal inspector job and move them to Washington DC. They hadn't bought a home of their own until after the apartment down the hall had been vacated—its renter gone to New York in pursuit of his dreams.

Might Esther have said something just like Brad Hanes had? *"There's another man willing to treat me right,"* Charlie could almost hear her sob. *"And his name is George Snyder."*

CHAPTER EIGHT

No, of course not!" Esther replied without hesitation to the question her husband had asked as he entered the house from his latest golf cart excursion. She had been sorting beads all evening, and she was exhausted. Her hands ached and her eyes stung. To tell the truth, she wasn't absolutely positive she had put the beads in the correct compartments of Ashley's plastic container. Preparing to head for the bathtub and then to bed, she was surprised at Charlie's big announcement.

"Why should I mind if you help Brad build the new room?" she asked him. "I'm delighted, honey. That's a very neighborly thing to do."

Crossing the living room, she stood on tiptoe, slipped her arms around her husband's neck, and gave him a peck on the cheek. Charlie smelled of the outdoors—chimney smoke, fallen leaves, the hint of rain. His jacket was cold, and she rubbed her hands up and down his arms.

"Brr! I can't believe you were outside for such a long time." She knelt and petted the dog. "Poor Boofer. Were you about to freeze? Well, why didn't you tell Daddy to bring you home? You were talking to Brad Hanes? Is that what he said? Really? My goodness!"

Usually Charlie chuckled when she pretended to have a conversation with the little black mutt they had rescued from an animal shelter nearly eight years before. Tonight, her husband didn't crack a smile. He walked over to his recliner, dropped onto the cushioned seat, and flipped up the footrest. As he reached for the remote control, Esther put her hand over it.

"Not so fast on the trigger tonight, Roy Rogers," she told him. "I want to hear more about this project. Is the room going to be a nursery or a garage?"

Charlie turned to her, and for the first time in a long while, she thought he looked old. It happened now and then, catching Esther by surprise. In her mind, they were much as they always had been. Two happy-go-lucky young lovebirds chirping along, building a nest, rearing fledglings, sending the young off to try their wings, and then settling down for a long summer's rest.

But once in a while, she would notice that she was seated across the table from an old man. He had white hair and trifocals and a fascinating webwork of lines around his mouth and eyes. Where had this fellow come from, and what was he doing in her dining room?

The same thing happened when she spotted herself in a store window. Who on earth was that elderly woman staring back? She was an awfully short, rounded-off little creature with silver hair, stumpy legs, and stodgy shoes. What had become of the girl with saddle oxfords, a swingy skirt, soft brown curls, and a giggle that drew boys like honeybees to a new rose?

"I don't know what to make of that pair," Charlie said, and for a moment Esther thought he was speaking about himself and his wife. Then he continued. "Brad loves Ashley down deep, but the boy has an awful lot of growing up to do. I'm not sure what made me offer to help him."

"You're just an old softie," Esther said, sitting on the edge of the sofa nearest him. "It doesn't surprise me a bit that you want to give the kids a hand. Ashley's having a terrible time of it, you know. She's afraid Brad is turning into a drunk. I think she's scared they're going to end up divorced."

"He is too."

"Did he tell you that?" Esther laid her hand on her heart and gasped. "Oh, Charlie, we can't let that happen. I want them to have a long, happy marriage like ours. Ashley is so anxious to have children, and she'd be a perfect little mother. Brad is handsome and hardworking. But you know what? He spends money like it was going out of style. And he never listens to poor Ashley. She's as lonely as a girl could be, even though she's in a brand-new marriage with a cute house and neighbors all around. If she didn't have me to talk to, I don't know how she would get through the day."

Charlie's mouth formed a crooked line—one that told Esther he had something on his mind. After all these years, she hardly had to look at the man. The sound of his voice or the way he walked across the floor could give him away.

"What's wrong?" Esther asked, knowing full well what he would say.

"Nothing."

"Good," she replied, "because I'm going to bed. I've been sorting beads till I could just about scream."

She made as if to stand but hesitated long enough to get the response she was waiting for.

"Esther?" Charlie spoke up. "Were you ever lonely? In our marriage, I mean. You said you hoped Brad and Ashley could have a happy life like ours. But has it really been happy for you?"

"You are the silliest goose in the gaggle," she teased him, swatting his knee. "Yes, I've been happy. Do I look like some miserable old hulk huddled up in a corner?"

"No, but in the hospital you said some things that bothered me. You blamed yourself for our problems. You said you had hurt me. And that has me wondering if the opposite is true. Maybe I hurt you, Esther."

"You never hurt me. Not once." She thought for a moment. These days, it was easier to recall events that had happened long ago than to remember what she had just been doing.

"Not ever?"

"Well, we had our spats, and maybe you did disappoint me a time or two," she conceded. "You forgot Valentine's Day one year. You didn't bring me a card or a gift or anything. And you gave me that snow globe one Christmas, remember? What was inside it? A filling station! Why on earth would you think I'd like a gas pump inside a snow globe, Charlie?"

"We were too poor for me to afford a gift you would really want. You had mentioned one time that you loved snow globes. I saw an ad in the newspaper saying you could get one free if you bought twenty gallons of gas at the local Texaco. Every time the car got low, I drove over there and filled up. The man behind the counter punched my gas card, and finally I had enough holes to get you the free snow globe. I thought you'd be thrilled, but I could tell you only pretended to be pleased with it."

"Well, for pete's sake, a snow-blown gas station? What woman would want to look at that?" As she spoke, Esther felt a familiar cloak of darkness wrapping around her.

Ever since the accident, a sense of frustration and gloom shadowed her, hovering, waiting to descend while she wasn't paying attention. She tried to see the good in people, but often they simply irritated the living daylights out of her. And so many things went wrong. Little annoyances—and most of them happened through her own carelessness.

"We'd been married at least a year, hadn't we?" she asked Charlie. "You should have known me better by that time. I like pretty gifts. Jewelry, flowers, even chocolates. I know we didn't have money, but how much could a box of candy have cost back then? Less than a tank of gas, I'll bet. I was always fun-loving and free-spirited in those days. You could have taken me to the zoo or even made me something. You're good with tools, Charlie, and I enjoy handmade gifts. Something artistic would have been nice. But a snow globe with a gas station inside? Well, anyway, it doesn't matter now. I gave that old thing to Charles Jr. years ago."

Esther could see her husband staring at her through his trifocals. She had forgotten what they were talking about to begin with—a sudden brain glitch that was happening regularly these days. She had no idea how they got off on the subject of snow globes. Charlie could dredge up the craziest things.

"I'm going to run my bath," she announced. "I'm so tired, and you just run me ragged around here. It doesn't matter what kind of pain or suffering I've been through; I still have to take care of you as though you were a little boy. I can't imagine how I used to have the energy to cook, wash, iron, and look after the kids—plus satisfy your needs."

This time she actually intended to stand, but Charlie caught her arm. "Esther, sit down," he said. "I'm not finished with this conversation."

She heaved an exaggerated sigh. Couldn't he see she wanted her bath? "What do you want to know?"

Charlie looked at the TV, staring at the black screen as if he, too, had forgotten the subject of their discussion. Then he turned to her. "It's about our marriage. Back in the beginning when we lived in that little apartment. I finally remembered George Snyder."

Esther's heart skipped a couple of beats. "George? The man who lived down the hall?"

"Did you talk to him much?"

"I suppose I did. You don't just walk past a neighbor without speaking. Honestly, Charlie, first you drag out the snow globe and now you've brought up someone from who knows when. I can't imagine what on earth you're getting at, but I'm starting to wonder if your arteries are clogging up too. Which reminds me . . . the doctor's office called from Springfield today. The receptionist wanted to schedule my plaque cleanup, and I decided right then I didn't want anyone fiddling around with me like that. So I told her to strike my name from the list. I figure if I've lived with it this long, I can go on for a few more years just fine."

This time it was Charlie who sat up straight. He dropped the footrest and leaned forward on his recliner. "What do you mean you cancelled? You can't back out of a procedure like that, Esther. Your carotid artery is halfway plugged. The doctor has to take care of it."

"No, he doesn't. It's *my* artery, and I'll decide whether anyone messes with it. Besides, I have a perfectly fine one on the other side of my neck."

"One is not enough!"

Now Charlie was agitated, and Esther began to wish she hadn't mentioned the phone call. Still, it took his mind off George Snyder.

"Listen to me, Charles Moore," she said. "I am not having that doctor stick a balloon into my artery. And I'm certainly not going to let him scrape off any plaque. Do you know how small these arteries are? Right here, take a look at this. Would you want someone putting a balloon into *your* vein? I didn't think so. You've opened many a clogged kitchen drain for me, and you know how that works. The dirty old gunk has to go somewhere. After you've run the snake through the pipe, that glop moves right on into the sewer system."

"We're not talking about plumbing, Esther. These arteries carry your blood supply."

"It's the same thing. The doctor could loosen a piece of plaque and have it float straight into my brain. Both of us know what that means. Do you want me to have a stroke, Charlie? Now think about it honestly. Would you really want me to suffer something as devastating as that? Even if I lived through it, there would be all that rehabilitation and physical therapy, just like with my mother. You'd run out of patience, and so would I. So no thanks. That's what I said today, and that's what I meant. Don't even bring up the subject again, or we'll have another spat."

Rising, she brushed his hand away as he tried to reach for her. Without letting him speak again, she padded toward the bathroom. She truly hated having these little quarrels with Charlie.

Some issues came up frequently, and even after almost fifty years, they had never been resolved. Esther hadn't been fond of her husband's parents, for example. They didn't think she was raising the children right. When Ellie got into trouble with drugs and alcohol, that gave them the trump card. Oh, they had looked so superior when they came over to the house to discuss what should be done with their granddaughter. Not even their deaths had erased the problem. Every now and then, Charlie would mention his dear mother or his sweet old dad. It was all Esther could do to bite her tongue—and sometimes she didn't bother to try.

She closed the drain in the tub and started the water running. Then she poured in a capful of fragrant bath salts. As she swished them around, she began to think of one thing after another that her husband did to annoy her. He left his big wet snow boots right in front of the door. He forgot to fill the birdbath. He was always watching those crazy talk shows or yelling out answers on game shows—as if he were a real contestant. And no matter how old he got, the man was forever after her to "make whoopee," as he put it. Didn't he have a clue what the word *osteoporosis* meant?

It was a wonder Esther bothered to encourage Ashley Hanes in her marriage. Charlie had been so difficult all these years, and Brad Hanes sounded ten times worse.

As she stepped into the tub and eased down into the warm water, Esther felt her nerves begin to relax at last. A husband could be such a trial. But really, when she thought about it, not too much more difficult than a dog. Boofer was always wanting to go outside. Then he would turn right around and bark to get back in. He'd had fleas and allergies and worms. The money they had spent on veterinary bills was downright obscene. And that didn't even take into account the dog's occasional accidents on the living room carpet or the kitchen tile.

Well, at least Boofer didn't bring home snow globes with gas pumps inside. Or ask irritating questions. What was bothering Charlie so much that he had to keep bringing up George Snyder? Let bygones be bygones—that was Esther's motto. And if it was up to her, the name of the artist down the hall would never come up again.

⚜

"You know who I was thinking about today?" Pete asked as he and Patsy sat side by side in the darkened, empty movie theater at the outlet mall in Osage Beach. "Esther and Charlie Moore."

"Esther came to the salon yesterday for her regular set-and-style," Patsy said. "It's good having her back. The TLC wasn't the same without her, and I missed seeing her in my chair every Friday afternoon. What made you think of them?"

Patsy had managed to fit into her pencil skirt, a warm nubby sweater, and a pair of knee-high leather boots. She had curled her blonde hair, redone her nails, and stuck on a set of false eyelashes. They were the wispy kind that looked natural enough to fool Pete. In her mind's eye, she imagined herself as a long, lean lioness prowling the savanna. But she felt like a sausage stuffed way too tight inside its casing. She was going to have to quit eating at the Pop-In or pretty soon she would start popping out.

"Charlie bought a tank of gas this morning," Pete told her. "We talked about the usual things—weather, fishing, football. He said the insurance company decided that Esther's car had been totaled in the wreck. He's not planning to buy another one."

"I'm happy to hear that. Esther told the TLC about both of them falling asleep on their drive home from seeing the doctor in Springfield. It was funny in a way. But when you think about what could have happened . . ."

Though Patsy had second-guessed her decision to go out with Pete, she felt fairly at ease after all. He sure looked handsome with that shaved jaw and combed hair. Pete had actually put on a real button-down oxford shirt instead of his usual T-shirt. He had tucked it into his jeans and was wearing a belt. Patsy couldn't remember ever seeing Pete in a belt. All in all, he didn't look half bad. The way he normally dressed, he came across as paunchy and haphazard. But tonight, she decided, he could better be described as stocky. His big shoulders filled the back of the theater chair from one side to the other. He had long, well-muscled legs, too. Good legs, if you could say that about a man.

"Crazy driving is never amusing to me," Pete said. "I'm a big NASCAR fan, and I've heard people complain about the number of wrecks. But let me tell you, Patsy, those drivers know exactly what they're doing. They take a lot of safety precautions, too. I think Charlie's wise to keep Esther in the passenger seat. Why risk another mishap?"

The local advertising on the big screen had ended, and now the trailers for new movies began. The lights went down until the theater was completely black. Behind them, someone dropped an open bag of Skittles, and the candies rolled down the floor toward the front of the room. The aroma of popcorn and nacho cheese drifted through the air. That's when Pete reached over the back of Patsy's seat and put his arm around her.

The moment Pete folded her into the protection of those big muscles, Patsy lost track of what was on the screen. Wow, did this man smell good. She recognized a piney-smelling aftershave she had always liked. His hand cupped her shoulder, and he tugged her a little closer.

"You know what I was thinking about the Moores?" Pete murmured against Patsy's ear. "I was thinking how well they fit together. Kind of like us."

"Us?" That single pronoun was all she managed to croak out before the feature film began.

Pete had chosen the movie, and Patsy tried to concentrate on the car chases; gun battles; and frequent loud, fiery explosions. But all she could think about were Pete's words. Did he and Patsy fit together? Were they anything at all like the long-married Esther and Charlie Moore?

From the moment Patsy had met her next-door neighbor in the Tranquility shopping strip, she had been able to see only their differences. He was noisy. She was quiet. He was so messy and disheveled that she often referred to him as a shaggy sheepdog or a big, hulking bear. Patsy loved fashionable outfits, pretty cosmetics, manicured nails, and expensive perfume. While she constantly updated her hair—experimenting with color and style, trying always to look her best—Pete rarely bothered to get his cut. It grew long and scraggly around his ears and neck. Until she objected, he wore an untrimmed beard.

As for their pasts, they couldn't be more opposite. Though Patsy's family had been poor, they knew the importance of good morals and strong values. Her parents' devotion to Christ and to each other had provided a firm foundation for her childhood. After her father died and her mother became ill, Patsy essentially gave up her social life to care for the woman who had raised her.

Pete, on the other hand, had grown up without the influence of religion or any other kind of virtuous principles. He'd been a heavy drinker. By his own admission he was a lousy husband to two wives. He'd even done jail time for driving while intoxicated. A stint in rehab and a few college business courses had set him on a better track. But only after moving to Lake of the Ozarks had he started attending church and holding down a regular job.

As some poor fellow on the screen got shot about eight times, Patsy decided Pete was totally wrong for her. They didn't fit together well at all. There was no *us*.

Just when she had settled her mind on this subject and started to figure out who was trying to kill whom in the movie, Pete leaned close and kissed her gently on the cheek.

"You sure do smell good tonight, Patsy," he murmured. "I'm glad you agreed to see a show with me."

Every single building block of reason and good sense in Patsy's mind tumbled down all at once. Thanking God that the theater was all but empty, she closed her eyes as he kissed her again. Why oh why did she feel this tangle of desire and yearning at the touch of his lips on her skin?

Patsy focused on forming a prayer for help. Surely the good Lord wouldn't allow her to succumb to a man just for the pure pleasure of it. Hadn't God helped her erect a strong barrier against that sort of thing? Her brain was nearly as full of Bible verses as Cody's. She knew it would be unwise to get involved with a man who didn't share her faith. Good relationships were founded on spiritual unity, friendship, mutual caring, and not . . . not . . .

Oh, that kiss sure was sweet. Now Pete's lips pressed against hers, and Patsy turned and slipped her arms around him. He cuddled her close and kissed her again. And then again. She touched his hair, discovering it was soft on her fingertips. So unlike his chin as it grazed hers.

My goodness, it felt wonderful to have Pete surrounding her with his man-smell and his man-muscles and his man-skin. So much of Patsy's life had been spent around women. But Pete was all male, and she didn't know if she could ever get enough.

"I'd like to kiss you forever," he whispered. "You're as sweet as maple sugar, girl."

"One more time," she murmured back.

He was more than happy to oblige, and Patsy realized she felt the same way. *Forever.* She wanted to be in this man's arms for the rest of her life. It had been too many years since anyone had brought her this much satisfaction and joy—and it had all happened in the length of time it took for a few car crashes and gun battles to kill off most of the characters in the movie.

No, that wasn't quite right. This whirlwind of emotion had been building between them for a long time. Over the months, they had fought and argued and stopped speaking to each other. They had laughed, teased, and flirted. But they had kept a careful distance, making sure not to reveal too much or act too confident about their feelings. Until this night, in this theater, in the dark.

"I love you, Patsy," Pete said against her ear. "I love you so much I don't hardly believe it myself. I've been feeling it for a while now, but I didn't trust it. With you here tonight, though, I don't have any more doubts. I love you, and that's all there is to it."

It would have been enough if he had only spoken the first three words. But Pete's confession of initial doubt and eventual certainty melted Patsy's heart. Like a block of paraffin softening in the manicure section of her salon, her own qualms, hesitations, and fears warmed and dissolved. Pete Roberts loved her. Truly loved her. And she loved him, too.

Swallowing back unexpected tears, Patsy watched the movie screen as a group of panting, bloodied men with torn clothes and smoke-blackened faces hugged each other and then strolled off into a jungle sunset. The music swelled, the screen went black, and the list of directors, producers, actors, and crew began to roll.

What on earth had happened? Most important—what next? Patsy could barely stand as Pete pushed himself up from the theater seat and took her hand. Her pencil skirt had managed to walk its way at least six inches up from her knees, and she tugged on the hem to lower it. Clutching her purse to her chest like a barricade, she stepped out from the row of seats and accompanied Pete up the aisle and into the lobby.

"Hey, Patsy and Pete!"

Cody's voice instantly brought Patsy to full alert, and she spotted the young man seated on a bench near the concession stand.

He stood and waved. "I didn't know you were here," he called. "I'm here too. How about that?"

"Were you in the theater just now?" Pete asked. "The one with the war movie?"

"No, we're getting ready to go in. But not that one. We're seeing a movie about chickens."

Patsy scanned the posters lining the wall for something that resembled Cody's description. "Who did you come with?" she asked.

Just then, Jennifer Hansen walked out of the ladies' room. Patsy could have dropped over dead. The young blonde, dressed in khaki slacks and a pale blue sweater, smiled when she saw them. Clearly trying to banish a coy grin, she joined the group.

"Hey," she said. "You two been having fun?"

Pete shrugged. "We saw that war movie. Pretty intense."

"Lots of shooting," Patsy added.

The whole time they spoke, Patsy was looking back and forth between the two young people. Was it possible? Had Cody asked Jennifer out on a real date? Had she agreed to go with him? What could this mean?

"Cody said you're seeing a movie about chickens," Patsy said. "Is it a cartoon?"

Jennifer glanced at Cody. Then she laughed and elbowed him. "Oh, it's a chick flick! That's what he means."

"Chickens," Cody repeated. He leaned over as if to confide in Patsy. "This movie is for girls, but I'm going to watch it anyway."

Patsy chuckled. He certainly looked handsome in a jacket, slacks, and a clean white shirt. His curly hair was the perfect length. Maybe Jennifer Hansen—with her generous, Christlike heart—was willing to overlook some of Cody's more unusual attributes in favor of sharing a friendship with the young man. Cody was not only good-looking, but like Jennifer, he was gentle, kind, and always sincere. Patsy hoped Jennifer knew what she was doing.

"Oh, there they are!" Jennifer sang out. "Jessica and her fiancé came up for the weekend. We decided at the last minute to throw a group together and see this show. Look, Cody, there are the other kids from church. Everyone's got snacks now." She smiled again at the older couple. "Sorry, but we've gotta run. Come on, Cody." Jennifer took his hand and hurried them off.

As they neared the others, Cody turned and called over his shoulder, "Patsy, you and Pete need to wash your faces. You have got lipstick everywhere."

With a gasp, Patsy turned to the man beside her. Pete Roberts' mouth and cheeks were smeared with Razzmatazz Raspberry lip gloss.

Pete studied her for a moment in silence. Then he shook his head and guffawed. "Heavens to betsy, girl," he chortled as he wiped his face with the back of his hand. "We make quite a pair, don't we?"

"I guess we do," she told him. Hurrying toward the restroom, she added to herself, *We fit together pretty well, Pete Roberts.*

CHAPTER NINE

Esther assessed herself in the salon mirror. Patsy was busy sorting out curls with a pick, and she didn't seem to notice as her client's head tilted one way and then another. *Definitely old*, Esther decided. There could be no other way to describe herself. The face staring back at her was old. Crow's feet fanned out from her eyes, and empty silk purses sat beneath them. Age had carved a set of parentheses around her mouth and a matched pair of exclamation points between her eyebrows.

But worst of all was her neck. Esther shook her head in dismay. What on earth could have caused all that skin to loosen up and let go of its hold on her chin? It reminded her of an old velvet theater curtain, swagged and draped from ceiling to floor.

"What's the matter?" Patsy asked. "You're frowning. Am I doing something wrong this afternoon?"

"It's not you," Esther assured her. "It's me. Do you want to hear the strangest thing? I can't remember ever being a woman. You know what I mean? A full-fledged woman—like my mother."

"You're a woman right now, Esther. And a lovely one, at that."

"I'm an old lady. That's what I am. Here's the trouble, Patsy. I can remember *wanting* to become a woman. But I never felt like I actually got there. In my mind, I've always been a young girl—dancing through life like a will-o'-the-wisp. When my hair started to turn white, I kept it colored. When my bones ached, I pretended not to notice. But all of a sudden there's no getting around it. I'm old. Just like that, I went from young to old. Somehow I completely skipped womanhood."

"I've been doing your hair a long time, honey, and I don't think of you as young or old or anything else. To me, you're just Esther. Pretty, sweet, kind, and generous Esther Moore. I don't believe age matters a whit. It's a person's character that counts."

"How old *are* you, Patsy? I've often wondered."

"Better watch out," the stylist clucked. "You're starting to sound like Cody. We might have to work on your social skills."

Esther laughed. "I'm sorry. It's none of my business. I do worry about you, though, sweetheart. You've been running this salon for years, but what have you ever done for yourself? You never take a vacation. You don't have a husband or children. You're too busy to take up a hobby or even volunteer for anything."

"Now hold on there. I'm a member of the Tea Lovers' Club, don't forget. And I've done my fair share of helping out with the neighborhood get-togethers. Not to mention providing plenty of entertainment at the last Fourth of July picnic."

Esther was pleased to see that Patsy had arrived at a point of finding humor in her Independence Day pratfall. Esther's flying car incident had been the talk of Deepwater Cove more recently, and she had decided to make light of it. In life, she had learned, it was best not to dwell too much on past events. Things happened—right or wrong, good or bad, funny or sad—and a smart woman moved forward.

"I hear a new manicure place moved in beside the tattoo parlor," Esther said. "I know that must be bringing you some competition. Have you ever thought of selling your business and starting off on a new path?"

Patsy raised the hair spray but didn't push the button. "Sell my salon?" she asked. "Sell Just As I Am? Why would I do that?"

"As I said, there's the new manicure business, and I hear Brenda Hansen has considered putting a decor shop into that last empty spot past the Pop-In."

"She sure is. It's going to be called Bless Your Hearth, and I can't wait for it to open up. Steve is building dividers out of shelving and lattice, and Cody's already painting the walls. Brenda plans to use blocks of color to break the shop into separate areas for bedding, living room items, bath goods, and kitchenware."

"All that color in one room?"

"It'll blend, Esther. Taupe, deep chocolate, and robin's egg blue. Don't those sound yummy together? Brenda's going to stock all kinds of local items, too—Ashley's beads, Color of Mercy's CDs, walnut bowls, you name it. I'm half afraid her store will make my salon look downright dowdy."

"Which is exactly what I was talking about a minute ago. Patsy, aren't you a little tired of running your salon day after day? I thought that after all these years, maybe you'd be leaning in another direction."

"What other direction?"

Patsy began to spray. To Esther, she seemed a little more animated than usual, filling the air around her client's head with a cloud of vapor. Patsy was nervous, but who wouldn't be at such a precipitous time in life?

Esther coughed and waved her hand in front of her eyes before she could reply. "Cody told me that he saw you and Pete Roberts at the movies last weekend. He mentioned that Pete was wearing . . . well, Cody said he was wearing lipstick. And with that information, I assumed that the two of you might be enjoying one another's company a little more than you let on."

Setting the spray can on the desk at her station, Patsy placed one hand on her hip. "Esther Moore, are you trying to sniggle information out of me?"

"I don't know that I'd put it quite that way."

"Well, I'm not a bit worried about Brenda's shop. And for your information, the new manicure place is no competition for Just As I Am either. It's not even much of a business. I went over there to check it out. The tattoo shop hired a woman who paints fingernails black, blue, green, or purple. She pierces anything you want a hole stuck through, and they gave her husband a job because he specializes in motorcycle tattoos. If you want to look young again, Esther, why don't you go and get yourself some sparkly green nail polish and an eyebrow ring?"

Almost the moment the words were out of her mouth, Patsy swung around and covered her face with her hands. "Oh, Esther, I'm so sorry. I don't know what came over me. That was mean, just plain mean."

Esther swiveled the chair toward her friend, then reached up and took Patsy's hand. "It's my fault for prying. I would never want you to sell Just As I Am, honeybunch. What would I do without my regular set-and-style? As for you and Pete . . . all I meant is that I would love to see you happily hitched. There's nothing sweeter than a loving marriage, but it's none of my business what you young people do these days. I'm old and nosy, and I'm a great big gossip, too. I know it as well as I know the nose on my own face. Please forgive me for butting into your privacy."

When Patsy turned around, Esther was surprised to see that big tears hung at the ends of her friend's long black eyelashes.

"Gracious," Esther murmured, standing to give Patsy a hug. "I had no idea my words would be taken so much to heart. Why don't you spray me a little while longer, and we'll change the subject? That way we won't say good-bye on a sour note."

"It's not that, Esther." Patsy picked up the can and again began filling the air with mist. "I really don't know what to say. I'm so confused about Pete."

"Then let's discuss Charlie. Do you know what that fellow of mine has done? He up and volunteered to help Brad Hanes build a spare room on the side of the Haneses' little house."

"Charlie's building the new nursery?"

"The jury's still out on the room's purpose, but I'm guessing it's more likely to be a nursery than a garage—at least if Ashley has her way. When Charlie came home and told me what he'd agreed to, I was sure surprised. He's been helping with the beads some, but truth to tell, he enjoys his retirement. He does nothing but watch TV day and night. I'll bet he could win us a million dollars on one of those game shows. He knows all the answers long before the contestants do."

"My goodness," Patsy said.

"Charlie's so smart, though you'd never know it to look at him. Anyway, he realized that something needed to be done about that eyesore Brad started building last spring. Brad and Ashley are too young to really know what they're doing. They up and got married, bought a house and a truck, and the next thing you know, she's starting a bead business. They're running themselves ragged. And let me tell you—that does not make for an easy marriage. I remember the days when Charlie was starting out as a mail carrier. We could barely make ends meet, and before we knew it, the babies came along. I was exhausted. He was tired and cranky. Those were difficult years."

"But look how well things worked out," Patsy said. She glanced at the dividing wall between her salon and Pete's Rods-N-Ends. Then she sighed. "What's your secret, Esther? How did you and Charlie manage to build such a happy marriage?"

A happy marriage? For a moment, Esther sat in the cloud of hair spray thinking of nothing but the multitude of troubles she and her husband had faced through the years. A meager paycheck. A cramped apartment. Fatigue. Messy diapers. Skinned knees. Moving from one house to another. Childhood sassiness followed by teenage rebellion. Not to mention the worries of seeing their children face more adult challenges once they'd left home. Arguments. Illnesses.

Disagreements. A thousand little annoyances. It was a wonder they had made it at all.

But as the fog cleared and she looked up at Patsy's hopeful face, Esther understood the desire of her dear friend's heart. Patsy didn't want to know about all the hardships and anguish in marriage. She wanted to hear the good news. The fun. The laughter. The warmth and celebration and love.

"Such a happy marriage," Esther repeated, reflecting on Patsy's words. "It's a matter of taking things as they come, honey. Put one foot in front of the other and keep going. Of course, it helps if you marry someone as wonderful as Charlie Moore. I simply adore that man. He's the light of my life, and I can't imagine ever being without him."

"So that's it, then?" Patsy asked. "The big secret? Taking things one day at a time."

The disappointment in Patsy's voice led Esther to reconsider. She certainly didn't want to discourage a romantic liaison by pulling out a list of all the challenges marriage could bring. Patsy and Pete were no starry-eyed teenagers. Pete had a difficult past, and Patsy knew that all too well. What she wanted was hope. A future she could look forward to with joy and eager anticipation. The last thing she needed was a reminder about dirty socks and ratty house shoes and a man who smelled to high heaven every time he walked in from working in his garden in the hot summer sun.

"Marriage is much more than one day at a time," Esther said as she focused on herself in the mirror. She made an effort to recall the good times and found it wasn't too hard after all. "Marriage is a blissful gift from God. When you wake up from a bad dream, someone wraps his warm arms around you until you fall back to sleep. When you look across the dining room table, you see the face of a man who has loved you through thick and thin. When you hold hands in church, you know every single bump and callus on your husband's palm and knuckles. Even though there were times in my life when I wished I'd waited awhile to marry, in the long run I wouldn't do it any different.

I truly am glad we married when we did, and I don't regret a single thing about our life together. I'd never want to be single and all alone, rattling around like a marble in an empty shoe box. I think I'd cry every single day if I had to live like that—wouldn't you?"

Esther looked up and realized all at once that she wasn't talking to Charlie. She was sitting in Patsy Pringle's salon chair. Not only that, but she'd been rambling about something to do with marriage and all its glories.

How could she have been so insensitive? There stood Patsy, looking about as forlorn as a lost puppy. Esther knew it was time to change the subject, and quick. But she couldn't leap into another topic without sounding like her brain had turned to mush.

"Marriage," she said. "Yessirree, marriage." She nodded her head a moment, struggling to think of something. Then it hit her. "*Marriage* is what concerns me about Jennifer and Cody. I'm sure she doesn't want to go off into the jungle without a husband to protect her from the natives. And we all know that Cody is head over heels in love with her. But the two of them together? It's a recipe for trouble, if you ask me. She can't be thinking about him seriously, can she?"

"Jennifer is my next client. Why don't you ask her?"

"Heavens, no! I wouldn't want anyone to suppose I was nosy. It's Jennifer's business what she does with her life. It's just that Cody is so . . . well, how would you describe it?"

"*Autistic* is the word Jessica used." Patsy picked up Esther's purse. "When she got back to college, she sent her sister a bunch of information from that education class she's taking. Jennifer has done some more research, and both girls are convinced that Cody is autistic. They say he's very high-level with his skills, and he's learned how to make up for most of his weak areas. Did you know some autistic people have strong areas of talent? You've heard of those math or music geniuses, I'm sure. Jennifer told me that Cody learned to read much faster than anyone would have thought possible. And his artwork is amazing."

"She would say that," Esther said, standing and giving her hair a last pat. "Every picture Cody paints is of Jennifer, including your entire mural. I've never seen so many Jennifers in my life. I can't imagine what she thinks of that wall."

"She seems to accept everything about him," Patsy said as they walked toward the counter. "Jennifer told me that once she found out Cody was autistic, everything fit together like a jigsaw puzzle. Not a single piece is missing. And Cody Goss is a pretty good-looking puzzle, if I do say so myself."

"Yes, but he's a puzzle all the same." Esther took out her checkbook and to her immense relief discovered that Charlie had already filled in all the blanks and written out the usual amount. Ever since she added an extra zero to the utilities payment, he'd been helping her with the bills. She didn't mind a bit.

"I'm certainly not autistic," she told Patsy with a laugh. "Goodness, math has never been my area of talent. That's for sure! I can't paint or play an instrument either. As a matter of fact, I can't seem to do much of . . ." She shook her head, trying to dislodge the dark cloud. "Well, never mind. I'll just sit over there and wait for Charlie. Oh, look—here's Jennifer. Isn't she the prettiest thing?"

Esther greeted the young woman and then seated herself near Patsy's station. She enjoyed watching the stylist work. Patsy had made an art form out of hair. There was nothing the woman couldn't do. Whether her customer's mane was straight or curly, long or short, thick or thin, Patsy could literally transform it from one fashion and color into another.

Setting her purse on her lap, Esther glanced toward the front door. Charlie was rarely on time these days, it seemed. The two of them had such trouble meeting up at the right times and places. Charlie faulted her for not checking her watch. Esther blamed it on the fact that her husband had refused to consider buying another car. Before the accident, they'd never had trouble tending to their own matters independently. Now she felt as though they were joined at the hip.

"No one had any idea Cody could create faux finishes," Jennifer was telling Patsy. Esther tried not to listen, but the young woman was talking loudly enough for half the salon to hear. "Miranda Finley often takes Cody to the library with the twins, and he checks out books. He can read anything, you know."

"Is that right?" Patsy had begun trimming the ends of Jennifer's long, straight blonde hair. "I guess I hadn't realized he'd come such a long way."

"He's amazing. He read a book about decorative paint finishes, and then one morning my mom walked into the new store to find that he'd done an entire wall to look like burnished leather. It's just gorgeous."

"Leather? On the wall?"

"It looks sort of rough—like cowhide—but it literally glows. Mom thinks Cody can get work faux-finishing walls for some of Dad's real estate clients. You know how much help Miranda has been with Ashley Hanes's bead business? Well, she says she's going to make business cards and a Web site for Cody. Can you imagine that?"

"Who would have thought!"

Esther eyed Patsy, wondering if she had any real concerns about Jennifer's enthusiasm for Cody. Faux finishes or not, that young man had a long way to go before he would fit comfortably into society. There were far too many people who didn't have the patience of sweet Jennifer Hansen.

"Cody wants to paint the sky on the ceiling," she was continuing. "Mom's not sure about that. She says clouds are very hard to get right. On the other hand, Cody can do almost anything he tries."

"With art," Patsy clarified. "I do believe that young man could make a thunderstorm appear on the ceiling of your mother's store. But there are things he struggles with, Jennifer. You know that."

"Oh, sure. He drives Jessica's fiancé up the wall. Dad struggles too when Cody gets going on one of his favorite topics. Dad says it's like he's a stuck record. I've never heard a stuck record, but I get the idea."

119

"Cody definitely has things he talks about over and over. Hot dogs. Chocolate cake cut into squares." Patsy reached around Jennifer to make sure the ends of her hair were even in front. As she did, she looked directly at the young woman and spoke more softly. "I'm sure you know how Cody feels about you. To tell you the truth, I'm a little concerned. He's smitten, sweetheart, and I'd never want to see him hurt."

"I wouldn't hurt Cody." The dismay was obvious in Jennifer's voice. "I care about him."

"But he loves you."

"He says that, but he doesn't really know what it means." Jennifer studied her hands in her lap. "He's never known about real love. Romantic love. He barely understands how marriages and families work."

"All the same, honey, his emotions about you are genuine. I know you wouldn't intentionally upset Cody, but you're so kind, so generous, so truly accepting and loving of all people. Please be careful that he doesn't misunderstand how you feel about him."

Jennifer fell silent for a moment, and Esther wondered if she was going to get mad. The young woman certainly had the capability of expressing herself strongly—as everyone had seen several times during TLC meetings. But now she shook her head and laid her hand over Patsy's.

"Don't worry," she said. "I'm not leading Cody on. He knows my goal in life is to serve on the mission field. He's not prepared or educated to do anything like that—and he's aware of that. But even more important, Patsy, I've told Cody exactly how I feel about him. I care about him—in the same way everyone in Deepwater Cove does. I won't hurt him. I promise."

Esther was in the process of thanking the good Lord for that when she noticed the salon's front door swinging open.

"Oh, look," she said loudly enough that Patsy and Jennifer both turned in her direction. "Here comes Charlie to pick me up. And wearing that awful green sweater. What is wrong with the man?"

Charlie ambled over as Esther stood and did her usual twirl in front of him. "What do you think, sweetie pie?" she asked.

"Pretty as the day I first laid eyes on you."

Charlie always said the same thing after her set-and-style. Esther slipped her arm through his and stood on tiptoe to peck his cheek. "Come on, you old goober. Let's go home."

As they headed out the door, Patsy ran after them with Esther's purse. She and Charlie stood chatting beside the car while Esther settled herself in the passenger seat. Esther didn't like it that he wouldn't even discuss buying her a new vehicle. But if there wasn't enough money in the bank, what good would it do to complain?

"Patsy sure did a great job on your hair," Charlie said as he climbed in and started the engine. "Did you two have a nice visit?"

Esther set her hands on her purse. For some reason, she couldn't remember a thing she and Patsy had discussed, but wasn't that the way it always was with women? You chatted and shared and poured out your heart, and then you went on your way—too busy with life to give anything else much thought.

"We had a good talk," she told her husband. "But honestly, Charlie, haven't I told you a hundred times not to wear your green sweater with those pants? You are so forgetful these days."

Every Wednesday morning, Steve Hansen and a group of local men arrived at Rods-N-Ends for their weekly Bible study. Charlie never missed a meeting. In fact, of all the events that floated through his week, this was the anchor. Not even a trip to Aunt Mamie's Good Food could beat the opportunity to get together with friends, drink a cup of steaming coffee, and talk things over in the storage area at the back of the bait-and-tackle shop.

"Mornin', Charlie," Pete called out from the cash register.

Pete was calculating change for a gas customer, so he couldn't stop to chat. Charlie didn't mind. He could see that Derek Finley had taken his usual spot already. Last week, the young Water Patrol officer had asked the group for prayer. He told the men that his mother was thinking about buying a house in Deepwater Cove. She had been looking at the small place beside Brad and Ashley Hanes' property. It was far less grandiose than the home she had owned in St. Louis. No chandeliers or winding staircases or twelve-foot ceilings. No need for a maid or a yardman. But it stood only five houses away from the Finleys' property, and Miranda wanted to live near her son and his family.

The idea was all right with Derek. Kim had agreed to it too. The main thing, Derek told the Bible study group, was that for everyone's sake, Miranda needed to get out on her own again. She had been helpful with the twins during the summer, but now too many toes were getting stepped on. A blended family was difficult enough without adding a mother-in-law to the mix.

"Hey, Charlie." Derek looked up from the open Bible he'd been reading. "How are you this morning?"

"Couldn't be better if I was twins." Charlie eased himself down onto one of the cold metal folding chairs Pete had rounded up. Chilly autumn mornings made his joints ache a little more than usual. "Been keeping you in my prayers. Any news from the home front?"

"Well, speaking of twins, Luke had a problem with his diabetes at school the other day. It wasn't a major crisis, but it upset Lydia all over again. They put the kids in separate classrooms, which means she can't keep an eye on him. She hates that—gripes about it all the time."

"I'll bet she does. But the school is probably doing the right thing. This way, Luke has a little breathing room, and the teacher and the other children are forced to pay better attention to him. That's how it should be. I imagine the separation doesn't hurt Lydia's concentration in class either. If she was always watching her brother, she'd never get anything done."

"You got that right," Derek told him. "Kim and I are happy with the situation, though she worries about Luke all the time he's out of her sight. You know women."

"I'd like to think I do." Charlie chuckled. "That wife of mine keeps me hopping, though. Did I tell you the latest? Esther has refused to get her carotid artery cleaned out."

"You didn't mention that. Charlie, you'd better make it a prayer request. Esther needs to get that taken care of. Angioplasty and carotid stenting are common procedures these days. Living with blocked arteries can lead to all kinds of problems."

"I know. That's exactly what the doctor told her. But she's afraid he'll knock a piece of plaque loose and give her a stroke. She compared the surgery to unplugging a drain."

Derek grinned. "It's a medical process, not a plumbing problem. Esther is more likely to have a stroke if she *doesn't* get her artery opened up."

"You try telling her that."

"I will, if you want me to. I've seen too many heart attack and stroke victims out on the lake. It's important for Esther to stay healthy as long as she can. She's still young."

Charlie thought about that for a moment. "I guess we're not as old as we think. Once in a while I feel the years, but staying busy keeps me young. I'm already itching to get back to my garden, and I've only just put it to bed. Spring is months away, but I can't wait to get my hands down into the dirt again."

"I hear you're going to help Brad Hanes finish that nursery he's been building on the side of the house. Kim thinks it's wonderful that you've volunteered your services."

"I'm not sure what I've gotten myself into, to tell you the truth." Charlie scratched behind his ear. "That boy has some things he needs to figure out. Having a baby won't make it any easier."

"You and Esther started out pretty young, didn't you?"

"Oh yeah, we were dumb kids too."

Charlie stood and went to the coffeemaker. The memory of those early years instantly brought the issue of George Snyder to mind. Every time Charlie decided to confront Esther about the sketch in her dresser drawer, something stopped him. One or the other of them was busy. Or visitors suddenly dropped by. Or he fell asleep in front of the TV before she went off to bed. He had never managed to get the question out of his mouth. And he was beginning to think maybe he really didn't want to know the answer.

"I waited a long time to marry," Derek was saying. "If you ask me, it doesn't matter what age you are. It's never easy."

"Nope," Charlie agreed as he stirred creamer into his cup. "Not easy . . . but it does get better as the years go by. Most of the time, anyhow. I guess after a while you stop thinking about whether your marriage is working or not. You're doing it, and that's all that counts. You're working, taking care of kids, heading off on the occasional vacation. The way I see it, Esther's there, same as always. Sometimes I can't even remember when she wasn't. I sure can't imagine losing her."

Derek stuck a finger in his Bible and closed it as Charlie seated himself again. It seemed like the younger man had something he wanted to say, but now the other fellows in the group were entering the tackle shop, greeting Pete, and heading toward the Bible study area.

"Listen, Charlie," Derek said in a low voice, "you've got to get Esther back to the doctor. You've already had two driving incidents that could have turned out a lot worse. Kim says she's worried about Esther. Evidently there have been a few times they've spoken—and once or twice at TLC meetings—when Esther seemed to have blanked out for a few moments. Kim's concerned she might be having ministrokes."

Charlie sat up straight and sloshed a drop of hot coffee on his thumb. "Ministrokes?"

"The technical name is transient ischemic attacks. We call them

TIAs. I didn't want to scare you, so I haven't mentioned it before. For quite a while, I've been feeling like I ought to say something, but I'd heard Esther was going to have the angioplasty and stent. Now that I know she refused treatment, I think I'd better be blunt."

Swallowing down the sudden fear that lodged in his throat, Charlie nodded. "Go ahead. Give it to me straight, Derek."

"You probably wouldn't even have noticed these ministrokes, but they damage the brain's cortex. That's the area associated with learning, memory, and language. The lapses in Esther's short-term recall and the driving problems she's had could all be tied into it. This kind of memory loss—it's known as vascular dementia—is degenerative."

"*Dementia?*" The word sounded like something out of a horror movie. Charlie didn't even like to say it aloud.

Derek wasn't finished. "And when a person starts having TIAs, it's common for a major stroke to follow eventually. You've got to get her back to the doctor, Charlie."

The other men were settling onto the chairs. They'd been discussing the weather and how it was affecting fishing. Crappie were biting well right now, Steve Hansen told the others. He had been out the evening before and caught a stringer full. One of the fellows launched into a tale about hooking into a big gar, a story that soon had the rest of them laughing.

Charlie couldn't move. Couldn't focus on anything but the caramel-colored circle of coffee in his cup. Couldn't even think beyond that one word.

Dementia.

Wasn't it every person's nightmare? To be physically fit yet unable to recall a loved one's face or name would be worse than death, Charlie had always thought. He hated the idea so much, in fact, that he'd refused to give it the time of day. No one in his family had suffered from Alzheimer's disease, and he kept his own brain sharp by dueling wits with game show contestants. That and filling in crossword puzzles, working out the measurements for a building project, planning his garden. He intended to stay mentally alert and healthy right up until the end of his days.

It had never occurred to him that Esther might have a problem. Sure, she was forgetful, but who wasn't occasionally? Just the other day, Charlie had gone to put a casserole in the oven, but he had opened the dishwasher door by mistake. Sometimes he couldn't dredge up a name or a face. Once in a while, he couldn't even come up with the simplest word—and right in the middle of a sentence. Brain lapses were common, weren't they? Take George Snyder, for instance. How long had it taken Charlie to put that memory back together?

No, it couldn't be possible. Not Esther.

All the same, Charlie intended to buckle her into the car and drive her back to the doctor in Springfield right away—no matter how much she protested. Esther could be nagging, irritable, angry, and even confused. But Charlie wasn't about to lose her. No sir.

CHAPTER TEN

Cody was nowhere in sight when Esther entered the living room the following afternoon. She glanced at the dust on the coffee table, the scraps of dried leaves Boofer had dragged across the carpet, and the newspapers piled on the floor beside the couch. Not a single job done.

"I ought to tan your hide, Cody Goss," she grumbled. "Where have you gone off to now?"

"I'm right here!" Cody's head appeared in a space between the couch and the wall. Curly hair framed his bright blue eyes as he smiled at her. "You have dust bunnies, Mrs. Moore. I also found a pen. And part of a cracker. And this bone."

He held up the artifacts as he scooted backward into the open again. Before Esther could react, Cody had spread out the grimy objects—including the dust bunnies—on the coffee table as though they were jewels he had dug from a mine in Africa.

"Put that nasty stuff into the trash," she told the young man. "Don't scatter it all over my nice furniture."

Cody slid his hands into his jeans pockets and studied the collection. "That's Boofer's bone, you know. He might want it. I don't think I should throw it away."

"He's finished with it, or it wouldn't have been back there behind the couch. Honestly, Cody, you can be so frustrating. We hired you to dust, vacuum, and take the newspapers to the recycling bin. Instead, you go rooting around under the furniture."

Cody's eyes filled with sympathy as he looked at Esther. "That is part of vacuuming," he explained, gently patting her arm. "Jennifer told me to move all the furniture away from the wall, then pick up the dust bunnies, and then run the cleaner over the whole carpet—even the part under the couches and chairs. That's how you're supposed to do it, Mrs. Moore. Didn't anyone ever teach you?"

Esther shook her head in frustration. "You can't do all that work every single time, Cody. I just want you to take care of this central area where everyone walks. See the leaves near the front door? And there's a sock Boofer dragged out of the laundry. That's all I need—a simple vacuuming."

"But, Mrs. Moore, I *can* do all that work every time," Cody said solemnly. "I'm very strong. I know how to move things around without breaking them. Besides, you have so many dust bunnies that we might need to start a bunny farm. That's a joke."

Lately the young man had been trying to learn how to kid around. Esther had noted from the beginning that Cody didn't seem to understand humor, and he took most playful jests in all seriousness. Someone—probably Jennifer Hansen—had taken it upon herself to teach him about joke-telling. Clearly, her efforts had been in vain.

"It's funny because rabbits are very . . ." Cody paused, searching the ceiling. "*Prolific.* That means grown-up rabbits make lots of baby rabbits. I read about rabbits in one of the animal books I got at the library. Last Saturday, Mrs. Finley took me there with the twins, and I checked out all the animal books I could carry, which was a lot because, as I said, I'm very strong. So, anyhow, my joke was that if you had too many rabbits, you would need to put them on a farm. That's why I said you might have to start a dust bunny farm. Get it?"

Esther pursed her lips and gave Cody a hug. "Very funny. But if I'm going to pay you to clean this house, you'd better stop making jokes and start working. They always say women are big talkers, but you and Charlie chatter like a couple of chipmunks. He's probably out there right now, rambling on and on to poor Brad Hanes, who only wants to get his new room built."

Picking up the objects he'd found behind the couch, Cody spoke again. "How come you're always mad at Mr. Moore these days? Have you forgotten how nice he is? He's the kindest man of all the old people in Deepwater Cove. When I went to Kansas to see my aunt, I used to think about Mr. Moore a lot. I decided he was one of my favorite friends."

Esther had been starting toward the kitchen, but at Cody's words, she paused. "I'm not mad at Charlie. Whatever would make you say a thing like that? He's my dear husband of almost fifty years, and I love him very much."

"You gripe at him."

"Everyone gripes now and then. No one can be in a good mood all the time. Besides, Charlie is a handful, let me tell you."

"A hand full of what?"

"Of irritating comments and muttering and annoying behavior, that's what."

"Are you sure? Because that's not how I see him. He's friendly to me. He stops and talks to me when he's driving his golf cart with Boofer. He laughs at my jokes too, and he tells me new ones that I never heard before."

Remorseful that she hadn't been more understanding about Cody's efforts at humor, Esther let out a breath. "My husband is a wonderful man or I wouldn't have married him. You know I love him, Cody. And Charlie knows it too."

"I think love is something you *do* more than something you

know." Cody took the vacuum cleaner from the entryway closet and plugged in the cord. "You shouldn't gripe at Mr. Moore, because then he might think you don't love him. People trust what you do more than what you say. That's what I explained to Jennifer. She can see that I love her because I painted pictures of her on Patsy Pringle's wall. Also because I listen to her when she's talking about important things like taking the gospel to foreign lands. And on top of that, I buy hot dogs for her from Pete's Rods-N-Ends. Jennifer likes hot dogs nearly as much as I do, and when I buy them with my own money, then she can see how much I love her. She doesn't have to know it. She can see me doing it."

"Aha," Esther murmured.

She realized this afternoon's housecleaning effort was going nowhere, and her feet were already killing her. She settled down on the sofa and curled up her legs. Might as well be comfortable if she was going to listen to Cody. The boy was a sweetheart, but my goodness, he could yammer on and on until Esther completely lost track of what he was talking about.

She propped a pillow behind her back and settled in for a long conversation. "What did Jennifer say when you told her how much you love her?"

Cody gave her an uncomfortable look and then turned on the vacuum cleaner. The loud whine obliterated any hope of a discussion. Obviously he didn't want to talk about Jennifer's reaction. Esther guessed that the young woman's response must not have been what Cody was hoping to hear.

She sat for a minute, watching as he worked the machine under and around Charlie's big recliner. The boy was right about how strong he was. Cody could probably pick up the couch all by himself.

But what about those things he had said earlier? Did Esther really gripe at her husband? In public? Surely not. Charlie could be troublesome all right, and she did have plenty to complain about. But if she was ever unhappy, she kept it to herself. Didn't she?

In the midst of Esther's reflections, Cody turned off the vacuum. "You'll have to get up now, Mrs. Moore. I need to clean under the couch. I could scoot it over, but you might fall off."

"Now you just sit down here a minute, Cody. And don't turn that machine on again until we're done talking." She pointed at the chair across from the couch. "Tell me why you said I gripe at Charlie."

"I said it because it's true." He perched on the edge of the seat, clearly reluctant to pause in his work. "When I first came to Deepwater Cove, you were happy all the time. You took strawberries to Brenda when she was feeling bad. You helped start the TLC, and you let me be the first and only male in the club. You said I was sweet and you called me punkin'. I thought you were the most cheerful person in the whole world."

"I was—and I still am."

"I'm sorry to disagree with you, but you're grouchy now, Mrs. Moore. You blamed me for wrecking your car even though I didn't. You wouldn't let me come and clean your house because you thought I would break things. And every time I listen to you talking to somebody, I hear you complain about Mr. Moore. You have changed from who you were into someone different. That's okay if it's a good change, like me learning how to read and paint. But not if it turns you into a grump."

Esther leaned back and regarded Cody. "A grump? Do you really mean that?"

"Mrs. Moore, why would I say something I didn't mean? I always tell the truth."

"Yes, you do, Cody." She sighed. "Well, I'm just bumfoozled about this. Charlie said almost the exact same thing last night. We were sitting right here in the living room sorting Ashley's beads, and all of a sudden he told me that he wants me to get back to the doctor before I have a stroke. And furthermore, he said I was forgetful, impatient, and irritable. He said I had changed."

"I think Mr. Moore tells the truth too." Cody fingered the vacuum cleaner button. "You are a grouch."

"A grouch *and* a grump?" Esther frowned. She had always cherished the image of herself as a lighthearted sprite of a girl who laughed in the face of trouble and hard times.

"Grouch and grump are the same thing," Cody informed her. "And it's not good. I think you're grouchy because Mr. Moore wants you to get your veins unclogged."

"But I don't *want* to have surgery," Esther cried in frustration. "I just don't! The idea of someone cutting into me is the most horrifying thing in the world. And do you know what that crazy doctor wants to do? He wants to slice open the top of my leg, float a balloon through my artery all the way up to my neck, and then blow up the balloon. He says the balloon will mash the plaque and open the artery. Then he's going to push a piece of mesh up through my artery and leave it there. Right inside my neck. I'll be walking around with a foreign object in my artery."

"It's a scary idea, Mrs. Moore," Cody admitted. "But you should not be grouchy at Mr. Moore about it."

"You'd be grouchy too if you were me. That surgery sounds like something doctors would have done in the olden days before they had figured out about medicine. I don't see why I can't simply take some pills to solve this problem."

"Sometimes pills don't work, Mrs. Moore. There is no pill for autism. If you've got it, you can't get rid of it. I'm going to be autistic for the rest of my life until I die."

"Well, at least you don't have someone pestering you all the time. Charlie won't hear of anything but putting me in the car and driving me to Springfield and making me have that surgery. Last night, we argued about it all the way from dinner through the talk shows—way past our bedtime. I said no, no, no. But Charlie would not give up. Can't you see why he irritates the living daylights out of me? It's *my* neck! I ought to be able to say what happens to it."

"It's your neck, but you are his wife. He wants you to get it fixed, and you should stop being grouchy—"

"Will you stop saying that word?" Esther stood and crossed her arms. "All right, maybe I have had a bad attitude lately. Maybe I have been negative and critical of Charlie."

"There's no *maybe* about it, Mrs. Moore. There are so many good things about your husband, but you're looking at the bad ones. Everyone does irritating things. Even you."

Esther stared at Cody. "Me?"

Cody nodded. "Definitely."

"Oh, what would you know about it anyway?" Esther said. "I love you, Cody, but you certainly can be aggravating."

"I love you, too, Mrs. Moore. And you certainly are a grump."

They regarded each other in silence. Esther considered all the rebuttals she might make to Cody's blunt analysis of her personality. But the fact was, Charlie *had* been getting on her nerves lately. Ever since the accident, she felt achy and tired and . . . yes, grumpy. A big part of it was this dark cloud around her head all the time. She couldn't think straight. She lost track in the middle of conversations. She forgot what she'd been doing. It was so annoying, and it frightened her.

"I'm going to vacuum some more now," Cody said.

"Hold on a minute there, young man." Esther narrowed her eyes as she studied him. "You didn't answer my question. You didn't tell me what Jennifer said after you expressed your love for her the other day."

The young man rolled his eyes and flopped back on the chair. "What does she always say, Mrs. Moore? 'I love you, too, Cody. Everyone does.' Jennifer loves me the same way you do. But I love her different from the way I love you. When you hug me, I don't mind, even though I'm not crazy about people touching me. But when I get near Jennifer, I start to wish she would hug me. Kiss me too. I think I would like a kiss from Jennifer. A kiss from her would be a good thing."

"But, Cody, you and Jennifer are poles apart, honeybunch. Can't you see that? She was raised by Steve and Brenda in a lovely home, and she has a good education. A college degree! She's studying to be a missionary because she feels God has called her to tell people about Jesus—people who live far away from Deepwater Cove."

"I know all about Jennifer. And you didn't even mention the main things that make me love her. She's pretty and nice and honest."

"Those are important, but not in the long run." Esther paused. "Maybe some of them are. Well, maybe all of them are. In fact, maybe those things are more important than her upbringing and her education. Oh, never mind, Cody. Jennifer is truly a sweetheart in every way. She would make a wonderful girlfriend for you. Even a wife. She'd be a great wife."

"I think so too."

"But what about *you*?"

He shrugged. "I'm handsome. I'm nice and honest too. Everyone says so. I think Jennifer and I would live a very happy life together, especially because I love her so much."

"But you and Jennifer are *different*, Cody." Esther struggled with how to express her fears in a gentle way. The idea that Cody might be deeply hurt by love was almost more than she could bear. And yet, she didn't want to injure him herself.

"I'm very different," he was saying. "I haven't met too many men my age, but I can tell you I'm nothing like them. I would never beat up someone or call them names the way those guys did to me before I came to Deepwater Cove. I'm very strong now, and I could protect myself and Jennifer. I also know how to earn money. I can keep a house clean and arrange flowers and paint pictures. I can say Scripture verses better than almost anyone. Plus, I'm autistic, which is definitely different. Most people don't have that. God made me just the way He wanted me, and that is something special."

Esther could feel the tears building. She was afraid they might start to roll down her cheeks and she would make a scene. All those fancy psychologists had labeled autism a disability. They called it abnormal—as if anyone in the world knew what normal really meant. But Cody thought autism was an exceptional gift from God! A blessing! Oh, how would he ever understand the harsh realities of this cruel, sinful world?

"Well, Cody," she managed, "you are indeed a wonderful, amazing, and talented young man. It is my privilege to know you."

"Even though I'm aggravating and you're a grump, we're good friends. That's a great thing, Mrs. Moore. All the same, I think you should get your artery cleaned out. Every time I look at you, I think about your clogged-up neck vein. And to tell you the truth, it makes me want to vomit."

With that, he stood, turned on the vacuum cleaner, and headed for the television.

🍂

Nail gun in hand, Charlie climbed the ladder. Of all the foolish things he had done in his life, this had to rank among the top ten. What business did a man his age have climbing ladders, wielding compressor-driven nail guns, and power-sawing lumber? If Esther could see him now, she would have a fit. Any minute, he could lose his balance and topple to the ground, shattering every bone in his old, worn-out body.

"How're you doing up there, Mr. Moore?" Brad Hanes called from below.

"Oh, fine. Just fine." Charlie shot several nails into a two-by-four. Each time the gun fired a nail, a burst of air nearly knocked his glasses off his nose. What had become of the good old days when a man used a bona fide hammer to pound in a nail? Well, come to think of it, Charlie probably wouldn't be much use at that anymore, he realized. Way back when he was a young whippersnapper, hauling heavy mailbags around all day had given him bulging biceps, a trim physique, and plenty of stamina. But on this project, it was all he could do to keep up with his partner.

"The last of the insulation should be here tomorrow," the younger man said. "I've had to buy it little by little when I had cash on hand. Ashley maxed out the credit cards again. The washing machine died the other day, and before I even got home from work, she had bought and installed a new one."

"Ashley set it up?" Charlie tried to picture the tall, thin, beaded redhead muscling an old washer out of a house and hauling a new one into its place. "You mean she hooked up the plumbing?"

"Electricity, too. The whole nine yards. Didn't ask for my help, even though that's the kind of thing I do for living. I'm sure we could have gotten the old machine repaired. But no, she had to have a new one. Top-of-the-line stainless steel."

Charlie descended gingerly from one rung to the next. When his feet finally touched the plywood floor of the new room, he let out a sigh of relief.

"Ashley said she'd pay down that credit card with her necklace money," Brad was telling Charlie. "But so far, her little business venture has been nothing but a cash drain. She keeps saying the bead business is going to make a lot of money one of these days, but if you ask me, she sounds exactly like her dad."

"Ashley's father runs a snack shop, doesn't he?"

"Yeah. He's got that dinky little hot dog and ice cream shop in Camdenton. You know the one I mean? It's over by the high school. Ashley worked there forever."

"I believe I remember her telling Esther and me that the two of you met at her father's little restaurant. She said you kept coming by for ice cream—even in the winter."

"I may have. You do dumb things when you're young."

Charlie recalled the first moment he ever laid eyes on Esther—right down to her purple sweater and matching purse. Brad was so cynical and hardened, he wouldn't even acknowledge courting Ashley. What a kid.

Though Charlie was ready to leave the job site and get on home, he had done quite a bit of praying that Brad would open up to him in a more personal way. Most days, the young man jabbered about his job or about tools, trucks, movies, and electronic games. Half the time Charlie had no idea what he was saying. So this afternoon when Brad began talking about his wife, Charlie put off his departure.

"I used to like Ashley's father," Brad said while he and Charlie gathered up tools and arranged the toolbox. "But these days he bugs me. Bottom line—the guy's an idiot. I wouldn't tell Ashley that, but it's true. Her dad is always talking about how he wants to expand his business. He thinks he's going to turn a huge profit with one of his crazy ideas. First he decided to install a frozen yogurt machine—it was the sure thing that would transform him into a millionaire. Next it was onion blossoms. Then it was jalapeño poppers. He has one get-rich scheme after another, so he invests in new equipment and all kinds of ingredients. Then he's shocked when tax time rolls around and he hasn't made any more money than he did the year before. I'm not going to stand by and let Ashley run us into the ground like that."

"I'm sure Ashley's father is no fool," Charlie observed. "The food industry is very competitive, and he's kept that shop going for a long time. Still, those schemes can cost a fellow. Maybe he ought to just stick with what sells."

Rolling up a heavy-duty extension cord, Charlie began to wonder what Esther had made for dinner. All this talk of hot dogs, onion blossoms, and ice cream was making him hungry. They had finally eaten the last of the frozen casseroles that friends and neighbors had brought over after her car accident, and now she was back to creating meals from scratch.

"It's feast or famine with Ashley's family." Brad spat tobacco juice on the floor of the new addition—a habit that had not endeared him to Charlie. But the kid kept talking, so Charlie kept listening.

"All summer, the hot dog place does a booming business with the tourists in town," Brad said. "Then in the winter, Ashley's father relies on high schoolers to stop by on their way home. Those kids don't spend anywhere near what he makes in the summer. Ashley told me there were years when all the clothes and shoes she and her sisters wore came from the thrift shop. And even though the family owned a restaurant, her mom would have to go to a free food pantry to get enough for their own table. That's pretty pathetic."

"You may not care for the father," Charlie said, "but it sounds like you care an awful lot about Ashley."

"I married her, didn't I?"

Brad said this with such contempt, sarcasm, and hopelessness that Charlie felt a strong urge to grab the kid by the shoulders and shake some sense into him. Ashley was sweet and innocent. It wasn't her fault that her father had mismanaged his business. Didn't Brad even remember why he had married the pretty redhead?

Charlie swallowed his ire and focused his eyes on the work the two had accomplished this afternoon. He couldn't remember ever feeling as angry or frustrated with Esther as Brad was with Ashley. Charlie had always looked forward to coming home to her and the children each evening. Weekends were the best—days of laughter, games, picnics, and rest. What had come between the Hanes kids to cause such strife?

"I'd say we got a lot done today," Charlie observed. When Brad didn't respond, he added, "Ashley ought to be happy about all we've accomplished so far. Have you two decided whether we're building a garage or a nursery?"

"It's a spare room. I told her I didn't want a baby right now. What's the point? She doesn't even like me half the time. I don't think it's a good idea to bring a kid into that kind of marriage."

"You're a wise man," Charlie remarked. After a pause, he asked, "So why can't you figure out what Ashley's mad about these days?"

Brad shook his head. "If I ask her what's wrong, she starts crying. Then she clams up. Then she talks and talks until I can't stand to listen to another minute of it. I have no clue what her problem is. All I want is what every man wants, you know? A wife, three square meals, clean clothes. I thought we'd really like being married. Ashley used to be a lot of fun. Now . . . forget it."

"You sound like a man from my generation, Brad. But you didn't marry Susie Homemaker. You've got a wife who can set up a new washing machine all by herself. Ashley works full-time at the country club, and she's doing her best to keep up with the bead orders that keep coming in. She's got to send those necklaces and bracelets out before Christmas, you know. And you expect her to do all the cooking and laundry too? Don't most young fellows help out with that kind of thing these days?"

"Not me. I'm no pansy. I work construction all day. Now I'm working on this project every afternoon. I'm not about to do the ironing or put dinner on the table. That's Ashley's job."

"I see." Charlie scratched his chin. He'd had pretty much the same idea about Esther throughout their marriage. Only Esther had never worked outside their home. Caring for the family and house was her chosen vocation, and she did it extremely well.

"You sure you've really talked this over with Ashley?" Charlie asked Brad. "Maybe you need to try a little harder to get everything out in the open. Tell her how you feel, and let her do the same. Nothing beats a good, honest conversation for resolving problems."

A smirk on his face, Brad hooked his thumbs into the pockets of his jeans. "So, when is Mrs. Moore getting her artery cleaned out? Did you ever get that problem resolved?"

Charlie shook his head and had to laugh. "You've got me there, kid. No amount of talking can convince her to let the doctor operate. She won't hear of it."

"You know what I think, Mr. Moore? I think women only hear what they want to hear. And half of what they do hear, they imagine. Like, I'll be sitting in the living room watching a football game, and Ashley will start crying and saying I ignore her. I'm not ignoring her. I'm just trying to watch the game. She imagines stuff. Totally dreams it up. Admit it, Mr. Moore. There's no point in trying to talk to women, and there's no use in listening to them either. If you're married, you have to just do your own thing and hope you survive another day."

With that, he spat another stream of tobacco juice on the floor.

Charlie thought about Esther for a moment. It certainly *seemed* like they'd had a good marriage. But she did tend to chatter on and on until he often lost interest—or found himself distracted. Listening to Esther could be a chore. And, now that Brad had brought it up, Charlie realized he hadn't had much success in talking to his wife lately either. Esther had point-blank refused to hear another word about her artery. Come to think of it, Charlie had never been able to get her to discuss George Snyder and the sketch in her dresser drawer.

Had they been fooling themselves all these years? They had imagined themselves happily married . . . but in reality, had they been more like Brad and Ashley, simply doing their own thing and hoping to survive another day?

Charlie and Brad eyed each other. The setting sun cast long shadows on the skeleton of the spare room. All at once, a sense of calm defiance filled Charlie's chest. He was not going to let his marriage go one day further without putting everything in order. He had set himself up as a role model for Brad Hanes, and by golly, he was going to confront Esther about his concerns and clear the air between them.

"Marriage can be good," he told the young man. "I'm not telling you it's easy living with another person every day. And I'm not saying it's ever totally perfect. But Esther and I have made it nearly fifty years together, and I wouldn't trade a single one of them. Now you and Ashley chose to marry each other, and you owe it to God and to yourselves to give it all you've got."

Brad studied Charlie from under hooded eyelids. "Yes, sir, Mr. Moore," he drawled. "But if it's no fun, why bother?"

"You answer that question yourself, Brad. I'll be eager to hear what you decide." Shouldering his tool belt, Charlie stepped out of the room. "See you tomorrow, kid."

As he climbed into his golf cart, he heard another splat hitting the wooden floor behind him.

CHAPTER ELEVEN

Esther had cooked an exceptionally fine pot roast this evening. As she brought it to the table, she couldn't hide her pride. Potatoes, pearl onions, and carrots made a colorful wreath around the savory chunk of beef that had been slowly browning all afternoon. In fact, the fragrant aroma had been so strong, she had opened the kitchen window to let a cool autumn breeze waft through the house. Only when Charlie came in the front door after working with Brad had she closed the window again and turned up the furnace.

"There you go!" she said, setting the platter before her husband. "The perfect dinner for my meat-and-potatoes man. I've got rolls in the oven and a salad in the fridge, but let's pray first."

Delighted with her success, Esther seated herself at the table. But just as she folded her hands and bowed her head, she caught sight of the dour expression on Charlie's face. He was staring at the roast and frowning.

"What's the matter?" she asked. "You look like you just ate a lemon."

"What have you done to the meat, Esther?" he asked. He adjusted his trifocals with one hand and began poking at the roast with a fork.

"I cooked it—just like always. What do you think I did?"

"Something's wrong here." Charlie speared an onion, held it to his nose, and then dropped it back onto the platter as if it were poison. "What is *that*?"

"It's a pearl onion," she told him, growing more annoyed by the second. "I don't use them often, but I spotted them in the store today, and they were so little and cute that I decided to add them to the roast."

Charlie looked up at her. "That's not an onion, Esther. That's an entire clove of garlic. You must have cooked fifteen or twenty of them here."

"Garlic? What do you mean? It's an onion."

He poked at the glossy white orb again. "Honey, this is garlic. I knew something was wrong the minute I drove up to the house. The odor goes all the way across the road out there. When I pulled the golf cart under the carport, I couldn't imagine what was causing such a strong smell."

"What?" Esther set her palms on the table and pushed herself up to her full five-foot-three-inch height. "Charles Moore, don't you think I would know a clove of garlic from a pearl onion? You are just like my mother. Insulting my cooking every time I turn around. You've never thought I was a good cook, and now you're treating my roast like roadkill! Well, I'll just take care of this problem for you then!"

In one swift movement, she swept the platter off the table and headed for the trash can.

Charlie caught up to her and deftly lifted the dish out of her hands. "Now let me have that, Esther."

"Oh no you don't!" Tears streaming, she swung around and tried to grab it back. As they both yanked on the platter, the roast made a swan dive, hit the floor with a thud, and slid straight under the table. Carrots and potatoes fanned through the air, landing in a perfect arc around the couple. Hot gravy splattered the counters and cabinets in a brown polka-dot pattern.

Esther covered her face with her hands and sobbed. "It's ruined! You ruined my lovely dinner with your insults and your awful behavior. Oh, you're a horrible, horrible man!"

In all her life, Esther couldn't remember ever feeling such desperate hatred for her husband. Not the time he had thrown out her favorite childhood doll during one of his garage-cleaning binges. Not the time he had broken her precious Limoges bud vase by knocking it off the dresser with his elbow. Not even the time he had confessed to going to a bar with his friends and ending up at a strip club. So what if the men had been celebrating a best buddy's engagement? So what if Charlie had never been drunk before or since? She had certainly reviled him then! She hadn't been able to imagine ever loving him again. Somehow, against all odds, she had forgiven him and learned to accept his many flaws.

But now! *Now!*

"Esther," Charlie murmured, laying a hand on her arm. "Esther, look at me."

"Get away!" she cried out, slapping at him. "Don't touch me, you beast!"

Feeling as if she might faint, Esther grabbed the countertop and let herself sag down onto the floor. Through her tears, she could see Charlie on his knees, crawling under the table and trying to wrest what was left of the roast away from Boofer. Esther gulped as she attempted to quell her misery. Her russet-colored slacks were spattered with gravy, and she could see a flattened carrot on the bottom of Charlie's shoe.

This was awful. The worst, worst thing in the world. How could two decent, civilized people end up like this? Shouting at each other. Throwing food. Crawling around on the floor. They might as well be barbarians.

Esther picked a pearl onion off the floor and sniffed it. Maybe it *was* garlic after all, but did that give Charlie any excuse for saying the things he'd said? So she'd made a mistake. It wasn't her first and it wouldn't be her last. Charlie made mistakes too.

"You threw out my doll, don't forget!" she yelled at him. "You pitched her into the garbage as though she meant nothing. But she was mine! My grammy had given her to me for my fifth birthday, and my mother sewed her clothes, and I loved her. And you tossed her out as though she were nothing but a piece of trash!"

"What are you talking about?" Charlie peered through the forest of chair and table legs. "Did you say something about your doll?"

"You don't ever listen to me, do you? You tune me out so you can watch your silly game shows. Well, Mr. Smarty-Pants, you make mistakes too. You threw out my doll—that's what you did. So what if I used garlic instead of onions? You're not perfect either."

"Esther, I'm trying to clean up this mess. Call Boofer, would you? He's got his teeth sunk into this meat, and I can't get it away."

"And don't forget about my bud vase, Charles Moore! My uncle Bob brought it to me from France after the war. It was Limoges, you know. The only pretty thing I had. The only valuable object I've ever owned in my whole life. And you knocked it right off the dresser with your clumsy elbow as if it meant nothing. There's no telling how much that bud vase would be worth today if you hadn't broken it. Don't talk to me about garlic cloves. Those are nothing compared to a Limoges bud vase."

The memory of how she had swept up the delicate pieces of the vase and tried to glue them back together blew into Esther's mind with the force of a tornado. She could see herself on her knees, plucking shards of French porcelain from between the wooden floorboards with tweezers. But it had been hopeless. The precious gift was irredeemably shattered.

Not only had Charlie carelessly broken her vase that day, but he had broken her heart. *"It's only a vase,"* he'd said. *"I'll get you another at the five-and-dime store."* He'd had no idea what that unique, fragile thing meant to her. Every time she looked at it, she had felt as though she were a French princess—gowned in some airy trifle of a dress with a purple cape on her shoulders and a diamond tiara on her head.

Now, sobbing even harder at the realization that she would never, ever be a French princess . . . that life had brought her nothing but the ordinary lot of a housewife . . . that not even her two children, in whom she had invested all of her time and love and energy for so many years, had turned out to be perfect . . . Esther curled into a ball on the floor.

The dark cloud wrapped around her, and she saw Ellie, her darling daughter, looking haggard and alcoholic. She saw dusty picture frames and cobwebs on the ceiling, mocking her futile efforts at housekeeping. She saw cakes fallen in the middle, pies with runny meringue topping, burned gravy, and lumpy mashed potatoes. She saw weeds in her rose garden. Wrinkles on her face.

And now . . . now twenty cloves of garlic in her pot roast, their odor seeping through her house and out into the street so that all the neighbors would look at each other as if to say, *"Yes, we know what an awful cook that Esther Moore is. It's a wonder Charlie has put up with her all these years."*

"There!" Charlie said triumphantly, as if announcing his superiority over his lowly failure of a wife. "I got the roast away from Boofer. And the vegetables are cleaned up too. Now all we need to do is run a mop over this floor, and we'll be as good as new. We can eat that yummy-looking salad I saw in the refrigerator. A salad and a couple of hot rolls will do me up jim-dandy."

Esther could hear Charlie fooling around with the plastic trash bag—no doubt taking her failed effort out to the Dumpster where it belonged. He turned on the water in the sink, getting it hot enough for his mopping job. He would make everything better, and the kitchen would look brand-new, and they would pretend that nothing bad had happened between them.

But Esther knew. She knew it now. She was losing her mind.

Charlie bit into a half-burned dinner roll and studied his wife across the table. Esther was still sniffling. It didn't seem to matter that he had cleaned up the entire kitchen, mopped the floor, lit some scented candles, and set out the salad and bread.

It didn't even register with her when he apologized for finding fault with her pot roast. He had considered reversing his declaration about the garlic cloves and declaring them to be pearl onions after all. But that was taking it too far. Apologizing was one thing. Flat-out lying in order to make peace was another.

"Esther," he said, trying to get her attention for the umpteenth time, "did Ashley tell you that she and Brad have finally decided to turn the new addition into a room? Brad gave up on having a garage. I'm not sure it's going to be a nursery, though. I don't think he's ready to become a father just yet."

Head bent, Esther dabbed at her eyes with a tissue. Her perfect hair had somehow come apart. The shellacked coiffure seemed to have cracked open down the middle, and both sides had collapsed. Charlie could see her scalp, pale and ashen, and it made him realize all over again that she was aging and fragile . . . and that he loved her dearly.

"Esther, honey, please talk to me." He rose from his chair, circled the table, and knelt on one knee beside her. "This isn't a big deal, sweetheart. It's nothing. Pearl onions or garlic cloves—who cares? We're having a nice supper, and there's plenty to eat."

"Oh, Charlie!" With a sob, Esther threw herself onto his shoulder and began weeping as if her heart were broken. "I have Alzheimer's. I know I do! How could I have thought those were pearl onions? They look and smell exactly like garlic. And I drove off the end of the carport. And I put the electric can opener in the dishwasher. And I fell asleep while I was driving. You should put me into a nursing home, lock the door, and never look at me again until I die!"

"Now, Esther." Charlie rubbed her back, realizing how truly fragile her small body felt under his work-callused hand. "Do you remember what Derek Finley said about your blocked artery? This fogginess you've been having lately must be caused by that. You're not getting enough blood to your brain. Let's talk about that procedure again. I'll bet if you have that done, you'll be as good as new."

"I can't. I'm too scared. You remember what happened to my father, don't you? He went into the hospital for pneumonia, and he never left again! He died right there in that awful steel bed with monitors and beepers and nurses all around him."

"He was nearly ninety-two, Esther. That's old enough, isn't it?"

"But what about my brother? The doctor found a lump, and he died in the hospital too. And my cousin was only in there a couple of days—"

"God was ready to take them all home, Esther. But that doesn't mean He's ready for you. Going to the hospital isn't a ticket to the cemetery. This procedure is supposed to help you stay well. By not having it done, you could get worse and worse."

She cried out in exasperation and pushed up from the table, heading into the living room. Charlie followed, only to find that Boofer's stomach had redirected most of the pot roast he'd wolfed down onto the carpet.

Seeing the mess, Esther wailed in despair and hurried for the bedroom. "I've probably killed him!" her voice echoed down the hall. "I've killed my dog by feeding him garlic roast beef, and I'll be next. I'll lose my mind and then die a terrible death in some nursing home."

Clenching his teeth in frustration, Charlie spotted Boofer under the coffee table, a guilty—or was it queasy?—look on the poor pooch's face. Unable to find words to express his emotions, he scooped up the mess, disposed of it, spot-cleaned the carpet, and coaxed the dog out into the open.

"Come here, Boof," Charlie said. As he sank down on the sofa, the little dog bounded into his lap. Charlie stroked the long black fur. "What are we going to do with your mama, Boofer? Why don't you go in there and talk her into letting the doctor put a balloon in her artery? Would you do that for me?"

The dog's dark brown eyes gazed up at his master as if pleading to be released from such an onerous duty. For a few minutes, Charlie leaned back on a cushion and tried to let the tension seep out of his body. It had been a long day. Beading in the morning, building in the afternoon, and a pot roast fiasco to top off the whole deal. Many of the hours had been spent in service to Brad and Ashley Hanes. Maybe *they* could return the favor by convincing Esther to get her artery cleaned. He might just put the task to Ashley and see if Esther would listen to her young friend.

Charlie couldn't deny he was worried about his wife. Esther had done plenty of crazy things while learning how to cook. But this garlic and onion snafu was the first major culinary mistake in many years.

What if she truly did have some sort of dementia? How would the two of them handle the coming years? Charlie couldn't imagine putting his wife into a care center, but he wasn't a medical professional by a long shot. He wouldn't have a clue how to take care of Esther if her mental faculties declined too far. Just the thought of losing his sweet, silly wife to such a terrible fate sent a shudder through him.

After reassuring Boofer that everything was all right, Charlie rose and made his way down the hall to the bedroom. There he found Esther, fully clothed and lying on top of the bedspread, fast asleep. Now he would have to rouse and undress her, put her into a nightgown, and help her slip back into bed. Trouble was, he just didn't know if he had the energy.

Sinking onto the edge of the bed, he stared at the dresser and tried to remember the vase that had so upset Esther that evening. He did recall the day he'd accidentally knocked it off that very same dresser onto the floor. But what did a broken vase have to do with a garlicky pot roast?

The vase incident had happened so long ago, almost at the start of their marriage. Esther had placed the trinket along with several other knickknacks on the dresser. Charlie had never even noticed the little collection until one winter morning when he was dressing in the half-light of an open curtain and hit the vase with his elbow. For days, all Esther could do was mourn that little French vase, until Charlie began to believe it must have held all her hopes and dreams. All those fantasies, like her vase, had been shattered by a clumsy husband who had no idea what the word *Limoges* even meant.

As the memory of that early, difficult time filtered into his mind, Charlie recalled something he had long ago dismissed as unimportant. On the day of the broken vase, he had returned to their apartment after walking his mail route and found Esther sitting in the living room with a neighbor. She had been crying—drinking cups of tea and weeping into her handkerchief. At her side on the sofa sat a golden-haired young fellow Charlie had seen once or twice in the hallway.

George Snyder.

At the time, Charlie hadn't thought much of it. Esther said George had heard her crying and had knocked on the apartment door to see if she was all right. They'd discussed the morning's events, and George understood both sides—how much the Limoges vase had meant to Esther and how easily it might have been broken by a man dressing in the dark. Charlie had thanked George for looking in on Esther, and the two men shook hands. In the following months, Charlie rarely saw him again and only at a distance.

Frowning, Charlie studied the bottom drawer of the dresser. What had George Snyder written on the bottom of that sketch?

All my love . . .

Love always . . .

Loving you forever . . .

It was something like that, but Charlie had forgotten the exact wording. He glanced at Esther and found her still asleep. So he bent over, pulled open the drawer, and located the sketch. As he slid it out of the envelope, he was again captured by the beauty of the young woman depicted. She looked fresh and lively and full of eager antici-pation. Her eyes sparkled. And her lips, parted just a little, almost begged to be kissed.

Was Charlie imagining things now? Or had George and Esther's friendship gone far beyond a couple of chance meetings? Had there been a true romance between them? Had they had an affair?

At the thought of Esther in another man's arms, Charlie winced. For nearly fifty years, he had believed Esther belonged only to him. She was his prize catch. His little woman. His darling wife. His better half. Esther was mother to his children, companion through good times and bad, and the only lover Charlie had ever known.

Could she have kept a dark secret from him these many years? Had there been a time in their marriage when her heart belonged to an unemployed artist with curly blond hair and an apartment two doors down?

"What are you looking at?"

Esther's voice at Charlie's shoulder startled him. He made a stab at stuffing the sketch back into the envelope, but she was already beside him, gazing down at the picture of herself. And there at the bottom were the words he had read earlier.

I will always love you, Esther.

Charlie held out the sketch so his wife could see it. "George Snyder drew this. That fellow down the hall."

"Where did you find it? What were you doing in my dresser? You had no business rooting around there. That's where I keep all my cards and letters and treasures. You should have asked me first."

"Why did George Snyder sketch you, Esther?"

"He's an artist. That's what he does."

Charlie looked at her. Her words made it sound as though they all still lived in the same apartment building. Was Esther lost back in time, or did she still stay in contact with the man? Were

George Snyder's letters among those tied in ribbons in her bottom drawer?

"When did he sketch this portrait of you?" Charlie asked.

"Well, when do you suppose? It certainly wasn't yesterday. I haven't looked like that in years."

"So, did you sit for him? Did you pose?"

"It's not a pose. When people pose, the life goes right out of them. That's what George always said. Do I seem lifeless to you in this picture?" She took it from Charlie's hand. "I think this is the best portrait of me ever made. George captured the real me, don't you think? That's what he said when he gave it to me. He said, 'This is the true Esther. This is your beating heart put down on paper.' I'll never forget that. Those were the very words he used—*beating heart put down on paper*. George always said things like that. Doesn't it sound wonderful and imaginative? In the portrait, that's exactly the way he captured me. See? I'm young and alive and fresh. Oh, dear. How time does fly!"

She picked up the envelope and slipped the sketch inside. Then she slid the envelope back into the drawer and pushed it shut.

"That was such a long time ago, wasn't it?" Esther leaned her head on her husband's shoulder. "Oh, sweetheart, I'm sorry. I'm just so sorry."

Every muscle in Charlie's body went rigid at her words. "Esther, what did you do?"

"All that garlic. I admit it. I truly believed those were pearl onions. I never should have argued with you about the pot roast, honey. And I shouldn't have fought with you over the platter. You had to clean up the whole kitchen and then Boofer's mess. All by yourself, you took care of everything. I didn't help one bit. Can you ever forgive me?"

Charlie let out a deep breath. "Of course I forgive you, Esther. Things like that don't matter. You made a mistake, but who doesn't?"

"It was such a silly blunder when you think about it." She covered her mouth with her hand and giggled. "What if we'd eaten that roast,

Charlie? What if you hadn't noticed those pearl onions were really garlic? I can just see myself at the TLC, knocking everyone over with my breath while I read the minutes! And poor Brad. What would he think when you arrived to help him with the house addition? He'd probably fall off the ladder!"

By the end of this humorous little trip into her own imagination, Esther had left the bed and wandered into the bathroom. Charlie could hear her brushing her teeth and washing her face. Once again, he had failed to confront his wife. He was no closer to talking her into the artery cleaning. And he still had no idea how intimate her relationship with George Snyder had become.

Almost as distressing, Charlie didn't know what he would do if he did learn some terrible truth about Esther. Would it affect him now, so many years later, to discover that she had been unfaithful? Would knowing that secret earlier have made any difference in their marriage? Perhaps if she'd confessed back at the beginning, they wouldn't even be together now—arguing over pot roast and arteries.

On the other hand, what if she had kept a small part of her heart for George Snyder? What if Esther never had truly belonged to Charlie?

The way she had been yelling at him lately made him wonder. Esther's moods seemed to swing back and forth a lot more than usual. For a while, she would be her chirpy little self. And then, out of the blue, she would get irritable, cranky, and even furious. She'd dredge up something like that old doll he had thrown out with the trash. Or the Limoges vase he had broken. If he didn't watch out, she might surprise him by throwing his venture to the strip club back in his face.

Oh, that was a terrible memory. What a mistake. But he had been so young and foolish. Out with his buddies for a night on the town. Coerced into a bar for a celebration, Charlie had started drinking. So unlike anything he'd ever done before. And then somehow the men had wound up inside a strip club. Charlie would never forget staggering home and blabbing the whole thing to Esther. It's a wonder she'd ever forgiven him.

Maybe she hadn't.

"Peekaboo!" Esther's head emerged from behind the bathroom door. She blew him a kiss. "I see you, Charlie Moore!"

He looked up and couldn't help but smile. This was one of their many secret codes. Esther's arm snaked out into the bedroom, and she waved her chiffon bathrobe around before dropping it onto the floor. As usual, every thought and worry in Charlie's head went right out the window.

Sure Esther was moving up in years and her body had changed shape over time . . . but the minute she sauntered through that bathroom door in her all-togethers, Charlie's heart began to thump.

"I see you, too," he said, waggling his eyebrows at her.

She tossed back her head and laughed. With a neat twirl, she fell into his arms and began kissing him. As Charlie slid his hands across the fragrant silken skin of his wife's back, all he could think about was how much he loved her and how grateful he was that God had given him such a beautiful, wonderful, and downright delicious woman for his very own.

CHAPTER TWELVE

You have the thickest hair I've ever seen on a man your age." Patsy lifted a swatch between her index and middle fingers and scissored off an inch. "It grows so fast too. I can't figure it out. This is like something I'd see on a kid. You don't have a single white hair either."

Pete studied the pretty woman in the mirror as she worked on his latest cut. He had been due for a trim, but this appointment to sit a spell in Patsy's salon chair wasn't motivated by shaggy hair. They needed to talk.

Their recent trip to the movies had been something Pete thought about night and day. The more he thought about it, the less he could do anything but keep on thinking about it. He supposed the obsessive pondering over the situation had something to do with his astonishment. And delight. And worry.

In the darkened theater, Patsy had willingly slipped into Pete's arms. She had welcomed his kisses. She had even kissed him back— more than once. In fact, that particular activity had taken up a significant portion of their evening. But only inside the theater.

The moment they stepped into the lobby, all the zing went right out of Patsy. At first, Pete had thought the change in her attitude must have something to do with their unplanned meeting with Cody and the Hansen girls. Patsy seemed to have a way of embarrassing herself in Pete's presence, and that night had been no different. In the bathroom mirror, he'd seen the pink lipstick on his mouth and cheeks, and he had a bad feeling his evening would not end on a high note.

Sure enough, by the time they got into his truck for the drive back to Deepwater Cove, Patsy had fallen silent. When he dropped her off at the door to her little house, he didn't get even a peck on the cheek.

That just wasn't right.

During the movie, Pete had confessed his love for Patsy, and she had definitely responded in a positive way. But they had not spoken about it since. The few times they passed each other in the parking lot or talked for a couple of minutes at Bitty's Pop-In, Patsy didn't mention their date or the intimacy they had shared.

It might have been her sense of mortification over the lipstick incident, Pete admitted. Patsy had been mad at him plenty of times for drawing unwanted attention to her. But lately he was wondering if something else had triggered her silence and withdrawal.

"I know you don't color your hair," she was saying as she trimmed his sideburns. "I can spot processed hair a mile away. But you ought to be thinning a little on top or at least sprouting a few silver hairs."

"It's my bloodline," he told her. "Cherokee. That's what my daddy always claimed. Although my mother said it was the Welsh in her ancestry that gave us kids our dark hair and blue eyes. Either way, I'm grateful. I have enough trouble keeping my physique as fine-tuned as I do. Going bald would be painful."

"You have a fine-tuned physique?" Patsy said, tilting her head and grinning at him in the mirror.

"Well, not as fine as yours, of course."

Her cheeks went pink. "Oh, hush, Pete Roberts. You know good and well I'm about to bust the seams on these slacks. Don't you dare humiliate me in my own salon."

"I thought the name of this place was Just As I Am. You accept everyone just as they are—except yourself?"

"Just as I am is how Jesus takes a person. You know the hymn. 'Just as I am, tho' tossed about with many a conflict, many a doubt.' When I was a little girl, I used to think it said *man, ya doubt*." She giggled for a moment. "Oh, come on, you must have heard that song in church, Pete. Seems like we sing it every Sunday. 'Fightings within, and fears without.' Something like that."

"I've probably heard it, but I don't recall."

She hummed and then began quietly singing the words. "'And waiting not to rid my soul of one dark blot . . . O Lamb of God I come! I come!' It means God accepts us even though we're full of sin and doubt and worry. We can come to Him no matter what. That's how I try to welcome people here in my salon, too."

"What did you say about a dark blot?"

"You know how it feels when you've been doing something wrong and your conscience finally wins out over your denial? That's when you see your sin as one dark blot."

"I've got more than one," Pete said.

"No matter how many you have, God doesn't care. He wants you; that's all. He wants your heart, whether it's just a little bit off track or black and evil and full of guilt."

"Does this have something to do with that 'born again' stuff we talked about on the dock a while back? In the Bible study group this morning, I got to thinking that I'd heard so many different things about religion, I couldn't keep them all straight. Fishing for men. Being born again. Giving your heart to the Lord. All to Jesus I surrender. Just as I am with one dark blot. It's confusing. Kind of makes me want to turn tail and run the other direction."

Patsy had begun to whisk snippets of hair off the back of his neck with her soft brush, and Pete could see that she was weighing his words. A little furrow ran between her eyebrows, and her lips were pinched tight. What had he gone and said now?

As she took the cape from around his shoulders, Pete noticed the mural Cody had painted on the wall across from Patsy's station. The lineup of women had a variety of hairstyles and colors, but they were all recognizable as Jennifer Hansen. No doubt about that.

Cody was as smitten with Jennifer as Pete was with Patsy. But both women were equally out of reach to the men who adored them. The more Pete thought about this, the more he realized it was for the same reason.

Jesus.

Jennifer Hansen was planning to be a missionary. Her parents, her church, and her education had prepared her for a life that would take her to some far-off country where she could proclaim the gospel. At least, that's what Patsy had told Pete. Even if Cody was as regular as the next guy, he didn't stand a chance with Jennifer. She might as well be locked behind a big iron gate with one word stamped across it—*Jesus*.

Same thing with Patsy. She had set high ideals for herself and everyone else. In the salon, she wouldn't tolerate gossip or rough language, and she played Christian music all day long. She wanted people to march in the Jesus parade—onward, Christian soldiers, like the hymn said. No doubt any man Patsy dated would have to be as holy and perfect as she was. That sure didn't describe Pete.

He and Cody were both out of sync with perfection. Cody couldn't help being kind of odd. Lately people were saying the young man was autistic. Pete didn't know much about autism, but he did know that it wasn't Cody's fault. He was simply born that way. But Pete was responsible for messing up his own life. He couldn't lay the blame for his dark blots anywhere but on his own two shoulders. He certainly couldn't lay it on Jesus, no matter what Patsy was singing. *Just as I am* couldn't include Pete Roberts. No way.

"You're not a coward, are you?" Patsy asked as she swept the floor around her chair. "You want to turn tail and run from God—even though He loves you just as you are? That's about as lily-livered an attitude as I've ever heard."

"Patsy, honey." Pete caught her arm as she tipped the dustpan's contents into the trash can under her table. He lowered his voice. "We've got to talk. And I mean serious talk. At the movie, things happened between us. You know they did. I want you to give me a few minutes to square the situation away in my mind. Otherwise I'm going to go crazy trying to figure it out."

She glanced around the salon. "Pete, it's almost time for the Tea Lovers' Club to meet. I can't talk to you today. I'm sorry."

"Now listen here, gal. If you've cleared your appointment book for the TLC, you can clear it for me. I'm at least as important as those women. That's sure how it seemed the other night."

"You are important, Pete. But . . ." Again she swept her gaze over the room as if worried that someone might see her speaking to him. "Pete, I care about you. I truly do. But I think we ought to go on being friends. Nothing more."

The words every man dreaded. Pete felt like he had swallowed a rock. He slumped in the chair and looked down at his work boots. *Friends. Nothing more.*

"Pete." Patsy's hand covered his. Her long nails glowed a frosty pink in the afternoon sunlight that shone through the salon's big windows. Patsy's hands were so pretty and perfect—just like her.

"Pete, I'm sorry about the movie," she murmured. "I shouldn't have let myself go like that. I have emotions and needs like every woman, but I know better than to surrender to my feelings. What I did wasn't right. I stopped thinking clearly, and I led you on. Please forgive me. I do like you. I like you a lot. Maybe even more than that. But don't you see? It's not going to work out between us. It can't."

"Why not?" He looked up at her, trying to gulp down the grit in his throat. "It's because of my past, isn't it? The divorces. Alcohol problems. Jail."

She sighed. "No, Pete. Haven't you been listening to me? My salon is called Just As I Am. And like I said, that's how Jesus accepts people, and it's how I try to take them too. I realize you have a rough past, but I can live with it. I can see you've changed your ways."

"Then it's because I don't own Rods-N-Ends or my mobile home or anything. I'm nothing but a poor, dumb country boy."

"Oh, for heaven's sake, I don't care about that either. Some of my richest customers have been the mean ones. So persnickety and critical. It doesn't matter to me whether a person is wealthy or poor as dirt. It's their character that counts."

"So you don't approve of my character?"

"I think you're a fine man, Pete. In fact, I admire you. You saw the error of your ways and pulled yourself up by the bootstraps. I'm glad you're my neighbor here in Tranquility. I couldn't ask for anyone better."

That left only one thing. Pete knew it already, but he'd been hoping it was something else that had pushed Patsy away. Now he had no choice but to spit it out.

"I'm not born again," he said. "I still have my dark blots. I haven't been fished up by Pastor Andrew. I'm not what you'd call a committed Christian, and for you that's a deal breaker. Am I right?"

Patsy stroked her hand up Pete's bare arm and then down again. Her gentle touch made him weaker than he'd ever felt in his life. He would swear that rock he had swallowed had suddenly started burning red-hot and melting him all over Patsy's salon chair. There was nothing he wouldn't do for the woman. Nothing.

"I'll get baptized," he managed. "I swear I'll be as good as gold, Patsy. I'm already going to church and Sunday school and the men's Bible study. I'll start buying canned peaches and giving them to the food pantry. I'll sign up to shovel snow in the church parking lot this winter and mow the grass around the building next summer. I can be a decent man, Patsy. I really do believe I can keep going like this for the rest of my life. I wish you'd talk to me about what it is you want from me and what I can do to measure up."

Pete had noticed tears filling Patsy's eyes as he spoke, but he didn't trust them. More than once, he had provoked her too far and made her cry. But he meant what he had just told her, and he hoped to goodness that she understood.

"Esther is already here," she murmured. "Kim and Miranda Finley walked in while you were talking. And I see Brenda in the parking lot. Pete, I can't walk out of here with you. This is not the right time to talk. I need to go to that meeting."

She wiped under her eyes, then bent toward the mirror. "Oh, why didn't I use my waterproof mascara today? I'm such a mess." With a tissue and some cream, she began working to remove the black trails on her cheeks and repair her makeup. "Pete, everything is complicated. I don't know how to explain my heart to you, and I'm not even sure I should try. Why don't you get on back to Rods-N-Ends now? Maybe we can talk on Sunday after church."

Sunday was a long way off for a man afire. Pete didn't like the idea of waiting, and on top of that he resented Patsy's obvious preference for the company of her female friends. All that smooching in the movie theater must not have meant a thing to her. His profession of love—words that had come from the deepest place in his heart—had been insignificant.

Despite her tears, Patsy was cold and indifferent to him. Pete had never thought of her as the sort of woman who would lead a man on, but she had admitted it just a few minutes ago. She'd been playing with him. Messing with his mind. Pete could endure a lot, but not that.

"You don't have to explain your heart to me," he said, standing and brushing off his jeans. "Your heart is as hard and icy as a stone. I may not be born again, but I'm not dead and buried either. I have feelings, Patsy, and I don't like anyone stomping on them."

"I know you have feelings." Tears welled again. "And I have strong feelings for you, too. But I'm scared. I've been alone a long time, and I'm used to it. If I keep going the way I was in the theater, I'm liable to end up in a real pickle. Can't you see that?"

Shaking her head, she stepped closer and pointed in the direction of the women now gathered in the tea area. Esther Moore had risen from her chair and was reading something to the group. Cody, grinning like a skunk in a cabbage patch, sat beside Jennifer. He had no idea that girl was going to break his heart into tiny pieces.

"You know how I feel about gossip," Patsy whispered to Pete. "If you repeat any of what I tell you right now, I'll be so mad I won't ever speak to you again."

"My lips are sealed."

"See Kim Finley over there? She told me that she'd made a mistake when she ignored the Bible's teachings about marriage. Derek is a good man, but he doesn't share her faith, and that has brought trouble to their marriage. They're working hard to build a strong foundation, but it's almost impossible without that common ground."

Pete regarded the thin, dark-haired woman across the salon. Kim was beautiful in a silent, mysterious kind of way. She had always fascinated Pete, and he was glad Derek Finley was married to her. They were both fine people, so it surprised Pete to hear that they'd had marital problems.

"Now, see Brenda Hansen?" Patsy murmured. "She and Steve have had problems too. But they're both committed to God. I think that has made a big difference in the way they've gone about working through the difficulties."

Pete scratched his head. Kim and Derek. Brenda and Steve. Had those decent, hardworking couples really struggled in their marriages? Who was Patsy going to bring up next—Esther and Charlie Moore?

"You and I," she said. "We're too different. My faith is what I cling to, Pete. It's all I've had for years and years. It's all I really need in order to have a fulfilling life—and you don't even understand it.

You're doing all the right things, and you're trying your best. But I'm scared that you and I don't have what we need to make things work out well between us. That's all I'm trying to say. I'm scared, okay? I'm just too scared, Pete."

Before he could respond, she laid the cape on the back of the chair and hurried toward the tea area. Pete considered putting his ball cap on and stalking out of the salon. He deserved to be mad. Nothing like pouring your heart out to a woman—offering to behave like a saint every single day for the rest of your life—and then finding out you don't have what it takes to please her.

Sure, Pete knew he didn't understand living for Jesus the way Patsy did, but he figured he was close enough. When he died, he might not get inside the pearly gates, but he'd probably be able to see them, anyhow.

Besides, how important was faith if it didn't keep you from having problems like everyone else? If Brenda and Steve Hansen—Mr. and Mrs. Perfect Church Couple—had trouble in their marriage, who wouldn't? What was the point of having a relationship with God if it didn't make life easier? And why did it matter so much to Patsy Pringle?

For a few moments, Pete studied the women sipping their tea and chatting with each other while Esther Moore tried to make herself heard. There they all sat—a flock of peacocks in their matching outfits and sparkly jewelry and well-sprayed hair.

Then Pete's attention focused on Cody. By golly, that was a handsome kid. If he wasn't marching to his own drummer, he'd probably have Jennifer Hansen swooning in his arms. But Cody didn't seem to notice that he was different. He was smiling, eating cookies, drinking tea, and gawking at the girl beside him.

Come to think of it, Cody never missed a meeting of the TLC. If that kid could attend, why couldn't Pete? The fellow he'd hired to help out now and then planned to be at Rods-N-Ends a few more hours. Maybe Pete would just ... well, why not? He'd become the second full-fledged male attendee of the Tea Lovers' Club.

Patsy noticed Bitty Sondheim slipping into a chair near the hot water urn. She was late for the TLC, but no one minded things like that except Esther Moore. As usual, Bitty looked pretty and strange all at the same time. She had on a red skirt, blue leggings, and a pink polka-dot sweater. Bitty's blonde hair hung loose and full around her shoulders, and Patsy could almost feel her fingers itching to snatch up a pair of scissors and snip-snap that glorious mane into shape. She had even hinted around a few times, but Bitty never took the bait. Clearly the transplanted Californian enjoyed her long tresses and had no intention of letting Patsy anywhere near them.

As Bitty settled in, another movement caught Patsy's eye. The sight of Pete Roberts taking the empty chair beside Cody Goss almost made her gasp aloud.

He was saying something to Cody and Jennifer, who both laughed and then turned to look right at Patsy. Pete set his ball cap on the table and leaned back in his chair to ponder the glass container of baked treats near the hot water urn. Obviously not listening to Esther's reading of the minutes any better than Patsy was, he stood up again and went to fetch himself a cup of tea.

Patsy could not help following Pete with her eyes as he selected a bag of Earl Grey and put it into a delicate china teacup. Just as she had taught him, Pete filled the cup with hot water, then set it aside to steep while he chose a dessert.

Oh, he truly was a decent, well-meaning man—and it wasn't as though he had asked her to marry him. He'd only said he loved her and wanted to talk to her about their relationship. And Patsy had informed him that he couldn't ever live up to her high-and-mighty Christian standards. As if she herself was any good at following the teachings of Jesus.

Feeling worse than the night she saw her lipstick-smeared reflection at the movie theater, Patsy watched Pete carry his teacup and a lemon bar back to the table beside Cody. So what if Pete hadn't figured out how to surrender his life to Jesus? Though Patsy called herself a Christian, she believed that becoming Christlike was a gradual process—two steps forward and one back. Maybe in time, the men from Pete's Bible study group would help him understand what Jesus had meant when He said a person had to be born again.

"Now where was I?" Esther Moore said. "I don't think anyone's paying a bit of attention to me this afternoon. Patsy, what was I talking about?"

Tearing her focus from the man at the next table, Patsy could feel her cheeks heating up. "I'm not exactly sure myself, Esther," she said. "But I was wondering about the Thanksgiving get-together in Deepwater Cove. Did you already discuss that?"

"Thanksgiving?" Esther blinked several times. "Have we had Halloween yet? I don't remember. . . . Oh, nuts, Patsy. Now you've gotten me all mixed up."

"It's already November, Mrs. Moore," Cody spoke up. "Halloween passed us by like a witch on a broomstick, which is a metaphor. Brenda says I'm very good at metaphors. When you compare two things inside a sentence, then you've made one. Like . . . Pete and Patsy are as cozy as two worms in an ear of corn. Or . . . Patsy is as pink as a rose."

"Thank you, Cody," Esther said. "And to my surprise, I see Pete Roberts himself sitting right beside you. Pete, are you just visiting today, or do you plan to become a member of the Tea Lovers' Club?"

As if Patsy weren't already mortified enough by Cody's metaphors, now Pete stood to address the group. "I hear the TLC is open to anyone who likes a good cup of tea and wants to help the community. That fits me to a tee, and if no one minds, I'd like to enlist."

Esther beamed. "Are there any objections? No, of course there aren't. Pete, we're delighted to have you. I would invite Charlie to join, but he's making me crazy about my arteries. You know how he can be. One thing after another. Mutter, mutter, mutter. He won't buy me a car because of the accident and the problem we had with falling asleep while we were driving. Well, *I* was driving, so Charlie blames me, naturally."

As Esther spoke, it occurred to Patsy that the older woman was now talking only to Pete—as if she had forgotten she was standing before the members of the TLC.

"Besides all that," Esther went on, "Charlie insists on checking on me all the time. 'How're you doing, Esther?' he says, even though he asked me the same question not two minutes before. Yesterday, I got so fed up that I told him to go to California and visit Charles Jr. and the grandkids. Or go to Florida and see Ellie. With winter coming on, I'm not about to travel anywhere, but Charlie could make a trip without any problems. He won't leave my side, though. It's like living with a vulture hovering over you all the time. The TLC is the only place I can get any rest from the man."

And then Esther seemed to notice she was back in the room.

"Oh well," she said, waving a hand as if she could brush away everything she'd just been talking about. "Does anyone remember where we were in the meeting, because I cannot find my place in these minutes."

"We were adding Pete Roberts as a member of the TLC," Cody reminded her. "And Patsy wanted to know about the Thanksgiving get-together."

Disturbed at Esther's revelation of the tension between herself and Charlie, Patsy glanced around the table. How could Esther have said such things in front of the whole group? And why did she appear to be drifting in and out of awareness about her surroundings? Everyone in the room, it seemed, had noticed Esther's confusion. The usual chatter ceased, and now only the whirr of a hair dryer and the splash of running water sounded from the salon area.

Patsy could see that Ashley Hanes, who had spent the most time with Esther recently, was frowning.

Esther was rapidly turning pages in her club notebook. "Are you sure Halloween is over, Cody? I don't remember it at all. Did the children come around this year?"

"Not too many, Mrs. Moore." Cody didn't seem the least bit aware of Esther's odd behavior. "It was raining that night. Jennifer says the rain was God's way of showing His disapproval of Halloween. The other Mrs. Finley says it was nothing more than a weather pattern. But they didn't get into an argument this time. They're trying to be friends about Halloween and Buddha and Jesus and if many paths lead to heaven."

"I have a report on the Thanksgiving plans," Kim said suddenly, standing and drawing everyone's attention from Esther's befuddlement. "Bitty and I have been working hard on this for several weeks now. Derek talked to the subdivision committee, and we'll be able to hold our event on the Saturday afternoon before Thanksgiving. We're planning various activities on the commons area in Deepwater Cove. Bitty, do you want to share our ideas?"

"I certainly do." Bitty rose, flipped a handful of blonde hair over her shoulder, and read from notes she had scrawled on a napkin. "We'll have apple bobbing and a cotton candy machine. I'm going to set up a stand for people who want to dip caramel apples. Steve Hansen found a wagon and tractor we can use, and Brad Hanes knows where to get hay—so we're planning a hayride around the neighborhood. Charlie Moore and several of the other men are gathering wood for a big bonfire."

"Instead of bringing grills down to the lake this year," Kim continued, "everyone will roast hot dogs over the fire."

"Oh boy, hot dogs!" Cody crowed. "I love hot dogs! Hey, Jennifer, did you hear that? Hot dogs!"

"This is a sign-up list." Bitty displayed a sheet of yellow legal paper. "We need marshmallows, baked beans, salad, cornbread, buns, desserts—that sort of thing. Each family has to provide its own wieners. Write down your name, the number of people coming, and what you plan to bring. If Patsy will promise not to do any of her lawn chair gymnastics, I promise not to have a hissy fit about how unhealthy all this food is. Though I've got to say, you can now find vegetarian hot dogs in the stores, and they're every bit as good as the regular ones."

"Vegetarian hot dogs?" Esther had closed her book of meeting minutes. "That sounds like the worst thing I can ever imagine. Don't you agree, Pete?"

Patsy held her breath as the big man pushed back his chair and got to his feet. "To each his own is what I believe," Pete said, walking toward Esther. "If Bitty wants to eat vegetables and I prefer pork, well, so be it. We ought to all do our best to get along with each other—especially us members of the TLC."

Gently, he slipped an arm around Esther's shoulders and helped her sit down. "I think we've about covered all we need to discuss today," he said, dropping the notebook into her purse and snapping the clasp. "You can adjourn the meeting now, Mrs. Moore."

Esther smiled up at Pete. "Thank you, sweetie pie. Yes, let's end the meeting. Why don't you sit down here by me and tell me what's going on with you and Patsy? I hear the two of you went to the movies the other night. How about that? A real date!"

CHAPTER THIRTEEN

Charlie was climbing into his golf cart when he spotted Cody walking toward him.

"Hey there, young fellow," Charlie called out. "What are you up to this fine autumn day?"

"I'm up to the Haneses' house, but I still have a long way to go," Cody said. "I have to walk all the way to Tranquility to work at Just As I Am."

Charlie couldn't help but chuckle at the typical Cody comment. Laughter was a welcome respite from his glum mood. This morning, he had risen before dawn and found that he couldn't stop thinking about George Snyder and the sketch. Each time Charlie tried to bring the man's name into conversation, Esther deftly changed the subject. That was a pretty good trick for a woman who had taken to putting nearly everything in sight into the dishwasher. Charlie regularly opened the machine to find artificial flowers, lace doilies, place mats, and even candles set in among the plates and glasses.

Not only was Esther putting things into the dishwasher and refusing to discuss George Snyder, but she wouldn't let Charlie even broach the subject of her artery condition. Everything he did annoyed her, it seemed, from his TV game shows to his muttering to his efforts at bead sorting. The more Charlie thought about these things while lying in bed watching the sunlight creep across the wall, the more he wanted out of the house for the day.

So he had eaten a hasty breakfast, left Esther a note, and driven his golf cart over to the Hanes work site. He arrived early enough to greet Brad and discuss the construction problems they'd been working on. Both were concerned that the seam where the old roof joined the addition might leak.

Ashley left the house a couple of hours after Brad had driven off to his job. She was on her way to make beads at the Hansens' house. In all, it had been an uneventful morning—Charlie stapling insulation to the studs and visiting with the occasional passerby until he decided it was time for lunch.

For once, Charlie had been able to concentrate on the job rather than on his wife, and that gave his nerves a chance to begin untangling. But at the sight of Cody coming along, he felt himself tighten up again. Cody had a way of being warm, kind, and helpful while at the same time driving Charlie a little wacky with his talkativeness and oddities. But Charlie had answered Cody's cheerful wave and greeting with one of his own.

"It's high time for window washing, Patsy told me," Cody was saying now, as he paused beside the golf cart. "And I'm the man for the job."

"I'll bet you are."

"If I had a driving slicer . . ." Cody paused. "I mean, a driver's license, then I wouldn't have to walk everywhere. But I don't have one, and also I don't have a car. Sometimes Jennifer drives me to Tranquility when she's on the way to her missionary classes at Hidden Tribes near Camdenton. But not today. She's packing her suitcase because she's going on a trip to help build a church in Mexico. She'll be gone for two weeks. That's seventeen or maybe twenty days. It's a long time."

"It's shorter than you think. Only fourteen days," Charlie said. "I hadn't heard about the mission trip. I guess you'll miss her."

"My spirits are as flat as a turtle that got run over on the highway, and that's a very good metaphor for how I feel about saying good-bye to Jennifer."

"It's difficult to see someone leave, but she'll be back." Charlie glanced down at the empty section of cushion beside him. "How about if I give you a ride to Tranquility, Cody? I was thinking of buying one of Bitty's wraps for lunch today. I can drop you off right at the door to Just As I Am."

"Thank you, Mr. Moore," Cody said, climbing into the cart and seating himself.

Charlie stepped on the gas pedal and guided the vehicle along the roadway toward the entrance to the Deepwater Cove neighborhood. He knew Esther would be all right if he didn't show up at the house for lunch, but he considered phoning her just to check in. On the other hand, both of them needed a break from each other, and he might as well leave her in peace.

"Saying good-bye is much harder than you think, and I have said good-bye to a lot of people." Cody was gazing out at the lake. "What if Jennifer likes Mexico so much that she doesn't come home? I went to Kansas and I missed everyone, so I decided to come back. But Jennifer told me she loves Jesus more than anyone or anything, and she is planning to tell people about Him no matter what. I think I'm the *what* that is no matter."

"Aw, now, that's not true," Charlie said, hoping to cheer Cody up. "Jennifer likes you a lot. I've heard her say that myself. Besides, she won't live in the jungle all the time. Missionaries return to the States to be with their families every few years or so. She'll take a break from the jungle, and you can see her then."

"Here's a metaphor for that idea. It stinks." Cody gripped the rail that held up the golf cart's roof. "That's not really a metaphor, but it's how I feel about only seeing Jennifer now and then. What if she dies in the jungle, Mr. Moore? I nearly died when I lived in the forest. I nearly died two or three times or even more. If Jennifer dies, I won't be able to think about anything but going to heaven to be with her."

"Now, hold on just a minute. You wouldn't want to do that, Cody."

"Yes, I would. Heaven is a much better place than earth. I can hardly wait to go there."

"You don't mean . . . kill yourself, do you, Cody? Surely you wouldn't feel that bad."

"No. I would never want to suicide myself, because think how sad everyone would be if I died that way. Everyone loves me a lot. A *whole* lot. People say I'm handsome and funny and artistic and also autistic. They'd really cry a lot if I died. But let me tell you for sure that I'm looking forward to heaven. It's my favorite place, and I wish I was there right now."

As the golf cart meandered up the hill toward the road to Tranquility, Charlie considered the young man's words. He had never given heaven a lot of thought. Life had always been so full of work, children, hobbies, books, television, and all the things that had occupied his mind and hands through the years.

When he did ponder the afterlife, Charlie quickly snuffed out the image. He had given his life to Christ as a child, and he knew he was destined to spend eternity with God. Though he didn't have to fear the fiery lakes and endless torment of hell, he hadn't ever been too crazy about the idea of heaven either. The Bible called it a place without pain or suffering. No one cried there. People worshipped God all the time. But truth to tell, it sounded fairly boring to Charlie—especially in light of the almost incomprehensible idea of eternity.

"Heaven will be a happy place, I know," Charlie told Cody, "but you don't want to be in any hurry about getting there. Even if Jennifer or someone else you love dies, you wouldn't want to be in heaven rather than here on earth, where the autumn leaves fall, and the snowflakes drift down, and summer brings fresh vegetables. Earth is a beautiful place."

"Maybe so. But heaven is better."

"Now why would you say that?"

"'For me to live is Christ, and to die is gain,'" Cody quoted, "'For I am in a strait betwixt two, having a desire to depart, and to be with Christ; which is far better.' That's from Philippians 1. My daddy used to talk about heaven a lot because he thought it was going to be wonderful to live there. Me too. You know Hebrews 11, don't you? That's the chapter in the Bible where all the people of faith are listed. In verses 13 and 14, it says, 'These all died in faith, not having received the promises, but having seen them afar off, and were persuaded of them, and embraced them, and confessed that they were strangers and pilgrims on the earth. For they that say such things declare plainly that they seek a country.' We're strangers here on earth, Mr. Moore, because our real home is afar off in heaven. Heaven is a country, and God has built a big city for us there."

Charlie drove in silence. He had probably heard those verses before, but they hadn't meant much to him. No doubt while some minister was reading them, Charlie and Esther had been trying to control their restless children with glares or occupy them with cereal and crayons.

"'They desire a better country,'" Cody said, "'that is, an heavenly: wherefore God is not ashamed to be called their God: for he hath prepared for them a city.' See, Mr. Moore, heaven is better than earth because God will be walking around with us there. 'God hath said, I will dwell in them, and walk in them; and I will be their God, and they shall be my people.' That's Second Corinthians 6:16. If God is in heaven and so are my daddy and my mother, then that's where I want to be."

"Well, that does sound nice," Charlie admitted. "It's just that I do love this good ol' earth."

"Just you wait and see, Mr. Moore. God is the King of heaven, and He has a new heaven and a new earth all ready for us. On this old earth, we see through a glass darkly. My daddy and I had a glass darkly in our old trailer. It was in my bedroom. I used to try to look out of it, but I couldn't see anything except blobs of color. If I opened the window, I realized that the blobs were trees and rocks and a river and the big house of the grouchy man who didn't know we lived in a trailer on his property."

"Where was that?" Charlie asked.

"I don't know, but one time my daddy was outside the trailer and he knocked on the glass darkly to get my attention. I got really scared. I couldn't see him too well, so I thought it was the grouchy man from the big house. But then I stood on my bed and opened the glass darkly, and there he was. My daddy. I saw him face-to-face, just like God."

Charlie pulled the golf cart to a stop in front of Patsy Pringle's beauty salon. It bothered him that Cody understood a lot more about the Bible than he did—and he'd been reading it practically his whole life. When Cody had come to Deepwater Cove, he couldn't even read. He and his father had memorized reams of Scripture, though, and Cody could rattle off verses at the drop of a hat. Even more impressive, he understood what the words meant.

"Here we are," Cody announced. "Time to wash windows in the salon. Nobody likes to look through a glass darkly, Mr. Moore. That's why heaven will be so much better. Okay?"

"Okay, Cody." Charlie nodded as the young man loped toward the salon's front door. What an odd kid. It seemed as though God had forgotten to put a filter between Cody's brain and his mouth. One thing for sure, no one could ever accuse him of lying. He said exactly what he was thinking, no more and no less.

Pondering heaven and Cody's surprising eagerness to go there, Charlie drove over to the Pop-In. He couldn't imagine being in heaven without Esther. Or living on earth without her either. No matter how often they got on each other's nerves, no matter that she had distressed her husband by keeping a sketch drawn by another man, no matter that she seemed to be getting foggier by the week. In fact, no matter what, Charlie loved his wife.

He loved her with a passion that went beyond all reason. That passion went down deep into the very center of who he was as a human being. If anything happened to her, he knew he would feel bereft—as though part of himself had died too.

"Hey there, Charlie Moore! I didn't expect to see you here for lunch. Come on in!"

Bitty Sondheim's cheery voice dispelled Charlie's gloom the moment he stepped into her little restaurant. Although he and the other men from the Wednesday morning Bible study had planned to build Bitty some tables, Charlie had gotten caught up in the construction of the Haneses' room addition. Nevertheless, he noted that she had set up a little wrought iron bistro on the sidewalk, and someone had put several tables and chairs inside near the large front window.

The place was bustling with lunchtime customers, and Charlie realized he would have to wait in line. Not an easy task. The aroma inside the place always made his mouth water. Cheese, onions, garlic, fresh tomatoes, basil, thyme, and all sorts of other herbs, vegetables, and meats melded into a fragrant blend that filled the room and caused his stomach to growl.

"I've got my fajita wrap on special today, Charlie," Bitty called out as she handed a heavy sack to a customer. "If that's not enough for you, well, I have the meat-loaf-and-dinner-roll special going too. You look like you've been working hard. You've got sawdust on your cap."

Charlie removed the offending cap and shook it over the large waste bin in one corner. As he tucked it under his arm, he spotted Jennifer Hansen headed toward the door with her hands full. He tipped his head in greeting. "So you're off to Mexico. Cody tells me that you and some of the other missionaries will be building a church down there."

The lovely young blonde awarded him a broad smile. "I cannot wait, Mr. Moore! This will be my second trip outside the country. We're going to a remote part of Mexico near Oaxaca, and I'll get to practice my Spanish while we work."

"Sounds like fun."

"It'll be great!" She was fairly bouncing up and down on tiptoes as she spoke. "Most of our team will be doing construction, but I get to work with children. I've planned all the Bible story lessons I'll be teaching. My mom is helping me sew puppets today, so I thought I'd run over here and get us a quick lunch. The team leaves tomorrow morning."

"I guess you know we're all going to miss you, young lady. Especially a certain curly-haired fellow who thinks you hung the moon."

Her cheeks flushed a pretty pink. "I'll be back, Mr. Moore. Cody is taking this way too seriously. He's acting like he'll never see me again."

"We never know when the Lord may call us home, and I'm sure you're aware of Cody's feelings for you."

Jennifer's expression grew serious. "Mr. Moore . . . can I . . . ?"

Before he could respond, she leaned against him, cupped her hand at his ear, and began to whisper. "Mr. Moore, please pray for me. I know what God wants me to do with my life . . . but . . . but I'm really confused about a few things . . . about Cody."

Charlie held his breath as she gripped his arm.

"Will you pray for me?" Her eyes filling with sudden tears, she backed away from him.

Charlie nodded. "Sure I will. You have my word on it."

Dazed, he watched her hurry out the door. He hadn't quite processed Jennifer's request when Bitty called him to the counter. He ordered the fajita wrap, and it wasn't but a moment before he was holding a lunch sack in his hand.

"Where's Esther?" Bitty asked. "I hope she's feeling all right."

"She's at home," Charlie mumbled. "I was working. The Haneses' addition. You know."

"Oh, sure. I drove by there the other day. It's looking so much better. I was beginning to wonder if Brad had given up on it. He was just in here for lunch, as usual, and he looked positively cheerful. I'm sure that's your doing, Charlie."

She smiled, and for the first time, Charlie noticed the freckles scattered across her cheeks.

"Do you suppose Esther would mind if you and I sat outside together?" she asked. "Looks like the lunch crowd is thinning out, and I could use a break. Pedro can take over for a few minutes."

"That'll be fine. Please join me."

"Hey, Pedro," Bitty called over her shoulder. "Cover the front for me, would you?"

Charlie noted Bitty's new employee moving from the kitchen area toward the counter. Pedro Baca didn't speak English too well yet, but he and his family were settling comfortably into the lake community.

"It's a perfect autumn day, isn't it?" Charlie tugged his cap onto his head again as he and Bitty left the Pop-In and sat in the bistro chairs outside. He excused himself, bowed his head, and offered up a silent prayer of gratitude for the meal. Then he spoke aloud again. "Blue sky, the last few leaves on the trees, and a breeze blowing in from the lake. My kind of weather."

Bitty chuckled as she stirred a cup of steaming coffee. "This will be my first winter ever. Southern California doesn't have much to offer when it comes to seasonal changes. I'm enjoying the lake, and even the cooler weather is nice. Winter will be a big adventure, though. I guess you're used to it. Esther told me you've lived in Missouri all your life."

Charlie studied the woman across from him as he chewed his first bite of lunch. He had never given Bitty Sondheim much heed except to marvel at the crazy outfits she wore. Today, her straw-colored hair was pulled back into its usual braid. As they left the warmth of the restaurant, she had tugged on a bright turquoise sweater with big black buttons. Underneath, she wore some sort of loose, wrinkled red dress that Esther wouldn't be caught dead in. Charlie thought he had noted black-and-white checkered socks and a pair of leather sandals on her feet, but they were tucked under the table now.

Despite her clownish getup, Bitty was pretty. It had taken Charlie a while to see it. Now that he did, he was almost astonished. Not only did the woman have the cutest sprinkling of freckles he'd ever seen, but her green eyes twinkled with happiness and her full lips parted over perfect white teeth.

"Bitty, have you ever been married?" Charlie asked.

Realizing immediately that he'd been as blunt as Cody, he cleared his throat. "I'm sorry. That's your personal business. It's just that the topic has been on my mind lately. Not you. Marriage. Marriage in general is what I mean."

He was digging a deeper hole the more he talked, so he decided the best option was to take another bite of his wrap. "Very tasty," he mouthed as he chewed.

Bitty tipped back her head and laughed. She had a big, hearty chuckle that couldn't help but lift a person's spirits. Pulling up the hem of her long skirt, she stretched out her legs and set her feet on the chair across from Charlie. Then she tucked a loose sprig of blonde hair behind one ear.

"Not legally," she said. "Married."

"Oh." Charlie took another quick bite.

"Back in California, I lived with one guy for about four years. He turned out to have a mental illness, but he wouldn't take his medicine. So that didn't work out too great. Then another guy and I were together for ... let's see ... oh, I guess ten years off and on. That one didn't work out either. After that, I decided I wasn't any good at being with men. About that time, an old friend of mine announced he wanted to marry me, but I told him no and ran away. So now I'm here—happy as a lark and determined never to set one toe into a relationship again."

At this, she lifted her foot and waggled it around, checkered stocking and all. Charlie joined in her laughter in spite of himself. Bitty was a little crazy, but then who wasn't these days? Esther sure had her moments. Cody did too. And what on earth was going on in Jennifer Hansen's pretty head? It felt to Charlie like he was riding on a Tilt-A-Whirl.

Seated on the porch, Esther was studying a case of Ashley Hanes's homemade beads when Charlie pulled up to the house in his golf cart. Boofer bounded across the yard to greet him, but Esther couldn't muster the energy to stand. She was so tired, and it felt as if she'd been looking at beads for hours. The way Ashley had organized them made no sense at all. No matter how hard Esther tried, she couldn't figure out how to straighten the mess.

"Insulation's done," Charlie announced as he strode up the steps and onto the porch. "Brad and I will start hanging drywall next week."

He paused and cocked his head. "Esther? Are you feeling okay?"

She shook her head. "I've been dizzy all day."

"Dizzy?" He sat down beside her and turned the bead box in his direction. "That's odd. I'm feeling a little off-kilter myself."

"Maybe it was something we ate."

"I think I've got too much on my mind. What have you done to the beads, honey? You've mixed them all up."

"Really? Did I do that?" She took a sip of lemonade and studied the bead box with her husband. The ice in her glass had melted long ago, but the drink was still cool.

"No, I think the problem is Ashley's directions," Esther told Charlie as she pointed to the array of objects on the table. "This afternoon, she brought over all these bags of beads and asked me to sort them, but I can't follow this nonsense she wrote. Can you make heads or tails of it?"

Charlie took the note card with its scribbled instructions. "Honey, this is the grocery shopping list I took to the store last Monday. Look here—eggs, milk, bacon, oatmeal. This is your handwriting, Esther."

She focused on the words, and all at once they made sense. "Oh, for pete's sake. If that isn't the silliest thing. I must have picked up the grocery list when I went inside for lemonade."

Charlie bent down and tugged at a piece of paper wedged against the leg of the wicker table. "Here's what Ashley wrote. Same as always. 'Please organize beads by colors and shapes.' She's drawn a little diagram for you."

"Let me see that." Esther scanned the instructions. "All right, but look at the container. Why are there red beads in with the blues? And see this gold one in here? Why would Ashley set up the box this way if she expected me to follow what she wrote on that note? That girl can be so loosey-goosey. I have to say, Charlie, sometimes I wonder if she's taking drugs. You know what a bad influence Brad is with all his drinking."

Charlie silently rearranged the beads. Then he opened one of the plastic zip bags and began filling the compartments.

Esther didn't like the look on his face, so she decided it was time to make her big announcement.

"By the way, I've decided to get my artery cleaned out." She tried to make her voice light, but for some reason the words came out in a gush of tears. "I love you so much, Charlie, and I know I've been a terrible pain in the neck about this whole thing. Letting that doctor put all those balloons and tubes and mesh pipes in my artery scares me to death, but I'm going to do it anyway because I want you to be happy again. You've been such an irritating old goat these past couple of months, and I know it's mostly my fault."

"Now, Esther." He reached out a hand to her.

"No, let me finish." She took the grocery list and began dabbing her cheeks with it. "Cody said I've been mean to you lately. People think I've changed since my accident. While I was getting my set-and-style last week, Patsy told me she felt I ought to have the balloon thing done. She said she was worried because at the last TLC meeting I didn't remember Halloween, and I don't. Then Brenda paid me a visit this morning, and she said that she and Kim had been talking about me. Imagine that! Gossiping about a person behind her back."

At this, Esther couldn't do a thing to stop the tears. Charlie kept saying, "Now, Esther," but it didn't do any good at all. The very idea of people discussing their neighbor and her arteries in secret was so mortifying that she hadn't been able to concentrate on anything else all day.

"Brenda and Kim want me to have the balloon put in too," Esther sobbed. "Kim's husband—oh, I can't remember his name right now—anyway, he knows all about arteries and CPR and heart attacks and strokes because of his job. He told Brenda that I might be demented. Can you believe it? Demented! And all because of my silly artery."

"Now, Esther, you're not demented." Charlie patted her hand. "Derek talked to me about his concerns too. I told you about that, remember? He said there's a condition called vascular dementia. All it means is that the plaque in your artery is blocking the blood flow to part of your brain. So maybe that's why you forgot about Halloween—not that there was much to remember. We only had three kids at the door, and you had gone to bed by the time they came around."

"I had? Did you give them anything?"

"Uh-huh. Bubble gum."

"Bubble gum! Oh, that's not a treat, Charlie. You know I always make little sacks of goodies. Miniature candy bars, lollipops, red hots, peppermints, chocolate drops—all the treats in a little black net bag tied up with orange ribbon."

Her frustration again shifted into a flood of tears. "Never mind about that, Charlie. What I'm trying to tell you is that I love you so much, and I want you to be happy, and I know you won't be happy if you have to live with a demented woman for the rest of your life. So Brenda called the vein doctor while she was here because— wouldn't you know it—I had misplaced his phone number. She found him in the book, and she set up the appointment. So the day after Thanksgiving, you and I will have to drive to Springfield again. Brenda says the surgery is an in-and-out kind of thing, and they probably won't even put me to sleep—though the truth is, I wouldn't mind it so much. All that cutting and pushing things through my veins . . . well, never mind. I'm going to do it, so that's that."

Charlie heaved a long sigh. "I'm glad, Esther. I'd dance a jig if I hadn't worn myself out hanging insulation all day. Have you told the kids?"

"Not yet," she said. "I think Cody must have done something with our address book the last time he was here. I can't find it anywhere."

"We'll let modern technology take care of that little problem." Charlie tugged his cell phone from his pocket and pressed a few buttons. Esther knew he would call their son first. Charles Jr. had always been calmer and more practical than Ellie. Even though their daughter had settled down and held a good job for several years, neither Charlie nor Esther could predict how she would react to issues that arose in the family.

"May I speak to Charles Moore Jr. please?" Charlie asked. "You can tell him that his father is on the line . . . with good news."

Esther pictured the receptionist outside their son's office. What a lovely young woman. And how wonderful that Charles Jr. had risen to such a prestigious position in his job. Some people might sniff at the fact that his place of employment was only an onion factory, but Esther regularly reminded herself how important that particular vegetable was in the greater scheme of life. Food simply tasted better with onions, and good food made the world a happier, healthier place.

Charlie's voice brightened. "Hey there, Son. This is your ol' dad. How are Natalie and the kids?"

Esther sat patiently awaiting her turn to talk while Charlie made small talk and then discussed the upcoming medical procedure and its importance for her health. Hearing the scenario explained all over again in such detail worried Esther. Maybe she shouldn't have agreed to it, after all. She certainly loved Charlie and hoped to live many more long, happy years with her husband. But the thought of lying on one of those hard hospital beds with lights all around and doctors peering down—

"He wants to talk to you," Charlie said, handing Esther the cell phone.

"Hello?" Esther cradled the device, uncertain exactly where her ear was supposed to go and how loudly she ought to speak. One slip of the hand and the phone could fold up on itself or even dial some random unknown number.

"Mom, how are you feeling?" Charles Jr.'s deep voice flooded through Esther's heart in a warm wave of love and delight. "Dad says you're having a little procedure done the day after Thanksgiving."

"Well, I wouldn't call it little, sweetheart. They are putting a balloon in your mother's artery, you know. That's quite a serious matter."

"Would you like for me to come and be with you and Dad? Natalie and the kids could fly out there with me. We'd be happy to do it."

Tears welled in Esther's eyes. "Oh, that's so thoughtful. Do you really mean that, Charles?"

"You bet I do. School will be out for Thanksgiving, and we can stay a few days. It seems too long since we've been with you and Dad."

"But the cost."

"It's not a problem, Mom. I got another promotion, remember?

I'm a vice president now. I make a good living. We can be by your side if it would make you feel better."

Esther reflected on that happy information. A vice president. Had she told Brenda Hansen about the promotion? Did the ladies of the TLC know that Charles Jr. had risen so high in the company?

"I'd love to see all of you," she said. But as she spoke the words, reality set in. "Only not after stitches in my leg and a balloon in my artery. We couldn't have a bit of fun. I'll be lying around moaning and griping like I did after my flying car incident. I know—why don't your dad and I drive out to California for Christmas? I realize it sounds impulsive, but I miss you and Natalie and the grandkids so much. I'll be feeling better by then, and we can bring a car filled with presents for everyone. Just like Santa Claus!"

Charles Jr. laughed. "The kids are a little old for that. But we'd love to have you here. Let's plan on it. Maybe we can talk Ellie into joining us too."

"Wouldn't that be great? All of us together, just like when you were little. Bless your heart, honey. I'll hold on to that dream while they're starting my surgery."

"Good deal, Mom. I'll tell Natalie after work today."

"I love you, baby boy," Esther cooed. "You take care of yourself now. Here's your daddy."

Charlie took the phone and spoke for a minute or two longer. Afterward, he dialed Ellie's number, but as usual she didn't pick up. It seemed the church kept that young lady busy day and night.

Charlie left a message and then slipped the phone into his pocket again. "She'll call us when she has a free moment," he told Esther.

"You know, Charlie, we do have the best children in the world."

"We sure do. It will be fun to see them at Christmas. Honey, if you'll have this procedure, we can get back to normal. I know surgery is a frightening thought, but you won't feel a thing. People have it done all the time. It saves a lot of lives, and I intend for it to save yours. I don't know what I would ever do without you."

A glow spread through Esther's chest at her husband's words. "I love you, sweetie pie. I'm sorry I've been finding fault with you so much lately. Cody told me I've been a grump and a grouch, and as much as it pained me to admit it, I decided he was right. Can you forgive me?"

"Yes, I can. And I do. You've forgiven me for a lot more than that."

"Well, yes, I have, now that you mention it. I'll never forget the time you went to that strip club.... Oh, what am I saying? I forgave you for that years ago. It's all in the past. The important thing is to focus on the good times we've shared and the things we love about each other. You know what I love the most about you, Charles Moore?"

"What's that?" he asked, taking her hand and kissing it.

"Your faithfulness. Through all the ups and downs, the good and the bad—"

"For richer, for poorer," he added. "In sickness and in health."

"Till death do us part." Esther stood, walked around the table, and sat down on Charlie's lap. "Thank you for loving me, my darling honey bun."

His arms slipped around her, and she laid her head on his shoulder. It felt good this way, she thought. Almost as if she were a child again and he was cradling her safely within his protection and strength. A woman could count on a man like Charlie Moore. She could trust him too. And thank God for that.

CHAPTER FOURTEEN

Patsy was thrilled about the new decor and gift shop that Brenda Hansen was planning to open the weekend after Thanksgiving. Every time she had a little break at the salon, Patsy hurried past the Pop-In and the tattoo parlor to peek through the window of Brenda's store with its bright new sign over the front door—Bless Your Hearth.

The place wasn't large, but Brenda had creatively divided it up into different sections. Patsy loved the rich colors Brenda had selected. Steve Hansen had built interesting dividers of shelving and lattice, and as the days ticked by toward the grand opening, the store gradually filled with an array of wonderful items.

"What are you looking at in there, woman?"

The voice at Patsy's shoulder startled her, jerking her gaze from a display of Ashley Hanes's beads on the front counter of the new store. She focused on Pete Roberts, who had somehow approached her in silence and was now standing just a hair too close for comfort. His arm touched her elbow, and she could feel its warmth through her thin sweater.

"It's Brenda's new shop," Patsy told him. "She had Cody help her finish painting the walls, and now she's stocking the shelves. Do you have a problem with me watching the excitement?"

"No, but I'm curious. Seems like every time I leave my place to pump gas or fish out some minnows for a customer, you're standing here gawking. It's only a bunch of towels and lamps and stuff, isn't it?"

He stepped closer and peered through the window. When his shoulder pressed against hers, Patsy shivered. For a split second, she couldn't even speak.

"Well, aren't I right?" he asked. "I can't figure out why you've got ants in your pants about this. What's the big deal?"

"It's the things Brenda has chosen and the way she's putting them together. Don't you see? The wall colors are so rich and beautiful. And look at how Brenda has fixed up her checkout counter. And then there's the sign her customers will read as they pay for their purchases. See? It says, 'Go home to your family, and tell them everything the Lord has done for you and how merciful he has been. Mark 5:19.' Isn't that lovely? It expresses everything Brenda stands for."

Pete nodded. "It is nice, Patsy. I see what you're saying. In fact, the whole lineup of stores here in Tranquility is getting downright classy. I might even have to rearrange my own window. Maybe I'll have a harvest sale. Coolers aren't moving too fast these days, and the swimming season is kaput. Rods-N-Ends could use some sprucing up inside, too. You've got a nice Bible verse over your counter. Reckon you or Brenda could come up with a sign like that for a tackle-and-bait shop?"

Patsy couldn't repress a grin. "Maybe something about fishers of men?"

Pete chuckled. "Not a bad idea. If we could think of Bible verses for the tattoo shop and Dr. Hedges's chiropractor business, we'd be sending waves of holiness all over the place."

Patsy frowned. "It's not a joke, Pete."

"I know. I'm only trying to get you to lighten up. The other day when you trimmed my hair, we didn't end things on the best note. You said I had scared you. You were afraid we didn't have the same beliefs in common. I know what the problem is. You don't think we share the important things that would make a marriage between us work out."

"I didn't say anything about marriage."

"Well then, I guess that was in my own mind. Anyhow, I've given this a lot of thought. I even wrote it down. I made a list of all the wrong I've done in my life—which took more than one page, I have to admit. I probably even left out a few things. Then I tried to think of every good change I've made. Needless to say, that list turned out to be pretty short. I sure couldn't make the good things outweigh the bad."

"It's not the number of items on a list that matters, Pete. It's your heart."

"I knew you'd say that. So I started a second list—the things I like about the Christians I know. Plus the qualities I don't like, and I have to tell you, there are quite a few of those."

"I'm sure there are. Christians are humans. If you want to make a list of positive aspects to our faith, you'd better start and end with Jesus."

"I figured you'd say that."

Patsy put her hand on her hip. "If you know what I'm going to say all the time, Pete Roberts, why bother telling me anything? The truth is, you don't know me well enough to predict what my reaction will be."

"Purt' near." He smiled at her. "Anyhow, I knew it would be easy to list the good things about Jesus, but I decided I'd rather take a look at the effect He has on His followers. The *fruit*, as Pastor Andrew calls it."

"Hold on now. That's not fair. Some Christians can be downright nasty—to each other and to outsiders. But that's not what Jesus wants."

"I've met a few of those nasty folks. On the whole, though, I'd say the faith has a good outcome. So that's why I've decided to talk to Pastor Andrew. He's got his work cut out for him because I'm one ornery ol' fish. But maybe he can reel me in."

Patsy held her breath for a moment, allowing the information to soak in. But wariness quickly tempered her elation.

"You're not doing this because of me, are you?" she asked. "Pete, I'm not sure we're right for each other even if you do decide to follow Jesus."

Pete turned from the window, where they had been watching Brenda tug a cute slipcover over a plain brown sofa. He took Patsy's shoulders and forced her to look him straight in the eye. "You know as well as I do that God brought us together, Miss Patsy Pringle. He did it for my benefit and for yours, too. But no, that's not why I'm going to talk to Pastor Andrew. It's because I finally understand the pond."

"Which pond?"

"Heaven's pond. The other afternoon I was out on the dock wetting my line, and that's when it hit me like a bolt out of the blue. I realized that when Jesus goes fishing for men and someone gets caught, he doesn't get jabbed through the gills, hung on a stringer, gutted, and then fried like a crappie. No . . . that's when he gets 'born again.'"

"Really?" Patsy wasn't certain she understood, but clearly this made perfect sense to Pete.

"Sure. The fellow gets yanked out of his old pond, and then Jesus throws him straight into heaven's pond. He starts swimming with a whole new school of fish. He sees life from a different perspective, because he has already looked death square in the eye and knows he's been given a second chance. He's been born again in heaven's pond. That pond is full of algae and minnows and mosquito eggs, so he grows and gets to be a better, bigger fish. And that's how it works."

"My goodness!" Patsy exclaimed. "Pete, I believe there's a preacher inside you just ready to bust out."

A crooked grin tilted one corner of the man's mouth. "You reckon?"

"Oh, Pete!" Patsy gasped as an idea hit her. "I know what your cash register sign could say. 'Heaven's Pond: Home of the Greatest Fisherman Ever.'"

He slipped an arm around her shoulders. "Would you make me a sign like that, Patsy?"

"I'll put Cody on it. That boy can paint letters better than anyone." She leaned against him. "Pete, you don't have to talk to Pastor Andrew to be born again, you know. Anyone who knows Jesus can lead you into heaven's pond."

"I'd like to talk to him anyway. There are a few questions I need to ask."

"Like what?"

"Like how does God feel about a twice-divorced, formerly drunk jailbird pursuing the hand of a lovely, sweet, and virtuous lady?"

Trying not to blush, Patsy wanted to answer, but she felt that Pastor Andrew would do a better job. Besides, she wasn't exactly sure what she ought to say. How *would* God feel about that? Just as important, how did Patsy feel about it? Did Pete truly want to marry her?

As they stood together gazing into the window of Bless Your Hearth, Patsy imagined herself and Pete years from now. They'd be together, just like the couple reflected in the pane of glass. They would live in a warm home decorated like Brenda's new shop. Maybe they'd even have a child or two. Patsy wasn't too old, after all. Pete might put his arm around her, and she might lay her head on his shoulder. Perhaps they would reminisce about the old days when Pete ran a bait shop and Patsy owned her beauty salon. They'd be like Charlie and Esther. Comfortable. Quiet. Satisfied. And still in love.

That would be nice, Patsy thought. Very nice. So nice, in fact, that if Pete decided to ask her to marry him one of these days . . . well, she might even say yes.

Esther couldn't quite believe she had forgotten the weekly meeting of the Tea Lovers' Club. She sat on the porch in a wicker chair and stared at the lake in utter befuddlement. How had it happened? She always went to the TLC gatherings on Wednesday afternoons.

But a few hours ago, Charlie had gone to work with Brad on the room addition. Then Esther had taken an unplanned nap on the sofa. When she woke up, she realized her left arm had gone to sleep. She could hardly move the thing. It felt numb and useless, and it seemed to take forever to get it to come back to life.

"That's what you get for snoozing in the middle of the day," her mother would have said. Esther's mother had never believed in naps. She'd always been so busy tending to the kitchen, the yard, the house, the children. *"Essie,"* she would say, *"get yourself off that sofa this instant. Get busy, Essie!"*

Smiling at the memory of her fussy mother, Esther thought of her own children. Once again, the Thanksgiving dinner table would seat only her and Charlie, all by themselves. Oh, the kids would call, of course. Charles Jr. would hand his phone to each family member in turn until they'd all wished Gramma and Gramps a happy holiday.

No doubt Ellie wouldn't even remember her parents until late in the day, after she and the other church members had finished making rounds of the various homeless shelters in the area. She would call—out of breath and flustered—and pour out everything about her life in one long, uninterrupted sentence. All her activities would flow through the receiver, and then she would say good-bye and hang up. Ellie had changed so much in the past few years, but she still forgot to talk about anyone but herself.

As Esther pondered her children, she saw Charlie's golf cart pull up under the carport. Boofer bounded down from the porch and scurried over to greet his master. Charlie bent and stroked the dog's head for a moment, rubbed behind his ears, patted his back. Then he straightened and stepped to the porch.

"Hey there, sugar bear," he called as he climbed the steps. "You look like the queen of Sheba—sitting there on your throne and surveying your territory. Mmm, so pretty I can't resist a little kiss." He leaned over and pressed his lips to her cheek.

Esther smiled. "I've been thinking about Charles Jr. and Ellie. They're so absorbed in their own affairs, aren't they? Charles is caught up in the doings of the onion factory. In his free time, he's so busy with family activities. Seems like the grandkids are involved in everything. And Ellie can hardly take a breath with all her church business. I sure do wish they'd come home for Thanksgiving, don't you? We could buy a great big turkey and feed the whole bunch. What about giving them a call?"

Charlie settled into the chair across from her and took off his hat. "Thanksgiving is just around the corner, Esther. They won't have time to change their plans. We'll go to California at Christmas like we planned."

"Did we plan that?"

"We talked about it."

"Do you ever wonder why Charles Jr. and Ellie chose to move as far away from us and each other as they could? One in California and the other in Florida. Maybe they were glad to escape us. Do you think we were bad parents, Charlie?"

"No! God took them down separate paths, that's all. Charles got that great scholarship to USC, and then he fell in love with a California girl. And Ellie . . . well, you know how she ended up in Miami."

"The rehabilitation center. What was it—the third or fourth one we'd tried?"

"Third. But that wasn't our fault. Ellie had her own mind the moment she was born. She was a stubborn little gal. Still is."

"Do you ever miss those years when the children were little? The birthday parties and Thanksgivings and Christmases? We did have a lot of fun, didn't we?"

"We sure did. All you have to do is open a photo album to remember the good old days."

Charlie fell silent. Esther watched the sun sinking over the lake. Across the road at the Finleys' house, Derek Finley's mother was beginning her daily yoga exercises. The chill evening air had led Miranda to dress in a black leotard and sometimes a sweater. Thank goodness. Esther had gotten a little tired of Charlie gawking at the woman—all the while pretending to be busy sorting beads or reading the newspaper.

Men! The poor creatures. Always driven by their hormones. Fighting wars. Conquering nations. Building great machines. Discovering new lands. So powerful, yet so easily seduced by the flutter of a woman's eyelashes or the coy pout of a pair of lips.

Esther was thankful that she had always been stalwart. People thought of her as flighty, and she did enjoy her own moments of silliness. But life had been a serious business all in all. Despite her occasional doubts about herself, she felt she had done a pretty good job of things. She had been dependable. Stable. Loyal.

Looking at Charlie, she felt a measure of pride. Marriage wasn't an easy undertaking, and they'd worked hard at making theirs successful. Lately, things had gotten a little difficult—as they did now and then. Esther had been finding Charlie annoying. But she had determined to do something about it. She had tackled her own bad attitude and was working hard to focus on the good in the man. There was a lot of good. Charlie had always been such a gentle, placid sort of man. All his life, he had worked hard, treated Esther fairly, and now and then even remembered her with a special gift. Once in a while, Charlie would walk in the door with a bouquet of roses. Or buy Esther a necklace and earrings set.

Yes, she was glad she'd made an effort to focus on Charlie's positive traits again and made sure to tell him often how much she loved him.

As Miranda posed in various awkward positions on the deck, Esther leaned back in her chair and sighed in contentment. Charlie would always be there for her, she knew—even if she didn't do yoga.

"Esther," he said, his attention trained on the dog in his lap, "I want to ask you a question."

She had to smile at how hard he was working not to stare at Miranda. "All right, honeypot, what is it? If you're wondering when I'll take up yoga, the answer is *never*. I don't care if osteo-whatever-it-is makes every bone in my body crumble. I'm not going to do anything as silly as that."

Instead of cracking a grin, as he usually did, Charlie ran his fingers through Boofer's thick, dark fur. "No, Esther. This is serious now."

He looked up at her, and Esther could see the strain on his face.

"What is it, Charlie? You know I've already agreed to get my artery augured out. What else can be troubling you?"

"George Snyder. There, I've said it. If you want to talk about the old days, Esther, let's talk about him. I want to know why George Snyder sketched that picture of you. And more important, I want you to tell me why he wrote on the bottom that he would always love you."

At first, Esther could only sit in stunned silence. Where on earth had that question come from? She had thought they were looking at Miranda Finley, discussing Thanksgiving, relaxing from the day's labors, and watching the sun go down as they reminisced about their children. Now this?

"I told you why he sketched me," she said, her irritation rising in spite of herself. "George is an artist. He draws and paints with water-colors and oils. And he pens ink illustrations. That's what he does."

"What he *does*?" Charlie's eyes narrowed. "Esther, why are you talking about that man as though he still lived in an apartment down the hall from us? We haven't seen George Snyder for nearly fifty years. At least I haven't. Have you?"

"Of course not. He moved to New York." She tried to think of a way to change the subject, but her arm was still bothering her and she couldn't concentrate.

"What did he mean when he wrote that he would always love you?"

"Isn't it obvious? A sentence like that doesn't need translation."

"It does if it's written about another man's wife." By now, Charlie had crossed his arms and was positively glaring at her. "You didn't meet George Snyder until after we were married, Esther. I'd like to know when that man had the time to sketch you."

"Sketching was all he ever did. He didn't have a regular job. You know that. George was taking art lessons. He worked on his paintings and illustrations day and night."

"Did he come over to our apartment other than that one time? Was he with you more often than the evening I found the two of you sitting together on our sofa with him mopping up your tears?"

"Oh, Charlie, what are you getting at? George was my friend. He came occasionally. We visited back and forth."

"Back and forth? You went into his apartment?"

"Well, sure. He always wanted to show me his latest project. He's quite a talented artist, I'll have you know. I could see that from the very start."

"Do you mean to tell me that you and this . . . this . . . man . . ." Charlie's face had turned bright red as he tried to sputter out the words. "That the two of you . . ."

"George Snyder was my best friend back then, Charlie. I won't have you making something ugly out of it! I loved him, and he loved me, too. But not in the way you're thinking. He visited me and brought me little gifts. I admired his work. We enjoyed chatting. That was all there was to it."

"That was not all!" Charlie stood and paced down the porch and then back toward Esther. "He drew you in a way I've never seen you. He made you look . . . different . . . in that sketch. And he wrote that he would always love you. While I was out pounding the streets delivering mail and earning our keep, you and George Snyder were dallying around! Am I wrong?"

Pursing her lips, Esther pushed herself up with her one good arm and headed for the house. "I'm not going to have all the neighbors hearing you yell at me, Charlie Moore. If you want to discuss this, you'd better come inside. And lower your voice while you're at it."

Esther made her way down the hall to their bedroom. She was so tired, even after her nap, and now Charlie was shouting and wagging his finger at her as though she were a misbehaving dog. Oh, this was no way to end a difficult day!

"Did you have a love affair with George Snyder?" Still barking, Charlie stepped into the room and set his hands on his hips as Esther lay down on the bed. "You'd better tell me the truth, woman. I want to know every detail."

Esther crooked her arm over her eyes and let out a breath. She wanted to be angry. But she couldn't even summon the energy for that. It was a terrible thing to grow old and run out of steam. "Open the bottom drawer, Charlie. Take everything out and spread it all here on the bed beside me. You won't be satisfied until you've seen it all."

She could feel tears building as she heard the wooden drawer scraping and felt the weight of the objects—always so private, so dear to her—tossed onto the bedspread. Charlie was muttering, as he usually did.

"There," he said. "Now you'd better start talking, Esther, because I have the sickest feeling in my stomach I've ever had."

"Oh, relax," she told him. "There's not a thing to get worked up about. Open that folder. The one tied with pink ribbon. Those are the sketches and little paintings George gave me. They're worth a small fortune now, by the way."

Her head on the pillow, she watched as Charlie sorted through the sheets of heavy art paper. "There's our apartment building," she told him. "That's the bed of tulips just outside the front door, remember? He used watercolor. George never thought he was good with watercolor, but he was. I kept telling him that until finally he believed it too. There's another sketch of me. And another. George drew whatever was in front of him. He couldn't keep his fingers still. He would draw on a paper napkin if he didn't have his sketch pad."

"He was in love with you." Charlie's voice sounded like it was coming from the bottom of a barrel. "That man was in love with *my* wife."

"Oh, he was not. He never touched me or said anything inappropriate."

"He wrote that he would always love you!"

"And I've always loved him. There's nothing wrong with loving a dear friend, is there? Untie those letters. The bigger pile."

"They're from him."

"Do you think I would have kept this correspondence if George and I had done anything wrong? You can read the letters yourself. You'll see what sort of friends we were. He wrote to me from New York. At first his letters came often. You must have seen them. I don't know why you're getting so worked up."

"He *writes to* you? *Here?*"

At the growl in her husband's voice, Esther suddenly feared Charlie might have a heart attack over this. She pushed herself up and took hold of his arm.

"Don't be ridiculous!" she snapped. "We stopped corresponding ages ago. Stop being so foolish. I've told you over and over that George and I were only friends. Nothing more. He's been working in New York all these years, and I'm sure he's forgotten me by now. He became a famous illustrator, just the way he dreamed. Look at the magazines there by my bed. I've collected nearly everything he's done over the years. I'm proud of George for following his ambition and making a success of himself, and I will not apologize for being the man's friend years ago when we were both young and lonesome. So just calm yourself and get down off your high horse. You're making a big fuss over nothing."

"Nothing?" Charlie buried his face in his hands.

For a moment he didn't speak, and Esther began to worry in earnest. She hadn't expected her husband to remember George Snyder. And she'd convinced herself that even if he found the letters, he wouldn't be upset. They were all so innocent. Just friendly wishes for a happy life. The magazines had meant a lot to her, but she knew someone would toss them out one day. Probably no one would even realize what they had meant to her.

But now Charlie was terribly agitated. He might even be crying. What had she done that was so wrong? Surely he could understand how a woman might want to have keepsakes of a friend.

"Charlie?" She laid her hand on his shoulder. "What's wrong?"

"Secrets." He shook his head and rubbed his fingers over his eyes. "Esther, you kept that man a secret from me all these years. You never told me about your friendship. When we were young, you didn't say a word about him. Through the years, you never mentioned his letters. Our whole marriage—every second of every minute—you've known about him. You've cared about another man, and he's been a part of your life. And you never even told me."

Esther could hear the pain in Charlie's words. She moved her hand down his arm, but he shrugged away from her.

"Keeping a secret is the same as telling a lie," he said through clenched teeth. "Living a lie. You hid this from me because you knew how I would feel. You knew I wouldn't like it, and I don't. It's not right. I should be the only man in your life. I'm the man you married, and I'm all you should ever have needed."

"Well, you weren't," she blurted out, hurt by his unfair accusations. "In the beginning, you were rude and crude and demanding, and it took me years to soften you into a nice person. George was nice from the very start. He knew how to give gifts, and you still can't think of anything better than that old snow globe! When we moved into our first apartment, I was lonely and scared and terribly afraid I'd made a big mistake in marrying you. But George was always there, calming me down and drying my tears. When he went off to New York, I was pregnant, and it just about devastated me to lose his companionship. But then Charles Jr. was born, and life began to have meaning again. Things made sense to me. I understood what my purpose was. I finally knew who I was and what I wanted out of life. And I began to figure out how to truly love you. George and I stayed in touch for a while because we cared about each other. But it wasn't love. Not like us. You and I are husband and wife, Charlie. I've always been faithful to you."

"How can you say you were faithful to me when you had a secret boyfriend? You kept his letters and gifts, and you bought and saved every magazine that ever published his work. That's not commitment. That's adultery!"

"Adultery? It is not!" Esther squared her shoulders in defiance. "I never touched George or kissed him or anything. I didn't commit adultery! How dare you say such a thing? I never got drunk and went into a strip club. You did! You've always kept one eye on pretty girls passing by. You've looked at catalogs with ladies in their underwear. I know you have. And you look at Miranda Finley doing yoga in her bathing suit too! Do you suppose I don't notice those things? Well, I do. You've hurt me plenty of times with your wandering eye, Charlie, and don't think you haven't. I was friends with George Snyder, and so what? It's no more wrong than you going into a strip club."

"I did that once, and I apologized," Charlie shot back at her. "I knew what I did was wrong. I admitted it, and I never did it again. But you've had feelings for that man for nearly fifty years! You never said a word about it. You kept it a little secret. A private thing between the two of you. That's wrong, Esther! Dead wrong!"

She swallowed down her hurt. "But I wasn't in love with George Snyder."

"Then why did you hide him from me?"

"I knew you'd be mad—and you are. You don't understand."

"Tell me this, Esther. Would you like it if I had visited back and forth with a woman every day at work while you were home with the kids? How would you feel if she gave me little presents and wrote me letters? Don't you know how awful you'd think it was if you learned that I'd saved her letters and notes and presents for fifty years?"

Esther hung her head. "I wouldn't like it. But you don't understand how it was with George and me."

"I don't have to understand. It was wrong for you to carry on a friendship with another man! It was wrong for you to have him over to our apartment and for you to go over to his! These letters were wrong!" He scooped up the letters and hurled them against the far wall, scattering them on the floor. "All of it, Esther. All of it was wrong, and you know it or you would have told me!"

At that, he stood, walked over to the stack of magazines, and gave them a kick. As they exploded into the air like a flock of chickens, he stomped out the door and slammed it behind him.

CHAPTER FIFTEEN

Charlie pressed the end of a strip of tape into the gray mudding compound and ran it down the seam between two sheets of drywall. Once he and Brad started this phase of the room addition, the kid had stopped spitting tobacco on the floor. Charlie was grateful. He'd begun to think if he heard another splat, he was going to wrench the kid's head off and drop-kick it into the lake.

"You're going a little crooked there, Mr. Moore," Brad called across the empty space between them. He was mixing fresh drywall mud. "Try to stay straight, because I can't mud over a wrinkle in the tape. It's got to be perfect the first time or it won't look right."

"Yeah, yeah, yeah," Charlie muttered. "The voice of experience. Mr. Perfection himself."

"What's that? Did you say something?"

"Just doing my job here," Charlie said over his shoulder. "You got that compound ready?"

"Coming your way."

Brad carried the heavy bucket toward the ladder on which Charlie was standing. As the younger man set to work on the next seam,

Charlie stepped down and drew in a deep breath. He was dog tired, and there wasn't a thing he could do about it.

Life simply wore him out these days. Especially with Esther acting so snippy and defensive. Since their conflict two days ago, she kept trying to convince Charlie that her friendship with George Snyder had been perfectly innocent.

It was going to be hard to work his way through this one, Charlie had realized. No matter what Esther claimed about the innocence of the relationship, it didn't feel right to Charlie. A man and a woman alone together for hours on end. Talking. Giving each other presents. Him sketching her. Her crying on his shoulder. No, it was wrong no matter which way you turned it.

Last night, Charlie had driven Boofer around the Deepwater Cove neighborhood so many times the golf cart nearly ran out of gas. He kept thinking about Esther's accusations—all the ways he had failed her through the years. Plenty of things came to mind. He'd been far from a saint, and she was right about his wandering eye.

Charlie had always struggled to keep his focus on Esther, especially during the times in their marriage when she had declared herself "not interested" in his affections. "Off-limits" was the way she put it. That didn't happen often, but it was enough to frustrate him plenty. Besides, Esther had never been much of a go-getter in the bedroom. In fact, that part of their marriage had been something of a disappointment. Still, he deeply loved his wife, and he had learned to adjust to their different levels of desire.

Little had he known that George Snyder was always lurking in the background of Esther's mind. Was that what had kept her from wanting Charlie at times? She had insisted that she and George never touched each other. But according to Esther, the artist down the hall certainly knew all the right things to do for a woman. The memory of her smile in the sketch made Charlie's gut ache. She had never looked at him that way. What had George Snyder done to earn Esther's eternal loyalty and unabashed adoration?

"I guess you heard what happened between me and Ashley the other night," Brad commented as he slapped gray mud onto a seam in the drywall. "Seems like everyone is talking about it. I don't even know why I'm working on this stupid room except to be able to sell the house and get my money back out of it."

Charlie tried to focus on the young man. Willing away thoughts of Esther and George Snyder, he lifted the ladder, moved it down to the next joint, and began to unwrap the tape. Charlie had no idea how he could concentrate on anything except his own worries and frustrations, but at the moment, he had no choice.

"I haven't heard anything about the two of you," he told Brad. "I try to keep my nose out of other folks' business. If you want me to know what happened, you'd better just spill the beans."

"I'm not sure I can talk about it without cussing. I'm so mad I could just—"

"Give it a try, boy, because I'm in no mood for your filthy mouth."

Charlie could feel Brad's eyes on him as he climbed the ladder. Placing the end of the tape at the top of the seam near the ceiling, he began pressing it into the damp mud. Truth to tell, Charlie didn't have much heart to serve as a marriage counselor for Brad Hanes this evening. Obviously he hadn't done such a bang-up job as a husband himself.

"It's all about Thanksgiving," Brad said. "Her mother expects us to go to their house, and I told Ashley I'm not eating a turkey cooked by that obnoxious mother of hers. After working in the family snack shop for so many years, the woman can't cook anything but chili dogs and onion rings. I told Ashley I figured we'd go over to my mom's place but—right on cue—she burst into tears at that. Boo hoo hoo. 'You don't like my family,' she says. 'You hate my mother. You don't respect my father.' Blah, blah, blah. On and on until I couldn't stand to hear another word."

Charlie paused with the tape and reflected on the battles he and

Esther had initially fought over Thanksgiving, Christmas, and the other traditional holidays. Those times had been nightmares for sure, especially after the babies were born. Both their families got involved, each putting on the pressure, until it began to feel like World War III. Come to think of it, that was one reason Charlie had pressed for the move to Washington DC and the postal inspector position. Anything to get away from their parents.

"So I go outside and I'm getting into the car," Brad was saying, "and here she comes, running after me, tears streaming, sobbing so loud the whole neighborhood can hear. She starts pounding on the window until finally I roll it down. That's when she grabs my shirt and tells me if I ever go to Larry's again, she'll divorce me. She says I'm a drunk. Hah. She doesn't have any idea what she's talking about. You want to know what a real drunk looks like? You should've seen my dad. Now there was a fall-down-and-puke-on-the-lawn alcoholic. He couldn't hold a job. He treated my mom like dirt. He smacked us kids around. He used to—"

Brad cut himself off and spat on the floor. For once, Charlie couldn't blame him.

"Anyhow," the young man continued, "I'm not a drunk. Ashley has no right to keep me from Larry's if I want to go. It's my bar, and it's where my friends hang out. People there treat me right, especially the women. I told Ashley that too. I said if she didn't watch her mouth, I'd find someone to take her place. And I would, too, Mr. Moore. Don't think I wouldn't."

"You really believe you could find a woman better than Ashley?"

"You bet I could! Ashley's nuts. Crying all the time. Blaming me for everything. She says I don't do nice stuff for her. Well, I bring home a paycheck, don't I? You'd think she might be a little grateful for that. No, she just whines at me. 'You used to take me to the movies, Brad. You used to buy me flowers. You used to dress up when we went out to eat. You were always so sweet. You always listened to me.' Yakety yak."

With his trowel, Brad dug a mound of mud from the pail and hurled it at the wall. The mud hit the seam dead-on, and the kid gave a victory whoop. "I used to play first base, Mr. Moore. Did you know that? And I was quarterback, too. There was nothing I couldn't do back in high school. I was *it*. I was *something*. Ashley couldn't get enough of me. Now, nine times out of ten she pushes me away. Says I'm mean. I'm too rough. I'm not gentle enough."

Brad scraped the drywall mud as he spoke. "I told her, 'I'm an athlete, you lamebrain. You expected me to turn into a ballroom dancer or a piano player once we got married?' These hands are callused because I use 'em all day long. I work hard. Ashley says what's the point in working so hard if I'm just going to drink up half my paycheck? But that's a lie. At least I'm not buying beads and string and junk like that. I don't know, Mr. Moore. If you ask me, it's hopeless. After that fight the other night, I'm figuring I'll get this room finished and put the house up for sale. Ashley's already talking about moving back to her parents' place. That's fine with me. She can sling hamburgers and make necklaces until her dying day. I'm going to have a *life*."

Stepping down from the ladder, Charlie ran the rest of the tape along the damp seam to the floor. He and Brad were almost finished with the mudding and taping, and it wouldn't be long before they could paint. The room was really beginning to take shape, and Charlie had come to appreciate Brad's workmanship and enjoy the camaraderie between himself and the younger man.

But this evening, Charlie could hardly even think what to say in response to the sudden flood of anger and resentment Brad had expressed about his marriage. How could Charlie blithely encourage another couple's relationship when his own suddenly seemed to be hovering on the edge of a steep cliff?

"You're never going to find a better woman than Ashley," he said finally. "I can promise you that. You might find a different gal, sure, but she'll come with her own set of irritations. You can count on it."

"Not those women at the bar. They're fine—"

"Good gravy, kid, you're not serious about taking up with a barfly, are you?" Charlie's ire rose as he spoke. "You want to marry some dame that can't think of any better way to spend her time than drinking and flirting with married men? You're upset because Ashley expects you to soften up and treat her nice. Wait till you hook up with a gal whose pastime is drinking beer and dancing the two-step. You'll come home wanting dinner, and she'll be over at Larry's with some other man."

Charlie shook his head as he continued. "You said you want to have a life, Brad? Well, you've got one. So what do you want out of it? You want to be sixty years old and still drinking at Larry's? Married to some toothless hag who's trying to look twenty-five? Or have three or four divorces under your belt? That's the direction you're headed, buster."

The two men stared at each other across the darkening room. Brad tossed his trowel to the floor.

Charlie dropped the roll of tape into the toolbox. He let out a hot breath and pointed his finger at the younger man. "If you let Ashley get away, you're dumber than I thought. Where to spend Thanksgiving isn't important. Drinking at Larry's bar isn't important. Ashley's beads don't really matter, and neither do your hard-working hands. What matters is that you kids found each other, loved each other, and made a vow to keep on loving each other no matter what. Now get yourself over to the country club and apologize to Ashley for being such a dad-blamed fool."

"A fool?" Brad's chest swelled.

"Yes, a fool, and don't argue with me. You called Ashley a lame-brain? You're a total numskull when it comes to women. You're even dumber than most men. So stop strutting around like you have the world on a string just because the floozies at some bar give you the eye. Any man can walk into a tavern and land himself a one-night stand. But you've married yourself a sweet little lady who used to think you hung the moon. You really want to be a man? Pull yourself together and hang that moon back in the sky for your wife."

Without waiting for a response, Charlie stormed through the door and out toward his golf cart. Ridiculous kid. Life was too short to have to listen to the kind of nonsense that Brad Hanes could spout. And he complained about Ashley being a talker? Brad jabbered like a blue jay. His head was so swollen that his brain had just about quit working.

"'I used to play first base,'" Charlie mumbled as he drove along the road toward his house. He could imitate Brad's bragging voice to a tee. "'I was the high school quarterback. I bring home a paycheck. I work hard. All the women at Larry's treat me right.'"

"What are you muttering about now, Charles Moore?"

Charlie looked up to find Esther walking toward him, sweater around her shoulders and purse hanging on her arm. In the waning sunlight, her silhouette looked small and fragile. She was limping a little, as if the arthritis in her knees was bothering her again. White hair aglow, she paused and smiled at him.

"I thought I'd come get you," she said. "Dinner's in the oven."

Disconcerted, Charlie stopped the golf cart and reached toward her. "You shouldn't have left the house at this hour, Esther. It's almost dark. You could have fallen."

"I wanted to bring you something." Her breath shuddered as she took his arm. "Drive me down to the lake, Charlie. Will you?"

"We'll need a flashlight in a few minutes. Where's Boofer?"

"I left him at home. This is just between you and me." She leaned against him as they rode to the commons area and then stepped out onto the crisp, brown, wintry grass. Her voice sounded small in the growing darkness. "How was work? Have you finished the drywall?"

"Nearly," Charlie said. "That Brad Hanes is as dumb as a box of rocks. No wonder Ashley's frustrated. I don't know how much more of him I can take."

"Ashley said Brad graduated near the top of his class," Esther protested. "Oh, are you talking about the fight they had the other night? Did Brad tell you about their argument over where to eat Thanksgiving dinner?"

Charlie had to chuckle. "Is there any neighborhood gossip you don't know, Mrs. Moore?"

"Not a drop."

"I guess Ashley must have confided in you," he said. "Did you give her some good advice?"

"Yes. I told her they should do what we did. Simple as that."

Consternation furrowed Charlie's brow. "What did we do?"

"We had all the holiday meals at *our* house, silly! Don't you remember? We decided that if our parents wanted to celebrate with us and spend time with Charles Jr. and Ellie, they had to come to our home—not the other way around. It was the perfect solution. No arguing, no fighting, no problems. When I told Ashley about it, she was so relieved she burst into tears."

"I understand she does that a lot."

"What woman doesn't? I don't know a female worth her salt who won't break down and sob now and then. Surely you and Brad have figured that out by now."

"Maybe we both fell off the turnip truck yesterday."

"Not you, Charlie. You're very wise. Much smarter than I am."

He could hear Esther swallowing again and again while they strolled down the length of the dock. She sniffled as she clung to his arm on the swaying wood plank flooring. Was she trying not to cry?

Charlie began to worry. What was this trek to the lake all about? Did Esther have a big announcement to make? Maybe after almost fifty years of marriage to a dull man who didn't know how to give a present better than a gas station snow globe, Esther had decided to run off with her artist friend.

The thought of losing his wife made Charlie nauseous. No matter how upset he'd been with Esther, he didn't want to lose her. Not to another man. Not for any reason.

As they arrived at the end of the dock, he sat down on his favorite fishing bench. "What's going on, Esther? What are we doing down here?"

Instead of answering, she opened her purse and lifted out one of the glass pickle jars she always saved. Charlie could see some sort of gray substance inside—maybe pepper—filling it halfway to the top.

Holding the jar up in the last rays of golden-orange sunlight, Esther turned it one way and then another. "Ashes," she announced finally. "Cody helped me. I explained to him that there are some things in life that you wish you could do all over again. People make mistakes, I told him. By the time we're old, sometimes we have regrets, and the best thing to do—if we can—is to set everything right again. Cody seemed to understand. So he found the chain to open the damper in the fireplace, and then he helped me put everything into a big pile on the grate. We stacked all of it—the magazines, the sketches, the letters. I struck the match, and Cody and I sang a hymn as the fire took hold and burned it up. You know what we sang? 'Just As I Am.' Like Patsy's store. Cody had reminded me that everyone has a black blot. Evidently Pete Roberts was talking about his blot the other day. Cody said that Pete actually cried a little bit, so it was okay for me to cry too. I was crying more than a bit because I felt so awful, and Cody put his arm around me and patted me on the back. Wasn't that sweet? He's such a dear boy."

Charlie had held his breath most of the way through the speech. Now he let it out in a rush as he spoke his wife's name. "Esther . . ."

"It took me a while to admit you were right," she went on, unscrewing the lid of the pickle jar as she talked. "I didn't want to let go of my memory and all the little things that had once been important to me. Oh, I had given myself all kinds of excuses to hang on to that stuff. *He was just a friend. Charlie wouldn't mind.* I suppose I even blamed it on you—I told myself that if you'd been more attentive in those early days, I would never even have noticed George. And besides, the artwork is valuable now."

She shook her head. "But you *did* mind, and in my heart I knew you would—otherwise I wouldn't have kept it hidden." She paused, and again it sounded as if she was swallowing and sniffling. "Charlie, what you said the other day . . . it was absolutely true. A married woman should not have *any* kind of friendship with another man. There, I've said it. No matter how innocent it seems, it's just plain wrong. I saw the hurt in your eyes the moment you first spoke his name." She sighed. Her voice grew small again. "I never meant to hurt you, honey. But I did. And now I realize what a dark blot my actions cast on our marriage. It wasn't your fault; it was mine. I'm so sorry, Charlie."

Before Charlie could respond, Esther knelt on the dock and dumped the contents of the pickle jar into the lake. The ashes swirled for a moment, spreading over the surface of the water. And then they vanished. She rinsed out the jar, put the lid back on, tucked it into her purse, and sighed again. "All these years, I've thought if we just put the past behind us and kept looking forward, we'd be fine. I'm sorry it took me so long to see the problems with that. I hope and pray you'll forgive me and believe how very much I love you. I always have loved you, and I always will. Shall we go home to dinner now? Cody and I just put a meat loaf in the oven."

As Esther moved to leave, Charlie caught her arm. "Sit down with me here a minute longer," he said, patting the old bench. "I want to make sure I understand this."

"I've told you everything." She seated herself beside him. "I'm so silly, you know. Oh, you won't believe what I did today. Remember our plan? After my set-and-style, Patsy was going to take me over to the grocery store for a few minutes to pick up some things for our Thanksgiving dinner next week. Well, she did, so I was pushing my cart down the aisle and studying all the different kinds of cranberry sauce. I chose one, put it into the cart, and kept on going. Suddenly, a lady started calling out to me, 'Hey, hey! That's my cart!'"

Esther laughed. "Can you believe it? I had put my cranberry sauce into someone else's cart and gone off with it. She and Patsy helped me track down my own cart, which was back at the tuna fish. Oh, what a day! But my hair looks pretty, don't you think? Patsy always does such a nice job on my set-and-style."

Charlie took Esther's hand and wove his fingers through hers. As always, his wife bounded from one topic to another until he could hardly keep track. But that was one of the things he had always loved about her. Chasing Esther's conversations kept things lively. Sometimes she went so far afield that neither one could remember what they'd been talking about to begin with. Usually they ended up laughing. But not tonight.

"Let me make sure I comprehend what you've told me," Charlie said. "Are you saying that you and Cody burned up everything I took out of that bottom drawer?"

"Not everything. I had saved cards the children gave me and sweet notes you left me on the toaster before you went off to work and little bookmarks from my mother's Bible. I didn't burn those. But all the rest of it is gone. The old magazines, too. Poof. Just like that. It didn't take but a minute or two to turn everything to cinders."

"You burned that sketch?"

"It was the first thing to go. It finally dawned on me how foolish it was to want to hang on to anything that might harm our marriage. It's all gone in a flash of flames. I didn't even want the ashes in our house. Cody helped me sweep them up and put them into a jar. And now they're all at the bottom of the lake with the muck—exactly where they belong."

She leaned against Charlie. "I hope you feel better, honey. I sure do."

"Does this mean you agree with everything I said the other day?"

"Yes, I do."

Charlie's heart was beating harder than he could ever remember.

"Esther, did you tell me the truth when you said you and . . . George
. . . never touched each other?"

"No more than a handshake."

"But did you love him? In your heart, did you ever care for him
more than you did me?"

She pondered a moment. "I wish I could say I didn't. But that
first year of marriage, I was so young and scared and frustrated. You
were gone, and he was there. Once in a while, I would get it into my
mind that an artist was somehow better than a mailman. How silly.
It's not what a man does that matters. It's who he is. And once you're
married, that's not even the most important thing."

"What is the most important thing, Esther?"

"Well, the vows, of course. On our wedding day, I promised to
love and honor you. No matter what. I shouldn't have nourished
and dreamed about a friendship that filled the holes in my heart.
That was wrong."

"Do you still have holes in your heart, Esther?"

"Sometimes I feel a little ache when you and I don't see eye to eye,
or when you start acting bullheaded and deaf to what I'm trying to
tell you. But you've learned a lot. Once I gave you the chance, you
figured out how to meet my needs pretty well. Well enough that I
wouldn't ever want to lose you."

Charlie had to think about this. It bothered him that he hadn't
been able to make Esther completely happy. But then, she never had
been the ideal wife either. They both had flaws; they did little things
that annoyed one another; they made mistakes. Charlie knew Esther
hadn't filled his every desire and dream—in the bedroom, with the
children, even in the kitchen, though he'd never admit to that last
one. Evidently he hadn't been all he should have for her, either. Was
that so bad? Was it enough to give up on a marriage?

For nearly fifty years, it hadn't been bad enough to ruin them. And
it wasn't bad enough now.

"I'm sorry too," Charlie said, putting his arm around Esther and drawing her close. "Brad Hanes is so ignorant about how to treat his wife . . . but I bet I was nearly as ignorant myself."

"It took me a while to train you."

"I wish I hadn't needed training."

"Well, you did. Anyone foolish enough to get drunk and go into a strip club needed a lot of work. But then, I had plenty to learn too. By having a male friend outside our marriage, I put everything that was happening between you and me on hold. All the things we needed to work out, everything we had to learn—it all stopped in its tracks. We could have fallen apart at the seams, Charlie. And then we would have missed such a wonderful life."

"Do you really mean that, Esther? Has our marriage been good? Are you satisfied?"

"Satisfied?" she asked. Leaning forward, she kissed his cheek. "Utterly."

Charlie chuckled. "Good, then let's go start on that meat loaf."

"Meat loaf?" Esther stood. "Did I say meat loaf? Oh, what was I thinking? I knew I put something with ground beef into the oven. I meant lasagna. Cody and I made lasagna. You should have seen the boy trying to hold on to those noodles, Charlie. Oh, it was the funniest thing in the world!"

CHAPTER SIXTEEN

Hurry up, Charlie!" Esther called to her husband from the master bathroom that Saturday. "We're going to be late to the Thanksgiving weenie roast. I don't care how goofy I feel today; I'm going on that hayride. If you fiddle around and make us miss it, I'll be hopping mad, and don't you doubt that for a minute!"

Esther pressed the button on her hair spray and gave her curls another shot of mist. God had provided Deepwater Cove with the most beautiful sunny and bright autumn afternoon imaginable, but Esther knew that even the slightest whiff of humidity could make her hair collapse like a soufflé. She was wearing her favorite fall outfit: a lovely violet sweater set with embroidered leaves and tiny purple seed pearls made into bunches of grapes. The matching slacks with their elastic waist would provide comfort and warmth for the evening to come.

A hayride. Apple bobbing. A bonfire. A weenie roast. Lots of friends and plenty of fun topics to discuss. She could hardly wait.

Thank goodness she hadn't forgotten about the event, Esther thought as she opened her cosmetics drawer. Missing Halloween had bothered her, even though everyone insisted that few children had come through the neighborhood. No matter what people said about the dark aspects of the holiday, Esther viewed Halloween as a time to enjoy giving little gifts. Nothing pleased her more than the shine in a child's eyes when she handed out one of her net bags filled with treats.

"Are you ready, Charlie?"

He was in the bedroom getting dressed, Esther knew, and she still had to apply her lipstick and a little mascara. For some reason, throughout their marriage, her husband had always dawdled. One might suppose a mail carrier would be prompt and efficient. But not Charlie. He would search for a jacket or a pair of shoes until Esther nearly went out of her mind.

"Wear your green jacket," she called. "The corduroy one. It'll look nice with my grape leaves."

Esther had forced herself not to think about the surgery scheduled for the day after Thanksgiving. In a sense, God had given her a great gift by putting the procedure right behind a holiday. This way she had so much on her mind that she couldn't dwell on the horrible image of that probe sliding through her artery.

It wasn't fair that she should be the one to have plaque. In his mail-man days, Charlie had eaten enough doughnuts to encircle the earth. What could be worse for arteries than doughnuts? But no, Esther had to be the one with clogged-up blood vessels. Charlie would have handled this problem so much better than she. He was a strong man. Valiant, even. He would brave a balloon and a stent without blinking an eye. Dear, sweet Charlie.

Esther was so glad she had burned all those magazines and letters from George Snyder. Why hadn't she done it years ago? How could she have been so weak as to fall into a friendship with another man, innocent as it was? Thank goodness it was behind them now. Ever since she had dumped the ashes into the lake, Charlie had been his usual kind and gentle self. It felt as though a high wall between them had tumbled to the ground.

"Did you find that jacket?" Esther asked as she stepped out of the bathroom. "It's hanging in the hall closet beside the—"

The sight of the crowd standing in the bedroom nearly buckled Esther's knees right out from under her. With a gasp, she caught the edge of the dresser for support. Brenda Hansen, Kim Finley, Ashley Hanes, Patsy Pringle, and Bitty Sondheim surrounded Charlie.

Wearing a big grin on his face, he stepped toward Esther. "Madam," he said. "Your gown."

Across his arms lay a pouf of orchid-colored netting and silk, velvet ribbons, and delicate lace.

"My prom dress!" she exclaimed. "I thought it was in the attic. What on earth?"

"We're having a Thanksgiving parade," Kim told her. "And we've elected you and Charlie as queen and king for the day."

"Queen?" Esther laid her hand at her throat. "Me? I'm the queen of the parade?"

"Yes, you are. And now, Your Majesty, if His Royal Highness will kindly step outside for a moment, your handmaidens will prepare you for your carriage ride."

"Oh my!" Esther could hardly believe it. The women shooed Charlie out the door, and then they began to lay out the old gown. It had been in the attic for years, and Esther was sure it must be full of holes.

"Brenda repaired it," Patsy said. "I swear that girl can sew anything. Look at this tiara Ashley made for you. Here, let me fix your hair so everything will look right. Kim, would you open my bag and start heating the curling iron?"

"Oh my!" Esther said again. Before she knew it, Kim and Ashley began helping her out of the sweater set. Patsy lowered Esther to the bed and started tucking the tiara—a soaring creation in crystal beads of every hue—into the older woman's curls.

Brenda gave the gown a shake to set the ruffles and netting in place. Then she and the others carefully eased Esther into the fragile garment.

"It still fits!" Esther exclaimed.

That might have been a bit of wishful thinking, Esther admitted to herself, but she didn't care. So what if her curves had drooped and spread in various directions. Brenda managed to zip up the gown, Patsy added a few tissues to fill out the bodice, and Bitty unfolded one of her own large shawls. For once, Esther couldn't find fault with Bitty's choice of accessory. The length of light purple wool would go perfectly with the gown, and it would keep the queen of the parade warm in the evening chill.

"Come on, everyone!" Ashley said. "We've got to hurry before the sun goes down."

Ashley fastened a three-strand necklace of pink pearls around Esther's throat while Kim helped her into the white gloves saved from the Moores' wedding. It was almost too much to bear, this amazing bustle of lovely women—dearest friends and beloved companions. Esther knew she shouldn't cry, because Patsy had been dabbing all sorts of cosmetics on her face while the others arranged ruffles and netting. But how could she hold in the tears of joy? All her life, Esther had loved parades. She had gazed at homecoming queens and Dogwood Festival queens and Country Days queens with admiration and even a touch of envy. But never had she permitted herself to dream of being a parade queen herself.

"Here we go!" Patsy sang out, taking Esther's arm. "Right this way, Your Majesty."

Giggling and crying all at the same time, Esther hurried down the hall and out the front door. And there stood Charlie. Oh, so handsome in his gray deacon suit, white shirt, and a new tie.

"A purple tie?" she cried as he bowed before her. "Where did you get that?"

"Lady Brenda Hansen sewed it for me." Charlie was smiling as though he really did have a lovely queen on his arm. He led her down the sidewalk to the carport, and there—lo and behold—sat the old golf cart covered with purple chrysanthemums, billowing ribbons, flags, streamers, and strings of beads.

"It's beautiful! Just beautiful," Esther gushed. "Charlie, did you know? Did you keep this secret from me?"

"Some secrets are meant to be kept," he murmured, giving her a wink. "For a little while anyway."

As the crowd gathered around them, Charlie helped Esther into the passenger side of the cart. The seat had been covered with a length of purple velvet edged in gold fringe, and all the women bent to help tuck the gown's billowing skirt into place. Charlie settled in behind the steering wheel and gave the horn a little toot-toot.

At that, he pushed on the gas pedal and off they went, with everyone following behind. Luke and Lydia had decorated their bicycles. Someone was pushing a baby carriage. Two other golf carts pulled in behind the Moores'.

And that's when Brad Hanes stepped to the very front of the parade, a large boom box in his hands. He raised it over his head as music began to play.

Esther felt it was almost too beautiful to bear. "Charlie, it's a miracle!" she exclaimed. "A miracle I never expected in my whole life."

He laughed. "Who ever expects miracles? That's what makes them so special. Like the day I saw your smile for the very first time. I could not believe God had actually created such a beautiful, perfect woman. But there you were right in front of me."

"Perfect? That's so silly."

"But true. I was thunderstruck. And when you spoke to me and said you'd go to the diner with me and then to a picture show . . . well, it was all a miracle."

Esther giggled as she waved at the few neighbors who weren't already in the parade. "I'm the Thanksgiving Queen!" she called to Opal Jones, who was sitting on her front porch. "Charlie's the king, and I'm the queen!"

Opal probably didn't have her hearing aids in, Esther realized, but it didn't matter. Anyone with two eyes could see the glittering golf cart and the handsome couple seated inside it. Esther had the sensation that she was floating along on a lavender cloud as the breeze lifted and played with her skirt. What a lovely evening. What wonderful neighbors. What a delightful place to live. And what a perfect man to be her gallant king.

As the golf cart neared the commons, the youngsters on bicycles veered away from the parade and headed toward a huge pile of driftwood that had been stacked up near the lakeshore. Esther watched as Brenda and Steve hurried hand in hand to set up tables. Patsy started toward the picnic area, and Pete Roberts quickly took off behind her, trying to catch up as she went about organizing the festivities. Kim and Miranda Finley were chatting amiably when they turned toward the commons to keep an eye on the twins. And then Ashley skipped up to where Brad was just turning off the CD player.

"Look," Esther murmured, elbowing Charlie. "They seem happy this afternoon, don't they?"

"Happy enough," he said. "But not nearly as happy as we are."

"Hey, Mr. Moore!" Cody cried, nearly deafening Esther as he stuck his head under the golf cart's canopy and leaned across to shout at Charlie. "Let's go around again. I'll play the music this time."

"Sure!" Charlie and Esther said in unison.

Esther watched as Cody took the CD player from Brad, held it over his head, and once more set off along the road that circled the neighborhood. Charlie pressed on the gas pedal and they started off, a parade of three.

"And how are you on this fine evening, my queen?" he asked as he slipped his arm around Esther's shoulders.

She snuggled against him. "I don't believe I've ever been happier."

Cody led the Thanksgiving King and Queen around Deepwater Cove six more times, giving them plenty of opportunity to admire the sunset, watch the bonfire go up in a burst of flames and sparks, gaze at the yellow moon rising over barren tree branches, and marvel as the stars came out across a velvet sky. They heard the same songs over and over—"As Time Goes By" . . . "When You Wish Upon A Star" . . . "The Look of Love" . . . "Moon River"—but Esther didn't mind. She loved every single one. Even better, she loved the man beside her. When his kiss brushed her cheek, a flood of warmth burst open inside her heart.

"I love you, my dearest Charlie," she said. "I love you so much."

"You're the queen of my heart." He pressed his lips to her gloved hand. "Always have been. Always will be."

"Hey, guess what!" Cody's face appeared again under the golf cart canopy. "It's weenie time, Mr. and Mrs. Moore! I love hot dogs. Let's get 'em!"

"You go ahead," Charlie told the young man. "We'll be there in a minute."

"I'll save you some. How many do you want? Five? Or eight?"

"Three ought to do us."

"Okay!"

The cart slowed to a stop as Cody hightailed it toward the pile of embers around which the Deepwater Cove neighbors stood in silhouette.

"Come here, you sweet little thing," Charlie said against Esther's ear. "A real king needs a real kiss."

Esther wrapped her arms around her husband, happy to oblige.

❦

Pete had decided a long time ago that sitting on the ground was for the birds. And as Cody would confirm, this was a good metaphor.

In the light of the dying bonfire, Pete could see he had no other seating option but the cold, hard earth. The picnic benches in the commons area were filled with people chatting, laughing, and eating hot dogs. But Pete could not count himself among the contented. His belt buckle was digging into his midsection. His legs were starting to prickle and fall asleep. Even his hands, on which he had propped himself in a half-reclining position, were going numb.

"Isn't this beautiful?" Patsy sighed. "I can't imagine feeling more thankful than I do right now."

Pete would be a lot more thankful if he had a lawn chair under his backside, but then he wouldn't be able to sit so close to the woman he loved. He had doubted many things in his life. His father. His mother. Marriage. The detox center. Most of all, Pete had doubted himself.

But he had no doubts about his love for Patsy Pringle.

She was the second-best thing to ever happen to Pete. Her smile lit up his heart. The sound of her voice made his head spin. Just touching her arm gave him goose bumps down to the tips of his toes. But Patsy was much more than a gorgeous woman. She was kind, generous, fun, opinionated, stubborn, smart, loyal, and most of all, pure. She was love in human form.

Pete had been through enough living that he knew how to be realistic. Patsy wasn't perfect and neither was he. He was, in fact, flawed up one side and down the other. But what he saw in Patsy was right and good and plumb near perfect. She was the woman he wanted. The woman he needed. Most of all, the woman he deeply loved.

"Are you thinking about that leaf-blower engine again?" Patsy asked, leaning against his shoulder. "Because if you are, then you're missing the prettiest sight on earth. Look at all the people out here. These are our friends and neighbors, Pete. Aren't we blessed? We have full stomachs, good businesses, and more of life than we could ever deserve. All that and a night like this. Do you see it?"

"I'm looking at the prettiest sight on earth right now," Pete said. "She's sitting beside me, and you can bet I'm not thinking about that busted leaf blower."

Patsy glanced at him, her lips forming a little smile. "You are such a tease."

"I'm not kidding, gal. Hey, Patsy, do you want to go for a walk?"

Pete had realized the entire lower half of his body was at risk of atrophy for lack of blood circulation. And besides, he wanted to spend a little time alone with Patsy. "We could stroll along the shore. The moon is bright enough to see our way."

"No thanks," she said. "I'm enjoying the smell of the bonfire. You know, when I was a little girl, we had a woodstove in our house. My daddy would let me help him build the fire. It was so cozy in the kitchen—and on really cold nights, we all slept around the stove. It's hard to imagine we lived like that just twenty, thirty years ago, but we didn't think a thing about it. In the early days, we even had an outhouse. But then we got a septic tank and plumbing and all that. Sometimes I wonder if the old house is still standing. After Daddy died and my mother got so sick with Alzheimer's, I had to sell the place and move to town. Every now and then, I get a whiff of woodsmoke, and it's like my whole childhood comes right back to me in an instant."

Pete was trying to think of a good response, but first he had to rearrange himself. He stretched out his legs, rolled over on one hip, and propped his head on his hand. That wasn't much better, but at least the blood started flowing again.

"Did you have a happy childhood, Pete?" Patsy asked.

"It was all right. I don't remember much of it, to tell you the truth. I recall I got into trouble a lot. I didn't do too great in school either. I guess my childhood was about average, and so was I."

"Sounds right for a kid from Halfway, Missouri."

He laughed. "*Halfway. Average.* I guess I'm not real impressive. About as good-looking as a tree stump. Not real smart. I don't have much to brag about, do I?"

"You can repair any engine that comes into your store," Patsy said. "You built the planter boxes outside our shops in Tranquility. You kept them weeded and filled with pretty flowers this spring and summer. Besides that, I hear your house is as neat as a pin, you can cook like a chef, and your yard is as green and tidy as a golf course."

"Where'd you hear that?"

"You told me."

Pete shook his head and chuckled. "I probably did."

She pushed her hair off her shoulders, looked up at the sky, and let out a deep sigh. "I could sit out here all night. The memory of Esther's smile when she saw her old prom dress will stay with me for the rest of my life. I'll never forget the sound of those songs on Brad's CD player as we marched around Deepwater Cove. And Cody's excitement over the weenie roast—that was a sight to see, wasn't it?"

At the vision of the woman looking so beautiful and serene, Pete couldn't stand it a moment longer. "Patsy, listen. I really do want you and me to take a walk. How about it?"

"No, Pete. I'm not going to stroll off into the darkness with you. I won't have anyone starting rumors about us."

Pete knew there were already rumors aplenty, but this wasn't the time to remind Patsy of that. He had a more important mission. Not only did he need to get up off the cold ground, but he had something important to say to Patsy. It wasn't going to be easy, and he had been sweating it for several days. But now, on this crisp autumn night when she was in such a happy mood, he was going to have to spit it out. Or else he never would.

He didn't have the patience to try to convince her to go for a walk, so he would just have to tell her right in the midst of their neighbors. Someone might overhear him, but he would risk it. Sitting up cross-legged again, Pete raked his fingers back through his hair. Then he scratched his chin a little, missing his beard but knowing it was gone for good. Finally, he flopped down on his back, rested his head on his hands, shut his eyes, and spoke the words.

"Patsy, I've got something to say to you. Something personal. Okay?"

She didn't say a word. Pete opened one eye. He could see her blonde curls highlighted in the golden embers of the bonfire. He opened the other eye.

"Is that all right?" he asked.

"I guess so," she breathed out. "But I'm not sure you should say anything. You know what happened the last time we tried to have a deep discussion."

"Well, tough beans. This is something that has to be said, and I need you to hear it."

"All right. Go ahead."

Pete studied the moon for a moment. Then he let it all out. "I'm going to get baptized two weeks from Sunday, and I don't want you to think it's because I love you, even though I do. It's because I went to Pastor Andrew, and we talked out the entire situation. First I told him about fishers of men and heaven's pond, and he said yes, my ideas were pretty much right. Then he explained what the word *surrender* means—which is something I was never any good at, being as bull-headed as I am. But I've known for years that I never was successful at running my own life, so why keep trying and failing? Right there in Pastor Andrew's office, I was about to surrender when I remembered my dark blot. Actually, all my many dark blots. That's when he told me about repenting—which is saying sorry and turning away from doing wrong. Until that moment, I had never believed apologizing was going to be good enough—not for God, anyhow. You were telling me about your happy childhood around the woodstove?"

"Yes," Patsy said. Her voice sounded small in the darkness.

"One thing I do remember about being a kid is that saying sorry was never good enough. If I did something I shouldn't, I could apologize until the cows came home, but I was going to get a whipping anyhow. After a while, I gave up on repenting because it never was any use. But Pastor Andrew said God accepts our apology as long as we really mean it. I assured him I did mean it, but I couldn't guarantee to be perfect for the rest of my life. Pastor Andrew told me that was okay. The main thing is to believe, repent, surrender, and submit to God's leading through the Holy Spirit."

"Did he tell you how to know what God is leading you to do?" Patsy asked. "I have a lot of trouble with that."

"You do?" It had never occurred to Pete that Patsy might have problems in any area of religion. She seemed to understand it all and be so good at living the way the Bible said people should live.

"I can't always tell who's pushing on me," she continued. "Sometimes I think it's God, but sometimes I think it might just be my own desires urging me to do what I want. And once in a while, I'm pretty sure it's Satan—all gussied up in a wrapping of what looks like truth—trying to mislead me with a bunch of his lies. It's hard, Pete. It's very hard to know."

For the first time in his life, Pete felt confident he could help a person with something other than repairing an engine or choosing the right bait.

"If you're not sure about something," he informed her, "you put it to the test. Pastor Andrew gave me the rules. You ask yourself questions. Does this thing go against any teaching in the Bible? Do my Christian friends approve? What does God say to me about it when I pray? And how does my conscience feel with it? If you get the green light on all that, then you can be confident God is guiding you."

Patsy sat in silence for so long that Pete wondered if he might have said something wrong. It was entirely possible. In his mind, he had gone over and over his conversation with Pastor Andrew. Pete felt sure he had believed, repented, and surrendered and that he was ready to let the Holy Spirit guide him. He had confessed that he didn't know all there was to know about matters of faith, but Pastor Andrew had assured him that no one did. Finally, he and the minister had agreed that Pete was born again, a full-fledged Christian, swimming in heaven's pond, and ready to be baptized.

But maybe Pete had said something wrong. Patsy sure did look upset. In fact, if he wasn't mistaken, she seemed to be wiping at her eyes. His legs weren't numb from lack of blood, but half of his body felt nearly frozen on the icy ground. If he had goofed by telling Patsy about the conversation with Pastor Andrew, then he would have to make it up to her later. He sure couldn't stay out here in the cold much longer.

"Patsy?" He reached for her hand. "Patsy, you okay?"

"Yes." She tucked her legs up under her chin, put her arms around her knees, and buried her face.

When she spoke again, Pete couldn't make out anything but a mumble. A mumble or a sob. He wasn't sure which. Neither was good. No doubt he had offended her in some way. He was chilled to the bone, and now he felt foolish trying to explain how he had gotten born again in Pastor Andrew's study.

He never should have said a word. In a couple of Sundays, he could have just shown up at church to get baptized and surprised the socks off Patsy. That would have been a lot better than fumbling around and telling her about the whippings he had gotten as a boy and all that.

"Okay." Patsy lifted her head. "Okay, Pete, I love you, too."

"What?"

"I said I love you, Pete. And not because of your talk with Pastor Andrew. Well, that might be part of why I love you. I love that you care about your soul. That you want to change. That you've tried to understand. I do love that, and I'm glad you're going to be baptized. But mostly I love you because it's all right. I see now that God has been trying to tell me it's okay to feel the way I do."

Pete couldn't move. He wasn't sure if it was because he had actually frozen to the ground like a discarded Popsicle or if it was because of what Patsy was telling him.

"You see, I wasn't sure until tonight," she said. "I couldn't tell where all these feelings and emotions were coming from. I didn't know whether my love for you was part of God's plan or if it was my own selfish desire. I even wondered if it might be Satan's way of tempting me into doing something wrong. But when you explained how to know God's will—by searching the Bible, talking to friends, praying, and examining my conscience—I realized that loving you is all right. It's all right, and I can say it, Pete. I love you. I do. I love you so much."

For a man whose full six feet four inches of height was mostly numb, iced over, and cramped, Pete had a sudden burst of energy as white-hot as a flash of lightning on a summer night. He bolted up from the ground, caught Patsy in his arms, and kissed her dead center on the lips. She laughed and buried her head in his shoulder.

Then she kissed his neck so softly he thought he would melt. He threaded his fingers through her hair, enjoying the touch of her soft curls.

And that's when Opal Jones poked Pete in the calf with the toe of her shoe.

"Now then, you two!" she said, much louder than Pete thought necessary. "I don't have my hearing aids in, but I've got my glasses on. I was married for fifty-eight years, and I know better than to carry on like that out in public. If you all want to go to spooning, you'd better find a chaperone and a porch with a great big light by the front door. And don't wait too long to get married, because it's neither right nor fair to either one of you. You hear?"

Pete nodded, suddenly feeling like that little boy who'd been caught in a misdeed. "Yes, ma'am. I'm sorry."

"Well now, how about if you give me a ride back to my house, kid?" Opal stared at Pete through her glasses. "I've stayed out here too long, and I won't be able to get back in the dark. And you, Patsy Pringle, you go on home like a good girl."

With his heart overflowing, Pete gave Patsy a last peck on the cheek, took Opal's arm, and headed for his pickup.

CHAPTER SEVENTEEN

Y̶ou and Ashley sure looked happy at the celebration last night," Charlie remarked to Brad.

"Yeah, I guess. It's off and on with us," the younger man said. "The bonfire was my kind of fun, even though they didn't allow beer. At least we got to enjoy the commons. Not like the Fourth of July, when we can't even shoot off fireworks. I didn't even mind the parade. I rode a float in every parade at Camdenton High School all four years until I graduated. Athletics, you know. I could have been on the Honor Society float, but I didn't want to hang with a bunch of nerds."

Following church, Esther had wanted to rest up from her queenly activities the evening before. She had encouraged Charlie to go over to the Haneses' house and help Brad with the new room. In a way, this construction work was a ministry to the young couple, Esther pointed out, and that made it a perfectly appropriate activity for the Lord's Day.

Charlie had to admit, Esther made a good point. He had come to see himself as something of a father figure to Brad. He dispensed tidbits of advice here and there. Slapped the kid on the back now and then. And whenever Charlie offered a word of praise, Brad drank it in like a thirsty man in a desert. Most afternoons they talked and joked around. They both kept up with the NFL, and it turned out they were rooting for the same teams. If it wasn't football, they discussed the weather, fishing, plans for the room, or some other topic of interest to both of them.

Charlie had come to admire Brad's willingness to work long hours at such hard labor. Brad was respectful, too. When they disagreed, the younger man often capitulated, even though he probably knew more about construction than Charlie.

During the past week, the two men had begun painting the addition. Now Brad was giving the white ceiling a few touch-ups while Charlie started cutting in with a soft yellow semigloss that Ashley had chosen. The couple still hadn't decided the purpose for the space, but Brad felt it would add to the sale price of their home if—as he regularly predicted—the marriage went down the tubes.

"I thought I spotted you and Ashley snuggled up under a blanket while you roasted marshmallows," Charlie observed. "Looked mighty cozy to me."

"Yeah, we had a good time. She had taken the night off from waitressing at the country club, and for once she wasn't nagging me about Larry's."

"Have you gone back to the bar since her ultimatum?"

"No, but that doesn't mean I won't." Brad slapped the paintbrush on the ceiling so hard that droplets spattered across his face like bright white freckles. "She can't expect me to sit around the house by myself watching TV every single night. That's ridiculous."

"Maybe you could take up a hobby."

"What—collecting model trains or postage stamps?"

"As a matter of fact, I collected stamps for years." Charlie mused on the hours he had spent gazing through a magnifying glass at the bright colors and detailed pictures of butterflies, flowers, portraits, and other objects indigenous to the countries where his stamps had originated.

"I wonder what I did with my collection," he murmured. "I hope it didn't wind up in the attic with Esther's prom dress. Brenda Hansen had to work a miracle to patch that thing back together. If my stamps are up there, no telling what condition they're in."

"You liked stamps because you were a mailman," Brad said. "I couldn't care less about that kind of stuff. The only things I enjoy are football, baseball, and building houses. Unless you go to college, there's no football or baseball after high school. And the softball teams are all tied to churches. You aren't getting me anywhere near a church—ball games or not. And as for building, that's what I do all day long. So I guess you could say my hobby is hanging out at Larry's, shooting pool, having a few beers, listening to the music, and talking to my friends."

"Dangerous territory," Charlie intoned. "What about college? If you were in the National Honor Society, you must have a good GPA. I'll bet you could get financial aid and take some classes. I hear they even offer online computer courses these days."

"College is for geeks."

"Is a good salary and a better job for geeks?"

"All I want to do is work construction. You don't need a college degree for that."

"Couldn't hurt. If you were studying for classes in the evenings, I doubt you'd have time to shoot pool at Larry's bar."

"I like shooting pool, Mr. Moore. Didn't you ever want to hang out in a bar and have a few drinks with your friends?"

Charlie gave a mirthless chuckle. "Yes, and I nearly lost my marriage over it. Twice."

"Twice?"

"Women have long memories, kid. You do something stupid now and you may end up paying for it years down the line."

"Yeah, but do I care?" Brad stepped down from the ladder. "I thought I loved Ashley. Now . . . I don't know."

"Nothing can beat a long marriage. Let me tell you that for sure. Last night while Esther and I were riding around in our golf cart, all I could think about was how much I love that woman. And how glad I am for our years together. You don't want to miss out on having that with Ashley, do you?"

Brad shrugged as he stepped out of the room to wash the paint residue from his roller. As Charlie worked his favorite paintbrush around the room, he reflected on that long-ago time when he was about Brad's age and newly married. Just like Brad and Ashley, the Moores' romantic love affair had turned into a daily rut with neither meeting the other's inmost needs.

They could have fallen apart so easily. Too much pressure. Too many strains. Conflicting desires and unspoken pain. How had they made it almost fifty years?

"You and Mrs. Moore had it easy," Brad said as he stepped back into the room. He knelt and poured paint into the roller tray. "The world is more complicated now than it was in the olden days. People don't think of things the same way anymore. Some of the guys in my construction crew are on their third or fourth marriages. That's just how it goes, you know?"

"Is that so?"

"Yeah. If things don't work out, you have to move on. You and Mrs. Moore didn't have so much coming at you. You were a mailman, and your wife stayed home to raise the kids. Everything was simple and clear-cut. It's not like that now. Life is a lot harder these days."

Charlie had to work to hold back a retort. But he knew each generation believed itself to be living in the most difficult age. His father had talked endlessly about the First World War. Charlie himself was born during the Depression, and he had barely missed the Korean conflict. He knew that as soon as a cure was found for one disease, another cropped up. Presidents were assassinated, volcanoes erupted, riots broke out. This old earth—so obviously under Satan's thumb—hadn't been a happy place since Adam and Eve left the Garden.

"I hope you realize," Charlie said finally, "that what's going on in the outside world isn't nearly as important as what's happening in your marriage. You can make this marriage work or let it go."

"Whoa, Mr. Moore, are you sure this is the right color? It looks yellow to me." Brad was staring at the paint can.

Charlie rolled his eyes and set his brush on the edge of the can. "It looks yellow because it is yellow. That's the color Ashley chose." He fished in his pocket and pulled out the note on which she had written the information. "Buttercream. That's the shade your wife picked, and that's what we bought."

"Man, I thought cream meant white. This is yellow. I don't want a yellow room. It'll look like someone's been smoking cigarettes in here for fifty years."

"It's only paint, Brad. Once Ashley decorates the room, you won't even notice."

"Nah, this isn't cream. This is tobacco-stain yellow. I'm not having this color in my house."

Charlie reached for his jacket. "I'm going to head for home, kid. You and the wife will have to work it out, and I'll be back tomorrow afternoon. Don't forget we've got Thanksgiving this week. That'll tie up my Thursday at least. Maybe Friday, too."

"How could I forget about Thanksgiving?" Brad knelt and pushed his roller into the tray of yellow paint. "It's all Ashley talked about for weeks. Nag, nag, nag. But we worked it out—thanks to Mrs. Moore."

"What did you decide?"

"We're having dinner at our house. Ashley's folks and my mom are coming over here. They're bringing side dishes, and Ashley thinks she can cook the turkey. Personally, I'm not so sure. She grew up making chili dogs and onion rings in the snack shack, just like her mother. But she says the directions are in her cookbook, and Mrs. Moore is going to teach her how to do some kind of fancy stuffing. So I guess that's it."

Charlie didn't want to tell Brad that Esther's stuffing was not one of her best dishes. She was sensitive enough about her cooking. All the same, the thought of everyone in the Haneses' house biting into a mouthful of that dry, bland dressing was not pleasant.

"I'm sure Esther will do all she can to help," Charlie said. "Besides, I'll bet there are plenty of good stuffing recipes out there. Your mom might even have one she likes."

"Hers is dry. It tastes like sand." Brad was rolling yellow paint across the new wall. "I'm not a big dressing fan anyhow. So, whatever . . ."

"Yep. Whatever."

Muttering to himself about turkey stuffing and yellow paint and bullheaded young men, Charlie said good-bye to Brad for the evening and got into his golf cart. He probably should have taken a little snooze after church. The parade and weenie roast had been a lot of fun the night before, but he was tired now. He just didn't have the energy to listen to Brad spouting off nonsense about the "olden days" and how good they supposedly were.

Winter was coming on fast, Charlie realized as he motored along the street toward his house. Missouri always ushered in the seasons with a flair. Esther had a cousin who lived in west Texas. He said spring and fall lasted a week at the most. But summer went on and on.

Not here by the lake. Autumn had unfurled in a slow revelation of glory. Golds, reds, browns. Mums and asters. Shocks of ripe corn. Pumpkins.

Now the chill was beginning to peek around the corner. Icy wind whipped at the fallen leaves. The ground hardened and went cold. Charlie knew that winter would play hide-and-seek with autumn for a while longer—maybe as much as a month. And then the humid cold would blast in with a vengeance. A Missouri wind could knife right through a wool coat. Ponds would freeze and ice storms would snap branches off trees. Cattle would huddle miserably together while cardinals and squirrels scurried around in search of something to eat.

Charlie pulled the golf cart under the protective roof of his carport. He couldn't look at the support posts without remembering Esther's wild ride through the backyard. That had been the start of a difficult season, and Charlie was eager to put it behind him. He and his wife would enjoy their dinner on Thursday. Talk to the kids and grandkids by phone. Get a good night's sleep. And then head for Springfield and Esther's procedure. Both of them would be glad when it was over and done. Life could return to normal.

Esther's idea of the two of them going to California or Florida for Christmas sat well with Charlie. The family hadn't been together for months now, and he was long overdue for a hug from Charles Jr. and a kiss on the cheek from Ellie. As he pushed open the door, Charlie could see Esther in the kitchen.

"Hi-ho!" she called. "How's the new room coming along, sugar bear?"

"It's yellow." Charlie took off his hat and jacket. Then he rubbed the lenses of his glasses on his shirt to clear the mist that always clouded them when he walked into a warm house. "Brad doesn't like the color much. Says it looks like the room has tobacco stains."

"For pete's sake." Esther carried her recipe file into the living room, where Charlie was searching for the television's remote control. "That color is buttercream, and it's a perfectly gorgeous shade. Ashley showed me a sample of it yesterday, and I told her it was beautiful. Can you help me find my stuffing recipe, Charlie? It's always been here, and suddenly I can't locate it."

As Esther leaned against his shoulder, Charlie took the small metal box. "Did you file it under *S* or *D*?" he asked.

"Well, it's stuffing, silly. Why would I file it under *D*?"

"*D* for *dressing*."

Esther looked up at him in surprise. "Oh," she said. Then she sank down into Charlie's favorite television-watching chair.

"Oh." She spoke the word again in a slight gasp.

Charlie had begun to flip through the alphabetized dividers when he noticed that Esther's head had sagged to one side as if she'd fallen asleep. Her legs, always so carefully tucked into a ladylike position, stuck out in different directions.

"Esther?" Charlie set the recipe box down on the side table. "Are you feeling okay, honey?"

When she didn't answer, he dropped to one knee. Eyes closed, Esther's face was unmoving, and her pink cheeks had gone an ashy white. Charlie took her hand, expecting her fingers to tighten on his as always. They were limp.

"Esther? Esther, what's wrong?" He took her shoulders in his hands and raised his voice a little. "Esther, sweetie. Esther!"

Nothing.

He placed his palm on her cheek and tried to jiggle her awake. She didn't move. And then he realized she wasn't breathing.

"Esther!"

Charlie grabbed the phone from the side table and dialed the emergency code. When the dispatcher answered, he blurted out their address. "Send someone!" he shouted. "Something's gone wrong here. Hurry up now; you hear me? I need an ambulance!"

Though the dispatcher asked him to stay on the line, Charlie knew he couldn't do that. Esther was lying there on the chair like a discarded coat. He bent over and scooped her up into his arms.

"Esther," he said, surprised that she didn't weigh more. He began to tremble. "Esther, don't do this. Wake up, honey!"

For a moment, Charlie stood paralyzed in the living room, unable to move or form cohesive thoughts. What was happening? What should he do?

Then he realized he ought to lay his wife out on the carpet. CPR—that was the thing. He felt for a pulse. Nothing in her wrist. His fingers pressed against her neck.

"No." He shook her shoulders in frustration at the lack of a heartbeat at her throat. "Esther, no! Stop this, now. We're going to the doctor on Friday. Come back here!"

She lay still and quiet, so unlike herself. Charlie shook his head in disbelief. This couldn't happen. No. Not this.

Wasn't she breathing? Maybe just a little? He leaned over and laid his cheek near her lips. Not even the whisper of a breath tickled his skin.

Trying to remember what he had learned about CPR while coaching his son's Little League baseball team, Charlie fumbled with the top button on Esther's blouse. *Press on the chest,* he thought. But where? Wasn't the heart on the left side? Or was it in the middle? *And breathe through the mouth.* But how many times?

Who would know this? How could he get help? Where was the ambulance?

"Derek," he murmured. Leaving Esther's side, he jerked open the drawer on the side table. *Derek, Derek.* What was his last name? *Finley.* Charlie flipped through the pages. As he ran his finger down the list of names beginning with the letter *F*, he could hear a siren in the distance.

"Esther, they're coming," he told his wife. "The ambulance is on its way. Just breathe for me, sweet pea. Breathe all you can. We'll get your heart going again in a minute."

Charlie punched in Derek Finley's telephone number and began to speak even while it was still ringing. "Hello? Hello? Derek?"

"Hello?" a woman's voice said. "Hello? Who's there?"

"I need Derek! This is Charlie. Charlie Moore. Send Derek over here. It's Esther. She's . . . she . . ."

The doorbell rang and Charlie dropped the phone. Figures in blue uniforms entered the house. Bags. Needles. Stethoscopes. People hovered over Esther. Then Derek Finley burst into the living room. And Kim. Miranda, too.

Charlie tried to get close to Esther, but hands pushed him back. He stood by the fireplace, watching the huddle around his wife.

"Esther," he called out. "Esther, I'm right here, honey. Don't worry. You'll be fine."

Someone put an arm around him. Kim Finley. She lowered him onto the sofa. And then Brenda Hansen's face appeared in front of Charlie. Other people moved around, talking, discussing. Two of them brought a gurney into the room and began to move his wife.

"Esther!" Charlie tried to stand. "Where are they taking her?"

"She's going to the hospital, Charlie."

It was Derek Finley. He pressed two fingers against Charlie's neck. "How are you feeling, Mr. Moore? Are you faint?"

"Not me. I'm fine, but I need to talk to Esther. She'll be confused about all this, Derek. These past few days she's been a little mixed up." Charlie again tried to rise. "I think it's that artery, like you said."

"Was she on the floor when you found her?" Derek asked.

"No, we were talking. We were looking for stuffing." He gestured vaguely at the recipe box on the side table. "Dressing. We're having Thanksgiving dinner this Thursday."

"All right," Derek said. His eyes intense, he was nodding at Charlie. "And what happened next? What happened while you were talking?"

"She said *oh*. Like that—*oh*. And then she sat in my chair. She might have fainted. It was kind of a sag the way she went down. I tried to wake her, but she wouldn't open her eyes. That's when I called 911. It didn't seem like she was breathing right, you know. And then I picked her up and put her on the floor because I thought I would do CPR. But it's been a long time and . . . and . . . and . . ."

"It's okay, Charlie." Derek laid a hand on Charlie's shoulder. "They're putting her in the ambulance. How about if I drive you to the hospital?"

"I'd better sit with her in the ambulance. She'll be upset when she comes to. In fact, she'll be embarrassed at the hubbub."

"You ride along with me," Derek said, leading Charlie out the door.

The ambulance sat in the driveway, lights flashing, back door open, motor running. Charlie stared at it. The paramedics were sliding the gurney inside. Was that Esther lying there? She looked too small. Too pale.

"I should ride with her," Charlie said.

Derek placed a supporting arm around his shoulders. "Kim's bringing our car around. We'll follow along right behind the ambulance. The EMTs need room to tend to Mrs. Moore. We'll get to the hospital at almost the same time. You'll see."

"But you don't know how Esther is about things like this." Charlie watched in befuddlement as someone shut the ambulance door and it began to roll down the driveway toward the street. "I think it would have been better if I'd gone along for the ride. I don't know what happened, Derek. Do you think Esther fainted? She didn't seem sick at all. It was so . . . odd."

"I'm not sure, Charlie." Derek led him toward the car that Kim now pulled into the Moores' driveway. "It's hard to tell what might have happened. The doctors will have a better idea once they've examined her."

Somehow Charlie found himself climbing into the passenger's side of Derek Finley's car. Kim and Brenda were in the backseat. And there was someone else.

"Brad? Is that you?"

"Hey, Mr. Moore." The young man clamped a hand on Charlie's shoulder. "I saw the ambulance and ran over. How are you doing there, buddy?"

Charlie looked across the back of his seat. "You've got paint on your face, Brad. From the ceiling."

The two men stared at each other. Charlie could remember that paint splattering across Brad's nose. Not long afterward, he had left the Haneses' house. Esther had been in the kitchen, hadn't she? Weren't they looking for a recipe? What could have happened?

"I called Ashley," Brad said. "She's meeting us over at the ER. Are you gonna be okay, Mr. Moore?"

Charlie couldn't move his focus from the young man's face. Gazing at Brad, he could suddenly see Esther. Her eyes had been closed and her chest still. She'd had no pulse. Her hands never moved. Her mouth never changed expression. Esther hadn't fainted, had she? No. She hadn't fainted at all.

The passengers fell silent as the car zipped along Highway 54 toward Osage Beach. Charlie tried to replay the events of the past hour, but they kept getting out of order, so he would start again. At some point, Derek's Water Patrol radio crackled on. Derek and someone began speaking to each other in code. That bothered Charlie. He wasn't sure the conversation was about Esther, but he didn't like to be kept in the dark.

Finally Derek brought the car to a halt near the emergency room, and everyone piled out. Brad came alongside Charlie, taking his arm. For a moment, Charlie considered pushing the kid away. He didn't need help getting across a parking lot. He wasn't a crotchety old man. But as they neared the door, Charlie decided he was grateful, and he leaned against his younger friend.

Inside, people moved far too slowly for a place called an emergency room. *What emergency?* they seemed to be saying. *This is just our job. We're in no hurry.*

Charlie stood beside Brad in the center of the tiled floor. Derek spoke to someone behind a desk. Over to one side, Kim and Brenda whispered back and forth.

"I have to see Esther," Charlie said, irritated that no one seemed to notice he was there. Didn't they realize he was worried about his wife? He kept seeing Esther's face, unmoving and pale. He remembered trying to find her pulse and then the ambulance arriving and people pouring into the house.

"When Esther wakes up," he told Brad, "she'll need me beside her. I want to be with her while the doctors tend to her."

"We've got to wait this one out, Mr. Moore." Brad pointed at a row of seats. "How about we park ourselves over there?"

Parking himself was the last thing Charlie wanted to do. But somehow he found himself sitting down. Handing Derek Finley his wallet with the medical and other identification cards inside it. Watching people come and go. Trying to eavesdrop on Kim as she spoke to Derek. Listening to Brenda, who was on her cell phone making one call after another.

"We came here this summer when Luke had his diabetic emergency, remember?" Kim asked, stooping in front of Charlie. "The doctors are very good. We were pleased with the way they took care of him."

Why didn't she sit in a chair? Why wouldn't anyone let him go talk to Esther? Didn't they understand what almost fifty years of marriage meant? You couldn't just take one person away without bringing the other along. He and Esther were a pair. A matched set, like salt and pepper or a left and right shoe. You didn't expect one to stay apart from the other. It wasn't right. Professionals ought to know that.

He stared at the doors between the waiting room and the rest of the ER. Why didn't someone come out and talk to him? He could picture Esther lying on a bed back there, her blue eyes filled with confusion as doctors poked and prodded her. She wouldn't like it, and she would expect Charlie to be right beside her.

"We're having her artery cleaned on Friday," he said aloud. "I'm going to be with her during that procedure."

The chattering around him stopped, and now he realized that the room had slowly filled with friends and neighbors. There stood Ashley Hanes, Patsy Pringle, Pete Roberts, Steve Hansen.

Pastor Andrew had come too. Now he was a man of authority.

"I need to see Esther," Charlie told his minister. "She was terrified to have the angioplasty and stent. This incident is going to upset her a lot. Could you ask someone to let me go back there?"

Pastor Andrew glanced at Derek Finley. Both men nodded and

stepped to the front desk. *That's better,* Charlie thought. *Get this thing moving along now.*

Relief spilled through Charlie as the men beckoned him toward the double doors. Brad started to help him to his feet, but that wasn't necessary. In a moment, he had joined Pastor Andrew and Derek in the short journey to a small, windowless room. He entered to find nothing but a few chairs around the perimeter.

"Wait . . . this isn't right," Charlie muttered. His irritation grew. "Where's Esther? Listen, I've had enough of this waiting around. I want to talk to my wife."

A doctor slipped into the room, shut the door behind him, and motioned for the men to take seats. That's when Charlie understood.

He wasn't going to see Esther again. Not his bright, chirpy little wife with the mischievous smile and busy hands. No more dishes clattering in the kitchen. No purple elastic-waist slacks and matching sweaters. No Friday set-and-style appointments. No long, gossipy reports about the Tea Lovers' Club. No sweet kisses on the cheek. No warm arms reaching for him in the night.

Charlie studied the doctor. The man was speaking, and Charlie understood the words. But they made no sense. None at all.

CHAPTER EIGHTEEN

With Boofer on his lap, Charlie sat in his recliner and pressed the remote control's channel-changing button again and again. The sun rose—golden and far too bright—slanting through venetian blinds that hadn't been adjusted in years. As a rule, Charlie didn't watch television in the morning. Usually his garden or workbench beckoned at dawn, and he didn't collapse into his chair until late afternoon. Today was different.

Laying a hand on the dog's head, Charlie reflected on his television habit. Esther hadn't approved, but he had always argued that game shows kept his mind active and alert. He told himself that filling out crossword puzzles or trying to beat the contestants on his favorite programs would prevent Alzheimer's disease. Now, as he flipped past cartoons, shopping shows, and sports announcers, he realized that particular goal no longer mattered. In fact, he wouldn't mind a good strong dose of amnesia.

"What's the matter, Boof?" he asked the dog, who was in the midst of shifting position. "Why can't you settle down, fella? Are you missing your mama? Well, I guess that makes two of us."

Charlie had never been much of a weeper. His father had taught him that a man never cried. Facing life with a stoic attitude and an unwavering confidence in oneself and God formed the essential core of a male.

That was hogwash, Charlie realized not long after the doctor told him about Esther's massive stroke. As it turned out, she had gone instantly. The ambulance ride, the long wait in the emergency room, the efforts of the doctors—that had been nothing but protocol. Derek Finley had probably known all along. No doubt everyone but Charlie suspected it.

To him, the news had hit like an earthquake—a gigantic seismic shifting of the earth, followed by ripples of aftershock. The doctor gently informed Charlie that his wife had died. Nothing could have been done to prevent the stroke—not even the angioplasty and carotid stenting would have helped in Esther's case. And then Charlie began weeping. He hadn't been able to stop since.

Charles Jr., Natalie, and their two children had arrived from California on the afternoon after Esther's death. Ellie came in a couple of hours later from Florida.

It was Monday, someone told Charlie, the Monday before Thanksgiving, and things had to move fast. He couldn't comprehend why that was so. To Charlie, the whole world had stopped in that tiny windowless room.

But the moments passed anyway, one after the other. Flowers came to the house. Ellie and Charles Jr. cried, made phone calls, hugged each other and their father. People knocked on the door and brought in casseroles or sandwiches or relish trays. The doorbell rang. More flowers. Charlie dozed off and on, but mostly he sat in the recliner with Boofer and watched everything through a blur of tears.

It was Tuesday, Charles Jr. had informed him on the way to church. He hadn't even noticed the passage of night. Seated in a pew with his children and grandchildren, Charlie studied the casket near the altar. Esther had never liked sitting near the front where everyone could look at her. She wouldn't be happy with this arrangement, Charlie realized, but nothing could be done about it now.

Esther wore her nicest suit. She had told Charlie the shape was flattering. But then the figure lying motionless in the casket wasn't really Esther. Charlie's wife was nowhere to be found, he slowly began to realize. Not in the kitchen or the bathroom or the bedroom. Not marching down the hall while singing out some news she had just learned. Not stringing beads on the front porch.

"Heaven," Pastor Andrew had said repeatedly during the funeral service. It was a place of joy. A land without pain. A home in the presence of the holy God.

What about earth? Charlie had wondered. That's where he had been left when Esther sighed and drifted away. What was he supposed to do now?

He could almost hear his wife explaining her death. *"It was silly of me, I know, sweetie pie. I hope you're not too put out."*

As he flipped through television channels now that his children and everyone else had gone away, Charlie heard the doorbell chime. Boofer's ears perked up, but when Charlie didn't move, the dog settled down again.

That doorbell had become a nuisance in recent days, Charlie thought. People dropped by at all hours and expected to be let in. They came before and after the funeral, even after Charles Jr. and Ellie had returned home. They came in the morning, and they came at night—in and out, in and out, crying, telling stories, laughing, setting food inside the refrigerator. Everyone tried to make it better . . . and failed.

"Go away," Charlie muttered after the doorbell echoed through the house a second time. "We've got enough relish trays, don't we, Boof? We don't need another ham or pot roast. We've got turkey tetrazzini coming out our ears, and I'm not even hungry."

Someone began knocking. Charlie flipped the channel. "Skedaddle," he said under his breath. "I'm busy."

"Mr. Moore?" Cody's voice filled the living room. "Hey, Mr. Moore, is that you in the recliner? Is that Boofer?"

"Well, who do you think it is, Cody?"

"I think it's you, Mr. Moore. Sorry to open the door and walk in without being invited. I know that's bad social skills."

Charlie shook his head. He'd just lost the love of his life, his best friend for nearly fifty years. The last thing he needed was to try to decipher whatever Cody Goss had on his mind.

The young man appeared in Charlie's range of vision. He was wearing a tan turtleneck, a brown leather jacket, and khaki slacks instead of his usual jeans and T-shirt.

Cody stood beside the TV for a moment. Then he let out a deep breath. "Aren't you going to invite me to sit down, Mr. Moore? Because that's manners."

Charlie set the remote on the side table. "Cody, what do you want?"

"I want to sit on your sofa."

"All right, sit, but I'm not in the mood to talk. I'm watching television."

"Okay."

Though Charlie made an attempt to focus on the show, it was impossible. So he reached for the remote and switched off the TV. Closing his eyes, he sniffled. He was awfully tired, and Esther would scold him for not taking better care of himself. Or rather, she would have scolded him if—

"Why did you come, Cody?" Charlie barked. He hadn't meant to sound so harsh, but he didn't have the energy to pretend niceness.

"I came to get you," Cody told him. "We're going to drive around Deepwater Cove in your golf cart. It's a plan made by Brenda and the two Finley ladies and also Opal and Ashley and Patsy. I'm in charge of it, because I don't have a house of my own. Besides, Brenda wanted me to go away because Jennifer didn't have a good time on her mission trip to Mexico, and it's better if I find something else to do. So here I am."

Charlie took off his glasses, wiped them for the umpteenth time. Then he blew his nose and put them on again. He leaned back in the recliner and stared at the ceiling. "Cody, I'm not going anywhere in the golf cart today. You need to find someone else to bother. Why don't you go see Patsy?"

"We will. She's last on our list." Cody fidgeted. "I think I'm going to have to tell you a secret, Mr. Moore, because this is important. Patsy Pringle loves Pete Roberts. She finally decided for sure. How I know is because I read a card that was sitting at her beauty station inside Just As I Am. I wasn't supposed to read the card because that is snooping and it's bad social skills. But I knocked over the card when I was dusting, and then I picked it up and it said *I love you, Pete* at the very bottom in Patsy's handwriting. That's how I know. Patsy tries to pretend she doesn't care all that much about Pete. But I saw the card and also I know Pete loves her. It's hard not to love someone who already loves you. It's also hard if you love someone and they don't love you. Love is hard no matter what."

Charlie squeezed his eyes shut. Boy, did he have a headache. He ought to take some aspirin. Esther would—

"Cody, go home," he said. Again feeling instant remorse for his tone, he added, "I understand about Patsy. I'm glad she loves Pete, and it is important. I just don't want to talk right now, okay? I want to watch television and that's all."

"But we have to drive around Deepwater Cove in your golf cart. That's the plan."

"What plan are you talking about?"

"The aggressive dinner. It was Mrs. Finley's idea—the older one. Miranda Finley bought the house next to Brad and Ashley Hanes. I'm not sure you knew. It was a secret, but now it's not. She's moving in next week. Yesterday she said we should have an aggressive dinner for Charlie Moore because what will he do without Esther? So the other Mrs. Finley, who is Kim, talked to Brenda. They all agreed, and that's why I came over here. We're going to ride on your golf cart."

Charlie rubbed his eyes. "Cody. Please."

"I can help you, Mr. Moore. I know how it feels to want to sit down and never get up. That's exactly the way I felt when my daddy said I was twenty-one and ready to make my way. Then he put me out on the road and drove off. I sat down, and I didn't think I could ever get up. But then I did. After that, I had a hard row to hoe, which is a metaphor. It means things were difficult. But in the end, I found Deepwater Cove, which shows that God is watching you and planning a happy life for you even without Mrs. Moore."

Charlie gritted his teeth, torn between wanting to knock the kid's block off and cry some more. Neither would do.

"Cody, you can't possibly understand what it feels like to lose a wife of almost fifty years. I don't expect to live a happy life. Not now and maybe not ever again."

"You didn't lose your wife, Mr. Moore. She's dead, but she's not lost, and that should make you at least a little bit happy. Mrs. Moore doesn't have to worry about getting her artery unclogged, which she was dreading a lot. Also, she doesn't have to try to remember old business for the TLC. She will never again fall asleep while she's driving or run her Lincoln off the end of her carport. Those are some good things about Mrs. Moore these days. In fact, if you could see her right now, you would cheer up a lot."

"Well, I can't see her, Cody. I'll never see Esther again. I won't touch her or hear her voice or eat her cooking or sleep at her side. And I don't . . . I don't . . . well, Cody, I don't see a single thing good about that."

The young man nodded. "You have a hard row to hoe, Mr. Moore. But here's a thing to remember while you're hoeing your row: 'Behold, the tabernacle of God is with men, and he will dwell with them, and they shall be his people, and God himself shall be with them, and be their God. And God shall wipe away all tears from their eyes; and there shall be no more death, neither sorrow, nor crying, neither shall there be any more pain: for the former things are passed away.' Revelation 21:3-4."

Charlie shrugged. "Pastor Andrew said something like that."

"Mr. Moore, the former things are what's happening now. One day, though, they will all be former. That means they'll be passed away. Gone. When the former things are passed away, you're going to feel a whole lot better."

"And in the meantime?"

"Well, we have a job to do, and I'm not talking about driving around Deepwater Cove in your golf cart—even though that is what we're supposed to be doing. Our job is to *'Go ye therefore.'* That's a command Jesus made at the end of Matthew."

"Cody, I'm not about to go to the uttermost parts of the earth and teach the nations. I'll leave that up to Jennifer Hansen and the other missionaries."

To Charlie's surprise, Cody's earnest expression suddenly went solemn. Even sad. It was the first time since Esther's death that Charlie had actually noticed much of anything outside himself, his children and grandchildren, and their loss.

A memory filtered through the haze of his confusion, anguish, and sorrow. A bright, golden-haired young woman was whispering something in Charlie's ear.

"Mr. Moore, please pray for me. I know what God wants me to do with my life . . . but . . . but I'm really confused about a few things . . . about Cody."

Jennifer Hansen. She had begged Charlie to pray for her. And he had. But what was happening now? Cody had said Jennifer's mission trip to Mexico didn't go well. The mention of her name a moment ago had brought a total change to the young man's face.

"Are you all right, Cody?" Charlie asked.

"I'm having a hard time hoeing my row."

"What's the problem?"

"Jennifer is the problem." Cody shook his head. "I don't know what happened to her in Mexico. She won't talk to me. She won't even look at me. I'm afraid I did bad social skills, but I'm not sure.

I love Jennifer a lot, and I want to marry her. I'm autistic, though, and that's a big problem for people who want to get married. I don't think Jennifer wants to marry me."

Charlie found he couldn't answer. He gazed across at the boy's blue eyes.

Cody clenched his hands into fists. "I don't know which is worse, Mr. Moore. Wanting to get married to someone who doesn't love you or getting married and then finding out at the hospital that your wife is as dead as a doornail, which is a metaphor I don't understand. Either way, you're left alone and that's hard, especially if you really love the other person a whole lot."

Charlie swallowed the lump in his throat. "Cody, I think you and I ought to go for a drive in my golf cart. What do you say?"

"I say we're late already. Probably the ladies of Deepwater Cove are as mad as hornets, and that's a metaphor I do understand."

Boofer stood up on Charlie's lap, stretched, and then leaped to the floor.

It turned out to be Thanksgiving Day, a fact that took Charlie by surprise. As he drove Cody toward the Hansen house, reality slowly crept up on him. Pumpkins beside doorways. Scarecrows and bales of hay arranged in yards for decoration. Cars lined up along the narrow street.

"'Over the river and through the woods,'" he muttered.

"Which river?" Cody asked.

"The one in the song that Esther used to sing."

"I miss her. She was president of the TLC, even though we didn't really have a president. Mrs. Moore kept minutes in her purse and read them out loud. She was my friend."

"I miss her too." Charlie could feel the tears well up again, and he dug in his pocket for a tissue. Crazy thing, crying so much. But every time he thought of his wife, of any little thing about her, he could hardly bear it. Her clothes hung in their closet. Her makeup lay on the counter by the sink. Her pillow had a dent right where her head used to rest.

"Here we are. Salad at the Hansens'." Cody hopped out of the cart as Charlie set the brake. "Salad is good for you even though it's made of vegetables, which are not my favorite. My aunt in Kansas eats vegetables all the time, and she loves salad."

As Cody threw open the Hansens' front door, a burst of warm air carried with it the fragrance of roasting turkey, pumpkin pie, and steaming sweet potatoes. People rose from the table, surrounded Charlie, and began greeting him. Justin, who almost never came home from college. A grandmother. An aunt. Steve and Brenda. Jessica and her fiancé. And finally Jennifer.

"You're late, Cody," Brenda said. "We had to start eating without you. Charlie, is your phone turned off? I must have called ten times."

"I'm not sure."

Charlie felt as though invisible strings were moving him along like a marionette. He sat at the table and picked at a bowl of fresh green salad, managing to eat a bite or two. People talked about the funeral, asked questions about Charles Jr. and Ellie, mentioned how much they had loved Esther. Charlie nodded and mumbled things he thought made sense.

He tried to remember what Cody had told him. One day, this meal at the Hansens' house would be *former things*. One day he would be with God, and he would see Esther, and there would be no more tears. But now . . . just for now, there was only one thing to do.

Go ye therefore.

What could that mean? What significance could it have for a man well past his prime, a man with no wife, no joy, no reason to keep breathing in and out?

"Time for Mr. Moore and me to move on," Cody announced. "The main course is at the Finleys' house. That's the turkey and dressing and hot rolls. It's the best part of an aggressive dinner."

"*Progressive*," Brenda said. "A progressive dinner."

Everyone laughed as Cody shrugged his shoulders and hurried toward the front door. The Hansen family had been in the midst of their dinner when Charlie arrived, and now they returned to the meal. Someone said to pass the mashed potatoes. Someone else asked about pecan pie.

Charlie was putting on his coat when a movement nearby startled him. Jennifer Hansen had stepped into the foyer.

"Mr. Moore," she whispered. Without another word, she slipped her arms around his neck and rested her head on his shoulder. Charlie felt the pain inside him soften just a little. He reached up and patted the young woman on the back.

"I'm so sorry about Mrs. Moore," Jennifer murmured. "I don't know how to say anything that will make you feel better."

"It's all right not to know," he told her. The warmth of her embrace was more comforting than he could have imagined.

"Mr. Moore, may I please talk to you sometime next week?" Jennifer said in a low voice. "It sounds selfish of me to ask such a favor at this terrible time in your life, but you're the only one I can think of to talk to. You know so much about life. Could you . . . would you please let me come over for a visit?"

As she drew back, Charlie looked into her serious eyes, almost a mirror of Cody's. "You're welcome to visit me next week, Jennifer. I'm not sure I have any wisdom to pass along to you, but I'm dandy at listening. Esther trained me well."

Her face brightened. "Thank you. I'll come on Monday."

She kissed his cheek before he went out the door to join Cody. The golf cart ride to the Finleys' house took less than a minute. Along the way, Cody talked about how embarrassing it was to mix up his words. *Progressive* and *aggressive* had sounded very much alike to him, but now he knew he had made an error. Right in front of Jennifer, too.

"Welcome, Charlie!"

Miranda must have been waiting near the door. Cody and Charlie had just stepped onto the porch when she sailed out to embrace them. Still feeling like a marionette, Charlie drifted into the dining room and took his place at the Finley Thanksgiving feast.

This was a louder family, the twins calling to each other across the table, Derek trying to calm everyone, Kim asking questions of Miranda. Turkey, dressing, cranberry sauce, mashed potatoes, marshmallow-covered yams, green bean casserole . . . each found a place on Charlie's plate.

"Good dressing," he told Kim after he had taken a bite. "Moist."

It was the first positive comment he had uttered since Esther died. Was she watching from above? Did she know he preferred Kim Finley's dressing to hers? Feeling guilty, Charlie laid down his fork. He did sense Esther nearby. In fact, he could almost hear her voice.

"Oh, just eat it, honeybunch. I don't mind. My dressing always was a little dry, wasn't it?"

Again fighting tears, Charlie tried to listen as Miranda Finley addressed him. The woman wore a beige sweater and chocolate brown slacks with a big gold necklace and matching earrings. With her spiky blonde hair, she seemed to glow as she spoke.

"A moving truck will be coming in on Thursday." Her voice had that too-friendly tone people used when they were trying not to mention something uncomfortable. "I guess that's a week from today, isn't it? I hadn't realized it was so soon! All the furniture I had put into storage will be here, and I have no idea where to place half of it. I had a huge home in St. Louis. Charlie, would you be so good as to stop by and take a look at the house early next week? I know you'll be working on the Haneses' room addition next door, and I'd be so grateful for your advice. I'll need a handyman, too, and Derek won't be any use to me in that department. He's always so busy, even in the cold months. And with Kim's pregnancy—"

A gasp went up around the table.

Miranda clapped her hand over her mouth. "Oops! I wasn't supposed to tell yet. I'm so sorry, Derek. Kim, can you ever forgive me?"

"Mom, you promised not to say a word." Derek's face clouded with frustration. "Charlie, we'd appreciate it if you would keep this under your hat. We just found out, and we wanted to wait awhile to make it public. Cody, can we trust you not to tell?"

"No," Cody said frankly. "I'm not good at keeping secrets. I found that out about myself. I can give it a try, but I would be surprised if I didn't tell."

"Don't worry, Dad-o," Lydia piped up. "If people find out Mom's pregnant, it's okay. What's the big deal?"

"That's because Lydia already told Tiffany," Luke chipped in. "Everyone at school knows. It won't be long before the whole neighborhood finds out."

"Lydia!" Kim exclaimed.

Charlie ate a last bite of turkey and tried to work this new information into his fogged mind. Kim Finley was expecting a baby? No wonder Derek looked so satisfied. The twins were excited too.

Esther had gone away, but so many things were still happening. A baby would arrive to join the Finley family. Miranda planned to move into a new house. Cody wanted to marry Jennifer. Jennifer needed to talk.

Life did go on, didn't it? Charlie thought about that as he and Cody thanked the Finleys for sharing their Thanksgiving dinner. The afternoon sun had begun to cast shadows across the road as they turned the golf cart toward the Haneses' small home. How many hours had passed since Charlie sat with Boofer in the old recliner and watched the channels changing on his television?

"You're not gonna like this." Brad Hanes opened his front door to Charlie and Cody. He spoke in hushed tones. "Ashley burned the pumpkin pie, so her mother bought one at the grocery store. It tastes like cardboard."

Inside, Ashley took one look at Charlie and burst into tears. Draped with necklaces and bracelets, she threw her arms around him and sobbed. "I can't think about anything else," she wailed. "How could it have happened, Mr. Moore? It doesn't seem possible, does it? She meant so much to me. We spent all our time together, and she helped me with my beads and my cooking, and I could tell her everything. I don't know what I'm going to do without her. Oh, it's the most awful thing in my whole life. I can't stand it. I really can't."

Overwhelmed with Ashley's red hair, beads, and tears, Charlie was surprised to discover a plate of pumpkin pie in his hands. Someone reached over his shoulder and squirted on a dollop of whipped cream from an aerosol can. Brad took him by the elbow and led him into the room where they had been laboring the day of Esther's death. Ashley's father and Cody accompanied them, admiring the fine handiwork.

"We're going green," Brad said. "I told Ashley I couldn't handle that yellow, so she agreed to change it. Sagebrush green. I've got the floor tile coming in on Wednesday, so we'll need to repaint before we can lay that. What do you think, Mr. Moore? It would help me a lot if you'd trim out the room."

Charlie nodded, trying to imagine himself standing on a ladder with a brush and a can of green paint. Things had been so different such a short time ago. Yellow paint. A search for the stuffing recipe. And Esther. Alive, laughing, making plans.

Before Charlie could slip into a daze of shattered memories, though, he realized that his plate of pumpkin pie, only half eaten, had been taken away. Cody was ushering him out to the golf cart again. Ashley made one last dash—enveloping Charlie in sobs, necklaces, wails of despair—and then Brad pulled her away.

"Patsy Pringle is last on the list," Cody told Charlie as they rode along. "We're having coffee with her and Pete Roberts. Even though I don't like coffee, not even decaf, I'm going with you. Patsy said she'll make tea for me. She's not sure she can get through Fridays anymore without Esther's usual set-and-style, but Pete said he would take her over to the Pop-In for a latte and a cinnamon roll. She said that wouldn't do any good and it would make her fat besides. I don't think Patsy's too fat, do you?"

Charlie drank in the crisp evening air. "I believe Esther told me the correct word is *ample*. I'd call her curvy."

"Yeah." Cody chuckled. "I used to get *ample* and *apple* mixed up. *Curvy* is a better word. Patsy works really hard on her hair and nails, and she worries about her figure all the time. But I don't see why. Everyone loves her just the way she is. Like her sign. Just As I Am. That's how Patsy loves people, but she doesn't know they love her back the same way."

"I never thought of that."

"Mr. Moore, there are lots of things I never thought of. In fact, I believe I'll never think of everything that can be thought. One thing I do think, though, is that Mrs. Moore was really glad about her life. She loved her Friday set-and-style. She loved the TLC. She loved all her friends. Most of all, she loved you. If you think about it, you'll know that for sure."

Pulling the golf cart into Patsy's driveway, Charlie felt the tears trickling down his cheeks again. He wondered if he would ever be able to stop crying about Esther. It had been such a shock. So unexpected. And yet, in some small place in his heart, he had known this would happen. He could see it coming, and he tried to stop it. But Cody was right. Esther had been glad about her life, and Charlie knew she had loved him most of all.

"We have to pretend that we don't know Patsy loves Pete," Cody said as they walked up to the front door. "Pretending feels like lying, doesn't it? I'm not good at pretending. Or keeping secrets."

"Hey there," Patsy greeted them, opening the door and welcoming Charlie and Cody into her living room. "I was about to give up on you. Pete and I are ready to float away, we've drunk so much coffee."

"We were progressing," Cody said.

"Well, progress right on in here and sit yourselves down on the couch. Pete, scoot over to that chair, would you? I'm going to get the tea. Charlie, do you want tea or coffee?"

He thought for a moment. "Tea. The way Esther drank it."

Cody walked across the room to Pete's chair, bent over, and peered into the man's face. "Why do you look scared, Pete? What's wrong with you?"

"Go sit down," Pete said, prodding the young man toward the sofa. "Sit by Charlie."

"Your face is different," Cody remarked as he obeyed. Plopping down too close to Charlie, he crossed his arms. "This is supposed to be Thanksgiving Day, but everywhere we go, something isn't right. At Charlie's house, Esther is gone. At the Hansens' house, Jennifer won't talk to me. At the Finleys' house, Kim is pregnant, which is a secret I wasn't supposed to tell but it's too late now. At the Haneses' house, Ashley burned the pumpkin pie, and Brad is making her paint the room green. And you look weird, Pete."

"Pete looks weird?" Patsy sashayed into the room bearing a tray with mugs of hot tea and coffee. She giggled. "Weirder than usual?"

"Hey now," Pete protested.

"Here's your tea, Charlie," Patsy said. "Cody, you're so close to Mr. Moore that you're about to sit on his lap. You've got the whole couch to yourselves. Remember what Brenda said about paying attention to other people's private space? You're in Charlie's space."

"Okay." Cody glanced at Charlie. "I'm sorry, Mr. Moore. I forgot about private space. That's one of my worst social skills. Also telling secrets. And mixing up words. I interrupt, too."

Charlie smiled. "That's all right, son. I've messed up a few things in my life too."

"I would feel a lot better if Jennifer would talk to me. Or even look at me. I don't know what I did, but I have a feeling—"

"Stop." Pete stood and held up his hands as if he were a traffic cop.

"Stop talking, Cody. Don't anyone say another word. I've waited all day for this, and I'm not going to wait another minute. It's my turn to talk, and this is what I have to say."

Charlie blinked as Pete took a step in his direction.

"Mr. Moore, you and your wife have meant a lot to me," Pete said. He swallowed hard. "A whole lot. See, I never had much of a father. My mother didn't do too well either. I botched up two marriages, and I had about decided the whole business was nothing but a bunch of hooey. And then I moved to Deepwater Cove and met you and Esther. I saw the two of you at church. I watched you drive your wife to Patsy's for her hair appointments. I studied you at the Fourth of July picnic. And I looked on as you circled the neighborhood in the Thanksgiving parade just the other night. I was amazed at how you treated your wife, Charlie. I never met such an honorable, upright fellow in my life. And the way she looked at you made me feel things I never felt before. That's why I wanted to do this in front of you. I hope it's the right thing, and I'd like to ask for your help along the way, if I might."

Charlie wanted to speak, but he wasn't sure he knew what to say. What did Pete mean? What was he going to do?

"Patsy Pringle," Pete said, turning to the woman and dropping down on one knee, "I'm not worth a plugged nickel, and I know that. But I love you more than I ever loved anyone or anything in my whole life. If I can be half the husband Charlie was to Esther, I'd consider myself a great success. So with that as my challenge, I want to ask you to marry me. Will you marry me, Patsy? If you're not interested, that's all right. I realize I'm no bargain, and—"

Patsy put her hand over Pete's mouth. Her eyes brimmed with tears as she replaced her fingers with a kiss. "Yes, Pete Roberts. I will marry you."

With a whoop of joy, he leaped to his feet and swept Patsy up in his arms. "You will? Did you really say yes to me, girl? Oh, Lord, thank You! Thank You for answering my prayers!"

"And mine!" Patsy sang out.

"Yours, too?"

"Oh yes, honey. Once I knew I loved you, I hoped and prayed you'd ask."

"What's going on?" Cody turned to Charlie, a look of wonder on his face. "Is Patsy going to get married to Pete?"

"She sure is," Charlie said.

"Mr. Moore, you've gotta help me." Pete was suddenly down on his knees in front of Charlie. "I don't think I can do it right. I'm afraid I'll mess up."

"You'll be fine."

"But will you help me? Can I ask you for advice?"

"I reckon so." Charlie nodded. "Might as well."

As Pete and Patsy snuggled up together in a love seat, Cody settled on the carpet at their feet. "I helped make invitations for Jessica's wedding," the young man said. "I tied on the apricot ribbons. I could make your invitations. Am I invited? Are you going to have nuts and a guest book? I think I might make a good usher by the time you get married. I'm going to be an usher at Jessica's wedding, and I'll get a lot of practice there."

Charlie leaned back on the sofa, sipped his tea, and thought about Esther.

"Cody," Patsy said, "you're in our space. Go sit by Charlie."

EPILOGUE

I'm glad you're up and about this bright Monday morning," Bitty Sondheim said as she took the chair across from Charlie. "Hope you don't mind if I join you outside. I need a break from the breakfast crowd."

"Not too nippy for your California blood?" he asked.

"I'm getting used to this autumn weather—though I guess it's probably about time to buy a pair of real shoes. Sandals and socks aren't going to get me through the winter. I can see that already."

Bitty's smile was warm, and Charlie noted that the freckles on her cheeks were growing more visible as her suntan faded. Her long braid was as blonde as ever.

"How's that breakfast wrap?" She propped her elbows on the bistro table and studied the meal in its parchment envelope. "I put in a little extra cheese for you today."

"Your omelets always start me off right, Bitty."

"I'm buying my eggs locally now. Nothing like fresh eggs for a hearty omelet."

"I couldn't agree more."

As Charlie sipped a cup of hot coffee, he waited for Bitty to comment about the events of the past week. Though Esther had been gone only a few days, he had already learned to dread the awkward moment. Some people tried to be far too chipper: *"Esther's funeral was lovely. It was wonderful to see Charles Jr. and Ellie looking so good. What a beautiful casket you chose."* Others assumed solemn expressions and poured their grief all over Charlie—as if he didn't have enough of his own. Finally, there were those who avoided him completely. They didn't know what to say, and he didn't know how to respond anyway.

"So, how was your weekend?" Bitty asked.

"Hard. I didn't sleep much. Couldn't eat."

"I suspected that."

Charlie took another sip of coffee, surprised at Bitty's refreshing, matter-of-fact tone. And suddenly, for some reason, he felt like talking. "I thought I'd cried all the tears I had in me. But this morning they started up again."

Bitty pushed her braid over her shoulder. "I doubt there's an end to tears. Mine seem to come from a bottomless well."

"You told me you've had some sadness in the past."

"My own kind. Not the same as yours."

"Still. It hurts." He studied the thicket of leafless trees across the highway from the row of shops. "You said you ran away."

"Yes, but it didn't help. Moving to Missouri changed the scenery but not the heart."

"I guess you're right."

"I am."

She propped her feet on the extra chair at the table. Charlie watched the breeze lift a wisp of golden hair and dance it across her forehead.

"I thought I might quit," he told her. He set the omelet wrapper on the table. "For a while this weekend, I could see how it might happen. I would sit in my recliner with Boofer, and gradually we'd fade right out."

"But here you are this morning," she said. "I'm glad you didn't quit."

"I realized I couldn't. I'm tangled. Tangled up with people. I think Esther did that to me on purpose." For a moment, Charlie reflected on his wife and the neighbors she had loved so dearly. "You know, Bitty, you may be the only person in Deepwater Cove who doesn't need me."

"Oh, I wouldn't say that."

"At least you're not asking me to run the grill or mop your floor, though to tell you the truth, I wouldn't mind. This afternoon, Jennifer Hansen is coming over to talk to me. What words of wisdom can I offer a fine young lady like her? Tomorrow, I've got to walk through Miranda Finley's new house and help her figure out where to put her furniture. Wednesday morning, I'll be expected at the men's Bible study, and Brad's got a load of floor tile coming that afternoon. We have to paint the new room sagebrush green. After that, I'm supposed to help the movers place Miranda's stuff. And then there's Pete."

"I hear Patsy told him yes."

"And I told him yes too." Charlie was surprised to hear himself chuckle. "Pete thinks I can help him be a good husband. If only he knew how many mistakes I made. How hard it was. What a long, difficult . . . wonderful . . . amazing journey."

Bitty smiled. "And yet, how very well you did it."

DISCUSSION QUESTIONS

The principles and strategies illustrated in this novel are taken from *The Four Seasons of Marriage* by Gary Chapman. In this book, Dr. Chapman discusses marriage as a journey back and forth through different "seasons."

- **Springtime** in marriage is a time of new beginnings, new patterns of life, new ways of listening, and new ways of loving.

- **Summer** couples share deep commitment, satisfaction, and security in each other's love.

- **Fall** brings a sense of unwanted change, and nagging emptiness appears.

- **Winter** means difficulty. Marriage is harder in this season of cold silence and bitter winds.

1. In *Falling for You Again*, which season of the year is it in Deepwater Cove, Missouri? Which season of marriage do you think Esther and Charlie Moore are experiencing? What are the signs that let you know?

2. At the start of the book, Esther has a car accident. What changes does this event bring about in her life? How does the accident affect Charlie? What do their reactions tell you about their marriage?

3. Charlie and Esther have had a long marriage. What have they done to make their relationship successful? In what ways have they failed to keep the marriage strong?

4. In this story we learn that long ago, Esther formed a friendship with the Moores' neighbor George Snyder. What was good about this relationship? What was unhealthy? Do you think husbands or wives should have close friends of the opposite sex? Why or why not?

5. Patsy and Pete are having a hard time with their relationship. What do you think each wants from the other? Why is it hard for Patsy to feel comfortable accepting her feelings for Pete? Why does Pete believe he is unworthy of Patsy?

6. In this story, Pete forms a very special relationship with Jesus Christ. Who helps him in his journey toward faith? Who hinders him? How does Pete finally figure out the biblical concepts of "fishing for men" and being "born again"?

7. Charlie tells Brad, "Any man can walk into a tavern and land himself a one-night stand. But you've married yourself a sweet little lady who used to think you hung the moon. You really want to be a man? Pull yourself together and hang that moon back in the sky for your wife" (page 210). How can one partner in a marriage do this for the other?

8. Charlie and Esther have strong opinions about the part of their marriage that takes place "in the bedroom." How do Charlie and Esther each feel about the other's attitude toward sexuality? What does each wish had been different throughout their nearly fifty years together? How do they act toward each other in this important area? Is it all right to feel one way and act another in marriage? Why or why not?

9. What are Jennifer Hansen's goals in life? How is she trying to achieve them? In what way does Jennifer express her faith in Christ? What is it about Cody that appeals to her? Something happened to Jennifer on her trip to Mexico. What do you suppose it was? Does God's will for a person's life ever change?

10. Strategy 1 in *The Four Seasons of Marriage* challenges couples to deal with past failures. Do past failures doom a person to fail in the future? How can we keep from making the same mistakes again and again? When Esther came to terms with her inappropriate relationship with George Snyder, what do you think of the way she handled it? Do you think she should have done something different?

11. Strategy 2 reminds couples of the importance of choosing a winning attitude. Dr. Chapman claims that a negative, critical attitude pushes you toward the coldness of winter whereas a positive attitude, which looks for the best in your spouse and affirms it, leads to the warmth of spring and summer. Esther struggles with her negative attitude toward Charlie. She describes it as a dark cloud that wraps around her. Was her attitude caused by her mental deterioration, or has she always been negative and critical? Does it matter? Who tells Esther about her negative outlook? How does she try to break the cycle of negativity toward Charlie? Does she succeed or fail?

12. Strategy 3 in *The Four Seasons of Marriage* encourages couples to discover and speak each other's primary love language. The five love languages are (1) words of affirmation, (2) acts of service, (3) receiving gifts, (4) physical touch, and (5) quality time. Charlie's love language is quality time. With whom do we see him "speaking" his love language? Esther's love language is receiving gifts. Is Charlie aware of this? Has he been able to speak her love language well during their marriage?

13. Charlie Moore is very good at empathetic listening—Strategy 4 in *The Four Seasons of Marriage.* Practical ways to do this include (1) listening with an attitude of understanding (not judgment); (2) withholding judgment on the other person's ideas; (3) affirming the other person, even when you disagree with his or her ideas; and (4) sharing your own ideas only after the other person feels understood. How does Charlie practice empathetic listening with Esther? with Brad? How might you use empathetic listening with your spouse or another loved one regarding an area of disagreement in your relationship?

14. Do you know anything about autism? In this book, the character of Cody is childlike in his faith and understanding. But he is maturing in many ways too. Recall some of the truths he speaks and how they affect the other characters. What was your favorite "Cody moment"?

15. The people in Deepwater Cove spend a lot of time together—celebrating life, mourning death, and doing a great deal of talking! Can you think of ways to add meaning to your own life by reaching out to others? Is there someone you know who would benefit from your friendship? Can you be bold yet vulnerable enough to talk openly and honestly? Try it! You'll be amazed at what may happen.

ABOUT THE AUTHORS

Catherine Palmer lives in Missouri with her husband, Tim, and sons, Geoffrey and Andrei. She is a graduate of Southwest Baptist University and holds a master's degree in English from Baylor University. Her first book was published in 1988. Since then she has published over forty novels and won numerous awards for her writing, including the Christy Award—the highest honor in Christian fiction—in 2001 for *A Touch of Betrayal*. In 2004, she was given the Career Achievement Award for Inspirational Romance by *Romantic Times BOOKreviews* magazine. More than 2 million copies of Catherine's novels are currently in print.

Dr. Gary Chapman is the author of *The Four Seasons of Marriage*, the perennial best seller *The Five Love Languages* (over 4 million copies sold), and numerous other marriage and family books. He is a senior associate pastor, an internationally known speaker, and the host of *A Growing Marriage*, a syndicated radio program heard on more than 100 stations across North America. He and his wife, Karolyn, live in North Carolina.

Turn the page for an exciting preview from

FOUR SEASONS

Winter turns to Spring

the fourth book in the

FOUR SEASONS SERIES

by Catherine Palmer & Gary Chapman

Available Spring 2008

TYNDALE
FICTION

www.tyndalefiction.com

Winter turns to Spring

Brad dipped a spoon into the box of chocolate ice cream tucked under his arm like a football. Ashley was undressing—always a favorite activity for him to observe—only now the puppy kept nipping at the legs of her black slacks or snatching a sock and racing around the bedroom with it.

"Stop him!" she said finally, turning on her husband. "I'm too tired for this. You have to lock him in another room. And put down some newspapers, too."

"Lock him up? Are you kidding?" The image of the dog crouched alone in a corner brought back memories of Brad's own childhood punishments—dark closets, his father's belt, a slap across the face. "He doesn't mean anything by it, Ash. He's just playing with you."

"I don't want to play, Brad. I want to go to sleep."

"Yeah, you never want to play anymore. I figured that out months ago."

She shot him a dark look as he set the ice cream box on the dresser and picked up the puppy. "And don't let him lick your spoon like that," she added. "Chocolate is poisonous to dogs."

"You don't think I know how to take care of him, do you?" He put the dog on the floor and sank down onto the edge of their bed. "Admit it."

"Brad, all I'm saying is dogs can die from eating chocolate."

"But you said we could keep him, right?"

"I don't care what you do with him. Just don't let him chew on me. And you'd better give him a bath. Tonight. He's probably got fleas and ticks and worms and who knows what else. You'll need to get him neutered, too, or he'll run all over the neighborhood looking for females. If he digs in someone's yard, they'll be furious. I guess you're planning to foot the vet bill out of your paycheck."

Brad stared at his wife. She was letting down her hair, a cascade of thick red-gold waves that tumbled to her waist. Any other time, he would have been unable to resist throwing his arms around her, easing her onto the bed, and kissing her all over. But now Ashley wadded up her slacks and hurled them into a plastic basket in the bottom of the closet. Boy, she was in a fine mood.

"If he's our dog," Brad said, "we'll pay for him together. That's what married people do, remember?"

"*I'm* not the one who has forgotten he's married. I don't hang out at a bar with my high school buddies, drinking beer all night and staring at girls. I work two jobs so I can pay the bills we owe. The bank already repossessed your truck. What do you want me to do next—sell the junker I've owned since my sophomore year in high school?"

She balled up her shirt and threw it into the closet. Uncertain how to respond to this tirade against him, Brad studied the puppy. The dog had sunk his tiny teeth into the toe of Brad's sock and was backing up in a mighty effort to tug it off. Though he wanted to grin at the little rascal, Brad knew there was nothing amusing about Ashley's accusations.

After all these months of marriage, they still hadn't figured out how to blend their incomes. When they were getting along, they agreed to put everything into one account and pay bills from it. But when they got angry, both decided their own paychecks were private. Money flowed and ebbed at the bank. Mostly ebbed. Credit card charges gradually mounted, and the company kept upping the interest rate while requiring timely payments to avoid hefty late fees. Worst of all, the mortgage check often failed to make it into the mail on time.

"Listen, Ashley, you're the one who's always ordering supplies for your bead business." Brad gave in and let the puppy have his sock. "I don't know why you blame me for all our problems. You've run the credit card up so high we'll never get it down. And you don't give a rip about our utility bills. I came home tonight and found every light in the house blazing like it was Christmas."

"Christmas?"

At that, she bit her lower lip and jerked on her favorite blue-flowered flannel nightgown—a garment he hated with a passion. Without speaking, she turned on her heel and headed for the living room. With a *yawp!* of delight, the puppy scampered after her.

Brad looked down at his one bare foot. He had no idea what to do. What could a man even say to a woman like this? Ashley was so emotional. If she wasn't laughing, she was crying or angry. Usually he couldn't even begin to figure out why.

"These are the papers you'll need to put down whenever you leave the house," his wife said, reentering the room with a stack of advertising tabloids in one hand and a bowl of water in the other. "And don't you dare let him into the new room. That's the only good thing we have. I don't want that dog chewing it up."

"*That dog?* What are you so mad about, Ashley?" Brad stood and followed her into the bathroom. "You should be happy. I didn't go to Larry's tonight. I didn't drink a single beer or look at any woman except my wife—who put on her dumpiest gown just in case I might be feeling a tiny bit of what's left of my desire for her. In fact, I came into an empty house with nothing to eat but some kind of leftover junk out of the freezer. I don't see what I've done that's so awful."

"You *exist*, Bradley Hanes!"

She paused, her back to him, and stiffened. A sob echoed off the tiled walls. With a loud sniffle, she dropped to her knees and set the bowl of water by the sink. Then she began spreading the papers across the floor.

Fighting the anger that roared through his chest at her declaration of disgust for him, Brad saw a tear fall from Ashley's cheek onto the ad sheet. Then another. She leaned her back against the bathroom wall, curled her knees to her chest, and buried her head in her arms. As her shoulders shook, Brad hooked his thumbs into the belt loops of his jeans and stared at her. How had he managed to be so stupid as to *marry* that huddled mass of hair, tears, and ratty old nightgown?

"I'm sorry." The muffled words emerged from Ashley and gradually began to seep into Brad's consciousness. She inhaled deeply. "I'm so sorry, Brad. I shouldn't have said that. I just can't believe our marriage is . . . I can't believe we . . . oh no! A flea!"

She bolted up off the floor, her index finger and thumb squeezed together. Covering her eyes with her free hand, she held the other out in his direction. "It's a flea, Brad! It was on my arm. I don't know what to do with it! Oh, yuck. This is disgusting. Here, take it. Take it, take it!"

He reached out for the miniscule pest. The moment Ashley opened her fingers, the flea vanished. Brad looked down to find the puppy staring up at him, tongue hanging out as he panted happily.

"We have to wash the dog," Ashley announced. She bent over the tub and began running warm water. "Pick it up and put it in here. We'll use your shampoo. Ugh, this creeps me out. What if the fleas get everywhere in the house? Pick it up, Brad!"

"*It?*" He looked into her red-rimmed brown eyes. "The dog is a male. And I'm going to bed."

"No, you're not!" She grabbed his shirtsleeve. "Put that puppy in the bathtub, Brad, and I mean it. I hate fleas. I can't stand bugs. I'm going to ask Jay which exterminator they use."

"Who's Jay?" Brad demanded as he lifted the puppy and set him into the tub. "You never mentioned Jay."

"He works at the club. He's in charge of customer relations."

"How old is this guy?" Dread dropped like a stone into the pit of Brad's stomach as he pushed the puppy toward the stream of water running from the faucet. In the time he'd known Ashley, she had never mentioned any men at the country club other than the bartender, the chef, and the busboys—all of whom were too old or too young to attract her interest. Knowing how hard he was fighting his attraction to Yvonne Ratcliff, Brad suddenly realized he ought to keep his eye on his own wife. If he could feel so strongly about—

"*Yow!*" As the puppy slid under the warm cascade, he let out an ear-shattering yelp, spun around, and began trying to run in the other direction. Tiny claws clattering on the tub's porcelain surface, he made no progress whatsoever to get away from the water.

"*Yow! Wow-wow-wow!*" Wailing piteously, he slipped and fell belly-first into the puddle that had collected around the plug. Trying to stagger to his feet again, he clunked his head on the side of the tub.

"Oh, my goodness!" Ashley lifted him out of the water with both hands and gathered him in her arms. "Are you okay? That was a bad bump. Let me see."

Dumbfounded by his wife for the umpteenth time that night, Brad watched as she carefully examined the puppy's furry little head. Finding nothing wrong, she pressed her lips to one floppy ear. The dog licked her cheek, and she giggled.

"Stop that, you silly goober," she murmured. "Now you've got to get into this tub and have a bath. No ifs, ands, or buts. Oh, Brad, I'll bet he's never been washed. Isn't that awful? He looks like he crawled out from under a barn somewhere. I bet he misses his mama and his brothers and sisters. Poor little fella."

Brad knelt beside Ashley as she placed the puppy into the tub again, held him firmly with one hand, and ladled warm water over him with the other. Knowing instinctively what she would want next, Brad squirted a trail of shampoo down the dog's back.

"Help me hold him," Ashley instructed. "He's not going to like this."

With both grasping the squirming pup, they worked the shampoo into a lather. Instantly, the foam turned brown as the dirt turned to sludge and began dripping into the tub. Ashley fussed and clucked over the dog while working shampoo through the long hair on his ears and body and down to the end of his tail. Just as she leaned back to take a breath, he gave a mighty shake, splattering the bathroom and its two human inhabitants with muddy suds.

"Oh no!" Ashley squealed, bursting into laughter. "Grab him, Brad. He's getting away."

The muck in the tub giving him traction, the dog was doing his best to leap out. Brad could hardly keep a grip on the slippery ball of bubbles.

"*Yarp! Yarp! Yarp!*"

"Run some clean water on him," he told Ashley. "I can't hold him."

"He's getting away!" she shrieked as the puppy shook himself again.

She cupped her hands under the running tap water and threw it over the dog. Brad managed to wrap both hands around the animal's tummy, spreading his fingers as if holding a football. Despite the howling and yowling, he shoved the puppy back into the warm stream and helped Ashley rinse him down.

"He's brown!" she exclaimed. "And here's a white spot on his head. Look at his legs—they're white too. I thought he was gray, didn't you? Let's shampoo him again."

"Again?"

Though Brad considered this a very iffy idea, he cooperated as his wife lathered the puppy one more time. Now the soap foamed up white, and the defeated dog submitted mournfully to his final rinse.

Grabbing a towel, Ashley wrapped the wet puppy and nestled him in her arms. "He's so sweet," she murmured. "Look at his big brown eyes, Brad. Isn't he adorable? And now he smells good too. Poor boy. You're lonely, aren't you? Yes, you are. Just a lonely little baby boy."

Brad perched on the toilet lid. It had to be one or two in the morning. In a few hours, he'd need to shower, drink some coffee, and head off to the condominium complex his employer was building near Sunrise Beach. His boss didn't like the men showing up late, and he had little tolerance for nonsense. The work was steady, it paid well, and he had made some good friends. But other than that, Brad couldn't find much to like about his job. The last thing he needed to be doing was washing a puppy in the middle of the night.

"He's really cute, Brad," Ashley said, her own brown eyes turning on her husband. "You found him in a parking lot?"

"Larry's. I was on my way in with Mack when we heard this hullabaloo coming out of a cardboard box. The little guy was inside. I couldn't let him freeze."

"Aww." She leaned up and kissed her husband's cheek. "I didn't know you had such a soft spot."

"Hmm." He rested his elbows on his knees.

"What?" she asked.

"Sometimes I'm not sure you know much about me at all, Ash. Seems like we fight most of the time these days. It's as though we're enemies instead of two people who are supposed to be in love. A few minutes ago you said you were mad at me because I exist."

"Don't bring that up, Brad. I said I was sorry. I didn't mean it." She shook her head. "I'm so tired, and the house is a wreck, and we work all the time, and nothing is ever fun anymore. We aren't fun. I don't know what happened to us."

"*Brrrp . . . brrrp . . . brrrp . . .*"

Ashley glanced down at the puppy in her arms and then smiled at

Brad. "He's asleep," she whispered. "He must be exhausted. And look at this bathroom. And us."

It was a sight to be seen, Brad had to admit. The white tile walls wore polka dots of brown mud. His shirt was sopping, and he was wearing only one sock. Ashley had the dog bundled up against her chin, but Brad had no doubt her nightgown would be dripping wet.

"I'll rinse the tub," he suggested, "and you find some kind of box for him to sleep in. How's that?"

"I love you, Bradley Hanes," she said, kissing him again. "I love you, and I want everything to be wonderful again for us."

Introducing the

CHAPMAN GUIDES

Simple solutions to life's most difficult problems

EVERYBODY WINS

*The Chapman Guide to
Solving Conflicts Without Arguing*

CONFLICT IS INEVITABLE.
ARGUING IS A CHOICE.

Relationship expert Dr. Gary Chapman provides a simple blueprint to help you and your spouse find win-win solutions to everyday disagreements and leave both of you feeling loved, listened to, and appreciated.

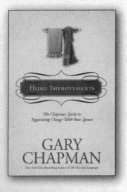

HOME IMPROVEMENTS

*The Chapman Guide to
Negotiating Change With Your Spouse*

IS YOUR SPOUSE'S BEHAVIOR
DRIVING YOU CRAZY?

Over time, annoying little habits can wreak havoc on a relationship. After years of counseling battle-weary couples, Dr. Gary Chapman has developed a simple and effective approach that will help you and your spouse turn those irritating behaviors around once and for all.

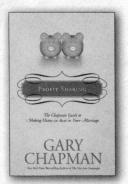

PROFIT SHARING

The Chapman Guide to
Making Money an Asset in Your Marriage

WHEN YOURS AND MINE BECOME OURS.

Money is often listed as the number-one source of conflict in marriage. In this simple and practical guide, Dr. Gary Chapman shows couples how to work together as a team to manage their finances.

NOW WHAT?

The Chapman Guide to
Marriage After Children

AND THEN THERE WERE THREE.

In his trademark simple, direct, conversational style, relationship expert Dr. Gary Chapman answers the age-old question, "How do we keep our marriage alive now that the children have arrived?"

Available now in stores and online!

CP0072

BOOKS BY BEST-SELLING AUTHOR
CATHERINE PALMER

FOUR SEASONS FICTION SERIES
(COAUTHORED WITH GARY CHAPMAN)

It Happens Every Spring
Summer Breeze
Falling for You Again
Winter Turns to Spring (COMING SOON!)

THE MISS PICKWORTH SERIES

The Affectionate Adversary
The Bachelor's Bargain
The Courteous Cad (COMING SOON!)

ENGLISH IVY SERIES

Wild Heather
English Ivy
Sweet Violet
A Victorian Rose

TREASURES OF THE HEART SERIES

A Kiss of Adventure
A Whisper of Danger
A Touch of Betrayal
Sunrise Song

A TOWN CALLED HOPE SERIES

Prairie Rose
Prairie Fire
Prairie Storm

FINDERS KEEPERS SERIES

Finders Keepers
Hide and Seek

CHRISTMAS ANTHOLOGY SERIES

A Victorian Christmas Tea
A Victorian Christmas Quilt
A Victorian Christmas Cottage
Cowboy Christmas

STAND-ALONE SUSPENSE

A Dangerous Silence
Fatal Harvest

STAND-ALONE

The Happy Room
Love's Proof
The Loved One
(coauthored with Peggy Stoks)

Visit www.catherinepalmer.com today!

CP0045

have you visited
tyndalefiction.com
lately?

Only there can you find:

- » books hot off the press
- » first chapter excerpts
- » inside scoops on your favorite authors
- » author interviews
- » contests
- » fun facts
- » and much more!

Sign up for your **free** newsletter!

Visit us today at: **tyndalefiction.com**

Tyndale fiction does more than entertain.

> *It touches the heart.*
> *It stirs the soul.*
> *It changes lives.*

That's why Tyndale is so committed to being first in fiction!

TYNDALE
FICTION